THE MAN IN THE PARK

This is a work of fiction. Names, characters, places, and incidents either are the product of the author's imagination or are used fictitiously. Any resemblance to actual persons, living or dead, events, or locales is entirely coincidental.

First paperback edition December 2019.

www.indiecrime.com
Facebook.com/ChrisCulverBooks

THE MAN IN THE PARK

A Joe Court Novel

BY

CHRIS CULVER

ST. LOUIS, MO

Other books in the Joe Court Series

The Girl in the Motel
The Girl in the Woods
The Boys in the Church
The Man in the Meth Lab
The Woman Who Wore Roses

1

When Logan first entered witness protection, he had been too young to understand what it meant. Now he did. He was no longer a human being. The moment he entered the program, he had become a protectee. That meant he couldn't see his dad, he never saw his old friends, and he had to leave the only home he had ever known. The marshals took everything from him, even his name.

One day, he had gone to bed as Logan Robinson. He had lived in Katy, Texas, and attended Jenks Elementary School. His family had a big house, and he had his own room with a TV. His brother didn't have a television, but he didn't share a room with anybody, either. Evan had just started kindergarten. Both of them had friends. Once a week, they had dinner at their grandparents' home in Houston. His parents lived apart, but he got to visit his dad whenever he wanted, and if he couldn't see him, at least he could call. Life was almost perfect.

Then their mom screwed it up.

The US marshals came in the night and flew them to a training facility in Washington. A guy with a badge told Logan his last name wasn't Robinson anymore. He was now Logan Alvarez. For some reason, the government had given him a Spanish name, but he didn't speak Spanish. They didn't live in Katy anymore, either. Now, they lived in St. Augustine, Missouri. The marshals told him to say he was born in St. Louis and had moved to St. Augustine because the town had better schools. It was all bullshit, and if the people looking for his mom ever spotted him, they'd know he was living a lie right away. He hated his fake life, but at least he had his dad now.

"Did you like the Arch?"

Logan looked to his father, Joel Robinson. For a split second, his throat tightened, and he wanted nothing in the world more than to throw his arms around his dad's neck and hug him tight. Since the guys at school would rip on him to no end if they spotted him doing that, he just shrugged, nodded, and looked out over the park.

"It was okay, I guess."

The smile slipped from his father's face, and he looked down.

"I bet you go there a lot, don't you? We'll find something cool to do next time. I read about a place called the City Museum. It's like a giant fun house. You can climb on everything. It's even got a ten-story slide through the building. You might have a good time assuming you're not too old to hang out with your dad."

At the mere mention of another weekend with his father, Logan's heart almost jumped out of his chest, but he kept his excitement down.

"I guess that'd be okay," he said.

"Maybe we can take your brother next time."

Logan darted his eyes to his left toward his father.

"Evan's too young," he said. "You're not supposed to know where we are. If he told Mom, you'd get in trouble, and the marshals would make us move. I wouldn't see you again."

Joel put a hand on his son's shoulder and squeezed.

"Nothing could ever keep me from you."

That time, Logan scooted toward his father and let the older man hug him. For a few seconds, they stayed there. In six years in witness protection, no one had threatened the family, come after them, or tried to hurt them. Justin Cartwright, the US marshal in charge of their protection, said they were safe in St. Augustine. The marshals, though, had never made Logan feel safe. A hug from his dad did. It also made knowing that his dad had to leave even harder to bear.

"You could come home with me," said Logan, his voice a hushed whisper. "What's Mom going to say? It's her fault we're here."

He could almost feel the change come over his dad. He took his arm from his son's shoulder, straightened, and folded his hands in front of him.

"Don't blame your mom for this. It's not her fault."

"Yeah, it is," said Logan, standing up and pacing in front of the picnic table. His black leather jacket stopped the piercing December breeze from reaching his chest and arms but did nothing to protect his face. Despite that, his throat felt hot. They were in Sycamore Park. Just a year ago, Logan had learned how to hit a fastball in the batting cages not thirty feet away, while Evan had played on the playground about two hundred yards beyond the cages. Their mom, Krystal, had flittered from one place to the other, cheering them on.

Logan thought he had been happy then, but he wasn't. A stranger with a US marshals badge had taught him how to shave the first time. A second stranger, also with a badge, had given him advice on how to talk to girls. Both men had been kind, but they weren't family.

Back then, he only saw his father once a year for "Christmas." Christmas in witness protection wasn't like the happy holiday most kids had. It could happen any time of year, and the marshals never told you when it was. Once, they had it in March. Another year, they had it in the middle of the summer. It didn't happen at home, either. The marshals flew the family somewhere on a private plane. Once they landed, they taxied to a private hangar, and someone shut the doors. Then, a marshal led them to an SUV with blacked-out windows and a metal plate that separated the driver from the passengers. According to the marshals, the vehicle could withstand a point-blank RPG attack and was like the ones the president's family rode in for parades.

The first family probably had working windows.

Once they reached their destination, they parked in a garage and stayed put until the door shut. Then, when the light disappeared, Logan and Evan would have "Christmas" with their father in a windowless concrete bunker. Logan was always glad to see his dad, so he pretended to enjoy the day for his sake, but it was hard to be happy in such a shitty situation.

"She's a criminal," said Logan, looking at his hands.

"Most people in witness protection are," said Joel, squeezing Logan's shoulder, "but she's the only mom you've got. She screwed up, but she's trying to make amends."

"She's trying to cover her ass," said Logan. "And I can't believe you're defending her. Because of her, I can't even see you. If we get caught, you'd go to prison, and she'd walk away like she did nothing wrong. How fucked up is that?"

"Watch the language," said Joel. "It'll get you in trouble. And I'm not defending her. I'm telling you the truth, even if you don't want to hear it."

Logan shoved his hands in his pockets and scowled. A geezer walking a scrawny, ugly dog stared at them from the far side of the park. Logan wanted to run over there and punch him, or at least scream at him. It made no sense, but nothing made sense anymore. He was angry every day and didn't even know why, and when he wasn't angry, he felt sad. His dad should have understood him, but they could barely talk.

"I'm fifteen. I can say what I want," he said, turning and cupping his hands around his mouth so his voice would carry to the old guy. "Fuck you, old man. Fuck you and your stupid dog."

The old guy stared at them. Joel waved as if to

apologize, which pissed Logan off even more.

"Don't apologize, Dad," snapped Logan. "You're always apologizing, even when you're the one getting screwed. Why aren't you mad? It's like you don't even care."

Joel stood and tried to put a hand on Logan's shoulder, but Logan threw it off and stepped back.

"I care, buddy," said Joel, his voice soft. "And I am angry. I've fought for you daily for six years. I've sued your mom, I've sued the government, I've even sued the judge who signed off on the custody order taking you from me. And you know where that got me? Nowhere. I've spent every dollar I've earned for the past six years, fighting to get you back, but I can't fight anymore. The system sucks, and I can't fight it anymore. You're fifteen. When you're eighteen, you can leave witness protection. I'll take you in and keep you safe. We'll move to Timbuktu if we have to.

"Until then, you've got to stay with your mom. I'm doing my best, but you've got to hold on."

Logan balled his hands into fists in his pockets.

"Your best sucks, Dad."

"Yeah, it does."

Hearing his dad acknowledge that somehow made Logan feel better, like he wasn't alone. He sat down and watched as the old man knelt to pick up his dog's crap. Then he looked at his dad.

"I could come home with you," he said. "Mom won't care. She's drunk most of the time, anyway."

Joel said nothing for a moment. Then he laced his fingers together.

"Have you told the marshals about her drinking?"

"They know. She puked on Justin two weeks ago. He got pissed."

Joel smiled just a little.

"Justin's the marshal who looks after you?"

Logan nodded. "Yeah."

"You like him?"

Logan tilted his head to the side and shrugged.

"He's a dork, but he's nice. He told me how to shave."

Joel smiled and ran a finger along his son's cheek.

"Looks like he did a good job," he said, winking. "It's like you don't have any hair there at all."

"Shut up, Dad. I've got hair growing everywhere now."

Both of them snickered but said nothing. Logan knew his dad meant well, but he wished Joel had the guts to do something. They could disappear together if Joel wanted. They could drive to Mexico and rent a home on the beach. Logan could get a job. Maybe they could open a father-and-son dive shop that catered to American tourists. Evan could come, too, but he'd have to stay in school until he was older. They'd be a real family. Their mom could drink her problems away in peace, then. Without her sons in the house, she could drop all pretenses of sobriety. The guys she testified against wouldn't come for Evan and Logan. They wanted her.

Logan sighed and looked at the ground.

"Why don't we just get in your car and drive? It'd be like a test. We could go camping, and then I'd come back in a week. We'd see what Mom does."

Joel said nothing for a moment. Then he blinked and furrowed his brow.

"You can't tell anybody this, but I've got a plan. I'll get you back sooner than you might think."

"Really?" asked Logan, a spike of adrenaline flooding his system. "Like how soon?"

Joel didn't respond. Logan followed his gaze toward a man walking toward them. He was in his early forties, and he wore a dark sport coat, dark slacks, a white button-down shirt, and a US marshal's badge around his neck on a thin chain. He had the thick arms and legs of a bodybuilder. Logan didn't recognize him, and that was a problem. His heart started beating faster.

As the marshal walked toward their picnic table, he reached to the badge at his chest but left it around his neck. Then, once he was sure Joel and Logan had seen it, he let the badge drop and raised his eyebrows. Logan leaned toward his dad. His lungs felt tight, his gut felt as if he had just dropped off a cliff, and a tremble passed through his hands.

"Hey, Dad," said Logan, his voice almost breathless. "We need to run."

"It's okay," said Joel. "The marshal and I will work this out. You go home. I'll talk to you later."

"You don't understand," said Logan, his heart now

thudding in his chest. He grabbed his dad's arm and tried to pull him up, but he was too heavy to move. "He's not a marshal. The marshals don't approach us like this. There are procedures. They call Mom first, and if they can't call, they'll send Justin. If Justin can't come, they send a guy by the house. If it's an emergency, he'll tell us he's there to remove the groundhogs. If it's not an emergency and he just needs to talk, he'll tell us he's there to check the windows. We're supposed to let him in. They never show us their badges, though. That's a rule, Dad. This guy's not a marshal. We've got to go."

By then, the fake marshal was maybe thirty feet away and walking closer. He looked smug. Joel stood, but he didn't run or even walk away despite Logan trying to pull his arm.

"Dad, you're not listening," said Logan, struggling to keep the terror out of his voice. "We've got to go."

"I am listening," said Joel, nodding. Logan, once more, tried to pull his dad's arm, but this time, Joel twisted his wrist and pulled his arm back. Logan let go when he felt his dad tremble. Still, he kept his voice soft. "Run, Logan."

Joel stepped forward and held out his hands, leaving his son at the picnic table.

"Looks like you caught us, Marshal," he said. "What now?"

"What are you doing?" whispered Logan, following behind his father. "I just told you. This guy isn't a marshal. That's a fake badge. He shouldn't be here."

Joel said nothing, but he reached to his side and nudged his son back.

"You must be Joel Robinson," said the fake marshal, stopping about ten feet from Logan and his father. His voice was gravelly and deep, and it sent tendrils of ice through Logan's body. He shuddered. "I'm sorry we met under these conditions."

"Me, too," said Joel. "I know I'm not supposed to be here, but Logan's my son. Have you got kids?"

The fake marshal considered and then shook his head.

"No, but if I did, and if I were in your shoes, I'd be doing the same thing you are," he said. He paused and looked around as if he were considering the situation. "I'll tell you what. Since this is a first-time offense, I'll give you a pass. Get in your car and drive away. You don't have to go home, but you can't stay here. I'll take Logan home. We'll pretend we never met."

"I appreciate that," said Joel. "Can I at least hug him goodbye?"

"Sure," said the fake marshal, smiling. "Hug your son."

Joel turned his back to the marshal and put his arms around his son. Logan, once again, tried to pull him away.

"What the hell are you doing, Dad?"

"Run, kid," said Joel. He squeezed his son and then let go and shoved him back. "Now!"

The moment the shout left his lips, Joel flipped his hips around and dove at the marshal's midsection with his shoulder. The two hit the ground hard. Logan brought his hand to his hair as his father and the marshal writhed on the ground. They both reached for the marshal's firearm.

"Fuck, Dad," said Logan.

"Run!" shouted Joel, his voice little more than a snarl. Logan did the only thing he could. He ran. His feet barely touched the ground. As he reached the road in front of the park, he looked over his shoulder in time to see the marshal standing. He had a gun in his hand, but Joel swatted it away. Then they tumbled to the ground again. As he ran, Logan prayed that his dad would be okay.

Then he heard the gunshots and knew he'd never see him again.

2

It was cold, and thick gray clouds draped across the skyline, blocking most of the late afternoon sun. The weather should have felt gloomy, but it didn't. That was mostly because of the company. Mathias and I were at the St. Louis Zoo. When he'd suggested a date at the zoo, I'd agreed, but I hadn't felt enthusiastic about it. It had seemed almost childish.

Then we parked and walked inside, and I realized it was wonderful. Most of the animals had fur coats or other adaptations that allowed them to thrive even on a cold day, so many were out and active, and since it was a weekday afternoon, most kids—the zoo's largest visitor demographic—were still in school.

We stopped in front of the Amur leopard's exhibit and read the sign with information about the animal's habitat and anatomy. The leopard lounged on top of her stone den. Her tail swung over the side. Even without moving, I could see the thick muscles of her back and sides. With a steel mesh separating us, she was beautiful and powerful, but she looked no more dangerous than a house cat. As she lifted her head and peered at us with cold black eyes, though, I knew she was a predator.

"She's pretty," said Mathias.

"Yep," I said, squeezing his hand but not looking at him. As if our trip to the zoo wasn't juvenile enough, we were holding hands like two teenagers. We left the Amur leopard exhibit and walked toward the snow leopard. It was relaxing and nice. A keeper drove by in a green, heavy-duty utility vehicle and smiled, but otherwise, we had the place to ourselves.

As we tried to find the snow leopard in his enclosure, Mathias squeezed my hand and pulled out his phone.

"It's a quarter to five," he said. "We should head toward the parking lot before they close."

"Yeah," I said, nodding. "That's a good idea."

So we started walking. The silence felt comfortable.

"You want to grab dinner after this?" he asked. "There's a Mexican place on Euclid Avenue I'd like to try."

"Sounds great," he said.

After a few more moments of silence, Mathias cleared his throat.

"How's life with George Delgado?" he asked. I groaned.

"I hate talking about work."

He shrugged but didn't drop my hand.

"Work's part of your life, and I enjoy hearing about your life. Plus, your boss is such an asshole it's almost comic."

I smiled, looked down, and nodded.

"I don't think he means to be an asshole," I said. "Now that he's been the sheriff for a while, I think he's growing into the role. Sometimes he's an asshole, but other times, he's a decent boss who lets me do what I have to do."

"I'm glad to hear it."

We walked for another few minutes. Then he glanced at me.

"I know you can't give me many details, but how's Peter Brunelle?"

I slowed and felt a shudder come over me. To mask it, I pretended I had tripped on a crack in the concrete. Mathias saw through that, but he had the decency to avoid saying anything.

"He's good," I said, shrugging. "He's in prison still, so I haven't talked to him recently. We've lost touch, although I plan to drive to Terre Haute and see him tomorrow. I'll tell him you said hello."

I had hoped he'd laugh and drop the subject, but he squeezed my hand instead.

"He's a serial murderer who persuaded someone to bury a bag of human heads in your backyard. That's scary. How are you doing?"

I forced myself to smile and act casual.

"To be fair, it was behind my backyard, and the heads all belonged to men. I don't think he intended to threaten me. I think he was bragging and showing me what he could do."

Mathias let my hand go.

"I'm serious, Joe. I'm worried about you, and I want to make sure you're okay."

"Then I'm fine," I said. "Roy and I are staying at Susanne's house until the FBI figures things out, and I keep two pistols in my bedroom and a shotgun in the front hall closet. Roy has bite training, and he's a very good watchdog. I'm as safe as I can be. Is that what you want to hear?"

"It is, and I'm glad you're safe," he said. We walked for another few minutes to the zoo's southern entrance. The gift shop had closed for the day, and the woman in the membership kiosk had closed her window. We walked through the open gate and passed a young father and his toddler son. Both were smiling and happy. The little boy waved at us. I smiled back and said hello.

"Are you and Ian still trying to find out who murdered your mother?"

Apparently, Mathias reserved button-pushing for the third date.

"My mom is Julia Green, and she's still alive and well the last time I checked. Erin Court gave birth to me, but she was never my mom. That was her choice, not mine."

Outside the zoo, a winding walkway led to a bridge over Government Drive. That bridge led to the parking lot. Since I was cheap, and since I hadn't wanted to pay for parking when free spots were available nearby, I had parked on the street about two blocks away.

"Ian thinks of her as his mom, though," said Mathias.

Ian was my half-brother. For most of our lives, neither of us knew the other person existed, but then he found me after breaking into the internal network of the law firm that managed the trust funds Erin had set up for us. He was a good kid, and he was coming to realize that Erin didn't deserve the pedestal he had put her on. Years ago, someone shot her multiple times with a .45-caliber pistol and left her to die in an abandoned lot in Dutchtown, a neighborhood south of downtown St. Louis.

"Erin Court was a drug-addicted prostitute who loved heroin more than her children," I said. "I've looked at her autopsy, read the original investigator's notes, and visited the site where she died. Unless somebody comes forward and admits to murdering her, there's nothing to find. Her case is closed."

We walked another few feet.

"Does your brother know that?"

"Are you trying to ruin our night?" I asked, cocking my head to the side and furrowing my brow. "Because you're getting damn close to pissing me off. I've got to drive to Terre Haute tomorrow morning to visit a serial murderer in prison. Until then, I don't want to talk about Brunelle, my brother, Erin Court, or work. Let's just focus on something else."

"I'm worried about you," he said. "You've got a lot going on, and I want to make sure you're able to deal with it. I'm allowed to do that, aren't I?"

I glanced at him, and he smiled.

"You are," I said, reluctantly. Then I paused and stopped walking. He stopped a foot in front of me. "Did my mom ask you to talk about this?"

He hesitated before responding.

"Why would you ask me that?"

"Because this sounds like something she'd do," I said. "She's been needling me to talk about all this stuff to somebody, and she knows I'd confide in you."

"If she's trying to get you to talk, it's because she cares about you," said Mathias. "I care, too."

I rolled my eyes, let go of his hand, and started walking toward my car.

"You can tell her I'm fine. You can also tell her the two of you ruined a nice date."

I got a few feet away before he hurried after me.

"Your mom didn't order me here," he said. "Now that she's retired, I don't even see her anymore. I'm asking because I want to make sure you're okay."

I turned to him and opened my eyes wide.

"You don't need to protect me. I'm fine, Mathias."

"Are you scared?"

I sighed and crossed my arms.

"You can't take a hint, can you?"

He shook his head.

"No."

I balled my hands into fists, squared my hips to him, and dropped my right shoulder back as if I were in a shooter's stance. Then I looked him in the eye.

"Then yes," I said. "Peter Brunelle scares me. I'd be stupid if he didn't. Is that what you want to hear?"

He nodded and held my gaze. For some reason, I couldn't keep looking at him, so I looked down.

"I'm here for you," he said. "For anything."

"Thank you," I said, "but I'm fine. I'm taking every precaution, I'm mindful of my surroundings, and I keep my schedule unpredictable in case anybody's watching me. Brunelle's not the first asshole who's come after me. The other guys are in the ground. I'm glad you're concerned about it, but you don't need to be. Besides, I'm a detective, and I'm armed at all times. I can take care of myself."

He gave me a sideways glance.

"Are you wearing a gun under that dress?"

I considered him but kept my arms crossed even as I softened my voice.

"If you hadn't screwed up our date by talking about Peter Brunelle, you might have found out."

He blinked and then caught my gaze.

"Any chance I can make it up to you?"

"At this point, probably not, but better luck next time."

He tilted his head to the side.

"So, there'll be a next time?"

"Unless you keep talking about Peter Brunelle, yes."

Mathias's face softened, and he smiled. Even if he annoyed me with his overprotectiveness, I enjoyed seeing that smile.

"Let's get dinner," he said.

We turned to my car and started walking again. Since Mathias lived on the way to the zoo, I had picked him up. Unfortunately, as we reached my Volvo, my phone rang. I pulled it out of my purse, glanced at the screen, and sighed.

"Damn," I said.

"Something wrong?"

I looked at my date and slid my finger across the screen to answer.

"It's my dispatcher," I said before putting the phone to my ear. "This is Joe Court. What do you need?"

"Hey, Joe. I'm sorry for calling. Trisha told me you were off tonight, but we've got a situation unfolding in St. Augustine. We have multiple shots fired in Sycamore Park and have at least one victim down. The suspect fled on foot, and we have officers in pursuit now. We need a detective."

The caller was Jason Zuckerburg, our evening dispatcher. I processed what he'd said and then nodded.

"Do we have anybody at the scene?"

"Marcus Washington. He called for paramedics and a detective."

I sighed. The paramedics were a formality. Marcus wouldn't have called for a detective this early unless the victim was dead.

"Tell Marcus to secure the scene. I'm in St. Louis, but I'll be there as soon as I can. I'll work the case, but I'm leaving town tomorrow for an assignment in Terre Haute."

Zuckerburg told me to drive safely. I thanked him and hung up and then looked to Mathias. He gave me a knowing but sympathetic look.

"I guess we'll have dinner next time."

I nodded.

"Sorry, but you know how it is," I said, reaching for both of his hands. I pulled him close and kissed him. He put his hands around my back and gave me a hug. It felt nice. Once he let go, I stepped back but continued to hold his hands. "You mind getting a cab to take you home?"

"Sure," he said. "Stay safe."

"I will," I said. I kissed him once more before climbing into my car. He waved as I put my car in gear. I turned around on Wells Drive and felt a bundle of nerves in my gut untangle. My last real relationship had been in college, almost eight years ago, and it hadn't ended well because I'd pushed the guy away at every opportunity when things had become serious. I hoped I wouldn't screw this one up. My past was…complicated. Mathias understood as much as he could, but we had led very different lives. I hoped he'd be patient.

For now, though, I couldn't worry about my love life. I had a murder to work. This would be a long night.

3

Logan sprinted the better part of a mile to the brick and cedar-siding home he shared with his mom and brother. Several unfamiliar cars had parked on the street out front, but that happened a lot. Their neighbor ran a salon out of her basement, so strangers went in and out of her house all day. It had freaked the marshals out at first, but they freaked out about everything. It was fine.

Their mom always kept the front door locked, so Logan ran to the backyard. His heart thudded in his chest, his belly ached, and his cheeks hurt from holding back tears. Their yard sloped downward, allowing the family to have a walk-out basement and a big deck attached to the first floor. Logan slid open the back door and walked inside. With its sliding glass door and big windows to the exterior, the basement was bright. Logan blinked tears from his eyes.

"Mom!"

When no one answered, he drew in a deep breath and walked deeper into the basement.

"Mom! We need to call Justin! Tell him the groundhogs are here."

The floor creaked above him, so he ran to the stairs. A woman with brown hair and light brown skin stood at the top. She was the same age as some of his younger teachers, but her green eyes looked older somehow. She looked at him the same way their principal did. In other circumstances, he might have thought she was hot. Logan gripped the stairwell tight and stepped back, feeling his breath catch in his throat.

"Who the fuck are you, and where's my mom?"

She smiled.

"I'm Gloria," she said, pushing back her maroon blazer to show him the marshal's badge and firearm on her hip. "What's this about groundhogs?"

He looked at her up and down. If this was a real emergency, the marshals would have sent Justin. Even though he felt cold, sweat slicked his back and armpits. She'd kill them, just like the guy in the park killed their dad. This was his fault. He knew it. He never should have bought that phone from Eric. That kid was trouble. Even Justin saw that, and he didn't see shit. Without that secret cell phone, he never would have been able to call his dad. This wouldn't have happened.

He squeezed his jaw tight and forced the tears from his eyes. He was too old to cry.

"We've got groundhogs in the backyard," he said, hoping she'd provide the countersign. "Mom's pissed because she thinks they'll eat the dill she planted."

She smiled a little.

"Oh," she said. "You should try putting out gum.

The smell draws them in, so they eat it, choke, and die. It sounds cruel, but it's the best way to get rid of them."

That wasn't the response he had hoped for, but he nodded anyway.

"I'll tell my mom. Do you know where she is?"

"I don't, but your brother and I are upstairs waiting for her. My partner, Diego, was supposed to meet you at the park. Did you see him?"

"No. There was nobody at the park."

She raised her eyebrows, surprised. Then she sighed.

"It's our first time in town, so he might have gotten lost," she said. "Come on up. Your brother's with me."

He took one step up but then stopped. If he ran, he could be outside before she reached the bottom of the steps. She'd never catch him then. He knew every yard, house, and fence between here and his school. He could disappear, but that would leave Evan alone with her.

"Why are you here?"

She considered him and then crossed her arms before answering.

"Why do you think I'm here?"

"Justin only comes if there's a problem or if he's worried about something," said Logan. "Is that why you're here?"

Again, she paused. Then she nodded.

"I can't get into a lot of details, but the US Marshals Service works with several other federal agencies to keep families like yours safe. Another government agency has heard some chatter that the people your mother testified against have found out where you live. We'll be evacuating you as soon as your mother gets here."

Logan had always known that was a possibility, so it didn't surprise him. He nodded.

"Why are you here instead of Justin?" he asked.

She looked down and drew in a slow breath.

"Marshal Cartwright is unavailable and will be so for the foreseeable future."

Logan's heart thudded against his chest.

"What does that mean? Is he dead?"

She shook her head and then chuckled a little.

"No. He's not dead, but I'll tell him you asked that. Again, I can't get into too many details, but Justin is at our headquarters building in St. Louis being debriefed by our boss. He's either had some serious lapses in judgment, or he's involved with a criminal organization. I doubt he's broken any laws, but you won't see him again. I'm sorry."

Even if that was the case, the Witness Protection Program still had procedures in place to deal with changes, and they didn't involve two strangers showing up in St. Augustine and flashing badges around town. He needed to get Evan out of here before Gloria realized he knew she was a fraud.

He nodded. His legs shook, and he almost felt dizzy, so he reached out to the wall.

"It's okay to feel scared, honey," whispered Gloria. "I'm here, and my partner will be here soon. We'll keep you safe."

He forced himself to nod and stay still even though

every muscle in his body told him to run.

"Thank you," he said, blinking. He hated that his voice trembled, but he couldn't force himself to stay calm. "Can I talk to Evan? If we're leaving, he and I should pack. We'll need some clothes."

"Sure," she said. "I need to find Diego, anyway. He should be here by now."

And once she made that call and got in touch with him and learned that her partner had already murdered Logan's father, she'd kill him and Evan. Neither of them had any value for her. Their mom had value, but they didn't. If Gloria were a real marshal, she'd know to check out bars for Logan's mom. She had a regular rotation. On Wednesdays, she was at the Neon Lady for two-dollar well drinks.

The fake marshal turned and walked upstairs. Logan followed a few feet behind as she walked into the kitchen. Evan was at the kitchen table near the backyard, eating what looked like an entire box of pizza rolls. He wore a hooded St. Louis Blues sweatshirt and jeans. Freckles marked his nose and cheeks, and his big front teeth made him look almost childish.

"Dude, where have you been?" he asked. "Gloria was looking for you."

"I found her," said Logan. "Come on. We've got to go upstairs to pack a bag. We're leaving."

"I'm eating," said Evan. "I just made these."

Logan glanced at Gloria. She was on the phone with her back to them. He grabbed his brother's arm and pulled hard. Evan spilled his snack on the floor.

"Pick them up and let's go," he said. "Move."

"You're a fucking asshole," said Evan, bending down to gather his stuff. "I'm telling Mom."

"Like she'll care," said Logan, waiting and staring at the marshal and feeling his heart race. Once Evan got his food back on his plate, Logan pulled his brother toward the hallway that led to the second floor and lowered his voice. "Dude, Gloria isn't a marshal. We've got to go."

"What are you talking about? She's got a badge."

He got right in his brother's face.

"When she got here, how'd she introduce herself?"

Evan shook his head and shrugged, a bewildered look on his face.

"She said she was Gloria and that she was a US marshal and that Justin had sent her."

"She told me Justin was in trouble and that she came to evacuate us," said Logan. "We've got to go. She's lying to one of us."

"Why would she lie to us?" asked Evan, reaching to his plate and taking a giant bite of a pizza roll. "You're so stupid."

Evan tried to walk back to the table, but Logan squeezed his brother's arm hard. Evan cried out, but Logan put his hand over his brother's mouth tight.

"They killed Dad," he said. "Okay? That's how I know they're bad guys. I've been talking to Dad for months on Facebook. He's been coming down to see me while you're in school. We went to the Arch in St. Louis today, and then he dropped me off at Sycamore Park. While we were there, Gloria's partner came and gave us this whole US marshal spiel, but we saw through it. Dad tackled him so I could run."

Evan scoffed and shook his head.

"Bullshit. How are you talking to Dad on Facebook? Mom sees everything you do on your phone. She'd kill you."

Logan gritted his teeth.

"I got an old phone from a kid at school. It's one of those prepaid things. To add more time, I buy cards at Walmart."

"Let me see it," said Evan.

Logan wanted to slap him, but that'd just start a fight. Instead, he sucked in a slow breath through clenched teeth.

"Fine. Will you listen to me once you see it?"

Evan nodded, so they took the stairs to the second-floor hallway. Logan kept the phone in a Ziploc bag taped to the back of the toilet tank in his ensuite bathroom. When Evan saw it, his eyes opened wide.

"This is awesome," he said. "How long have you had this?"

"Long enough," said Logan. "We've got to run."

Evan shook his head and carried the phone toward the bedroom.

"You can call whoever you want with this," he said. "You can even text people without Mom or the marshals knowing."

Every moment they wasted fighting in the bedroom over the phone was a moment they couldn't use to escape. Logan's hands trembled as he walked to his closet for his go-bag. It was a black backpack that held two pairs of clothes, toiletries, and a pair of tennis shoes. Evan had a similar bag. Justin had given each of them one and told them to keep it stocked with stuff that fit. Unlike Evan, Logan had added to his bag since meeting his father. He now had a cell phone charger, two hundred dollars cash, a Texas ID card in the name of Logan Robinson, and a credit card his dad had given him for emergencies.

"Just get your fucking bag," said Logan.

"Why?"

Logan balled his hands into fists.

"Are you listening? They killed Dad. They'll kill us. We've got to go. That lady downstairs isn't a marshal. Did she tell you she was there to remove the groundhogs?"

He paused and looked up, a curious expression on his face.

"No," he said. His mouth opened, and he blinked as if he had heard his brother for the first time. "Dad's dead?"

"Yeah, maybe, I don't know," said Logan, shaking his head. "A guy in the park said he was a marshal. He wasn't, though. He didn't tell us about groundhogs, either. This is all fucked up. Dad fought him, and I ran. I heard gunshots. I don't know what happened. Maybe Dad won the fight and shot him. Or maybe it was the police. I don't know. All I know is that lady downstairs isn't a marshal.

She's a liar, and we've got to go."

Evan lowered his hands.

"What do we do?"

"Get your go-bag. We've got to move."

He got up and handed Logan the phone before hurrying across the hall to his room. Logan slung his bag over his shoulder and checked to see that his brother couldn't see into his room before going to the bookshelf beside his desk and pulling out a hardback copy of *Ender's Game* by Orson Scott Card. It was his favorite book, and he had read it half a dozen times. Because it was bigger than most of the other books on his shelf, his mother had never noticed that it stuck out an inch from the wall.

He pulled out the canister of pepper spray he had hidden there and slipped the strap around his wrist and held the cylinder in his fist. Then he put the book back and walked to his brother's room. Evan was in the closet, throwing clothes around.

"Where's your bag?"

"Under here somewhere," said Evan, before moving an old towel to reveal the black bag. He pulled it out and slung it over his shoulders.

"Let's go."

As they stepped into the hallway, they found Gloria standing near the top of the stairs. She smiled, but it didn't reach her eyes. She had a hand behind her back.

"You guys ready?"

Logan nodded. His shoulders felt tight, and the hair on his arms and the back of his neck stood on end. His legs itched and told him to run, but he locked them at the knee so he wouldn't. Behind him, Evan started pushing him forward, using him almost as a shield. Logan couldn't stay put long or his brother would knock him over, so he did the only thing he could and started walking. Evan stumbled but caught himself.

Logan swallowed hard. His heart hammered against his chest. Gloria kept her hand behind her back for a reason. She probably had a gun.

"Did your partner find our mom?" he asked.

She shook her head.

"No, but he told me something interesting," she said. "You shouldn't have run from him. Your dad's disappointed, too."

Behind Logan, Evan whined like a lost puppy and pressed hard against him. Logan kept his back straight and his body between the crazy woman and his little brother. Logan had about thirty pounds on his brother. If Gloria had a gun, he'd have a better chance of fighting her off than Evan would. He gripped the pepper spray canister and flipped off the safety with his thumb.

"My dad's in Houston," he said, stepping forward.

She tilted her head to the side and sighed.

"I don't like it when you lie," she said. "We've got your dad in custody. He attacked my partner."

"He's alive?" asked Logan, a very real tremble in his voice. Muscles all over his body felt tight, and sweat had formed on his brow. "I heard gunshots. Your partner shot him."

She smiled. She wasn't nervous at all. Evan kept pressing himself against Logan's back, driving his larger brother forward. It annoyed him at first, but then he realized he could use that. He thought of his dad and how his father had died trying to protect him, and he allowed the tears to come to his cheeks.

"Your partner killed my dad," he said. His voice cracked as soon as he said *dad*, so he swallowed hard. "I heard the gunshots. Are you going to kill us?"

Evan whined again. That was good. This was just like his favorite book. People in *Ender's Game* saw Ender Wiggins as a child. They underestimated him and dropped their guard around him, just as Gloria was dropping her guard now. She wasn't even bracing herself.

"I don't want to kill you," she said. "Are you going to make me?"

"No," he said, stepping forward again. They were about three feet away now. Evan huddled against him. Logan didn't know how much his brother weighed, but it was at least eighty or ninety pounds. Gloria was bigger but not by much. "What do you want us to do?"

"My partner's on the way. You'll come downstairs, and then we'll wait for him. The police are looking for him, so we'll stay here until your mom comes home. Then we'll figure things out."

And if they waited that long, they were all dead. They had to get away before then. He closed his eyes and started sucking in air as if he were hyperventilating.

"You're fine," said Gloria. "Just take some deep

breaths and—"

Before she could finish whatever she planned to say, Logan jumped to the left, and Evan tumbled forward. His shoulder hit her in the leg, knocking her back. She didn't fall, though. Evan rolled to the right, and Logan lifted his hand with the pepper spray.

"Bad move!" shouted Gloria, kicking Evan.

"Hey, bitch!" shouted Logan.

She glanced up at him, and Logan squeezed the trigger for his pepper spray. A sharp stream shot from the nozzle and hit her square in the eyes. She stumbled back again and brought her hands to her face. Logan didn't waste time. He kicked her as hard as he could in the chest.

She fell backwards, and her head smacked into a step with a sickening thud. Then her legs tumbled backwards, and she rolled like a doll before coming to rest on the hardwood floor. Logan sprinted after her. She didn't move.

"Fuck!" he said, running his hands through his hair and then looking up to his brother. Evan clutched his side where Gloria had kicked him, but he looked okay. "She's not moving. I think I killed her, Evan."

Evan used the handrail to pull himself to his feet and then joined his brother at the bottom of the step. He looked down at Gloria and then to his brother.

"I thought people were supposed to shit themselves after you killed them," he said. "It's on TV."

"I think that's only if you shoot them," said Logan, his eyes wide as he grabbed his brother's elbow. "Come on. Her partner's coming."

This time, Evan came with him.

"Where are we going?"

Logan didn't respond until they reached the front door. He looked around, but nothing moved.

"Somewhere safe," he said, licking his lips.

Evan followed him across the lawn but stopped on the road.

"We should go to the police."

"We just killed somebody," said Logan. "Do you want to go to jail? I don't."

"Then where are we going?"

"Home. Now come on. I've got a plan."

Evan nodded and followed without asking a single question. Logan wished he knew what he was doing.

4

I hit the beginnings of rush-hour traffic on my way back to St. Augustine, stretching my hour-long drive to an hour and a half. By the time I reached Sycamore Park, the sun had set, and night had descended. Though the park closed at sundown, modern lights meant to mimic Victorian lampposts lined the sidewalks and trails. Much larger sodium lamps lit the parking lot as bright as day. Unfortunately, by the looks of things, our crime scene was in a dark area at the far end of the park.

I parked in the lot near the swimming pool. Three marked cruisers, our forensics van, and a hearse had parked on the grass near a pair of picnic tables at the far end of the park. For just a moment, I flashed back to a previous encounter I'd had near the swimming pool. A very sick man with a very high-powered rifle had tried to gun down families at the pool in some kind of twisted revenge fantasy. We stopped him, but it came at a cost that had given me nightmares for a long time.

I stilled myself and then drew in a deep breath before reaching into my glove box for a notepad on which I wrote notes about my time of arrival and the conditions of the area. Outside, the air was bracing, and my breath came out in a puff of frost. On my drive over, I had noticed several houses nearby had draped tarps over their flower beds to protect the plants from an early frost.

As I approached the scene, Officer Marcus Washington left the crime scene's perimeter and walked toward me with a smile on his face. I met him in the light cast by a cast-iron, faux-Victorian lamppost.

"Evening, Marcus," I said, taking out my notepad. "I heard you were the first responder. What's going on?"

He pulled his own notepad from his utility belt.

"We've got a homicide. Victim is Joel Robinson. According to his license, he's a thirty-nine-year-old Caucasian male from The Woodlands, Texas. His car's in the parking lot. Darlene and I searched it already but found nothing remarkable. The police in Houston arrested and charged him twelve years ago for driving under the influence, but other than that, his record's clean. He looks like a solid citizen.

"So far, Darlene and Kevius have collected eight spent .40-caliber Smith & Wesson casings, but we have yet to find the firearm. Shane Fox and Katie Martelle are searching the park and the surrounding area, but the shooter likely took the piece with him. I've checked out most of the houses nearby to see whether anybody saw anything or whether anybody has a surveillance camera overlooking the park, but I struck out. We have a witness, but he's an older guy, and he saw the shooting from a distance. When I got here, he was feeling faint and experiencing chest pain. Paramedics took him to St. John's for evaluation."

I nodded and jotted down notes. Then I glanced up.

"Before paramedics took him, did the witness say anything?"

"He said the shooter and victim spoke as if they knew each other. There was also a third party involved somehow, but he ran off before the shooting started. We've had patrols out in the neighborhood to find that guy, but no luck so far."

Marcus paused.

"You look nice, Detective. Sorry if we ruined your evening."

I glanced at him from my notepad and smiled. I liked privacy, and I tried to keep my personal and work lives as separate as possible, but when you were on call twenty-four hours a day, a little mingling was impossible to avoid.

"You didn't shoot anybody, so you didn't ruin anything. And thank you," I said. "Is the body still here?"

Marcus nodded.

"Yeah, but that's a little complicated."

I raised my eyebrows.

"Oh?"

Marcus drew in a breath and blinked a few times before turning his head and looking toward a stooped, elderly man with white hair near the picnic tables. I hadn't noticed him before, but he wore a black three-piece suit, black shoes, a white shirt, and a black tie. When he saw us looking at him, he turned and waved but didn't move from the picnic tables. I looked to Marcus.

"Who is that, and why is he in our crime scene?"

"That is Mr. Stan Rivers," he said. "He's St. Augustine County's new coroner."

I didn't respond, hoping he'd elaborate, but he didn't.

"Where's Dr. Sheridan?"

Marcus shook his head.

"I don't know. I called in a homicide, and they sent Mr. Rivers."

My mouth popped open, but I had nothing to say at first. Then I shook my head.

"You called him *Mister* Stan Rivers," I said. "So, he's not even a physician?"

"According to Missouri law, the coroner doesn't have to be," said Marcus. "Mr. Rivers and his sons own the Rivers Family Funeral Home in town."

"This won't work," I said, shaking my head and taking out my phone. Marcus grimaced and looked down while I dialed Dr. Sheridan's personal cell number. He answered on the first ring. "Doc, this is Detective Joe Court. I've got a body, and they sent me a mortician instead of you. We're at Sycamore Park in St. Augustine. Whenever you're ready, come on down."

Sheridan sighed.

"I guess they didn't tell you," he said. "Three days ago, the St. Augustine County Council sent my office a certified letter to let me know my services are no longer required. I'm sorry, but I don't work for the county anymore. According to the County Council, it was a cost-saving measure."

I shook my head and felt my skin grow warm.

"Let me call you back," I said. "I'll straighten this out."

"Your bosses fired me and my staff," said Sheridan. "There's nothing to straighten out. We're independent contractors, and my office manager has already started negotiations for a new contract with Madison County."

"This is insane," I said. "We need you here. You're good at your job."

Sheridan paused.

"And so are you," he said. "I've enjoyed working with you, Joe, but people like you and me don't get to make the rules. I know where I'm not wanted. Maybe I'll see you around."

"I'll make some calls," I said. "I'll talk to you soon."

I hung up before he could respond. I thought about calling my boss and demanding answers, but Sheriff Delgado would have no more power to fix this than I would. Instead, I searched through my phone's address book until I found the number of County Councilman Darren Rogers, the biggest blowhard I'd ever met. His phone went to voicemail after four rings, so I left a message telling him I planned to keep calling until he either turned off his phone or picked up. Then I dialed again. This time, he answered after three rings.

"Detective," he said. "I didn't expect to hear from you tonight."

"I didn't expect to see an old man with a hearse at my

murder scene, so I guess everybody's got a little surprise tonight."

Rogers paused.

"I see you've met Mr. Rivers."

"I haven't met him yet because I refuse to talk to a civilian about an open investigation," I said. "What the hell's going on? Trevor Sheridan told me you fired him."

Again, Rogers paused.

"Unfortunately, we had to part ways with Dr. Sheridan. He's a fine coroner, but his contract costs this county almost a hundred thousand dollars a year. We couldn't afford that."

I shook my head.

"We can't afford to lose him," I said. "He's a board-certified forensic pathologist with an extensive background in forensic medicine and organic chemistry. He's helped me close half a dozen murders in the past year alone. We'd be lucky to have him and his staff at two hundred grand a year."

Rogers sighed.

"I understand and appreciate your loyalty, but I think you're overplaying Dr. Sheridan's value. For a hundred grand a year, I expect an employee to work more than five or six days a month. We didn't have that many murders. We can't justify the expense."

Again, I shook my head.

"As high as that fee might be, it paid for his staff, his lab, his equipment, and his vehicles. He was available twenty-four hours a day, every day. His replacement doesn't even have a medical degree."

"I think you'll find Stan is a more than adequate replacement."

"He's not even a doctor," I said. "What formal forensic training does he have?"

"I've said all I have to say to you, Detective," said the councilman. "Good luck with your investigation."

He hung up before I could protest. Muscles all over my body trembled, and I squeezed my phone hard enough I thought I might break the screen. I wanted to drive to Rogers's house and throw him through a window, but that'd just get me arrested. Then again, if I shot him, I'd have a decent chance of getting away with it because we no longer had a competent coroner.

"You okay, Detective?" asked Marcus.

"No, I am not okay, but that's my problem, not yours," I said. I clenched my jaw and sucked in a deep breath through my nose, hoping that would calm me down some. "You said there was a witness. Tell me about him."

Marcus flipped through his notes.

"His name is Richard Ballard. He lives about a mile away and came here to walk his dog. His wife came about twenty minutes ago to pick up the dog, and she talked to Katie Martelle. The hospital plans to keep Mr. Ballard overnight for observation, but it looks like he'll be okay. They think he had a panic attack. I've got his address."

I nodded, so he recited the address. I wrote it down and then looked at the crime scene before focusing on

Marcus again.

"Did Mr. Ballard mention seeing the victim at the park before?"

"I didn't get the chance to ask," said Marcus. "He started clutching his chest shortly after I started my interview. The paramedics were already on their way, so I had him loosen his collar and sit down at the picnic tables. I thought he was having a heart attack, so I didn't want to stress him out with more questions."

"Good idea," I said, nodding as I wrote that down. Then I glanced up. "Okay. Good work all around. If our shooter tossed his gun, we need to find it before a kid does. I know you've already done it, but I want you to walk through the park and check the trash cans, bushes, and any other hiding spots for the weapons. If you find a gun, call for Darlene or Kevius. If you don't find it, keep looking. And consider getting the metal detectors from the station. They could speed things up."

"Will do," said Marcus. "Good luck, Detective."

I thanked him and walked toward the scene. The headlights from two police cruisers lit the area in an almost blinding light that forced me to blink and shield my eyes as they adjusted. The victim was on his back, and he wore a black sweater, dark fashionable jeans, and a pair of canvas tennis shoes. Numbered flags surrounded him, indicating those spots in which Kevius and Darlene had found evidence. The dirt around him was powdery and dry. It held footprints well, but this was a well-used public park. Dozens of people could have walked through there today alone.

The coroner, Stan Rivers, stood beside the picnic tables. He perked up when he saw me.

"Evening, Detective," he said, holding out his hand. "I'm Stan. I'm the new coroner."

I didn't bother shaking his hand, mostly because it had blood smeared across the palm.

"What'd you touch?"

"Excuse me?" he asked, narrowing his eyes. I blinked a few times and then held my breath for a ten count so I wouldn't snap at him.

"You've got blood smeared on your hand. What'd you touch?"

He looked down, and then his eyes opened wide as he looked around him. Then he focused on the picnic table.

"The edge of the table," he said. "I guess there must be blood there. I didn't see it."

"Next time you come to a crime scene, keep your hands in your pockets at all times so you don't contaminate anything," I said. "When we finish talking, tell Darlene McEvoy you touched a blood smear on the table. She'll swab your hands."

He nodded.

"Okay," he said. "Sorry."

"Me, too," I said. "Tell me about the victim."

Rivers hesitated.

"He's dead."

I forced myself to smile.

"Anything else?"

He blew a raspberry and then shrugged.

"He had a driver's license in his wallet. His name is Joel Robinson, and he's thirty-nine. Somebody shot him in the chest at least twice, but I can't see the gunshots well because he's wearing that dark sweater. The gunshot wound on his neck has a circular burn and some black grit around it. The killer must have held the pistol to his neck and fired."

I nodded and crossed my arms as I processed that.

"If he shot him from close range, the shooter should have blood all over him."

"Probably," said Rivers. "The dead guy's got a broken hand and cuts on his knuckles. I don't know the fancy medical term, but I've always called it a boxer's fracture. He punched something before he died."

Our new coroner wasn't useless, but he wasn't Dr. Sheridan, either. I wrote some notes and nodded as I looked around the scene. The picnic tables had been positioned in one spot long enough for the grass beneath them to die and for their legs to leave indentions in the soft earth. One of them—the one Rivers had touched—had been knocked askew, leaving blood on one corner. If the victim and the shooter had gotten into a fistfight, they could have bumped into it.

I looked around the scene and found Kevius Reed, one of our evidence technicians, collecting cigarette butts near the base of the oak tree.

"Kevius," I said. He glanced up and then walked

toward me.

"Evening, Detective," he said, nodding. "What can I do for you?"

I looked at the table and bit my lip.

"Could you pull prints off a wooden table like this?"

He grunted.

"Wood is always tough to pull latent prints from, and this table looks like it's been outside a while. The surface is rough. I can try, but I wouldn't be too hopeful if I were you."

"Then give it a shot and see what you can figure out," I said. "Marcus said that he and Darlene searched the victim's car. Do you know which one it was?"

He nodded toward the parking lot.

"Gray Subaru sedan."

"Do you know if they tried to print the door handles?"

"That, I don't know," he said.

"If you see Darlene, ask her," I said. "And if she hasn't, ask her to print the passenger side door handle. A witness reported that someone was with the victim before he died. If they drove to the park together, we might get his prints."

"Will do," said Kevius. I thanked him and started walking to the vehicle. Before I could go more than a few feet, Rivers cleared his throat.

"Anything you need me to do?"

I considered him and then shook my head.

"No."

He blinked and then looked down.

"I've heard about your former coroner," he said. "I know I've got some big shoes to fill, but I think if you give me a chance, I'll—"

"Stop," I said, interrupting him. "You seem like a nice man, Mr. Rivers, and I don't doubt your sincere intentions, but you can't fill Dr. Sheridan's shoes. I'm sure you're a great mortician, but you're not qualified for this job, and we both know it. The County Council hired you to save money. Until you come to your senses and quit, it's best if we keep our interactions short. Okay?"

He nodded.

"Sure."

I turned and walked to the car. My skin felt hot despite the freezing temperature, and my heart thudded against my chest. I was pissed, but I couldn't let that affect my work, so I drew in two deep breaths and focused on the car in front of me. It was eight or nine years old, but it looked clean both inside and out. Someone had left a parking pass from a hotel in Festus, Missouri, on the dashboard. I snapped a picture with my phone and walked to Marcus Washington on the periphery of the crime scene.

"Have you seen Bob Reitz today?" I asked. Marcus thought and then shook his head.

"I think he's on vacation."

I hadn't seen him for a few days, so that made sense.

"You want to earn some overtime and flex your detective muscles?"

He smiled a little. "Sure."

"Find someone to supervise the crime scene and then go to our station and pull the victim's credit report. We need to find out whether he's got any credit or debit cards, and then we need to find out where he's used them. If possible, I'd like to put together a timeline of his activities for the past day or so."

Marcus wrote that down and nodded.

"I think I can do that."

"Good," I said, nodding. "I'm heading to Festus to search his hotel room."

He wished me luck. I nodded and got into my car. Aside from my issues with the coroner, the case was easy so far.

I doubted that would last.

5

It took twenty-five minutes to drive to the hotel and another twenty-five to find my victim's room. The night manager was helpful, but Mr. Robinson hadn't checked in under the name Joel Robinson. Instead, he had checked in as John Rutkowski of St. Paul, Minnesota. He paid in cash, but he had given the young woman who checked him in a fake ID and a credit card with a false name on it.

I didn't know what that meant yet, but people didn't check into hotels under fake names without a damn good reason. After we had the ID sorted out, I checked out the room, but it was mostly a bust. Robinson had a single bag that held three pairs of jeans, three shirts, four pairs of socks, four pairs of boxer shorts, a pair of pajamas, and a bag of toiletry items. There were no guns, drugs, cash, or anything else worth killing for. He did, however, have a cell phone charging from an outlet beside the television.

I powered the phone on, but it required a passcode to access its contents, making it useless to me for the moment. I bagged and tagged the phone and charger before locking up the room. Afterwards, I drove toward St. Augustine and called Marcus for an update while I was still on the interstate.

According to Marcus, our new coroner had taken the victim's body to the morgue in his funeral home, and Darlene McEvoy and Kevius Reed were wrapping up at the crime scene. As soon as they finished, he'd go to the station and start looking up Joel Robinson's credit report. All of them had work to do, and all their jobs required specialized skills. I had a job that required specialized skills, too. I had to call Mr. Robinson's next-of-kin, and I already felt my stomach contort at the thought.

When I reached my station, I parked in the lot and walked to the side door that served as our main entrance at the moment. The men and women of the St. Augustine County Sheriff's Department worked out of a massive, historic temple formerly owned by the Freemasons. When the Masons left town, the county had purchased the building and reconfigured it to suit our department's needs.

Unfortunately, it was an old building, and things had gone to shit in the past few years. The old wooden windows and slate roof leaked, the basement flooded, and the HVAC system struggled to maintain a comfortable work environment in even mild conditions. In its infinite wisdom, the County Council decided we needed a top-to-bottom renovation. Considering it couldn't even pay our coroner, I had no idea where the multimillion-dollar renovation budget came from, but that renovation had begun a few months ago and promised to continue for the foreseeable future. Eventually, we'd have a gorgeous, modern facility. Until then, we worked in a construction zone.

I took the stairs to the dilapidated second floor and hurried to the storage room I was using as an office.

At twenty-eight, I had been a cop for six years, and social media had been a mainstay in my investigative arsenal from the very start. I knew of few better windows into a person's life than what they posted for their friends and family, and I planned to take advantage of that.

Once I reached my desk, I searched for Joel Robinson on every major social media site I could think of. He wasn't on Instagram, but he had accounts on Facebook and Twitter. Unfortunately, his tweets were benign—mostly he retweeted jokes and complained about the head coach of the Houston Texans football team—and the privacy settings on his Facebook profile prevented me from seeing anything but his picture.

Since I struck out there, I searched for him on the license database to get his address. Then, I searched for anyone else living at that address and got a name: Daisy Robinson. She was thirty-six, had black hair and brown eyes, and weighed a hundred and twenty pounds. Joel had blond hair and blue eyes, which likely meant Daisy was a spouse instead of a younger sister. Either way, I had my next-of-kin.

I dialed the number in the license bureau's database and waited through three rings before a woman answered with a tentative hello.

"Hi, is this Daisy Robinson?"

She hesitated.

"Yes, but I'm not interested in whatever you're selling."

I smiled, but my smile faded just as quickly as it had arrived.

"Are you married to Joel Robinson?"

Again, she hesitated.

"Yes. What's this about?"

My gut tightened.

"My name is Mary Joe Court, and I'm a detective in St. Augustine, Missouri. Are you somewhere we can talk for a few minutes?"

"I'm at home," she said, the pitch of her voice growing higher. "What's this about? Why are you calling me about Joel?"

Already, I could hear the panic in her voice. I grimaced.

"Unfortunately, I have some bad news. Are you sitting down?"

"Cut the shit and tell me what's going on. Is Joel hurt?"

I drew in a deep breath.

"I'm very sorry to tell you this, but your husband died this evening in St. Augustine. We're still very early in our investigation, so we don't have a lot of details yet. Anything you can tell me now would—"

"Wait a minute," she said, her voice husky. "Was my husband murdered?"

She deserved the truth, so I nodded even though she

couldn't see me.

"Yes, ma'am," I said. "I'm very sorry."

For about ten seconds, the line went silent. I thought she had hung up, so I pulled the phone from my ear and looked at the screen. Then a sob ripped through my phone's speaker. My arms and legs felt heavy, and my stomach contorted, as it always did when I made these sorts of calls. I hated next-of-kin notifications more than anything else in this job. No matter how delicate or sympathetic or kind I was, I ruined someone's life with every call. No amount of training or experience could ever change that.

Daisy cried, but then the phone went quiet once more.

"Are you still there, ma'am?"

"Thank you for the call, Detective," she said. "I need to go. I'll call you later."

Had she been local, I would have let her grieve for an hour or two before questioning her. Since she lived hundreds of miles away, though, I couldn't risk her running away and disappearing before I got the chance to interview her.

"I hate to do this, but I have to ask you some questions before I let you go. Everyone in my department will do our absolute best to find out what happened to your husband and put his murderer in prison, but to do that, we need information. Do you want to help me find the man who murdered Joel?"

She paused.

"Okay. Yeah. Just ask your questions so I can go."

She didn't like me, but she didn't need to like me for me to do my job. I grabbed a notepad.

"First, why was your husband in St. Augustine?" I asked. "We're about eight hundred miles from Houston. That's quite a drive."

"He went fishing there," she said. "He drove up to camp and go fishing."

On a superficial level, it made sense. St. Augustine had several deep, clear lakes that made for excellent fishing, and our campgrounds drew tourists from all over the Midwest. We hadn't found Joel's body near a lake, though, and his car had held neither fishing nor camping gear. He wasn't even staying in St. Augustine. Instead, he had checked into a hotel in Festus. I didn't know why he drove all the way up here, but, despite his wife's assurances, it wasn't to enjoy the great outdoors.

"Did he always make these trips alone?"

"Sometimes I go, too," she said. "I had to work this time, though."

"And on those previous trips when you came along, did you stay in hotels, or do you have a cabin around here, or did you go camping the entire time?"

She seemed to think for a second.

"We always stayed at the same campsite. I don't remember its name, but there was a lake nearby. It was pretty. We were thinking of coming up this spring for the fair."

"Did either of you have friends or family in the area?

Someone he might have visited?"

She didn't hesitate before responding.

"No. We didn't know anybody in town."

I couldn't prove it, but she was lying to me. As pristine as our lakes were, there were equally nice places in Arkansas, Oklahoma, and Texas for Joel and his wife to visit if they wanted to go camping and fishing. The story made little sense, but I didn't want to press her on it and have her shut me down.

"Can you think of any reason someone might have hurt your husband? Did he have a temper? Did he have gambling or drug problems? Anything like that?"

"No," she said. "My husband was a good, gentle man. He taught Sunday school. He had no enemies."

"I don't doubt that," I said. "And I apologize if my questions seem insensitive. I'm just trying to learn about your husband."

She hesitated before answering.

"I understand."

I wanted to ask how their marriage was, but that'd tick her off. That line of questioning could wait for a few days.

"A witness reported seeing your husband in the park with a man, and they seemed friendly. Are you sure you didn't know anyone in town?"

"No, and I don't like what you're implying."

I forced myself to smile and hoped it came out in my voice.

"I'm not intending to imply anything," I said. "He

was murdered in a park. A witness spotted him with another man before the incident. That man ran off before the shooting, so I'm wondering whether he told you anything about that meeting."

"No, Detective," she said. "Now if you'll excuse me, I have some very difficult calls to make."

"I understand. Thank you for—"

She hung up while I was midsentence. That could have gone better, but at least she hadn't told me to call her attorney if I needed to speak to her again. I pushed back from my desk to think. Obviously, she hadn't killed her husband, but she was holding back on me, and she was doing it for a reason.

Daisy Robinson had secrets. Under normal circumstances, her private affairs were none of my business, but a murder investigation changed the rules. I didn't have time to hold her hand and coax the truth out of her, and I didn't have time to be delicate. Murder investigations had to move, both because the killer could escape the area and because memories had a tendency to fade.

I'd worry about her later, though. For now, I needed to focus on her husband. I didn't know what he was up to before he died, but with Daisy holding back on me already, this case would get ugly before I finished. I just hoped no one else would get hurt.

6

It was dark. Even hours after killing Gloria, Logan's heart hadn't stopped pounding, and his hands hadn't stopped trembling. He and Evan had to get out of town. Diego wouldn't stop looking for them—especially after they pepper sprayed his partner and pushed her down the stairs. Logan could still close his eyes and hear the thump as the back of her head smashed into the carpeted step. It was like a cantaloupe dropping in the grocery store.

He hadn't meant to kill Gloria, but now that he had, he'd have to deal with the police. Logan wasn't stupid. He knew they'd never convict him for defending himself against a psychopath, but he understood the threat against him. The Marshalls had drilled into Evan and Logan how dangerous—and rich—the people after them were. The bad guys wouldn't hesitate to drop two or three million dollars to get their mom. Most of the local cops would turn down a bribe, but there were bad apples in every bunch, and the bad guys after them could sniff out every one. Until Evan and Logan found out who they could trust, they couldn't trust anyone—cop or civilian, stranger or friend.

So, they sat and waited in Theo Pascalone's basement for his older brother to come home from wrestling practice. They needed a ride, and Joey Pascalone, Theo's brother, had a car. Joey would charge them every dollar they had, but he'd get them to the train station in St. Louis safely. From there, they could go anywhere.

Theo Pascalone was cool. He was an eighth grader, so he was younger than Logan, but they had known each other for a long time. Joey was a senior in high school, and he'd do anything for money. He had a fake ID, and he wasn't afraid to supply booze to minors, so he had purchased beer for every boy-girl party Logan had ever been invited to. So far, that had only been one party, but a girl he liked had let him feel her boobs, which was awesome. Afterwards, she got so drunk she puked all over the floor. That put a damper on the evening, but Logan figured he'd get a second chance with her eventually.

"Dude, what's wrong with your brother?" asked Theo, pausing the video game he was playing. The three of them—Theo, Logan, and Evan—were in the basement. Theo sat on a big black beanbag chair, while Logan and Evan lounged on the sofa. Theo had offered them sodas earlier, but neither Logan nor Evan could force one down after what they had done and seen.

"He's okay," said Logan, looking toward Evan. The eleven-year-old's skin was pale and clammy, and he had brought his knees to his chest as he rocked. He had said little since they arrived. If Theo had known him better, he would have known something was wrong because Evan usually never shut up. "That's what he looks like when he's hungry."

"If he's hungry, we've got some pizza rolls in the freezer," said Theo. "We can microwave them."

"I don't want any pizza rolls," said Evan, his voice low. He didn't take his eyes off the carpet in front of him. Theo gave him a sidelong glance but then turned his game back on.

"Why are you guys going to St. Louis, anyway?"

"To see a concert," said Logan. He knew someone would ask him this, so he had his lie planned out beforehand. "It's, like, at a bar by St. Louis University. A friend asked me to go. She lives off Grand Boulevard in St. Louis."

"Sweet," said Theo, sitting up straight. "You guys are going to a bar? Can I go?"

Logan looked to his brother, but Evan wasn't any help.

"I only got the two tickets, and Evan already paid for one," he said. "I had planned to get a ride from some kid at Waterford College, but I think he forgot."

"If you've got money, Joey will drive you there, but he can't drive you home."

"My girlfriend will take us home," said Logan, the lies coming smoothly now. "We might even stay the night at her place, if you know what I mean."

"You're going to make it with her with your brother there? That's gross."

Logan shifted his weight before looking to Theo.

"He can stay on the couch and put his hands over his ears if Janet moans," he said.

"Dude, that is so awesome," said Theo, shaking his head and smiling. "How do you meet these people?"

"The internet," he said. "Like on Snapchat."

"What'd you tell your mom?"

"My mom won't care," he said, speaking honestly for the first time since he got in the house. "I haven't seen her for a few days, anyway. I think she's got a boyfriend in town. She stays at his place two or three nights a week."

"My mom won't let me do shit," said Theo. "Like going to a concert on a Wednesday? Yeah, she'd kill me if I even asked."

"Yeah, I'm lucky," said Logan, back to lying again.

Theo snorted and said it was awesome their mom let them do what they wanted. Had he known how much it sucked to have a mom who didn't give a shit about her kids, he wouldn't have said it. Theo resumed playing *Mortal Kombat 11* for about ten minutes. Then Joey came down the stairs. He was seventeen years old and had buzzed brown hair, wide shoulders, and thick arms. There was a big gap between his two front teeth.

"Hey, loser," he said, looking at his brother. Then he looked at Evan and Logan. "What are you two shit bags doing here?"

"They need a ride to St. Louis," said Theo. "Logan's got a girlfriend up there. He's going to get laid."

Joey snickered.

"Bullshit. Like any girl would let you put your

shriveled micro dick anywhere near her."

"It's true," said Theo before either Logan or Evan could respond. "I've seen her. She's hot. She wanted me to go to the concert, too, but I've got a math test tomorrow."

Joey narrowed his eyes.

"How old is she?"

"Sixteen," said Logan. "She can drive, but she had too much stuff going on to pick me up. Our first ride fell through, so we need your help. I'll pay you."

Joey looked to Evan.

"And what about him? He looks like he's going to puke."

"He's fine," said Logan. "He's just hungry and tired. He'll sleep on the way and wake up at the bar."

"How much money do you have?"

Before Logan could respond, the floor creaked, and a beautiful woman walked down. Maria Pascalone was the stuff of legends among the young men of St. Augustine. Twenty years old and fit, she had blond hair, blue eyes, and a body straight out of a fifteen-year-old boy's best dreams. Logan had only met her once, but he had thought about that chance encounter for weeks.

"Just take him, Joey," she said before looking at Logan. "And if you like this girl, show her some respect. And do not, under any circumstances, introduce her to either of my pervy brothers."

"You're real funny," said Joey. "It's kind of weird how a funny girl like you can't keep a guy interested for more than one night at a time."

Her lips curled into a tight but humorless smile.

"At least I won't die a virgin," she said. "Now drive him to St. Louis. Mom and Dad will be out until at least ten, and it's not like you plan to spend the night studying."

Joey scowled and looked to Logan.

"Gas, ass, or grass," he said. "How much money do you have?"

"Hundred bucks," said Logan. "All you have to do is drive us to the MetroLink station. We'll make it from there."

Joey glared at his sister before looking at Logan and holding out his hand.

"Hundred bucks," he said. "That's what you're offering?"

"Yeah," said Logan, reaching to shake his hand. Joey shook his head.

"No, kid, I want my money. I don't want to shake your hand."

Maria snickered and shook her head.

"You're such a dork, Joey. Just shake his hand," she said. Joey rolled his eyes and then squeezed Logan's hand tight. Finally, Maria looked to Evan before looking at Logan again. "Is your brother okay?"

Evan's mouth opened, but he said nothing.

"He'll be fine," said Logan. She gave him a tight smile but focused on Evan.

"Is that true? Is everything okay?"

His lips moved, so she walked to the couch and knelt in front of him. Logan swore under his breath. They had to get out of town. If he started crying or something, Maria would call her mom, and then Mrs. Pascalone would call the police. Logan and Evan would go to jail after that.

"Are you okay, buddy?" she asked. "I'm an adult. If something was wrong, you'd let me know?"

Evan blinked and then licked his lips.

"I like your boobs."

She closed her eyes and shook her head.

"I fucking hate boys," she said, already heading toward the stairs. Logan and the rest of the guys laughed as hard as Logan could ever remember laughing. As that died down a few moments later, Joey looked from Evan to Logan.

"You guys are all right," he said. "Let's get the hell out of here before she changes her mind and calls my mom."

Logan couldn't argue with that. He pulled out his money—five twenty-dollar bills—and then handed them to Joey. The sooner they were out of St. Augustine the better, even if it cost him every dollar he had.

Even hours after those two fucking kids attacked her, Gloria's eyes and nose burned, her head throbbed, and her ribs ached. She had gone to an urgent care center in Melville, a little town south of St. Louis, and said someone had mugged her. For twelve hundred dollars, they took X-rays of her chest to make sure her ribs were intact, did an MRI of her head to make sure she didn't have a brain injury, and gave her a thorough physical exam. The nurse and doctors who saw her were compassionate, but they couldn't do a lot except tell her to rest.

With Logan and Evan still missing, that wouldn't happen.

"Those kids are assholes," she said, looking into the rearview mirror of the SUV they had rented for the job. Diego sat in the passenger seat, lounging and paying little attention to the world around them. It was dark and had been for several hours, but the truck stop's massive lights lit the interior of their vehicle well enough that they could have read books had they wanted.

Diego nodded.

"Yep," he said. "If this makes you want to reconsider the whole kid thing, I'd understand."

He smiled. She glared at him but said nothing, and he held up his hands.

"Don't worry. I'll still knock you up if that's what you want," he said. "I get it."

"That's why I married you," she said, returning her gaze to the mirror. Eye drops had taken most of the redness from her eyes, but her face still felt dry and leathery.

"I thought you married me for my charm," said Diego.

"Nope," she said, shaking her head. "Your charm

helped, but I'm after your sperm."

"I'm glad to know where I stand in this relationship."

She glanced at him and smiled.

"I love you, too," she said. "So that's something."

"But mostly, it's the sperm," he said. She winked and reached over the console to squeeze his hand.

"Yep."

After the kids ran, Diego had found her at the bottom of the steps in the Robinsons' home. Gloria had been awake, but she hadn't been aware. He picked her up, put her in the back of the car, and cleaned her up as well as he could in the parking lot of a truck stop outside the town of St. Augustine. When she woke up enough to talk to him, he drove her to the urgent care center in Melville. It was sweet but unnecessary. She had a concussion but no broken bones or other long-term injuries. She'd be okay in time.

Afterwards, they had driven back to the same truck stop to wait. The kids would show up somewhere. They just had to have patience.

Gloria watched and shuddered as a gaunt young man —he was sixteen or seventeen—in a tight T-shirt and jeans climbed into the cab of a semi parked near them.

"He's the fourth kid working this parking lot," said Diego. "I suspect the guy who owns this truck stop isn't on the up-and-up."

"Fifth," said Gloria. "You missed a girl when you went to the bathroom. She knocked on the window and asked whether I'd like to chat."

"You declined, I assume," said Diego.

"Yeah," said Gloria, shaking her head and sighing. "This town may be pretty from a distance, but it sure is ugly when you get up close."

Diego nodded but said nothing. They waited another half hour before his phone buzzed. He pulled it from his pocket and ran a finger across the screen before looking at her.

"We've got them," he said. "They're in St. Louis, and they just spent two hundred bucks on Amtrak tickets. They're running."

Gloria nodded, turned on the car, and used the GPS to search for Amtrak stations in St. Louis. The city only seemed to have one, so she punched it in and started rolling toward the interstate.

"Where are they going?"

"Their credit card receipt doesn't say," said Diego. "But there aren't that many trains leaving tonight. Tickets to Chicago or Kansas City wouldn't cost that much, so I think our boys are taking the overnight train to Houston. They're going home."

It made sense, so she nodded.

"When's the train leave?"

"Little over an hour," said Diego.

She punched her foot down on the accelerator.

"We'll get them on the train," she said. "Reserve two seats for us. We're going to Houston."

7

After hanging up with Daisy Robinson, I walked to the second-floor conference room in which we had stationed our dispatcher during construction. Jason Zuckerburg sat behind a sturdy white table laden with computers, monitors, phones, and other equipment used to communicate with our officers in the field. When he saw me, he picked up a cup of coffee and nodded.

"Hey, Joe. What's shaking?"

"Keeping busy," I said. "Have you seen Marcus Washington around?"

Zuckerburg narrowed his eyes and clicked his tongue as he thought.

"Did you check the third-floor conference room?"

I raised my eyebrows and lowered my chin.

"We have a third-floor conference room?"

Zuckerburg smiled and nodded.

"As of two days ago. The construction crews finished roughing-in that floor. I think the plan is to move everybody from this floor to that one so the construction guys can tear the second floor apart. George mentioned it in the briefing yesterday."

I nodded and crossed my arms.

"I guess I shouldn't tune the boss out every time he talks."

Zuckerburg chuckled and nodded.

"Probably not. Anyway, I saw Marcus around earlier, so I bet he's up there."

I thanked him before leaving and taking the stairs to the third floor. The walls were white and unfinished, but gray Berber carpet covered the floor, while lights in the drop ceiling cast an even, bluish incandescence on the hallway. The construction crews still had some work to do —the walls needed paint, and the electrical outlets needed covers—but it looked nice.

I walked down the hall until I found a large open room with six wooden desks, each of which held a computer and monitor. Marcus typed at a computer, but he looked up when he saw me.

"Give me a second, Joe, and I'll be right with you," he said, focusing on his computer again. He clicked a few things with his mouse and then pushed back. As best I could tell, he and I were alone on the floor. "How do you like the new digs?"

I looked around and nodded.

"Not bad," I said, nodding toward a bank of windows on the far wall. "They replaced the windows, too. No more raining indoors, huh?"

"We're living large," he said before leaning forward and reaching for a printed piece of paper beside him. "As you asked, I pulled a credit report for Joel Robinson, our victim. He's got a mortgage but little debt otherwise. He makes a good salary and doesn't seem to have any money problems. I called his credit card company to check out his most recent charges. He checked into his hotel last night and then purchased dinner at Imo's Pizza. This morning, he got breakfast at Waffle House before going to the Arch, where he spent twenty-eight bucks.

"After the Arch, he drove to St. Augustine, where he got some gas and then spent twelve bucks at Rise & Grind."

I crossed my arms and blinked as I thought.

"Twenty-eight bucks doesn't buy you two tickets at the Arch, does it?"

Marcus shook his head.

"Not two adult tickets. Twenty-eight bucks is one sixteen-dollar adult ticket and one twelve-dollar child ticket."

I nodded as my mind processed that. Then I sighed.

"I called Robinson's wife in Texas. She said he was here to camp and go fishing."

Marcus furrowed his brow.

"Little cold to go camping," he said.

"I agree," I said, nodding. "He didn't come to camp, though; Robinson was here to see a kid."

Marcus nodded and laced his fingers behind his head as he leaned back.

"Twelve bucks at Rise & Grind will get you two cups of hot chocolate and four sugar cookies. I take the girls after school once a week."

I brought a hand to my chin as I thought. Then I nodded.

"Good work. I'll call Sheryl at Rise & Grind and see whether she remembers the victim coming in. Then I'll see whether anyone's reported a kid missing around here."

"You need me for anything?"

I shook my head.

"No. Finish your paperwork and head home. And thank you for sticking around. I know you'd rather be home, but I needed you, and you did good work. I appreciate that."

"Just doing my job," he said.

I wished him a good night and then walked downstairs to my office. A month ago, I had joined a book club at a friend's suggestion. We sat around a bar at five in the afternoon, we talked about a book, and then we went home. It was fun, and I liked the women involved—including Sheryl, Rise & Grind's owner.

Once I reached my office, I sat at my desk and called Sheryl's cell phone. She answered after three rings.

"Hey, it's Joe Court. I'm sorry I'm calling you so late."

She yawned.

"That's okay, but I can't talk long. I've got to be at the shop at four tomorrow to make the pecan rolls."

Sheryl's pecan rolls were the single greatest product ever created in St. Augustine. Without them, I never would have gotten out of bed most mornings.

"I won't keep you long," I said. "And this isn't a social call. I'm calling about a customer who came into your shop this afternoon. His name is Joel Robinson. He's thirty-nine years old, and he's from Texas, so he might have spoken with an accent."

"That's familiar, but afternoons are busy. I don't remember everyone."

"I understand, but anything you can tell me would help. Someone murdered Mr. Robinson this afternoon in Sycamore Park. We believe he was with a young person, possibly a young man. We're looking for the kid now because he might have witnessed a murder."

"Oh, man," she said. She paused. "Come by the shop. We can look at the surveillance video. I put in cameras after a customer started harassing Molly."

"Sure. How soon can you be there?"

"Five minutes if you don't mind seeing a grown woman in pajamas," she said.

I smiled.

"That's fine. I'll head over now."

I thanked her for meeting me on such short notice and then hung up. Since the coffee shop was just up the street, I grabbed a jacket and walked over. St. Augustine was a beautiful old town with hundred-year-old shops lining the main strip like row houses. The bars had yet to close for the night, but the old-fashioned candy shop, antique stores, and small, professional offices had long turned out their lights.

I hurried to Rise & Grind. The lights were on inside, and Sheryl held open the front door for me. Sheryl was at least a decade older than me, but she could have passed for my college roommate. She wasn't married, but she had a semi-serious boyfriend who taught psychology at Waterford College. I liked her a lot.

"Hey, Joe," she said, smiling.

"Thanks for letting me in," I said, allowing the glass door to shut behind me. "I know it's late, but this is a big help."

"No problem," she said, pulling a chair from a nearby table on which she had placed a laptop. "I've got the video ready, and I think this is the guy you're talking about. He ordered a chai latte, a cup of hot chocolate, and two blueberry scones."

I sat beside her at the table and looked at the video. The camera hung on the back wall near the ceiling, giving me a wide-angle shot of the cash register and most of the dining room. The man at the register was Joel Robinson, but I couldn't see anyone with him.

"Is this your only camera?"

She tilted her head to the side.

"It's the only one that works."

"That's Mr. Robinson, my victim. Let's play it and see who he sits beside."

She nodded and tapped a button on her mouse. Sheryl and I sat and watched as Mr. Robinson took a tray to a table near the window. A young man sat across from him. We didn't have a great picture of him, but he looked as if he were fourteen or fifteen. I looked at Sheryl.

"You recognize the kid?"

"No, but I know someone who might," she said,

reaching into the pocket of her bathrobe to take out her cell phone. She paused the video, zoomed in, and then snapped a picture of the screen. Then she typed for a moment and smiled at me. "You read this month's book yet?"

"I've started, but I haven't finished yet. It's good. It should give us a lot to talk about."

"Yeah, I'm looking forward to the meeting and seeing what Kathy says about—"

Sheryl's phone beeped, interrupting her. She looked down and read a text message.

"Molly didn't recognize him, but she showed the picture to her younger sister, who said his name is Logan Alvarez. He's a freshman at the high school and lives with his mom and his brother, Evan."

I leaned back and smiled.

"You're a saint," I said, standing and taking out my phone. "Thank you very much. And thank Molly and her sister for me."

She promised she would, which I appreciated. As I left, she locked the door behind me, turned off the lights, and disappeared into the back, where I knew she had a set of stairs that took her to her apartment on the building's second floor. I zipped my jacket and searched through my phone's call history until I found Daisy Robinson's number.

The phone rang five times before going to voicemail.

"Mrs. Robinson, this is Detective Joe Court in St. Augustine. Before his death, your husband had a snack with a young man named Logan Alvarez. Logan and your husband have a pretty strong resemblance. Is it possible your husband has a relative in town? Call me back. If I don't hear from you tonight, I'll call you tomorrow morning. Sound good? Thanks so much."

I hung up and slipped the phone in my pocket. My voice had stayed even during the message, but now that I was off the phone, I ground my teeth and balled my hands into fists. I didn't care if Joel Robinson had a love child in St. Augustine. His private life was his business. If his wife wanted to keep that secret from her parents or the neighbors, that was her right. When witnesses and family members held back on me during a murder investigation, though, people could get hurt. That pissed me off.

When I got to my office in my station, I used the license bureau's database to look up every St. Augustine resident with the last name Alvarez. That gave me nine names, but I could eliminate most of them right away. Logan Alvarez was a freshman in high school, which meant he was fourteen or fifteen. That meant his mom was somewhere between thirty and fifty. She could have been a little older, but I doubted she'd be younger than that. That brought my list of nine individuals down to two.

I called the first on my list, but she said she didn't have children and wished me luck. No one picked up at the second phone number, which meant she would get a visitor. I got the address and walked out of my office. It was time to get answers.

8

I signed out Old Brown, a decrepit but still roadworthy cruiser, from my station's motor pool and headed out. Krystal Alvarez lived in a split-level cedar-sided home on a big lot just outside the town of St. Augustine. The homeowner had cut the grass short, trimmed the hedges, and put yellow mums in cherry red pots beside the door. The flowers added a welcome splash of bright color to an otherwise dreary palette.

I parked behind a big pickup in the driveway and got out of my car. The moment my foot hit the pavement, a man opened the home's front door and stepped out. He was about six feet tall and had sand-colored skin, broad, rounded shoulders, and brown hair cropped close to his scalp. I figured he was about two hundred pounds, very little of which was fat. As I walked toward him, he dropped a foot back and turned so that his side faced me. He had a firearm on his hip.

I stopped and pushed my jacket back to expose my badge.

"I'm Detective Joe Court with the Sheriff's Department. Do me a favor and keep your hands away from that firearm."

He nodded but didn't move.

"I'm reaching for the badge in my wallet," he said. "I'm not going for my weapon."

"Sure," I said, forcing myself to smile even as every muscle in my body tensed. He reached behind him, and I inched my hand closer to my pistol. I had a tree to my left that'd give me some cover, and I could have half a dozen officers out there within ten minutes if I placed a call. None of that would matter if he pulled a gun.

My hand reached the exterior of my holster, and I popped the latch that held my weapon in place with my thumb. If he went for his piece, he'd have a bad day.

He pulled his wallet out and opened it to expose a round, steel badge with a star in the center. My shoulders relaxed some, but I didn't move my hand from my firearm.

"I'm Deputy US Marshal Justin Cartwright. My boss is Chief Deputy Marshal Kelly Babcock. She oversees the Marshals Service in the Eastern District of Missouri. She has a temper. If you call her at this time of night to verify my identity, you'll piss her off. Fair warning."

"I don't plan on calling her," I said, shaking my head. "Do you live here, Deputy Marshal Cartwright?"

He considered and then shook his head.

"No."

"Why are you here?" I asked.

"Why are you here?" he responded.

I forced myself to smile even though I was tiring of

this back and forth.

"I'm investigating a homicide, and I believe a potential witness lives at this address."

Cartwright looked toward the house and then back to me.

"Everybody's asleep. How about you come back tomorrow morning during regular business hours?"

"I'd love to do that," I said, tilting my head to the side. "But you know how this works. I've got a murder, and I'm following up on a potential witness. My shooter's a dangerous man, and a resident at this address can help me find him. You don't want to let a dangerous murderer walk, do you?"

He shook his head.

"No, ma'am," he said. "Dangerous men are my bread and butter. I'll tell you what: give me the details on your shooter, and I'll see whether I can find him for you."

"That's a generous offer, but I'll pass. I need to talk to Logan Alvarez. I believe he's inside, and you're preventing me from talking to him. Why is that?"

Cartwright sighed.

"Because Logan gets cranky if we wake him up," he said, crossing his arms. "Since you're insistent, I'll get his mom. You can talk to her."

I suspected I knew where this would end up, but I forced myself to smile and nod.

"Sure."

He walked into the house and shut the door behind him. About five minutes later, a woman in her late thirties or early forties emerged. She had long brown hair pulled back from her face and tanned skin. She wore jeans and a pink cable-knit sweater. The marshal kept an arm around her shoulder, but judging by the sway of her shoulders, it was more to prop her up than to show her affection.

"Ma'am, I'm Detective Joe Court with the St. Augustine County Sheriff's Department. Are you okay to talk for a minute?"

"I have nothing to say," she said, her voice so slow and deliberate I knew she had practiced it. Her eyes looked watery, and she had a dazed expression. I held her blank gaze for a moment before looking to the marshal.

"Is she drunk or high?"

Cartwright shrugged.

"Just drunk, I think."

I crossed my arms and looked at her again.

"Do you know Joel Robinson, ma'am?"

Her posture stiffened and her eyes popped open as she looked to the marshal, but she said nothing. I repeated the question.

"She's never heard of him," said Cartwright. "Next question."

Her surprise and the sudden shift in posture told me all I needed to know. She recognized the name. I forced myself to smile so I wouldn't clench my jaw tight.

"Can I talk to your son Logan?"

She shook her head.

"He's not here."

I raised my eyebrows and lowered my chin.

"You said he was asleep," I said, glancing at

Cartwright.

"He's asleep at a friend's house," said the marshal, pulling Krystal Alvarez back toward the house. "This conversation's over. If you need to contact us again, I'll give you the name of an attorney."

"This isn't over," I said, returning my hand to my firearm. "Now that you've both lied to me, I'm worried someone's hurt inside. I'm going to put you in handcuffs and walk through the house."

Cartwright straightened and stepped toward me. He was taller and broader than me, so he probably thought it would intimidate me. He wouldn't have been wrong.

"Do you have a warrant, Detective?"

"Not yet," I said. "But I'm worried about the safety of two minors inside this house."

"Logan and Evan are safe," he said. "I'm a United States marshal, and you have my word. If you or anyone from your department enters or attempts to enter this house without a signed search or arrest warrant, I will consider it a personal threat. Is that clear?"

My insides boiled, but I nodded and took a step back, anyway.

"Are you threatening a police officer?"

He shook his head.

"No, I'm warning you. This is a private home. If you want to search it, get a warrant."

"If I get a warrant, it'll be an arrest warrant with your name on it, and I'll bring half a dozen officers with me to serve it. You can either let me talk to Logan now, or I'll arrest you for interfering with my investigation."

"You're not talking to Logan, but good luck with your arrest," he said, smiling as he turned. "Have a nice evening, Detective Court, and good luck with your murder investigation. My office will be in touch."

He and Krystal disappeared into the home a moment later and shut the door behind them. I clenched my jaw and walked back to my car. After I fumed for a few minutes, worry began to replace my anger. Something was wrong in the Alvarez house. I needed to make sure Logan was okay, but I suspected the marshal would shoot me if I started peering into windows.

And that was the problem: I might have had exigent circumstances to search the home, and I had every right to talk to Logan Alvarez—with or without the marshal's permission—but if I did either of those things, I'd endanger people. I swore under my breath. As much as I hated talking to a kid after his mom refused me permission, Logan and I needed to talk. It might be nice to talk to Evan Alvarez, too, and see whether he knew Joel Robinson. No matter how I approached this, though, Cartwright was a serious problem.

I got back in my car and drove to my station, where I made phone calls for the next hour. As I sat on hold with the Department of Social Services, my mind wandered, forming a theory from the disparate and still incomplete facts I had gathered so far. My victim had some kind of relationship with Logan Alvarez. The video from Rise & Grind proved that. If I had to guess, they were father and son.

Justin Cartwright, the US marshal I found at Krystal Alvarez's house, had a relationship with Logan, too, even if I didn't understand the details yet. Not only that, Cartwright was familiar enough with Krystal Alvarez to not only be in her house this late but to also prop her up in a doorway so I could talk to her.

If Krystal had sole custody of her children, I could understand why their father's sudden appearance would piss her off. Maybe Krystal told her boyfriend—Cartwright—that her Joel was in town and that she was worried for her children. Then, maybe, Cartwright tracked Logan down and confronted Joel Robinson. That would have pissed Joel off, especially if he was just talking to his son. Joel and Cartwright then argued. The argument turned violent, and, unfortunately for Joel, Cartwright was both trained and armed to take down violent assailants. In this scenario, Cartwright shot Joel and fled.

I still had more questions than answers, but the theory fit the evidence so far. To prove it, I'd have to talk to Logan. I could also show Cartwright's picture to our witness once the doctors at St. John's cleared him for visitors. If our witness identified Cartwright as the shooter, I could get a search warrant for any pistols Cartwright might own and see whether any of those pistols fired rounds that matched the ones recovered from Robinson's body.

I hung up my phone—Social Services had kept me on hold long enough—and started pacing. It'd take some work, but I had a road map for my next few days. I wrote some notes and started to turn off my computer when my boss, Sheriff George Delgado, knocked on my door with a dour expression on his face.

"It's eleven at night, Joe," he said. "Can you guess why I'm here?"

"You like the free coffee in the conference room?" I asked, crossing my arms.

He sighed, crossed his arms, and leaned against the doorframe.

"That coffee isn't free, and no, I'm not here for a drink. Please tell me why the chief deputy marshal of the Eastern District of Missouri called me at home to chew me out for twenty minutes."

I sighed and raised my eyebrows.

"This may take a while."

"Oh, good," he said. "I hate going to bed at reasonable hours."

9

The train to Houston was late. According to the announcements over the PA system, there had been a storm somewhere north, and a bunch of trees had fallen on the tracks in the middle of nowhere. It had taken crews two hours to move everything and get the trains going again.

Every moment they were in St. Louis sent chills down Logan's spine, but he and Evan had taken refuge amongst the crowd in the station. Even if Diego and Gloria had fake badges, they wouldn't try to hurt them in such a public place. He and Evan should be safe.

"Maria Pascalone was hot, wasn't she?" Logan asked his brother, hoping to lighten the mood. "Theo says he's got pictures of her in the shower, but he won't show them to anybody. I think it's bullshit."

Evan nodded but said nothing. At least he had reacted this time. For a while, he hadn't even flinched when Logan poked him in the side.

"What should we do at Grandma and Grandpa's?" he asked. Evan shrugged but said nothing. "I bet Grandpa will want to go to Galveston Island State Park. He always liked it there. And remember that restaurant with gumbo and gyros?"

"Cajun Greek," said Evan, not taking his eyes from his shoes. Both of them were sitting on the floor beside their go-bags. Their backs were to the wall. Evan had brought his knees to his chest, but Logan sat with his legs stretched out in front of him. Exit doors to the left and right led out of the station. If needed, they could sprint down to the platform and escape there, too, but that would draw a lot of attention. They'd get caught.

"That's the name," said Logan, nodding and smiling much more broadly than he otherwise would have. "Grandpa always liked that place."

They waited another fifteen minutes in silence before they heard the rumble. The mood around the train station intensified as men and women began grabbing their bags. Logan stood and helped his brother up before looking again at their ticket. He had booked a private room with two beds. It didn't cost that much more than two reserved seats, and it came with breakfast. Plus, it'd be safer than sitting out in the open in the regular car.

"I'm hungry," said Evan.

"You should have eaten at Theo's house. He said he would have made you some pizza rolls."

Evan put his hands over his stomach and shook his head.

"I don't want pizza rolls again. I had one in my mouth still when you killed that lady."

Logan squeezed his brother's arm and leaned close.

"Don't talk about that," he said. "At least not until we get to Grandma and Grandpa's house. We'll get a lawyer."

"Dad's dead, isn't he?"

Again, Logan looked around before answering. Nobody seemed to watch them.

"Yeah. It was Diego, Gloria's partner."

Evan blinked a lot. His eyes were red, but nobody seemed to notice the crying eleven-year-old boy in their midst. The train pulled to a stop on the platform below them, so the men and women who worked at the station hurried about their duties, knowing time was short. Then, a voice over the PA system announced it was time to board the train.

Logan adjusted the grip on his bag and made sure his brother was with him before slipping into the crowd of people walking toward the train. The station was modern and clean, like a good airport, and it had wide hallways that allowed half a dozen people with bags to saunter toward their destination.

Logan's gut twisted, but he knew this was the right thing. Every time he closed his eyes, he saw his dad fighting Diego in the park. He heard him scream for Logan to run, and he knew his dad was dead. But he couldn't grieve, not until he and Evan reached safety.

Krystal Robinson, Logan and Evan's mom, had worked for a drug cartel. No one had ever told Logan that, but he wasn't stupid. The story made the papers. He even saw video clips on the internet of his mom exiting a courthouse wearing a bulletproof vest with men in tactical gear surrounding her.

Once, his mom had been a lawyer. She had worked in a big energy company in Houston and had specialized in international freight logistics and customs enforcement. Her company had moved billions of dollars' worth of equipment and supplies to South America, Mexico, Nigeria, and across the United States, so they needed someone like her, someone who specialized in that kind of law. Logan had been proud of her. They went to big parties and met lots of rich people. His dad had worked for the same company, but he was an engineer.

Then, one day, she came home in a Bentley that cost more than she made in a year. His parents argued for a week straight, and then their dad moved out. He tried to get the boys to move out, too, but their mom sued. It got ugly. Nobody realized she worked for a cartel. She told everybody she had made wiser investments than her ex-husband.

Logan and Evan showed their tickets to an attendant, who smiled and led them to their room. It was small but clean. It was the cheapest private room offered on the train, but it had two seats that folded into a bed and a second bed that folded down from the ceiling. The attendant said that when they wanted to sleep, he'd come and give them pillows and blankets.

"My brother's hungry. Are there vending machines on board?"

The attendant shook his head.

"No vending machines, and the dining car is closed,

but the lounge is open all night. They'll serve sandwiches and pizza and things like that."

Logan nodded and thanked him. The attendant reminded them to call him once they wanted to sleep. Then he left. They waited in their room for about five more minutes until the train left the station. The acceleration was smooth, and the ride felt comfortable. If it hadn't been for the countryside changing around them, it would have felt like they weren't moving at all.

After a few minutes, Evan started crying again. Logan thought about telling him everything was okay and that they were safe, but he said nothing. Things weren't okay. Their dad was dead, their mom was probably passed out in a bar or dead, too, and they had killed a lady. They may not go to jail for murder, but Logan didn't know whom they could trust. Not the US marshals, that was for sure. Justin said he'd keep them safe, but a murderer had walked right into their house.

His dad hadn't led the bad guys there. He had taken precautions. He had a fake ID, a fake credit card, fake everything. Someone at the US Marshals Office must have screwed up. The thought made his hands tremble and a nauseated feeling bubble up in his gut.

After a little while, Evan stopped crying. Logan didn't know where they were, but they had been on the train for at least half an hour, and his stomach rumbled.

"You want to get something to eat?"

Evan nodded, so they slipped out of the room, locked the door behind them, and followed signs to the lounge car. The attendants had turned the lights low, and most people were asleep or trying to sleep. About a dozen people sat in the lounge, drinking, eating, and chatting in low whispers. Big windows wrapped around the side of the train to the ceiling. It was a pretty night.

They took the stairs to the lower level and ordered sandwiches and Cokes in the cafe. The moon was nearly full, and the sky was clear. They sat at a booth and waited for their dinner in silence and watched as the countryside shuffled past their window. It was relaxing, and Logan felt his eyelids grow heavier.

"Hey, boys."

It was a woman's voice. Logan looked over, expecting to see an Amtrak attendant carrying their sandwiches. Instead, he found Gloria, the faux US marshal he had fought at their house. She smiled at him, but her eyes smoldered. Beside her stood Diego, the man who had killed his father.

"Scoot," said Gloria, shoving Evan toward the window. She lowered her voice. "If you scream, I'll shoot you."

Logan's mouth opened, and a shudder passed through him. He couldn't do anything but stare.

"I killed you."

The man with her laughed.

"Afraid not," he said. "That's good for your sake, too. If you had, I would have killed you."

"My husband is such a romantic," said Gloria, winking and sitting beside Evan. The guy sat beside

Logan. "What'd you guys order?"

"What do you want?" asked Logan.

"An apology would be nice," said Gloria. "If you had cooperated earlier, you'd be sitting in the back of a very comfortable SUV right now. Instead, you pepper sprayed me, kicked me in the chest so I fell down the stairs, and then ran. We were just hired to pick you up, but I'm a little pissed right now. I'm thinking about cutting off some of your fingers to remind you to be a little more polite."

The man laughed again.

"You're scaring them, honey," he said before smiling at Evan and then Logan. "I'm Diego. We haven't been formally introduced. My wife isn't usually violent, but she's had a bad day. We're here to take you somewhere safe. In the meantime, we're all going to enjoy a nice late dinner. We'll hang out on the train for a while, and then we'll get off at the Dallas station. I know it's not where you wanted to go, but it works for us. From there, we'll figure things out. If you cooperate, nobody will get hurt. If you fight us, though, we'll drug you, take you to a warehouse, and start peeling your skin back with a pocket knife. Sound good, guys?"

Evan said nothing, but Logan nodded.

"Just don't hurt us."

"Don't give us a reason to, honey," said Gloria, reaching across the table to touch his forearm. He pulled his arms back hard enough that his elbow thwacked into the seat. She smiled and then looked to her husband. "Honey, order some food. I'll stay here with the kids."

"You want anything in particular?" asked Diego, sliding out of the booth. She smiled once more.

"Surprise me."

He left, and Gloria smiled at Evan and Logan again.

"Anything you want to talk about, guys?" she asked.

Evan's nostrils flared every time he took a breath. He was almost hyperventilating. Logan reached under the table for his brother's knee and squeezed tight. Evan's breathing became a little more even, but his eyes were still wide with fear. Logan's chest felt tight, but his head felt light, like he was floating. He couldn't let his brother see how scared he was, so he forced a neutral expression on his face. Somehow, he'd figure a way out of this. They just had to survive until they could escape.

Diego came back a moment later carrying the sandwiches Logan and Evan had ordered. He put them in front of the boys and looked to his wife.

"Ours will be up soon."

She nodded.

"Good," she said. "Eat, boys. You never know when your next meal will come."

Logan unrolled his silverware and put the napkin on his lip. As he did, he tucked a butter knife behind his wrist and slipped his hand beneath the table. Gloria leaned toward him, the same smile on her face he had seen earlier.

"If you don't put that knife back on the table, I'll take it from you and use it to gut your little brother."

Logan did as she asked and put his knife beside his

plate. She winked at him and then focused on her husband's back as he waited for their dinner. Escaping would be harder than he'd thought, but they had to do it. If they wanted to survive, they didn't have a choice.

10

I spent the next half hour filling the sheriff in on my investigation and findings so far. When I finished, Delgado sighed and raised his eyebrows.

"Have you had any success accessing your victim's cell phone?"

"I haven't even tried yet," I said. "After I saw the surveillance video at Rise & Grind, I thought it was more important to make sure Logan Alvarez was safe. That led me to the Alvarez house and Justin Cartwright."

Delgado ran a hand across his chin and then glanced at me.

"The marshal's a little high-strung, isn't he?"

"That's one way to describe him," I said. "At the moment, though, he's not my primary concern. I need to talk to Logan Alvarez, and the marshal's preventing me. You talked to Cartwright's boss. Is there any chance she could persuade him to bring the kid to the station?"

Delgado didn't even pause before shaking his head.

"I'm not sure what's going on over there, but she didn't seem open to interagency cooperation."

"Meaning?" I asked, raising my eyebrows.

"She said that if Cartwright sees you anywhere near the house, he's within his rights to see it as a threat. Apparently, he's captured some high-level fugitives on behalf of the federal government, and those high-level federal fugitives have threatened his family. That's why he lives in Missouri instead of DC. He doesn't know whether he can trust you."

I rolled my eyes.

"I showed him my badge, and I rolled up to the house in a marked cruiser. If he doesn't know I'm a cop, he needs to get his eyes checked."

"Everybody's got a price, Joe," said Delgado. "Cops included. I'm not excusing Cartwright's behavior, but you have a tendency to overplay your hand. Maybe you came across a little more heavy-handed than you realized, and maybe Cartwright has reason to feel wary."

I shook my head and crossed my arms.

"I'm not the problem here," I said. "I'm doing my job and following up on a potential witness to a homicide. If Cartwright had concerns about me, he could have set up a meeting. I would done it on his turf, on neutral territory, or here. I would have met him and talked this through. He didn't do that, though. Instead, he called his boss. That boss then called you, and now you're arguing with me and telling me to back off on a suspect before clearing him. You're being manipulated, George."

Delgado narrowed his eyes and considered me.

"If I gave you a free hand to go after Cartwright, what would you do?"

"First, I'd talk to Logan Alvarez," I said. "We have a witness to the shooting who already talked to Marcus Washington. That witness described someone running from the scene before the shooting occurred. I'm willing to bet that was Logan, and I bet he knows who pulled the trigger and killed Joel Robinson."

"Even if you see Logan, he might not cooperate."

"And that'd be his choice," I said, nodding, "but Cartwright won't even let me see him. Not only that, the kid's mom was so drunk she couldn't even stand up. After seeing her, I don't trust that's a safe environment for two kids, so I've been trying to get in touch with someone from Social Services."

Delgado rubbed his eyes.

"Jeez, Joe. I get that you're pissed, but you don't have to go scorched earth on the guy. Don't try to take his kids from him."

"I don't know whether they are his kids, I don't know whether he stays at the house often, I don't even know whether the kids like him or whether he's good to them. All I know is that he was at the Alvarez house, Krystal Alvarez was drunk, and he's doing everything he can to prevent me from investigating. I'm just trying to make sure the kids are safe."

"Have you found any connection between your victim and Cartwright?"

I shook my head.

"No, but that's not surprising. My victim checked into his hotel under a false name, and his wife gave me a bullshit story about going fishing. I would suspect he was here to buy drugs or guns or something like that, but I couldn't find anything suspicious on him or in his hotel. As best I can tell, he came here to see Logan Alvarez. They went to the Arch, they got lunch, they went to Rise & Grind for a snack, and then they went to the park, where someone shot Joel."

Delgado drew in a breath and blinked as he thought.

"Could he be a pedophile here to pick up a kid?"

"It's possible, but I haven't found anything to suggest it," I said, shaking my head. "And Logan Alvarez and Joel Robinson look alike. If they're not father and son, they're related somehow. I think my victim was here to visit his kid. He doesn't have a criminal history, so I'm guessing he lost the kids in a custody dispute and is sneaking around to see them on the sly."

Delgado said nothing for about thirty seconds.

"Okay," he said, finally. "I'm not buying your argument that Cartwright is some kind of criminal. That doesn't mean you're wrong. It just means you've got to work the case. Talk to your victim's spouse again and ask whether he's got kids. She might lie, but it might spook her into revealing something she doesn't want to reveal. Then look for Logan Alvarez's birth certificate and see whether he's got a father listed. If we can catch Krystal Alvarez in a lie, we'll have some leverage over her. Build this thing slow and tight. We can't go after a US marshal without solid evidence."

It seemed like good advice, so I nodded.

"What if I find out Cartwright's a shit bag who killed the father of his girlfriend's children?"

"Then we'll send him to prison," said Delgado. "You've got to build the case from the ground up, though, and make sure it'll stick."

I knew how to do my job, but I smiled anyway as if it were advice that had never occurred to me before.

"Will do."

He nodded and turned to leave. It was getting late, but I was working a homicide. The clock didn't matter. I searched through my phone's call history until I found the number of Daisy Robinson, my victim's spouse. She answered on the fourth ring. Her voice sounded sluggish and tired.

"Evening," I said. "This is Detective Joe Court in St. Augustine. I'm sorry to call you so late, but it's important. I'm working your husband's murder, and I need to ask you something: did he have children?"

She paused for a good minute. I would have continued to ask her questions, but I needed to let her think.

"What makes you think he had kids?"

"I've got a video of him having a snack in a coffee shop with a young man to whom your husband bears a striking resemblance. Does he have a son or nephew in St. Augustine?"

"This sounds like you're accusing me of lying to you."

I forced a smile to my lips and hoped it came out in

my voice.

"Did you?" I asked. "When we spoke earlier, you said your husband came to fish and camp and that he didn't know anyone in town. I looked into him and found he checked into a hotel under a false name and didn't bring any fishing or camping gear. If your husband came here to visit his kids, now's the time to tell me. You talk to me now, and I'll forget that you lied to me earlier."

She paused again. Then she drew in a breath.

"I'll have my attorney call you tomorrow morning. If you need to talk to me again, you can contact their office. Good night, Detective."

I grimaced.

"Good night. And I'm sorry again about your husband."

She hung up. I put my phone down, pushed back from my desk, and rubbed my eyes. My victim was dead, so he couldn't get in trouble, and his kids—assuming he came here to visit them—wouldn't get in trouble, either. Hell, I kind of admired a guy who would drive hundreds of miles to spend a day with his son. No one had a reason to lie to me, but they did anyway. That annoyed me.

I filled out some paperwork and drove home at about two in the morning. Instead of going to my actual home, I drove past it and turned into a driveway with a metal mailbox with the word *Pennington* on the side in black and gold stickers.

At one time, it had been Susanne Pennington's house. She had been my friend for years, but I only truly learned who she was on the day she died. I wished things hadn't ended between us the way they had, and I wished I had told her what her friendship had meant to me, but life doesn't give second chances. Susanne left me her house and property in her will. One day I'd figure out what to do with it, but in the meantime, I'd been coming over a few times a week to flush the toilets and dust and make sure everything still worked.

I parked in the driveway, disengaged the alarm, and walked inside. Where my house had been an abandoned dump when I purchased it, Susanne's was a monument to a forgotten time. The woodwork was gorgeous and original, the antique furniture could have been in a museum, and the Turkish and Persian carpets would have been extravagant in a rich man's mansion. An appraiser I brought in after her death told me the house and property were worth almost eight hundred thousand dollars, which made me a wealthy woman.

I would have given it all back to have my friend.

Before going to bed, I texted Mathias and told him I was home and safe but busy. I also apologized for cutting our date short and told him I'd make it up to him when we rescheduled. Part of me hoped he'd respond right away, but it was the middle of the night. He had probably been in bed for hours.

I went to bed alone, but I wasn't lonely. That was a nice change of pace for me. As soon as my head hit the pillow, I fell asleep and dreamed of better days ahead.

11

Logan's shoulders and back ached with exhaustion, and his eyelids felt heavy, but a nervous energy coursed through him all the same. It was like an itch beneath his skin. Gloria and Diego had been drinking coffee all night, but they hadn't offered their two captives anything beyond the sandwiches the boys had ordered the night before. That didn't matter. They wouldn't have taken anything from those two, anyway.

As the sun rose, travelers began buzzing around the cafe car, ordering breakfast, and reading the news on their cell phones and tablets. The staff talked amongst themselves and smiled at the boys but kept a distance.

With every mile that passed, the knot in Logan's gut pulled just a little tighter. According to the announcements on the PA system, they were two hours outside of Dallas. Logan had been to Dallas a few times, but he didn't know the city well. Still, he'd get them out of this somehow. He just didn't know how yet.

"Can we get breakfast?" he asked.

Gloria looked up from her phone and then shot her eyes to Diego.

"You hungry, honey?"

He nodded and stretched his arms above his head, which opened his jacket and exposed the pistol on his hip. He had replaced his US marshals badge with one from the police department in Plano, Texas. It was a fake, but it looked real at a glance. It'd fool most people who saw it.

"I could eat."

Gloria looked to Logan.

"What do you want?"

He watched as someone walked past their table carrying a breakfast sandwich.

"Whatever that guy had," he said. "And get one for Evan, too."

Diego's lips curled upward into a humorless smile.

"Anything else, your highness?"

"No," said Logan. "Thank you."

Diego laughed and looked to his wife.

"You want anything, babe?"

"Breakfast burrito," she said.

He nodded and slid out of the booth. Logan didn't know how they could act so casually, like they were on a cross-country vacation instead of transporting two captives across state lines. Once Diego left, Logan looked to Evan. His skin was pale, and he had his head down on the table on his arms.

"What's your plan?" he asked, looking to Gloria. "You've got one, right?"

She smiled and leaned forward and spoke so that her voice was just above a whisper.

"I was thinking of spraying you in the face with pepper spray and then pushing you down some stairs. How's that sound?"

"Will you kick me, too?" he asked. "That was my favorite part."

She shrugged.

"We'll see," she said. "Maybe I'll kick you, maybe I'll use electrodes attached to a car battery to shock you, or maybe I'll just beat you with a stick while your brother watches."

Logan leaned forward. His heart pounded in his chest, but he wanted her to know that he wasn't afraid of her. No matter what else happened, she wouldn't beat him. He would never give up or give in.

"I got you first. I shot you with pepper spray, I kicked you in the chest, and I made you fall down the stairs. The world would give me a medal if I killed you."

"Stop," said Evan, his voice shaky. "Just stop, Logan."

"Looks like your brother's the sensible one," said Gloria, tilting her head to the side. "You've got too much of your dad in you. He tried to be a hero, too. You know how that worked out."

If the table hadn't been bolted to the ground, he would have thrown it at her. Every muscle in his body screamed at him to lash out at her and make her hurt. He couldn't, though, and that tore at him inside.

"I hate you," he whispered. "I hope you die."

"And yet somehow, I think I'll carry on," she said, looking over Logan's shoulder to her husband. He handed

Logan and Evan wrapped breakfast sandwiches before looking to Gloria.

"Something I missed?"

"Logan was just mouthing off," she said. "He wants to know what we plan to do."

"That's up to your mom," said Diego. "Now shut up and eat your sandwich."

He went back to the counter for a tray with coffee and food. The table went silent once more. The landscape outside their car was flat and a little dull, but it was familiar. Alfalfa fields interspersed with solitary, gnarled trees surrounded the roadside. In the distance, he could see a cell phone tower.

As the miles passed, though, neighborhoods and small towns began to replace the fields. Everything was big in Texas. The fields stretched as far as his eyes could reach, the trees were enormous…even the sun and sky seemed larger somehow. Logan had grown up two hundred miles away in Houston, but he had seen this sky—or one very similar—every morning for most of his life. He hadn't realized how much he had missed that. Despite the circumstances, he was coming home for the first time in years.

About an hour later, the train pulled to a stop at Union Station in Dallas. It was a big station, and a lot of people stood to leave, Diego and Gloria included.

"Okay, boys," said Gloria. "We're off."

"We need to get our stuff," said Logan. "It's in our room. You haven't let us go back."

"Too bad," said Gloria. "Let's go."

Evan started to slide out of his side of the booth, but Logan shook his head. His shoulders felt tight, and he knew that if he put his hands on top of the table, everyone would see them tremble. He swallowed the lump in his throat.

"You really are stupid, aren't you?" he asked. "You'd just leave our stuff in the room? It's like you want to get caught."

Diego stood straighter and said nothing, but Gloria raised her eyebrows and smiled.

"Shut it, kid," she said. "I'm tired of hearing you talk."

Logan leaned toward her.

"Don't you think the attendants will wonder why two kids walked off the train two hundred miles before their ticketed stop and left their stuff in their room after sitting with you two in the cafe car all night?"

Gloria started to respond, but Diego put a hand on her shoulder before she could.

"The kid's got a point," he said. "We should get their stuff."

"If we do that, it'll be two adults leading two kids to a tiny room on a train and then disappearing. It'll look even worse," said Gloria. "You want your shit, go get it, Logan. Diego and I will take your brother outside. If you don't join us, your brother will die. Then we'll find you and your mom and kill you two like we killed your father."

Logan narrowed his eyes at her.

"I hate you."

"I don't care," she said. "Now get your stuff. We'll be outside."

Diego put a hand under Evan's armpit and pulled him out of the booth. The three of them headed toward the exit while Logan walked toward their room. Even though Dallas was a major station, the train would only stop for fifteen minutes. Logan had to move. He slipped through the crowd and pressed his back to the wall to let other passengers with suitcases past.

Once he reached the room, he grabbed both of their backpacks before stepping into the hallway. Already, the crowds were thinning. He hurried up and down the car, but he couldn't find their attendant. He must have been helping other passengers with their luggage, so Logan ran downstairs.

Travelers crowded the first floor. His bags left him little room to maneuver in a hallway full of passengers with suitcases and carry-on bags, so he pressed his back to the wall and slid down the car toward an older man in a blue Amtrak uniform. Logan hadn't seen him before, but that didn't matter. He grabbed the arm of the older man's uniform.

"Sir, my name is Logan Robinson. My brother and I have a room upstairs. A man and a woman sat beside us in the cafe car last night and refused to let us leave. They've both got firearms, and they've forced my little brother off the train. They're on the platform now waiting for me. I don't know what they want, but the guy kept touching my brother and putting his arm around my shoulders. I'm scared."

With so much noise, Logan had to strain his voice. The older guy blinked a few times and then furrowed his brow.

"The door's right there, son," he said, nodding toward a door through which passengers were pouring. "You can get to the platform there and meet your family."

"You didn't hear me," said Logan. "Someone's trying to hurt me."

This time, he pointed toward the door.

"I'm sure your family's outside waiting for you."

Logan wanted to stand and argue with him, but the crowd had grown restless behind him. The weight of the travelers behind him pressed against his back. If he didn't move, he'd get knocked over, so he did the only thing he could and started walking. He'd have to find someone else, another Amtrak employee.

The platform outside was open air with vaulted awnings to keep the rain off passengers as they entered or exited their trains. To reach the station, he'd have to cross a small parking lot and a street full of yellow cabs. He had hoped he could find someone—a police officer, ideally—outside, but Diego and Gloria spotted him right away. They were standing, maybe, fifty feet from the train. Diego had a hand tight around Evan's arm, and all three of them stood still, waiting for him.

Cold anger began spreading through Logan's chest and stomach. He thought about charging toward them and attacking with everything he had. Maybe he wouldn't hurt them, but he'd call attention to himself.

Then he saw badges gleaming on lanyards around both of his captors' necks and the firearms they carried on their hips. They weren't cops, but they looked the part. Even if Logan screamed that he and his brother were being kidnapped, no one would help. People would see him and then they'd see Gloria and Diego's badges and think he was a delinquent being taken to the police station by a pair of detectives. They'd ignore his cries. Logan could run—and maybe he could even escape—but then Gloria and Diego would kill Evan. He had no options but to do what they wanted. So, he walked forward slowly, hoping for a miracle.

Then he got one.

Diego released Evan's arm and leaned into Gloria. His body looked stiff. Then, at once, she and her husband turned and started walking away, leaving Evan on the platform. Logan furrowed his brow, not understanding what was going on. Evan started to follow his captors, but then stopped after a few feet. Neither Gloria nor Diego turned. They just kept walking. They were leaving… without either of the boys.

As Logan watched the two criminals walk, he heard heavy footsteps pounding the ground near him. He looked toward the origin of the sound and found a pair of uniformed police officers hurrying across the platform toward him. At once, a weight lifted from his shoulders. The old guy on the train must have called for help. They were safe.

"It's the man and the woman," he said, pointing toward Diego and Gloria. "They kidnapped us. They're pretending to be cops."

The cops slowed and looked at each other. Then one of the cops started hurrying after the criminals while the second kept walking toward Logan. Logan breathed easier and closed his eyes. He and Evan were okay. He hadn't anticipated things working out like this, but they were alive. The police here would contact his grandparents, and his grandparents would keep them safe. His grandfather was a retired lawyer, after all. He'd know people. Logan could have cried.

Then everything went to shit.

"Sir, ma'am," shouted the officer following Diego and Gloria. "I need you to stop."

Diego looked to Gloria and nodded. Logan's heart began pounding again. This wasn't right. They were planning something.

"They've got guns!" he said. "They're armed."

The moment the words left Logan's lips, Diego turned and pulled out his weapon. Gloria ran. Time seemed to slow.

"Gun!"

Logan didn't know who shouted it, but both cops drew their firearms. Diego twisted his hips and aimed at a crowd of people on the train platform and fired three times. Logan wanted to shout and warn them, but he couldn't get the words out. People started screaming, and a woman holding a toddler hit the ground. One cop ran toward the crowd and started shouting for people to get down, while the other cop returned fire at Diego.

Diego zigzagged across the platform to avoid the gunfire and then ducked between cars in the parking lot. The cop ran after him and held his weapon in front of him.

Then Gloria popped up from behind a stone bench. She held her pistol in front of her and sighted down her arms before squeezing the trigger. It happened almost in an instant. She fired once, and then twice. The cop never even saw her. The rounds slammed into back. His body rocked. Logan had heard the shots that killed his father, but he hadn't seen them. Blood exploded in a fine mist around him before painting the sidewalk. This was surreal. This was wrong.

"Fuck, fuck, fuck!" he shouted, diving to the concrete as Gloria continued firing. Logan's heart hammed in his chest. He watched the cop fall, but he couldn't do anything. Then the gunfire stopped, and Gloria and Diego ran toward a white SUV with blacked out windows. They jumped in the back, and the vehicle accelerated. It must have been waiting for them. Logan and Evan were probably supposed to be in it, too. People were crying and screaming.

Logan didn't know what to do, so he pushed up from the ground and ran to his brother to make sure he was okay. His eyes darted around the station for threats, but nobody was looking at them. Evan wept.

"Evan, dude, we've got to go," said Logan. Every muscle in his body trembled, and it took every ounce of internal strength he had to keep the panic from his voice. "The cop is dead, and his partner's busy. We've got to get out of here before they come back."

Evan didn't move. Logan shot his eyes around the train station. A crowd had gathered around the fallen police officer, but already a few people were looking toward them. Sirens blared from every direction. A sour feeling began building in his gut. Logan pulled his brother to his feet.

"We've got to go, dude," said Logan, his voice warbling with strain. Evan didn't respond, but then an older man in a beige cowboy hat, white button-down shirt, and red tie split from the crowd near the officer and walked toward them. He put a big hand on Logan's shoulder and gently squeezed.

"Come on, son," he said. "The police will need to talk to you."

Neither Logan nor Evan knew how many partners Diego and Gloria had. This guy may have been a Good Samaritan just trying to help out, but he just as easily could have worked for Diego and Gloria. Logan had never seen him before. That meant he couldn't trust him. Their dad was already dead. Their mom was probably dead, too. Maybe even Justin was dead.

All Logan knew was that he and his brother were in danger, and they couldn't trust anyone but family. He squeezed Evan's arm.

"Fucking run!"

Finally, Evan listened. The boys ran and never looked back.

12

I got up at about ten the next morning in the guest bedroom of Susanne's house. Even though I owned the place, it still felt weird to wake up in there. I stretched, yawned, and sat up, already thinking through everything I had to do that day.

Ideally, I'd spend the entire day working Joel Robinson's murder, but I had an interview with a serial murderer named Peter Brunelle this afternoon. We didn't know how many people Brunelle had murdered, but at our first meeting, he had told me the location of where he had buried a previously unknown victim. Then, the next time I spoke to him, he described a location where one of his followers had buried three human heads belonging to three murdered men. They were behind my house. My dog found then them when we went for a run. I didn't know what to expect out of him at this visit, but he wanted something.

Brunelle was creepy and evil, and he had a morbid interest in me, but he wasn't the first asshole to threaten me. I could still breathe, and most of them couldn't. My friends and family were worried about me, but as long as I took reasonable precautions, I'd be fine.

Since I didn't need to leave for a few hours, I showered, dressed, and then called Preston Cain, a friend who had agreed to watch my dog. Preston was a former police officer who now built cabinets and furniture in his barn. He understood police work, and he liked Roy. One day, Preston and his fiancée would have children and a dog of their own, but for now, they were okay watching mine whenever I got stuck on a case. I'd pick him up in a day or two when my case slowed down. According to Preston, Roy seemed happy. I appreciated it.

After that, I spent a few minutes at my kitchen table, searching for Logan Alvarez on Instagram, Facebook, and Twitter. As best I could tell, he wasn't on any of them, though, which was odd for a kid his age. Facebook wasn't as popular with kids his age as it had once been, but most kids still had a profile—even if they didn't use it often. If I couldn't learn about him from his postings, I'd have to learn about him via the old-fashioned way: one-on-one conversation.

I left the house at a little before eleven and drove to the high school. Justin Cartwright and Krystal Alvarez had refused to let me talk to Logan Alvarez the night before, but I didn't need their permission to talk to a witness—even if that witness was a minor. Not only that, I didn't trust Cartwright. He may not have murdered Joel Robinson, but until I cleared him, I couldn't believe a word out of his mouth.

I parked in a visitor spot in front of the building and

walked to the front door. A security camera hung from the ceiling near an intercom panel on the wall. I buzzed the front office and showed my badge to the camera. The receptionist let me in.

I had worked several cases that involved school personnel and students, so I knew the building's general layout. I took the hallway to the front office and knocked on the door before stepping inside. The school had two receptionists, one of whom was on the phone. The second receptionist, an older woman with gray hair and deep wrinkles on her neck, cheeks, and forehead, smiled a greeting to me.

"Can I help you, Officer?"

I showed her my badge again and nodded.

"I'm Detective Mary Joe Court with the St. Augustine County Sheriff's Department, and I'm working a homicide witnessed by one of your students. Logan Alvarez. He's a freshman. I need to see him."

The receptionist typed and then picked up her phone before looking at me and smiling again.

"I'll call the principal, Mr. Brody. He'll be out shortly to help."

I thanked her and looked around for a seat. They didn't have any, so I stepped away from the desk and stood with my back to the wall. Eventually, a man in a navy suit, light blue shirt, and vibrant blue tie came from a back hallway. He smiled at me and held out his hand. I had met Mr. Brody a few times in the past, but I had never spoken to him for more than a few minutes.

"Detective Joe Court," I said, shaking his hand. "I'm here to talk to Logan Alvarez."

"So I've heard," said Brody. "Is Logan okay?"

"As far as I know, yes, but I believe he witnessed a homicide," I said. The principal opened his eyes wide with surprise but said nothing. "How's his home life?"

He cocked his head.

"I've met his mom once. She was…interesting."

I crossed my arms.

"How so?"

He smiled but said nothing at first. Then he looked up at his receptionists. Both women were busy behind their desks, but I suspected they were listening to every word we said. He lowered his voice and leaned toward me just a little.

"It was at a pub in town, and she was intoxicated. When my wife went to the restroom, Ms. Alvarez came to my table and propositioned me."

I didn't mean for it to happen, but my lips curled upward. Before Mr. Brody could say anything, I forced my smile away.

"Does that happen often?"

"I talk to parents almost every day," he said, lowering his chin, "but that was the first time a mom propositioned me."

"When was this?"

"Two weeks ago," he said. "My wife and I were out for our anniversary."

I nodded again as I tried to fit that into my puzzle.

Relationships were hard, and no single type of relationship worked for every single couple. Krystal Alvarez might have had an open relationship with Justin Cartwright, but it made me wonder all the same. If he were truly scared for his safety and the safety of his family after arresting high-profile fugitives, I couldn't see him dating a woman who propositioned strangers at bars. It just didn't add up.

I looked to Mr. Brody.

"Is there somewhere I can talk to Logan Alvarez in private?"

"I'd let you use my office, but Logan isn't in school today. His mother called him in sick."

I should have expected that, but I sighed anyway.

"Do any faculty members know him well? Maybe a coach or club leader?"

Mr. Brody blinked and screwed up his face.

"Maybe Mrs. Costandi, his homeroom teacher. As far as I know, Logan doesn't take part in our extracurricular activities yet."

"Let me talk to her, then."

Mr. Brody agreed and led me to Mrs. Costandi's room. Judging by the chalkboard when we arrived, she taught trigonometry, a difficult subject for a lot of high school kids. Despite the challenging material, none of the kids—even those far in the back—had their phones out or were talking to the students beside them. She must have been a good teacher.

She gave us a curt smile as Mr. Brody knocked on the

door.

"Mrs. Costandi, can I see you in the hallway for just a minute?" asked Brody. She looked to her class and then nodded to the principal.

"Of course," she said. She looked to her class once more. "Stay in your seats. I'll return shortly."

In the hallway, Mr. Brody shut the door, giving us some privacy.

"Morning, Mrs. Costandi," I said. "I'm Detective Joe Court with the St. Augustine County Sheriff's Department. I was hoping to talk to you for a minute about Logan Alvarez."

She crossed her arms and nodded.

"I know Mr. Alvarez," she said. "Is he in trouble?"

"Not at all," I said. "He may have seen a murder, though. I've been trying to track him down since yesterday."

She brought a hand to her face and then sighed.

"Kids face more these days than anyone should," she said. She sighed and then looked down. "As Logan's homeroom teacher, I only spend an hour a week with him, so I don't know him well. I do read every report written with his name on it, though. He's a promising young man. He's outgoing, friendly, and cooperative. I expect good things from him."

"That's good to hear," I said, reaching into my purse for a notepad. "Have you ever seen signs of abuse at home?"

"No, but I wouldn't. He's fifteen. Kids at that age are

good about hiding their emotions from the world."

I nodded.

"Any disciplinary problems?"

She hesitated.

"Nothing out of the ordinary. I confiscated his phone last week because I caught him using Facebook to message a friend in another classroom."

Now that was interesting because I hadn't found a Facebook profile with his name on it. When I mentioned that, Mr. Brody smiled.

"He's probably got an account under a fake name," he said. "Most of the kids do. They'll have a normal account under their real names for their parents, family, and college admissions counselors and a fake name for their real accounts. My office maintains a list of fake accounts, which we monitor to make sure the kids stay out of trouble. If they do something dangerous, we alert the proper authorities, but we let kids be kids otherwise. We can check Logan's account in my office."

"I'd appreciate that," I said before turning to Mrs. Costandi. "Thank you for your help."

She nodded and returned to her class as Mr. Brody and I walked to his office, where he consulted a list on his computer before looking at me and shaking his head.

"Unfortunately, we don't know whether Mr. Alvarez has a secret profile," he said, pushing back from his desk and pulling open the center drawer. He pulled out four Ziploc bags, each of which held a cell phone and a note card. "But we might be able to find one. My teachers confiscated these this morning. Give me a moment."

I nodded, and he picked up his phone and requested that his assistant call the four cell phone owners to his office. We waited about five minutes for the first—a young lady in a pair of navy jeans and a maroon polo-style shirt—to arrive. She smiled at me but focused on Mr. Brody.

"Mrs. Hurst said you wanted to see me."

"I did," said Brody. "Thank you for coming. Jessica, this is Detective Court. She works for the Sheriff's Department, and she's here to ask you some questions. Do you know Logan Alvarez? You're both freshmen."

She nodded.

"Yeah. I know Logan."

"Does he have a profile on Facebook?" asked the principal.

She hesitated but then shrugged.

"I…uh…I don't know."

She blinked and then looked down.

"It's important, miss," I said. "Logan's not in trouble, but I need to track him down before he gets hurt."

After a moment, she shook her head.

"I can't help you."

Being nice and hoping she'd do the right thing wasn't working. I crossed my arms and considered the situation. Jessica was fourteen or fifteen. It had been a while since I had been that age, but I doubted adolescence had changed much since I was last in school. Every teenager had secrets. Sometimes those secrets were innocuous, but other times they weren't. Jessica's particular secret didn't matter as long as she'd fight to protect it. I could use that.

"You can cut the shit, Jessica. We already know what's on your phone."

She smiled and tittered, but it sounded forced.

"What do you mean?" she asked.

The principal furrowed his brow at me but said nothing. I kept my eyes rooted on Jessica.

"I can talk to your mom about this, or I can talk to you," I said. "Which do you want?"

She considered me and then shook her head, a smile forming on her lips.

"My mom wouldn't care."

I had played that same card while sitting in the principal's office when I was her age, so I knew how to respond. I didn't take my eyes from hers.

"Principal Brody, get Jessica's mom on the phone."

Her smile faltered.

"You wouldn't do that."

I smiled at her.

"You don't know me. You have no idea what I'd do."

She cocked her head to the side and opened her mouth as if she couldn't believe what was happening to her.

"It was, like, one time," she said. "David said he wouldn't tell."

I raised my eyebrows and lowered my chin but said nothing.

"Okay, fine, we did it four or five times," she said. I

looked to Mr. Brody. He looked perplexed, but he was typing at his computer.

"Once you get Jessica's mom on the phone, put her on speaker," I said to Mr. Brody. "I want to hear her reaction when you tell her."

"This is so unfair," said Jessica. "It was just pot. It's not like I killed somebody."

At least she couldn't get pregnant from smoking pot. Good for her. I nodded.

"Show me Logan's Facebook or Instagram page, and I'll forget all about the drugs."

She rolled her eyes.

"Fine. Give me the phone."

She spent two or three minutes tapping the screen before handing the phone back to me. Logan had registered under the name Oliver Klothesoff. The name kind of threw me for a moment, but then I read it aloud and laughed. Then I focused again.

I couldn't search the kid's profile well, but at least I now had a name I could put on a subpoena. I wrote it down and browsed his list of friends until I found Joel Robinson. The dead man and Logan definitely knew each other. From what I could see, Logan didn't drink, he didn't smoke, and he rarely talked to girls. He did, however, play a lot of video games, but so did most fifteen-year-old boys.

I handed Jessica the phone back.

"So, I can go now?" she asked.

I looked to Mr. Brody.

"After the school resource officer searches your locker for pot," I said.

Her mouth popped open, and she stammered something but then stopped and drew in a breath.

"You said you'd forget about the pot if I showed you Logan's profile."

"I will forget about it," I said. "Principal Brody can't. He's got a school to run and can't have his students hiding their weed in their locker. Now, I've got to go. I've got an appointment in Terre Haute, Indiana, this afternoon, and I can't be late."

I stood and started for the door.

"I hate you."

"I get that a lot," I said. "Good luck."

13

I didn't enjoy leaving town with an open homicide to work, but time didn't stop moving no matter how full my schedule became. Terre Haute was a college town about seventy-five miles west of Indianapolis and two hundred and fifty miles northeast of St. Augustine. The drive took almost four hours with traffic, but it was easy.

When I got to town, I parked in the lot of a Denny's restaurant and grabbed a table. Neither Agent Cornwell nor Costa had arrived yet, so I ordered a sandwich, knowing I wouldn't get the chance to eat for a while. Special Agent Philippa Cornwell arrived first. She was somewhere in her early forties, and she had dyed blond hair and lively green eyes. I didn't know a lot about her except that she worked for the FBI's Behavioral Analysis Unit, but she seemed quite intelligent. Unfortunately, her intelligence was matched by her arrogance and disdain for everyone around her. She walked to my table.

"Detective Court," she said, her voice and lips flat. "May I sit down?"

"Please," I said, smiling. "I'm just finishing lunch. Or dinner. Or a snack. I don't know what you call a meal at four in the afternoon."

She forced a smile on her face and sat across from me.

"Agent Costa will be here soon. He got stuck at a red light."

"I would have just flashed my lights, put on the siren, and blasted through the intersection. Saves time."

She raised her eyebrows and gave me a brief, patronizing smile but said nothing. I put my sandwich down and wiped my hands on a napkin.

"That was a joke," I said. "I don't do that."

"I see," she said.

I had been ravenous when I walked in, but somehow, seeing Agent Cornwell had made me lose my appetite.

"Anything new on Brunelle?" I asked, reaching for the wallet in my purse. I put a twenty on the table for my waitress in case we needed to leave as soon as Agent Costa arrived. Agent Cornwell folded her hands together.

"If there was something we believed you needed to know, we would have informed you of it."

I forced myself to smile.

"I'm so glad."

Cornwell rolled her eyes and looked away. I ate French fries and waited for Agent Costa to arrive. Thankfully, it didn't take him long. Bryan had black hair that came to a pronounced widow's peak on his forehead. He reminded me of Dracula from the old silent films. Unlike Agent Cornwell, he was affable and easy to be around. I enjoyed working with him. As he walked to our table, he smiled at me and then nodded to Cornwell.

"Afternoon," he said, looking at my plate and then to Agent Cornwell. "Maybe we should all grab an early dinner."

"I'm sure we'll be fine," said Cornwell, sliding out of my booth to stand beside the table. "We've wasted enough time here already."

I didn't feel the need to eat anymore, but I picked up the remnants of my sandwich, anyway.

"I'll just finish up here. You guys start the interview with Brunelle. I'll meet you there."

Cornwell put her hands on the table and leaned down so that our faces were only a few inches apart.

"Do you think it's funny to waste my time, Detective?"

"Funny?" I asked, shaking my head. "No. It's not funny. It is enjoyable, though."

She straightened and looked to Agent Costa.

"I can't work with her. You're the senior agent here. You deal with her. I'm going to the car."

Costa and I watched as she stormed off and nearly took out a waitress carrying a tray laden with heavy drink glasses. The young woman pivoted as gracefully as a ballerina and smiled as Cornwell passed. The FBI agent mumbled an apology but didn't otherwise stop or slow down as she left the building. I looked to Agent Costa.

"She hasn't had the surgery yet, has she?" I asked.

Costa sat across from me and furrowed his brow. I put my sandwich down and pushed the plate toward the center of the table. He held his hand toward it as if asking for permission, so I nodded, and he grabbed a French fry.

"Which surgery is that?" he asked.

"The one that would remove the stick from her ass."

He smiled and nodded.

"She's just trying to do her job," he said. Then he paused. "And the stick's still there."

I sighed and crossed my arms.

"You have anything new to tell me?"

"Not really," he said. "Brunelle will only talk to you, but I'll be with you the entire time. I'd like you to ask him about the heads found in your yard. We've had difficulty identifying them, so it'd be nice if he could help. We also need him to talk for a while to give our technical team time to work."

"Okay," I said, sliding out of the booth. "Let's get to it, then. The more we dawdle here, the more pissed off Agent Cornwell will get."

Costa considered for a moment and then waved toward my waitress. She nodded, smiled, and held up a finger. Then he looked to me.

"Let's get coffee," he said. "Philippa can stew."

Brunelle's prison was a concrete fortress with very few windows. As a visitor, I almost found it peaceful. Every inmate in the building could have been screaming at the top of his lungs, but the concrete walls and thick, steel doors eliminated every sound but the tap of our shoes on the textured porcelain-tile floor.

A pair of guards were leading us to the interview room while other guards were strip-searching Brunelle in another part of the prison to make sure he didn't have any concealed weapons. Though the prison staff was professional, their jobs were too dangerous to allow Brunelle the dignity afforded prisoners in less restrictive environments. Everywhere Brunelle went, the guards would lock him in chains and pat him down for weapons. Considering he had murdered and dismembered at least three women, he deserved that and more.

Our interview room was a square about twenty feet on a side. In the center, the prison had bolted a steel table and benches to the floor. Narrow windows near the ceiling allowed a view to the hallway outside, but most of the room's light came from panels embedded in the ceiling. There were panic buttons beside the door and on the opposite wall.

Cornwell, Costa, and I sat at the table with our backs to the wall and facing the door. Two guards led Brunelle to the room a few minutes later. He smiled when he saw me and then faced the guards and held his arms out for them to remove the restraints that bound his wrists and legs together.

"Now that we're here, I'm not sure these are necessary," he said. The guard looked at us for confirmation.

"Leave them on," I said.

Brunelle turned and frowned at me.

"I had hoped you'd be a little more accommodating, Joe," he said. "After all, I'm here to do you a solid. The least you can do is treat me like a human being instead of an animal."

I shrugged.

"Life's full of disappointments. Get used to it and have a seat or go back to your cell and twiddle your thumbs. Your choice, dude."

He considered me and then looked to the guard.

"I'll be staying," he said. "I'll call you if I need you."

The guard led him to the table and unshackled him long enough to run the chain of his wrist shackles to a ring welded to the table. Then he squeezed the restraints tight again and looked at us.

"I'll lock the door behind me. There are two panic buttons inside. If you hit one, an emergency team will come running. I will be outside the door the entire time you're in here with Mr. Brunelle, but I won't be able to hear what you say. If you need me, pound on the door. Does that sound all right with you?"

We nodded, so the guard wished us luck and warned Brunelle to be on his best behavior. Then he turned and left. Brunelle smiled at me.

"It's good to see you, Joe," he said. "I've been thinking about our last conversation."

"Good for you," I said. "Let's talk about the heads in my backyard."

He shook his head. "Not yet. I have other things to talk about. Do you think it's strange that God hides from human beings? Think about it. If religious people are right, then a relationship with God is important, but to have that relationship, you've first got to believe God exists. Why doesn't he come down from his mountain and show himself? He could convert more people to his side doing the halftime show at the Super Bowl than Billy Graham could in a lifetime of work. If God exists, it just seems like he'd show up some."

I sighed and stood up.

"That's it," I said, looking to Cornwell and then Costa. "I told you I'd try, but he's not cooperating. I've got a case to work at home, so I'm heading out."

Brunelle's restraints jangled as I walked to the door.

"Sit down, Mr. Brunelle," said Costa. "The guard will be here soon. He'll take you back to your cell."

"We just got here," said Brunelle, a measure of anger entering his voice. "You're not going anywhere, Joe. I'm too important."

I stopped at the door.

"You're not important," I said. "You're a convict who lives in a seven-foot-by-twelve-foot cell, you sleep on a poured concrete bed, you have your meals served to you through a hole in the door, and you eat alone at a concrete table built into the wall. The only time you ever see another human being is when someone walks by your four-inch bulletproof window. Don't pretend you're something you're not. It's pathetic."

He tried to stand, but the restraints held him in a seated position.

"You don't know who I am or what I can do," he said, his voice a snarl. "If you did, you'd be shitting yourself."

I smiled.

"You're a child who picked up a philosophy textbook. You think you're interesting and important, but you're not. These visits waste my time."

His skin went red, and all light vanished from his eyes. Even with his hands secured to the table, it was terrifying to see—especially knowing that he had already persuaded someone to kill at least three people and bury their heads near my house.

"Go home and pet your dog and hug your mom. Be sure to tell her goodbye, too, because you and your whole family are dead."

I nodded and crossed my arms so he couldn't see my hands trembling.

"You'll forgive me if I don't take life advice from a man so stupid he'll spend the rest of his life in a prison cell."

I pounded on the door. The guard opened it within seconds, and I stepped outside where Brunelle couldn't see me. Then I exhaled and bent down so that my upper body was parallel to the floor. My stomach tightened, and I could feel my lunch rise, so I held my breath to prevent myself from vomiting. Thankfully, that feeling passed.

Costa and Cornwell joined me in the hallway a few

moments later, and I straightened and looked to the guard.

"You all right, ma'am?" he asked.

"I'm fine," I said, nodding and wishing I hadn't just lied. "Keep him in there for another half hour. Then take him back to his cell. And find somebody to escort me out. I'm done for the day."

The guard nodded and got on his radio. Within moments, the assistant warden came down from wherever he had been and led the two FBI agents and me outside. When we got to the parking lot, the two agents followed me to my car before I turned to them. Costa frowned at me and blinked a lot. He looked confused. Cornwell, though, looked irate. She opened her eyes wide and leaned toward me.

"What are you doing?" she asked.

I looked at her and then to Agent Costa.

"My job," I said. "He's contacting somebody on the outside. We know he's not doing it through the mail, and he's not doing it through his attorney because his attorney no longer returns his phone calls. Your teams have already searched his room, and you didn't find a cell phone. That means he's contacting his partner through a corrections officer.

"At this moment, your team is tossing his cell and installing hidden surveillance cameras. Now that I've riled him up, he'll contact his partner on the outside, and we'll watch. Then we'll make some arrests and shut him down. Clear?"

"You could have told us what you were doing," said Costa.

"If I had, would you have let me?" I asked, glancing at Cornwell. "Or would you have lectured me about operational procedure and reminded me that this isn't my case?"

"It isn't your case," said Cornwell.

"You're right," I said. "It's yours, and you've had Brunelle in prison for years, but you haven't found shit. Now go to your technician's van and monitor the video feed. Brunelle will probably make a move tonight. In the meantime, I'm checking into my hotel. See you later."

14

It had been a long and awful day, but it was nearing the end. After Diego and Gloria shot the police officer in Union Station in Dallas, Logan and his brother had run to the Greyhound bus station. Uniformed police officers had been on every corner, but they were looking for Diego and Gloria. They hadn't asked about the two boys traveling with them.

As soon as they got to the station, Logan had booked two seats on the first bus to leave the station. Within five minutes of arriving, they boarded a bus bound for Fort Worth and left the station five minutes after that. Once they reached Fort Worth, they transferred to another bus that took them to downtown Houston. Neither Logan nor Evan had been to Houston in years, but it was familiar all the same. Even Evan had smiled. They were going home.

"Do you remember the last time we saw Grandma?" asked Logan. "She made us vanilla ice cream."

"It was chocolate," said Evan. "It was the best ice cream ever."

Logan knew his brother was wrong, but he didn't correct him. They were sitting beside each other on a crowded Metro bus that stopped outside their grandparents' neighborhood. Neither of them had ridden that kind of bus when they had lived in the city, but they were both growing used to public transportation after their most recent adventure.

Both of the boys had removed their sweaters and jackets. It had been forty degrees and cloudy when they left St. Augustine, but it was seventy-five and sunny in Houston. It felt like spring.

"Grandma'll flip out when she sees us," said Evan. "You think she'll recognize us?"

"Dad sends her pictures," said Logan. "At least he used to before."

The mention of their father dampened their spirits some. Evan looked down. Logan swallowed and wished he hadn't said that.

"You think she knows?" asked Evan. "About Dad, I mean. That he's…you know."

"Probably," said Logan. "Daisy would have told her."

"Did you ever meet her?" asked Evan. "Daisy, I mean?"

"No," said Logan, shaking his head. "Dad showed me a picture, though. She looks nice. I bet she'll want to see us, so we'll meet her soon."

Evan looked like he would cry again, so Logan touched him on the shoulder.

"Hey, do you remember Thanksgiving at Grandma's house? She always made way more food than anybody could eat, and she always worried she didn't make enough."

"Her brownies were the best," said Evan. "I hope she makes them."

"I bet she will if you ask her," said Logan, his voice brighter and more enthusiastic than he felt. Once they reached their grandparents' house, their grandpa would know what to do. He was a lawyer, and he was smart. He had retired years ago, but he knew a lot of cops. This would all be fine.

As they neared their grandparents' neighborhood, Logan stood and reached for the buzzer to tell the driver to stop. Within moments, the brakes squealed, and Logan's heart began pounding again. It wasn't nerves this time. It was hope and relief. Everything around them was familiar. They had made it. Their grandpa had taken them for walks all around this area, and their dad had taken them to a park not two blocks away.

Logan looked to his brother.

"You ready, buddy?"

He nodded and stood. The bus stopped by the sidewalk, and they walked off. The air was humid, but it wasn't too hot or cold.

"What do you want to eat first?" asked Logan.

"Ice cream," said Evan. "Chocolate and then mint. Grandma liked mint. Do you remember?"

"It's been a long time since we've seen them," said Logan. "Maybe we should hold off on asking her to make us ice cream right away."

"She likes making it, though," said Evan. "She said

the hand crank gave her exercise."

"I remember," said Logan, smiling. "We'll see what she's up to. Maybe we'll get takeout. Grandpa used to like that barbecue place. He might want to go there."

"I could eat barbecue," said Evan. Logan nodded, and they started walking down the sidewalk. There were more pine trees than he remembered, but that was okay. St. Augustine had big, old trees that had already lost most of their leaves for the season. The pine trees, though, would stay green year-round. He could get used to that again. It'd be nice to live somewhere without such crappy winters, too.

They walked for about a quarter of a mile before they reached their grandparents' brick ranch-style home. The fire hydrant out front was painted like a rainbow, and the bushes in front of the windows had grown unkempt. Logan pointed to the hydrant.

"You remember when we painted that with Grandma?" he asked.

"Yeah, Grandpa was pissed," said Evan. "He thought the fire department would make him paint it back."

"They didn't," said Logan, shaking his head and sighing. The house didn't look as big as he remembered, but he hadn't been there in a long time.

"Grandpa's let the bushes go, hasn't he?" asked Evan. "And there are pine needles all over the driveway. Think he knows?"

"He's old," said Logan, crossing the lawn to knock on the door. "He's probably tired."

Even as Logan spoke, he knew this wasn't right. In all the years Logan had known his grandfather, never once had the old man allowed a single leaf to remain unraked on his yard for over twenty-four hours. If he had seen those pine needles on his driveway, he would have had a broom and the leaf blower out in a heartbeat.

When they reached the front door, Logan looked to his brother.

"Stand straighter and push your shoulders back," he said. "Proper posture reflects a proper state of mind."

Evan shook his head, but he pushed his shoulders back and straightened his back, anyway.

"You even sound like Grandpa when you say it."

Logan smiled and knocked on the door. It took a minute or two, but a woman with long blond hair eventually answered. She had a baby on her hip and an easy smile.

"Hey, guys," she said. "Can I help you?"

Evan stepped back, but Logan blinked a few times and drew in a breath.

"We're looking for our grandparents. They live here."

The woman's smile faltered as she shook her head.

"No, this is where my husband and I live," she said. "Are you sure you're at the right address?"

"Yeah. This is their house," said Logan. "They live here."

She blinked a few times and shook her head.

"What are your grandparents' names? Maybe you're on the wrong street."

"Doug and Beverly Robinson," said Logan. "This is their house. I know it is. Grandma and I painted the fire hydrant."

She nodded and sighed. Her smile was understanding and kind.

"And you guys did a good job, too, but the Robinsons sold us this house four years ago after…"

Her voice trailed off.

"After what?" asked Evan.

Her smile was tight this time, and she blinked and looked down.

"After Mr. Robinson passed away," she said. "It was sudden. I'm sorry. Do you want me to call your mom or dad?"

Logan grabbed his brother's forearm and started backing away.

"Our dad's dead," he said. "Our mom's probably dead, too."

The woman brought a hand to her mouth and said something, but Logan didn't understand her. Every part of his body felt numb. With everything else that had happened, he should have expected this. He pulled his brother from the house and started walking toward the bus stop again. Evan trembled, but Logan tried to hold his emotions inside. He felt sad, disappointed, scared, and frustrated, but overriding all of that was anger. This was his mom's fault. He didn't even care if she was dead now.

"What do we do?" asked Evan, his voice choked with tears.

"Just walk. She'll probably call the cops. We need to get somewhere safe."

"And where's that?" asked Evan, running so he could stand in front of his brother.

"I don't know," said Logan. "Just shut up and walk for now."

15

After leaving the prison, I checked into a hotel near the Indiana State University campus and took a walk. The cold air bit into my jacket, but it felt good to be outside. I watched the sun set while sitting in a little park and then called Mathias. We didn't talk long, but it was the highlight of my day, and I told him so.

Afterwards, I walked south until I found a pub. The tables were full, so I sat at the bar and ordered a drink and a hamburger with fried jalapeño peppers. St. Augustine was so small, half the county seemed to know me by name, and whenever I went to a bar, complete strangers would oftentimes come to me with requests. I was the county's only detective, and people seemed to believe it was their God-given right to get drunk and complain to me that their neighbor ran an unlicensed chainsaw-repair business in his or her garage or that their niece or nephew sold weed. Here, nobody bothered me. It was nice to sit and relax and enjoy the atmosphere.

About an hour after I got to the bar, and as I eavesdropped on the couple beside me on their second date, my phone rang. The caller had blocked the number.

It was half after seven, and I had started to enjoy my night, but I sighed and answered, anyway.

"Hey," I said. "It's Joe."

"Hey, Joe," said Agent Costa. "You free for a little while? I've got something to show you."

I smiled and looked down at my half-empty beer.

"With lines like that, I don't know how you fend the ladies off, Bryan. What do you want me to see?"

Costa chuckled.

"Sorry. I have video from the prison I'd like you to review."

I straightened.

"Brunelle's already made a move?"

"Not yet, but we think he will," said Costa. "Philippa and I have been reviewing surveillance footage from the past few days and have found something disturbing. Where are you? If you're free, I'll pick you up."

I closed my eyes and pushed a stray lock of hair behind my ear before giving him the name of the bar. He said he'd be over in a few minutes, so I called over the bartender to settle my bill before taking a big sip of my beer. It had been a nice evening while it lasted.

I met Agent Costa outside. We drove two blocks to a hotel and then walked into the lobby and then the business center, where Agent Cornwell was sitting and sipping a cup of coffee as she looked at a laptop.

"I'm glad you could make it, Detective," said Cornwell. "Bryan told me you were in a bar."

"I was having dinner."

She glanced up at me and then focused on her laptop.

"Are you sober enough to talk, or should we wait until tomorrow?"

"I guess we'll find out," I said. "I apologize in advance if I vomit on you. Otherwise, I think we're good."

Cornwell sighed and took her hands from her laptop's keyboard as she glanced at me.

"It was a simple question. You were at a bar, and I was asking you how much you had to drink."

I considered her and then shook my head.

"It was a rude question, and I responded rudely. I shouldn't have done that, and I'm sorry. We don't have to like one another, but we can act professionally."

She straightened and slathered a smile on her face.

"I'm always professional."

I wanted to say something, but Agent Costa spoke before I could.

"Before you two start, stop," he said. "You both have very different jobs, and you're both good at them. I'm not interested in being a referee, but if you two make me, I will send you both home and work this case without either of you."

I wanted to retort that she had started it, but that seemed juvenile. Instead, I said nothing. Costa sighed.

"Now that we've got that out of the way, show us the video, Agent Cornwell."

Her lips moved as if she were muttering something, but I couldn't make out what she said. She used her touchpad to open a video before turning the screen toward me and Agent Costa.

"As Agent Costa's already told you, he and I have been reviewing surveillance footage from the prison. We wondered how Brunelle was contacting the outside world, and now we know."

"Roll it," I said.

Cornwell tapped her touchpad, and the video started. The feed came from a camera hanging near the ceiling of a long corridor with beige tile floors and heavy steel doors painted blue every few feet. I knew it was the prison, but it reminded me of a high school. A corrections officer in navy pants and a bright white shirt strode down the hallway. He was forty-five to fifty, and he had buzzed hair. There was a radio on his shoulder similar to the ones patrol officers in St. Augustine wore. Unlike our officers, though, he didn't carry any weapons that I could see.

He stopped outside a room and used a key on a ring on his belt to open the door. Peter Brunelle emerged and looked up the hallway.

"The CO is supposed to lead him to the exercise yard for an hour of supervised recreation. It's on the schedule three times a week, rain or shine."

"Okay," I said, nodding. "Where do they go?"

"Just watch," said Costa.

So, I watched as they walked down the hall to an intersection, where the guard used his keys to open a gate. They hung a right and then disappeared off camera. Cornwell tapped a few more buttons on her laptop and slid her finger across the touchpad to open a new video.

"This video is from the security camera nearest that intersection, and it's spooled up to the same time as the video from Brunelle's cell."

I nodded and told her to play it. She did, but nothing happened. I would have thought her laptop had frozen, but the time stamp progressed in real time. After about a minute, I sighed.

"This is a problem," I said. "Brunelle apparently can turn invisible."

"The camera positioning leaves dead zones in the hallway," said Costa. "The guard led him through one."

I crossed my arms and nodded.

"Is it possible he did that accidentally?"

Costa shrugged. "Maybe if he had done it once. He did it in three hallways, though. Philippa and I watched video from every camera in the prison for the next ten minutes, but neither Brunelle nor the guard show up again until they reach the laundry room."

"What do they do there?"

Cornwell turned the laptop toward her and tapped the touchpad a few times before turning it to me again. This time, the video showed a big room full of metal cabinets and big wooden tables, all of which someone had painted white. The floor looked like concrete. There were piles of folded clothes, sheets, and uniforms on every flat surface and carts full of dirty laundry. Brunelle and the guard walked inside.

Then, the sheets in one of the laundry containers

began moving, and a young woman popped out. She had black hair, and she wore a black skirt and white blouse. The guard smiled and laughed before leaving. Brunelle smiled in response before focusing on the girl.

I groaned as he kissed her. She jumped and wrapped her legs around him, and he carried her to a laundry-sorting table.

"We can turn this off," I said. "I get what happens."

Cornwell tapped a button to stop the video feed. Then she leaned back.

"After the two of them have sex, they talk, and the girl gets back into the laundry tub and hides. About ten minutes later, a trustee wheels the tub to a truck, which takes it to the minimum-security prison camp, where the inmates do the laundry. The security at the camp isn't as tight as it is here. At the camp, she climbs out of the tub and into the trunk of a four-door passenger vehicle. From there, she disappears."

I nodded and let my mind process what I had just seen. Dozens of questions floated around in my mind, but I started with the obvious one.

"So, who is she?"

"We don't know," said Costa. "Have you ever seen her before?"

I shook my head but then shrugged as I thought better of it.

"I see dozens of strangers every day," I said. "St. Augustine's small, but we get a lot of tourists. Do we have a decent picture of her face?"

Cornwell reached to her side and pulled a glossy piece of paper from her briefcase. It was a photo, and it showed the young woman's face. She had closed her eyes and furrowed her brow but left her mouth agape. I took the photo and glanced at the two FBI agents.

"Do we have any pictures where they aren't mid-coitus?"

"We have a few others, but this is the clearest shot we have of her face," said Cornwell. "We'll feed everything through the Bureau's facial recognition software and see what we can get."

I nodded and put the photo on the table beside Cornwell's laptop.

"The prison's supposed to be secure. How'd she get inside?"

Cornwell picked up the picture and shook her head.

"That's our concern, not yours. If you haven't seen her, that's all we need to know."

Agent Costa rolled his eyes and shook his head.

"She had help, so we'll work with the Office of Internal Affairs of the Federal Bureau of Prisons to determine what happened," said Costa, glaring at his subordinate before looking to me. "They're flying in a team from Washington as we speak. In the meantime, the warden is increasing the number of patrols around the prison grounds and facilities and calling in additional manpower. Tasks that corrections officers would ordinarily complete alone are now being done by two officers. We're telling the staff that the Bureau's organized-crime division has received word of an impending prison riot in the facility."

"And they buy that?" I asked.

Costa tilted his head to the side and shrugged.

"We've worked cases involving prison gangs before," he said. "It's not unheard of for us to have intel of something that goes on behind prison walls. Plus, there's a certain mystique about the FBI. When people hear we're working a case, they pay attention."

It made sense, so I nodded.

"Corruption among the guard staff isn't your only problem," I said. "Brunelle didn't pick up this girl at a bar. She had to have contacted him first, but the prison's supposed to be monitoring his communication. Not only that, the guards aren't working for free. When Brunelle was on the outside, he worked as a stone mason. He made a good salary, but he wasn't raking in millions. And even if he'd had millions, his lawyers and the court system would have sucked that money away years ago. That means someone's funneling money to pay for access to a serial murderer."

Cornwell didn't react, but Costa blinked a few times and nodded.

"That's disquieting."

"Yeah, it is," I said. "As Agent Cornwell pointed out, though, it's your case. I'm just here because Brunelle has a crush on me. Good luck with everything. I'm going back to my hotel, and then tomorrow morning, I'll be going home. If you need me, you've got my number."

16

Logan and Evan walked until the sun went down, but no matter how many steps they took or how far they got from their grandparents' former home, they couldn't escape reality. They were alone in a strange city with no cash, no one to care for them, and no idea how to save themselves. Their dad was dead, their grandpa was dead, their mom was probably dead, and the people after them wouldn't stop until they were dead.

Logan felt like a giant had grabbed him in a fist and squeezed so tight he couldn't breathe. He didn't know what to do, but if he didn't do something, he'd die. Nobody could live like this. Everything was wrong.

"I'm hungry," said Evan.

"Yeah, well, I don't have any food," said Logan.

"There's a McDonald's up the street. We can go there."

Despite the wrenching, heavy feeling in his chest, Logan's stomach rumbled at the thought of food. He didn't know what street they were on, but it was busy. Restaurants, bars, and shops lined the roadway. Many of the stores had steel grates over their windows to prevent break-ins, but the heavy police patrols prevented the neighborhood from feeling dangerous.

"Do you have any money?"

Evan hesitated but then shook his head.

"No. Do you?"

"No," said Logan. "I spent all my cash already, so stop whining about food."

They walked another twenty or thirty feet before Evan stopped and sat on a bench beside the covered awning of a bus stop. He seemed smaller than he had even that morning. For some reason, that made Logan mad.

"I want to go home," said Evan.

"This is home now. We were born in Houston, and we'll die in Houston."

Evan said nothing, but then his shoulders hitched, and a tremble passed through him. Logan stepped closer and clenched his teeth.

"Stop crying," he said, looking around to make sure no one was watching them. An older woman sat, waiting for the bus with a paper grocery sack on her lap, but she didn't so much as turn her head. Evan wiped his face.

"I want to go back to Mom."

"No," said Logan, shaking his head. "Even if she's alive, she doesn't give a shit about us. Tell me the last time she picked you up from school. Tell me the last time she gave you a hug. Hell, tell me the last time you even saw her sober. I'd bet you anything in the world you can't."

Evan looked up and narrowed his eyes.

"Shut up."

"You going to make me?" asked Logan. He smacked his brother in the face. It wasn't hard, and he hadn't meant to hurt him. It was a release. Logan loved his brother, but at that moment, he wanted to stand over him and watch him beg, to know that he was strong. He wanted his brother to hurt, and he didn't know why. He smacked him again and again until Evan stood.

"Stop it," said Evan, his eyes red and his skin blotchy.

"Make me," said Logan, smacking his brother once more, this time hard enough to leave a mark. Evan tried to kick him, but Logan jumped back. The ground wasn't where he expected it, though, and he flailed his arms to maintain his balance as he fell into the road. Tires screeched as drivers pounded on their brakes. Logan scrambled onto the sidewalk again. The older woman with the grocery sack stood and looked from Logan to Evan.

"That is enough, you idiots," she said. "I have sat here and listened to you two bicker and fight, but this is it. This is my neighborhood, and you don't get to come into my neighborhood acting like spoiled brats. Sit down and shut up."

Both Logan and Evan sat down. It felt good to sit. The woman stood over them.

"Where are you two staying?"

"We don't need your charity," said Logan. "We're fine."

"Oh, is that what you think this is?" she asked, raising her eyebrows. "Charity? Listen, honey, I don't care about you or your welfare. I'm trying to keep you from running into traffic. I want to go home, and I can't do that if you two morons cause a traffic accident. Now where are you staying?"

Evan and Logan spoke simultaneously. Logan said his grandparents' house, but Evan said he didn't know. The woman crossed her arms and sighed.

"There's a shelter for homeless kids about two blocks away, and I'd suggest you boys get to it before they run out of beds and shut the doors."

"We don't need a shelter," said Logan. "We're fine."

She closed her eyes and shook her head as she sighed.

"Look, I'm trying to help you, kid, but if you're too stupid for help, that's on you," she said. She opened her eyes and turned and pointed to the street. "What do you see around you?"

Logan looked and shrugged.

"A liquor store."

"I see Latin King territory," said the woman. "Behind you, I see MS-13 territory. You are standing in a war zone. Do you know that? It doesn't look so bad in the day, but if you stay out here for another hour, you'll be lucky if you're just robbed. Go back to your mom in the suburbs. You don't belong here."

"We don't need your help," said Logan.

She snickered and shook her head but said nothing. Then, she picked up her parcel and walked toward the edge of the sidewalk as a Metro bus approached. Logan looked around again and found patterns in the graffiti.

One side of the street had crowns sprayed on the sides of buildings, but the other had MS or the number thirteen sprayed in an elaborate script. She was right. They weren't safe here.

"Where's that shelter?" he asked.

She glanced at him and pointed down a side street.

"Two blocks down there. There'll be kids out front. And get yourself a knife if you don't have one. You'll need it."

"Even in the shelter?" asked Evan.

She nodded.

"Yeah, but at least you won't get shot."

The bus's brakes squealed as it pulled to a stop. Logan looked to his brother and then started walking in the direction the lady had pointed.

"I don't want to go to the shelter," said Evan.

"You heard her," said Logan. "It's late, and we don't have anywhere else to go."

"You've got that credit card," said Evan. "We can stay in a hotel."

"My card has a four-hundred-dollar limit, and we already spent most of that on train tickets. To go over that limit, Dad has to give his permission, and he can't because he's dead."

Evan grabbed Logan's arm.

"What about Daisy? She was nice. I bet she'd help us, and she still lives here."

Logan had never met Daisy, but their dad had loved her. They were married, so she was almost like a stepmom. If nothing else, maybe she'd let them stay at her house long enough for them to track down their uncle Travis. He was in the Army; he had driven Logan and Evan all over his base in Kentucky when they last visited. That had been eight years ago, though, and they hadn't talked to him since. Still, he was family.

Somebody had to take them in. They couldn't run forever.

"We'll see Daisy tomorrow," he said. "She and Dad live in The Woodlands. It'd take us too long to get there tonight."

"It won't take us too long," said Evan, shaking his head. "We could take an Uber."

"If we had any money, we could," said Logan. "But we don't. We've already wasted all our cash. We'll get a bus tomorrow. Tonight, we'll stay in the shelter. No one will hurt us there."

"We could get stabbed," said Evan. "You heard that lady. We'll die if we go there."

"You won't die," said Logan. "I'm your brother, and I'll protect you. That's my job. Okay?"

Evan blinked a few times. Even as he nodded, he looked uncertain, but at least he agreed to go. Logan hoped he hadn't just lied to him and that he could keep him safe. Something told him, though, that no matter what he did, they wouldn't be safe as long as they lived.

Logan looked around. He couldn't get a knife, but he picked up a flat stone a little bigger than a golf ball from a planting bed beside the road. If it came down to it, he could bash somebody in the head with it. He put it in his pocket and looked to Evan.

"Let's go."

17

Sasha had been exercising in her gym when she got the call. Peter had needed a favor. That happened sometimes, so she had been ready for it. She wasn't Peter's only girlfriend, but she flattered herself to think she was his favorite. He was an important man, so she forgave his indulgences, and he filled her with the warmth of his light and the strength of his character.

Every time she spoke to him was a blessing because their conversations carried such risk. He couldn't keep his cell phone in his room at the prison—it was too dangerous—so a corrections officer had to bring it to him when he needed to make a call or receive a message. Even that was risky. Prison rules forbade the guards from carrying phones inside the facility, so if an uncooperative guard had learned that a colleague had hidden a cell phone for a prisoner, there would be questions no one wanted to answer.

Peter shouldered that risk for her. Though he had never said it aloud, he loved her. Sasha saw it in his eyes. He told her she was an extension of himself outside the prison walls. Through her, he touched the world. He gave her life purpose and meaning.

For this job, she wore a black sheath dress that brushed the delicate skin just above her knees and a black sweater over her thin shoulders. Her fiery red lipstick and dark eyeshadow contrasted with her almost porcelain skin. In college, she had taught yoga at a little studio on Delmar Boulevard. Afterwards, she had used her talents for an altogether different profession. She planned to put every skill she had to good use this evening. It was for Peter. He deserved her best effort.

She had been fourteen when she made her first kill. It was her uncle, and he had liked young women. Sasha's father had been a worthless drunk with very few talents. He spent most of her childhood in and out of prison, which minimized the amount of damage he could cause to a little girl. Then he disappeared when she was ten. Maybe he was dead, but maybe he was alive. She didn't care.

Her mother had done the best she could. She dealt blackjack at a casino in Reno, Nevada. She had been beautiful, so a lot of men requested her for private games, and since prostitution was legal in large parts of Nevada, many clients seemed to believe every woman in the state was for sale. That wasn't true, and Sasha's mother had let them know that right away. Sasha had always admired her mom. She had been strong and kind, but, unfortunately, ovarian cancer doesn't respect strength or kindness.

A porter held open the country club's door as Sasha approached. The building was old limestone with columns on the exterior, creating a facade that exuded the feelings of permanence, power, and wealth—three things demanded by every family whose names adorned the membership rolls. The interior was bright and cheery with crisp white wainscoting, a striped yellow and cream colored wallpaper, and elaborate crown moldings that led to a coffered ceiling twelve or thirteen feet high. It was a grand entry with an enormous vase of fresh lilies on a brass and marble table in the center of the room.

Sasha smiled hello to people she didn't know before signing in at the membership roll beside the door. Though she wasn't a member, she knew this crowd and how they thought. She understood their needs and even counted a few members as clients. The men and women who walked through those doors had power and multigenerational wealth that ensured their families would remain powerful for decades if not centuries. That power and wealth, though, made them vulnerable.

Tonight, though, she didn't care about the membership or her clients. She was there for Dylan Green, the younger, adoptive brother of Detective Joe Court. Detective Court had been naughty, and Peter wanted her punished. Sasha couldn't get to Joe, so she'd start with her family.

The first time Sasha had killed, she had used a fillet knife from the kitchen. Her mother had died two weeks earlier, and her uncle had moved into their house as her permanent guardian. Before she killed him, Uncle Andy had had a lecherous gaze. She had been fourteen, and she hadn't realized what that look meant. Now, looking back with adult eyes, she saw ample warning signs of his perversion.

It was a Thursday at ten in the evening when he forced himself on her. He said he'd kill her if she called the police, and she believed him. That was why she slit his throat as he slept in her mother's bed three hours later. When she cut him, the blood had gushed down his chest and shirt and had made his neck almost look as if it were smiling. He had tried to reach for her, but she had been too quick, and he had been too weak. He had died within seconds.

The police arrested her, which she had expected. When they asked her why she had done it, she told them the truth. An OB-GYN at the same hospital in which her mother had died examined her and confirmed her account of events. The prosecutor, an asshole who had just graduated from law school and who had yet to have his moral compass installed, had tried to charge her as an adult with murder, but the local news ran her story, and the public outcry overcame the young prosecuting attorney's ambition.

When the state dropped the charges, the courts released her to the foster care system. A nice couple took her in, but they weren't her family. She didn't need them. Sasha could protect herself, and everyone around her knew it.

She walked down the front hallway toward the club's restaurant overlooking the greens. With every step, her heels tapped against the solid oak floor. It wasn't a busy night, but there were still half a dozen couples in the lobby and side rooms, whispering to each other in hushed tones.

A group of men sat in a lounge to the left, laughing and drinking whiskey or bourbon from crystal glasses. She recognized one and smiled at him. When he saw her, his face paled, and he straightened. He was an attorney from an old St. Louis family. He used to brag that Al Capone had once gotten drunk in a speakeasy his great-great-grandfather operated in the Central West End. She doubted his friends knew he paid her a thousand dollars an hour and that she forced him to wear a studded leather collar and bark like a dog on command.

Sasha never slept with or even touched any of her clients. That was part of the mystique. She was unobtainable, remote, and powerful. She was the one thing in her very wealthy clients' lives they couldn't possess. It got them off, and it made her a very nice living. Peter Brunelle was the only man strong enough for her. He and he alone deserved her. He knew how to take care of problems—just like she did.

As she reached the club's restaurant, she paused at the threshold and cast her gaze over the room. Unlike the bright and cheery entryway and main hall, the dining room had subdued lighting and stained wood-paneled walls. Glass windows two stories high overlooked a massive pond and water garden on the golf course. A glossy black grand piano sat unused near a roaring fire. Couples and a few families with older children ate at the tables.

As she approached the restaurant's front desk, Dylan Green and an attractive, dark-skinned girl in a fashionable black sweater and slacks greeted him. They were the host and hostess. On a busy night or special occasion, the club would have employed at least two more young people to greet the membership, but tonight Dylan and the young lady could handle things themselves.

Dylan was handsome but slight of build, like his mother. He had his father's strong chin and big hands. When Peter first expressed an interest in Joe Court, Sasha had taken it upon herself to investigate her family and lifestyle. She had been to the detective's property half a dozen times and had walked through the woods behind her home half a dozen more. Joe seemed to enjoy solitude. She had a Facebook profile, but she kept the privacy settings so tight Sasha hadn't been able to see anything.

Joe's half-brother, Ian, had the same proclivity for privacy that Joe did, but her adoptive siblings, Audrey and Dylan, allowed the world to view everything they did. Dylan slept with a different girl every week. Audrey was a little more careful about what she posted, but she dated men. That made approaching her difficult. Dylan, though, was ripe for the picking.

The young woman behind the desk smiled at her.

"Will you be dining alone, or are you waiting for company, miss?"

Sasha ignored her and focused on Dylan.

"Hey," she said before biting her lower lip. "May I sit at the bar?"

He smiled, as she knew he would.

"If you're meeting someone, Tracy and I can prepare a table for you."

"No," said Sasha. "It's just me tonight. For now, at least."

She raised her eyebrows, and Dylan flicked his eyes down her body. She had him. Sasha was twenty-five, and she worked out six nights a week. She knew how to use what she had, so it wasn't hard to hook an eighteen-year-old boy.

"Have a seat at the bar," said Dylan. "Tony will take care of you."

She allowed her smile to slip into a frown.

"I was hoping you could, Dylan."

He looked to his co-worker. She rolled her eyes but then sucked in a deep breath and smiled when she noticed Sasha watching her.

"Do I know you?" asked Dylan, lowering his chin.

"I know your sister Joe," she said. "I'm Sasha."

"Oh, okay," he said, nodding as if Joe introduced him to women often. "If you have a seat and order a drink, I'll be by to check on you."

"I look forward to it," she said, winking before she turned toward the bar. As she walked, she knew half a dozen men were watching her, but she only cared about one. Dylan slept around, but he had never met a woman like her. Soon, she'd give Dylan a night he'd never forget.

More than that, she'd show Joe Court the danger of having loved ones.

This would be fun.

18

My brother Dylan called as I walked back to my hotel. I loved Dylan, and I loved watching him grow up, but he and I weren't as close as my sister and I were. He was so much younger than me that I had moved out of the house while he was still in elementary school. I saw him when I came home on breaks and on holiday, but we rarely spoke otherwise.

"Hey, dude," I said, my voice bright. "It's been too long. How are you doing?"

"Awesome," he said, his voice almost breathless. "Sasha is so hot."

I laughed and nodded. It was a little after nine, and this part of Terre Haute had shut down for the evening. I kept a close watch on dark corners and alleyways, but it didn't feel dangerous. More than anything, it just felt sleepy.

"I'm glad to hear it," I said. "She a girlfriend of yours?"

"You know who she is," said Dylan. "Is it cool if I hook up with her? She seems into it."

I paused, unsure what to say.

"Sure," I said. "I guess. I don't know. Why are you asking me?"

"Because she's your friend," said Dylan. I shook my head.

"Her name isn't ringing a bell."

"She said she works in the crime lab in St. Louis and that you know her."

That could have been true, then. Both the city and county of St. Louis had good-sized crime labs, and I had met several of their technicians while working shared cases. I tried to remember people's names, but I couldn't remember everybody.

"In that case, use your judgment and stay safe," I said. "And have fun."

"Oh, we will definitely have fun," he said. He paused. "You going to come home for Sunday dinner?"

"I'm working a case, but I'll try," I said. "If I don't see you then, I'll talk to you later. Okay, bud?"

"Yeah, see you later. I'm going to meet Sasha at Blueberry Hill after work and put my fake ID to good use."

Blueberry Hill was a bar and restaurant that had live music a couple nights a week. I smiled but shook my head.

"I'm a cop, and our mom's a retired cop," I said. "Don't tell me you've got a fake ID."

"In that case, I don't have a fake ID, and I don't plan to use it at Blueberry Hill tonight."

I laughed and thanked him for considering my situation. He hung up a moment later, and I slipped my phone into my purse. I thought about calling Mathias again, but he was probably busy. Instead, I sent him a text message to wish him a good night and let him know that I was thinking about him. He texted me back and said likewise. It wasn't as good as a goodnight hug, but it was nice.

When I got to my hotel, I went straight to bed and slept well through the night. The next morning, I called Agent Costa to see whether he needed anything, but he and Agent Cornwell seemed to be okay for a while. Costa said that a guard had come by Brunelle's room after our meeting to let him use a cell phone, but Brunelle had spoken so softly their microphones hadn't picked up what he said. The guard denied any wrongdoing when questioned and demanded a lawyer. He also refused to unlock the cell phone they found on him. Costa was confident they'd break the guard, but it'd take time.

I wished him luck, checked out of my room, and started driving home. While I was somewhere on the interstate in the middle of Illinois, my mom called. I put her on speakerphone so I could talk and keep both of my hands on the wheel.

"Hey, Mom," I said. "I'm in the car on my way home from Terre Haute."

"Oh," she said. "The Peter Brunelle thing. How's that going?"

I sighed.

"It's going," I said. "We don't know many details yet, but someone was paying off the guards and smuggling people in to see Brunelle. It's a mess, but the FBI's working the case with the Federal Bureau of Prisons' Office of Internal Affairs. They'll sort things out."

"Who would pay off the guards to visit a serial murderer?"

"Attractive young women, apparently," I said. "We've got a video of him *in flagrante delicto* in the laundry room with an unknown woman."

Mom stuttered something, but I didn't understand what. Then she laughed.

"I've got a lot of questions, but I don't imagine you can answer them," she said. "You doing okay otherwise?"

"Yeah," I said. "Life's not too bad."

She and I talked for about fifteen minutes. Neither of us had anything monumental to say, but it was nice to hear her voice. After our conversation quieted some, Mom sighed.

"You haven't heard from Dylan today, have you? He sent me a text message last night that said he planned to stay overnight at a friend's house. I've been trying to get in touch with him, but he hasn't been answering his phone."

"That's because his friend was hot," I said. "He called me last night to ask whether I minded if he hooked up with a woman I know who works at the St. Louis crime lab. He's probably still passed out at her place."

Mom sighed again and muttered something.

"That kid thinks with his penis more than anyone I've ever met."

"He's eighteen," I said. "Boys that age don't think

with their brains. I wouldn't worry about him too much. He knows what he's doing. It's Audrey I'd worry about. She could be dating anyone."

Mom grunted.

"I love your sister, but she's not here to defend her dating choices," said Mom. "But now that we're talking about men, how are you and Mathias doing?"

Even just mentioning his name made my stomach get a little fluttery.

"We're good. A murder cut short our most recent date, but things are going well. I like him. Even when I have a bad day, he can make me smile."

"I'm glad. You deserve somebody who makes you happy."

Mom and I talked about work and Mathias and my siblings and the wobbly kitchen table Dad was building in the garage for a while longer. It was a nice chat, exactly what I needed after my latest meeting with Brunelle.

I reached St. Augustine a few hours later and drove directly to Preston Cain's house for my dog. There was a big moving van in the driveway, so I parked beside it and walked around until I found Preston and Roy near the barn. Roy, my dog, bounded toward me with his tongue sticking out of his mouth. He was trembling with excitement. I knelt beside him and petted his cheek as he licked my arms and face.

"Hey, sweetheart," I said. "I missed you."

"I missed you, too, Joe, but you've got to understand that I'm engaged now. Whatever we may have had is over."

I glanced up at Preston and smirked but said nothing. He smiled. Preston was younger than me, but he had retired from the police force when an asshole shot him in the chest. He lost a lung and some mobility. Now, instead of chasing down bad guys, he built custom kitchen cabinets and furniture in his barn.

"I saw the truck in the driveway," I said. "Shelby moving out?"

"No, no," he said, shaking his head. "She's still madly in love with me, so she's sticking around. The truck's for a delivery. I finished some cabinets for a kitchen remodel in Webster Groves."

Webster Groves was an inner-ring suburb west of St. Louis. My parents lived one town over, so I had spent a lot of time in that area when I was a teenager. It was safe and clean, and many of the homes had big trees in their front yards. I liked it there.

"I'm glad to hear you're keeping busy."

"Me, too," he said, his voice bright. "Anyway, Roy's been great. You have his breeder's number? After having Roy around, Shelby wants a dog."

"I'll call my mom and ask," I said. "Thanks again for watching him. And thank Shelby for me, too."

He said he would. Roy and I walked to my car, and I drove him back to my property. The moment I parked in front of Susanne's old house and opened the back door, Roy jumped out of the car and peed on every tree in the front yard. Then he stretched, yawned, and lay down on the front porch. When Roy first moved in with me, I worried about him getting lost on the property or running away. Not anymore, though. He was home now, and he wasn't going anywhere.

"You want to take a walk?"

He jumped to his feet at the mention of a walk, which made me smile. We didn't go far—maybe a mile or two—but it was nice to stretch my legs. I checked out my house, but the windows and doors were all still locked. If Roy had smelled or heard somebody lurking about in the woods, he would have taken off running. He didn't, though. We were alone.

I was lucky to own two houses so close together, but I missed my home. Hopefully the FBI would catch Brunelle's partner, and I could move back in.

After our walk, I left Roy on the porch at Susanne's house and drove into work. I said hello to my colleagues and then went to my office to reorient myself to the Joel Robinson murder. The day Joel died, he had spent the day with Logan Alvarez. I wasn't clear on their relationship, but I suspected they were father and son. Unfortunately, Logan's mom and her US marshal friend had prevented me from talking to him so far. I needed a way around that.

I searched through my notes until I found the phone number of Daisy Robinson, my victim's spouse. She had told me she'd get me her lawyer's phone number if I needed to talk to her again, but she hadn't sent me anything. That was unfortunate because she and I needed to talk.

I dialed her number and waited through three rings for her to pick up. When she spoke, she sounded tired.

"Mrs. Robinson, hey," I said. "This is Joe Court from St. Augustine, Missouri. I'm sorry for calling again, but I'm still working your husband's case, and I need a little more information."

She sighed.

"Fine. Ask your questions."

"Thank you," I said, smiling and hoping she could hear it through my voice. "I'm hoping to create a timeline for the day your husband died, but I'm having a little difficulty. I've got his credit card statement, but I was hoping I could look through any text messages he might have on his phone. You know his passcode? It's a six-digit number."

She sighed again and then thought.

"Try 030804 or 011908."

I wrote the numbers down. At first, they looked like random strings of numbers, but if Joel had chosen random numbers, his wife never would have guessed them. These numbers had meaning for him. I considered them and then added some slashes, making the numbers *03/08/04* and *01/19/08.* They were dates. March 8, 2004, and January 19, 2008. If I had to guess, they were birthdays—one of a fifteen-year-old and one of an eleven-year-old.

"Is there anything special about these numbers?" I asked, a moment later.

Daisy paused.

"They're just numbers," she said. "That's it. Can I go now? My husband's dead. I just want to grieve."

"I understand," I said. "And I'm sorry."

"Everybody's sorry, but that doesn't bring Joel back. Goodbye, Detective. Please don't call me again."

She hung up before I could tell her I couldn't make any promises. I wished I could just leave her alone and let her grieve as she saw fit, but I had a body to investigate. That took precedence over everything else—even a widow's grief. I grabbed my notepad and headed to the evidence room in the basement. There, we stored money, guns, and drugs in a vault and everything else in an enormous open room full of heavy metal shelving and wire cages. Mark Bozwell, our evidence tech, stood from his desk when he saw me.

"Hey, Mark," I said. "I need Joel Robinson's cell phone. Marcus Washington brought it in a few days ago."

Bozwell nodded and typed something before glancing at me. His eyes lingered on mine, but when I turned my head, I caught him looking at my body. He was classy like that.

"Give me a few minutes, and I'll pull the box."

I thanked him and crossed my arms to wait while he walked up a nearby aisle. Two or three minutes later, he returned with a white cardboard banker's box with a case number written on the side.

"Thanks," I said, opening the box as soon as he set it down. It held a big plastic bag with a paper biohazard sign taped to the side—probably bloody clothing—and a dozen paper bags full of evidence found at the crime scene. I searched until I found a plastic bag with the victim's phone. Kevius had already dusted it for prints, so I didn't worry about wearing gloves.

I pulled the phone out, powered it on, and tried the numbers Daisy had given me as passcodes. The first didn't work, but the second did. I'd dump the phone's contents when I could, but in the meantime, I checked Joel's text messages. He and Logan Alvarez had spoken often, including the day Joel died. Logan called him Dad, and judging by the panicked text messages the kid sent after the shooting, he saw everything. Now I really needed to talk to him.

I looked up to Bozwell.

"Thanks, Mark. You may have just helped me break my case."

19

Logan felt the knife to his throat before he saw or even heard his attacker. The shelter was safer than the streets, but one look at the angry, scruffy, and much larger other kids told Logan everything he needed to know about them. They were predators, and he and Evan were easy prey. They didn't belong in this part of town or this world, and everyone there knew it.

"You got a phone and a wallet, and I want them both."

Logan felt the warm breath on the back of his neck, but he couldn't see the speaker. He didn't need to see him to recognize him, though. The other boys called him Alf. They had let him cut to the front of the line at dinner, and he was the first person out of the chapel after the previous evening's prayer service. He was big, and he had a mean look in his eyes.

Logan had hoped to be out of the shelter by the time Alf woke up, but the staff didn't open the doors until eleven. Some kids said it was the staff's way of making sure everybody had lunch before they left. Other kids, though, said the neighborhood association preferred to keep the shelter kids off the streets as long as possible and forced the shelter to lock its doors as a condition of its continued operation. Logan didn't know what was true, but it didn't matter with a knife to his throat.

He was sitting on a threadbare red couch, one of half a dozen in a big open room. There were three foosball tables but no balls, two ping-pong tables but no ping-pong rackets or other equipment, and a dozen bookshelves but no books. The shelter had plenty of TVs bolted and chained to the ground, though. Some kids played basketball in the gymnasium next door, but Logan hadn't been in the mood for games. Evan was in the bathroom. That was probably why Alf had attacked then.

"I don't have anything," said Logan, his voice shaky. "Please. Just leave me alone. After today, you won't see me again."

The bigger kid—he was at least sixteen or seventeen—pressed the knife harder against Logan's throat. The blade was so dull it felt like a butter knife, but Alf could still hurt him with it. Logan swallowed hard.

"You don't give me your wallet and your cell phone, nobody ever will see you again. It's your choice, Richie Rich. Do you want to die in a shelter or go home to mommy and daddy?"

"My dad's dead. Somebody shot him. My mom's probably dead, too."

He had hoped the story would generate some sympathy, but Alf laughed as he pulled the knife away.

"Sucks to be you," he said. He smacked him on the

temple hard enough for Logan to see stars. Logan brought his hands up to protect himself, but the bigger kid grabbed his wrists and pulled back, wrenching his shoulders. Then Alf leaned forward. Logan could feel his weight on the back of the sofa. "Your money and your wallet, or I will gut you and your stupid little brother the moment they open the doors."

Logan shook his head.

"Mike won't let you hurt us," he said. "He said we'd be safe here as long as we wanted to stay."

Alf laughed again.

"You think Mike gives a shit about you?" he asked. "He's here for a paycheck and a piece of whatever ass the girls next door give him. Them, he'll protect. You don't have anything he wants. You make me take your wallet instead of giving it to me, I'll break your arm."

Logan didn't doubt him. None of this should have happened. They shouldn't have even been there.

"You've got to let go of me so I can reach it," he said.

The pressure let off his shoulders, and Logan sat straighter. Then he reached for his wallet and phone and handed them over. Alf removed his credit card.

"I knew you were a rich kid," he said. "This your daddy's card?"

"My dad's dead," said Logan. "Like I told you."

Alf grunted, pocketed the credit card, threw the now empty wallet back to Logan, and powered on the phone. He nodded when he saw the welcome screen.

"I see you again, I want some cash. Twenty bucks a day keeps my knife away. Living in my house ain't free, boy. Remember that. Phone's mine now. Hope you don't mind."

Logan wanted to act tough and fight back, but Alf was probably six feet tall and close to two hundred pounds. Logan was five foot five and a hundred and thirty pounds at most. He wasn't small for his age, but Alf had the muscles of a much older boy. He wouldn't stand a chance. Until they were out of there, they just had to keep their heads down.

After slapping Logan again and telling him to bring cash next time they saw one another, Alf sauntered off to a group of laughing boys huddled around one of the TVs. Two boys looked at Logan and laughed. They weren't older or bigger than him, so Alf had probably done the same thing he had done to Logan to them on their first nights. Now, they were his friends. They couldn't beat him, so they had joined him. People sucked.

Evan walked toward him from across the room, a concerned look on his face.

"Hey," he said, his voice soft. "You okay?"

"Shut up. I don't want to talk."

Evan shut his mouth and sat beside him. Logan tried not to cry, but he couldn't help it. This whole place was just fucking wrong. Everything about it. If this was what their future had in store for them, if he and Evan had to become one of those laughing jackals who hung around Alf to survive, he might as well find a gun somehow and check out now. He couldn't live like that. It wasn't worth it.

After about half an hour, Mike, the social worker who ran the place, walked into the room.

"Everybody up and out," he said. "Grab a lunch and take a walk. Doors are opening now. They will close this evening at nine. And if you're drunk or stoned, don't bother coming because we won't have room for you."

Most of the boys stood to leave. Logan and Evan waited until the room had cleared out before standing. As they walked, Mike called out to them.

"How was your first night, guys?"

"It was fine," said Logan, remembering what Alf had told him. "We've got somewhere to be, so see you later."

Mike crossed his arms and shook his head.

"You guys shouldn't be here. You and I both know that."

Logan stopped walking.

"What do you mean?"

Mike considered him and looked him up and down.

"Your jeans are dirty, but they fit you and don't have any holes; your shoes are clean and new; and both of you are wearing fleece jackets from L.L. Bean. You're not shelter kids. You've got a home. This place is for kids who don't have anywhere to go. By staying here, you're stealing from kids who don't have anything. You don't seem like the kind of kids who'd steal from the underprivileged, though. Why are you here?"

Logan looked to his brother and then to Mike before

shaking his head.

"We lost our home. Now we've got to go."

"Losing your home…that's a story I can understand," said Mike. "I lost my home, too, when I was your age. My mom kicked me out. She and her boyfriend dealt crack out of my old bedroom. What'd your mom and dad do?"

Logan looked down.

"My dad's dead. I don't know about my mom. She may be alive, but she's a drunk."

Mike softened his voice.

"Let's go to my office and talk. I can't make any promises, but maybe I can help you find a new family. The world has good people, but sometimes they're hard to find."

Logan wanted to believe him, but he didn't even know what to tell him. They were on the run from two armed sociopaths who probably worked for the drug cartel their mother had testified against at a criminal trial, they were probably wanted for questioning in the shooting of a police officer at Union Station in Dallas, and everyone who had ever loved them was dead or gone. If they told Mike the truth, he'd have them carted off to a mental hospital—or to jail.

"Thanks, but we've got this," said Logan.

"You change your mind, my door will be open all day," said Mike, nodding. "I'm here to help you, but I can't do that unless you talk to me. You guys understand?"

Both Logan and Evan nodded, so Mike wished them luck. As they left the building, a red-haired woman in a gray cardigan and blue jeans smiled at them and handed them each a sack lunch with a peanut butter and jelly sandwich on whole wheat bread, a Ziploc bag of pretzels, an apple, and a banana. Logan's stomach was rumbling, so he appreciated the food.

They walked for about two blocks without saying a word to another before stopping at a covered picnic table beside an apartment complex. It wasn't a park, just a little outdoor area for residents of the apartment complex to eat outside. Nobody else was around, so Logan and Evan sat.

"You want to talk now?" asked Evan.

Logan shook his head and took out his lunch.

"Nothing's changed. We've still got to get to Dad's house."

"You were crying," said Evan. "That guy put a knife to your throat. He would have killed you."

Logan's hands began trembling, so he put his sandwich down and brought his arms to his waist so his brother wouldn't see how terrified he still was.

"It's fine. We're alive. Both of us. He wouldn't have hurt me there, anyway. There were too many witnesses."

"If you say so," said Evan, looking at him out of the corner of his eye and opening his own sack lunch.

Logan tried eating again. His hands didn't tremble, but he no longer felt hungry. His sandwich tasted like dirt, and his stomach churned so much he nearly threw up.

"He took my credit card and the phone," said Logan. "We'll still make it to Dad's house, but we have to walk."

"Dad and Daisy live in The Woodlands," said Evan. "That's, like, forty miles. It'll take us days."

"Yeah, so save half your lunch. It'll make it easier."

Evan considered him and then opened his pretzels before looking to his brother.

"I've got some money," he said.

"How much?"

"Twenty bucks," he said. "I stole it from Mom's purse two weeks ago and hid it beneath the padding in my shoe so you wouldn't find it."

Logan's mouth hung open.

"You shit head. I got in trouble for that. She thought I ripped her off."

"I was going to use it to buy something," said Evan, tilting his head to the side.

"What?"

Evan paused and then sighed. His face was a little red.

"Nick was going to sell me a character from *World of Warcraft*, okay? He was an 89-level warrior. It was awesome. I just needed a little more money."

"You're such a tool," said Logan. "Give me the money and finish your lunch. We'll take the bus. If we do this right, we'll have dinner with Daisy tonight and sleep at Dad's place."

Evan nodded and took a giant bite of his sandwich. It should have been easy to ride a bus across town and to the suburbs, but nothing had gone right since his dad had died. As much as Logan wanted to hope that they'd have dinner with Daisy, he doubted it would happen. Somehow, somebody would screw this up for them. He just hoped their screw up would leave them room to recover instead of putting them down for good.

20

I dumped Joel Robinson's text messages from the past six months and sent them to the printer in our dispatcher's conference room. As I waited for my documents, Trisha smiled at me from behind her desk.

"Hey, Joe," she said. "I thought you were in Terre Haute."

"I was, but I came back early. The Bureau's working the case and has a few leads. It's a terrible case, and I think I'm done with it. I don't want to go back."

"If it means anything, we like having you here."

I smiled and looked down as I arranged my documents. Then I blinked a few times.

"Thanks for being my friend, Trisha," I said, darting my eyes to her and then back to my papers. "I'm not good with feelings, so I don't say that kind of thing often. I appreciate you, though. I just wanted you to know."

A smile stretched across her face.

"I know, Joe," she said. "And I'm glad you're my friend, too."

I didn't know what it said about me, but I felt a little awkward after that admission, so I nodded and smiled to her before taking my documents back to my office. The entire floor smelled like paint and drywall dust. I looked forward to going an entire day without hearing construction workers hammer, saw, and shout at one another.

For a while, I sat and read the text messages, but more often than not, the messages between Logan and his father referenced other conversations they'd had on Facebook Messenger, Instagram, and the telephone. That gave me a lot more to read, but once I scanned everything, I had enough information to start a timeline of their conversations.

Logan had a fake Facebook profile under a false name, and, six months ago, he used that fake Facebook profile to contact his father. At first, Joel didn't respond, but Logan was insistent. He sent him pictures and messages until Joel relented and messaged Logan back to say he had missed him but, as they both knew, he wasn't allowed to contact him.

Logan continued to message Joel to remind him that family didn't give up on one another. He also messaged Joel every time his mom came home from a bar drunk—which was two to three times a week. After that, Joel gave Logan his phone number, and they switched to text messages and telephone conversations. From then on, they texted every day and spoke on the phone often. Every morning, Joel texted his son to tell him he loved him and that he was thinking of him even though they were far apart.

Logan usually responded and said something similar. They shared a lot of pictures. Joel sent pictures of his garden, his wife, his dog, and a pair of bedrooms in the house he had set aside for his sons one day. Logan sent his father pictures of his friends and of his brother and of himself. It looked like a very healthy, very loving relationship.

Because I had time stamps on everything, I could even put phone calls together with text messages. When Logan texted his dad to say he had a bad day, Joel almost always called right away. Then, after the phone call, he sent his son encouraging text messages for days to make sure he was doing okay.

I couldn't be certain about a lot in this case, but those text messages and Facebook contacts told me one thing: Logan loved his dad, and Joel loved and missed both of his sons. They also told me something else: If everything Logan said was true, his mom wasn't a fit mother. I might have dismissed them as a young teenager's angry impressions of his primary caregiver, but I had actually seen his mom once, and she had been so drunk she could only stand with help.

Logan and his dad met in person for the first time since Joel lost custody four months ago. They met at Sycamore Park, the same park in which Joel later died, but Joel didn't stay long. Afterwards, he sent his son messages apologizing for the short meeting but promising he'd stay longer the next time. He also warned that if Logan's mom found out they were visiting, they'd both get in serious trouble.

A month later, Joel returned to St. Augustine. Logan skipped school, and the two of them had lunch and went on a hike. After that, they met every two weeks, and their days together started and ended at Sycamore Park. Joel would meet Logan there in the morning, and then he'd drop him off there in the afternoon or evening. For days afterwards, Logan talked about how much fun he had. He also said some mean things about his mom. Joel didn't defend her, but he asked his son not to speak ill of her. She had problems, he said, and sometimes adult problems were hard to deal with.

Justin Cartwright, the US marshal I had found in the Alvarez home, came up a few times in text messages, but those references were brief. It was clear, though, that the marshal played a big role in Logan's life and the lives of his mom and brother. I couldn't tell whether Logan liked him from the messages, but he did what Justin asked. He seemed to respect him, which I doubted would be the case if Justin were abusive or mean.

After reading through the messages and putting together a timeline of Logan and Joel's relationship, I leaned back in my office chair to think. Krystal Alvarez and Joel Robinson had a relationship. Maybe they were married, but maybe not. Either way, their relationship produced two children of whom Krystal had sole custody and sole access.

The latter was important. The courts rarely denied a father visitation access to his children. They could restrict a father's visitation rights and put stipulations on when and where he could visit them, but they rarely severed a dad's rights—and they never severed them without very good cause. To prevent Joel from having any access to his kids, Krystal must have shown the courts he was a danger to Logan and Evan's health and well-being.

Based on all I had seen, that made no sense. The police had picked him up for driving under the influence once, but his arrest report didn't mention that he had children in the car—and it would have if they had been there. Aside from that, his record was clean. Krystal looked like the real danger.

More and more, this looked like a domestic situation that got out of hand. Maybe Krystal found out Joel was visiting Logan and became enraged. Maybe she shot Joel herself, but maybe she had her boyfriend—Justin Cartwright—do it. I couldn't say who pulled the trigger yet, but those two had just climbed to the top of my suspect list.

In a normal case, having two strong suspects made things easier. Here, it added difficulty I rarely had to contend with. Logan Alvarez was a witness to a homicide likely committed by his mother or his mother's boyfriend. I needed to see him, but so far, my suspects had prevented that. Worse, one of them was a US marshal.

This would be a nightmare. Given the circumstances, I didn't believe Krystal Alvarez could act in the best interests of her child, so I'd have to work with the Department of Social Services and see about having a guardian *ad litem* appointed for the kids. Once Logan and Evan had a third-party, trusted adult looking after their interests, I could interview them. I'd also have to work with the US Marshals Office of Professional Responsibility.

No matter what happened, this investigation would hurt these kids. They had lost their father, and I suspected their mom would go to prison for a while—or at least lose custody until she sobered up. I wanted to catch a murderer, but those kids were my priority. My job was to protect them, and that might mean breaking up their family. This sucked.

I wrote notes and then walked upstairs to my boss's office. Sheriff Delgado was on the phone when I arrived, so I waited outside until he hung up. He called me in, and I told him what I had found. I also told him my plan to call Social Services and work with them to ensure I could interview Logan. He crossed his arms while shaking his head.

"You're jumping the shark," he said. "We get Social Services involved, this whole thing will grind to a stop. How about you let me talk to Ms. Alvarez first? I'll see what I can do."

If Krystal didn't want to talk to me, I doubted she'd talk to him, but he was the boss. If he thought his presence alone could compel her to talk, I couldn't stand in his way.

"Sure," I said, trying to keep the annoyed edge out of my voice. "We can do that."

"Good," he said, reaching for his phone once more. "I've got to make a call, so give me a few minutes. I'll meet you in the parking lot."

"Okay," I said, nodding. "I'll meet you outside."

As he dialed a number on his desk phone, I slipped out of the office before heading downstairs. Outside, the sun was shining on a clear, cool day. At least it was pretty. I leaned against the sheriff's unmarked black SUV and waited.

And waited.

After about twenty minutes of sitting out there, I called his office, but his phone was busy. Then I called Trisha, our dispatcher, and asked her to check on him when she had the chance. She called me five minutes after that to say Delgado was still talking but promised to be down soon. I waited another fifteen minutes and felt my temperature rise the entire time before calling Trisha back to tell her I planned to get a cup of coffee at Rise & Grind. If Delgado wanted to waste my time, I might as well waste it in more comfortable settings than sitting in a parking lot. She said she'd let him know.

Two minutes after that, Delgado called me as I was walking to the coffee shop to let me know he was in the parking lot and was annoyed that I had left. I almost told him off, but that'd just give him a reason to write me up. Since becoming sheriff, Delgado had vacillated between being surly but competent and being a vindictive doofus who had no business being in law enforcement. Today, he was leaning toward doofus.

I told him where I was, and he agreed to pick me up. Within moments, I saw his SUV coming toward me on the road. I waved, and he slowed and rolled down his window.

"When I ask you to be somewhere, Detective, I expect you to be there."

I lowered my chin and raised my eyebrows.

"I was there. I stayed and waited for forty-five minutes. When you didn't come out—and after I had called you—I left to get a cup of coffee."

He narrowed his eyes but said nothing. I considered leaving. Instead, I tilted my head to the side and raised my eyebrows again, waiting for him to make the next move. He leaned over and opened the passenger side door.

"Get in," he said. "I'm not waiting all day for you."

I climbed into the SUV. Delgado already had the GPS spooled up and ready to navigate, so I stayed silent as we drove. Unfortunately, I might as well have just stayed in my station and written reports because nobody answered the door at the Alvarez house. I called the elementary school where Evan attended sixth grade and then the high school where Logan was a freshman. Neither kid had been in school since Joel's death, and nobody had answered the school's repeated phone calls. Not only that, their house was locked up tight, their car was gone, and none of the neighbors had seen the kids in several days.

As Delgado and I walked back to his SUV after interviewing the neighbors, he scowled before looking at me.

"When we get back to the station, put out an APB for Krystal Alvarez and Justin Cartwright. I want them brought in tonight."

I considered but then shook my head.

"They're on the run, but Cartwright's still a marshal. If we put out an APB, his buddies will tell him. That'll just drive him further underground."

Delgado slowed.

"What's your big idea, then?"

"We work intelligently," I said. "He's a suspect in a homicide, but he's got a life and a career, and he's got friends and family. He's not going to abandon everything he's ever earned until he doesn't have a choice. We'll take him out before he even knows we're looking at him."

Delgado nodded as we reached his SUV.

"Sounds like a plan. Good luck, Detective. I'm going home."

I raised my eyebrows.

"You going to drive me to the station first?"

He considered and then shook his head.

"Call Trisha and tell her to send somebody to pick you up. I've got somewhere to be."

Before I could say anything, he climbed into his car but didn't unlock the passenger side door. I stepped back so he wouldn't run me over, and he drove off without a second look, leaving me slack-jawed and shaking my head.

"You are such an asshole."

21

I called our dispatcher's back line and waited about four rings before Trisha answered.

"Hey, it's Joe. Our boss has seen fit to drop me off at the home of a murder suspect with no way of getting back to our station. Can you route somebody to pick me up?"

I gave her the Alvarez family's address, and Trisha chuckled.

"Sure," she said. She typed and then paused. "Katie Martelle is about ten minutes out."

"Thanks," I said, sighing and looking around. I had nothing to do except twiddle my thumbs and wait. "You know why our boss is being a bigger jerk than usual today?"

"Oh, you haven't heard," said Trisha. "Our good sheriff will no longer be running unopposed in the 2020 election."

I furrowed my brow.

"Who's challenging him?"

"A guy named Dean Kalil. He's a former lieutenant in the Greene County Sheriff's Office."

I narrowed my eyes.

"Where's Greene County?"

"Springfield, Missouri. It's a couple hours southwest of here," she said. "His wife got a job in St. Louis, so they moved here. He applied for a detective position, but George declined to even interview him. I guess that didn't sit well with him because he's running for sheriff now."

"Serves Delgado right," I said. "I hope Kalil wins."

"You're not the only one," she said. She paused and typed. "I've got calls incoming. Katie'll be there to pick you up soon."

I nodded and thanked her before hanging up. As Trisha had said, Katie Martelle pulled to a stop in the Alvarezes' driveway about ten minutes after I placed my call. Katie was the youngest officer we had in the station, but she was a quick learner, and she worked hard. I liked her. We didn't have much to talk about, but we chatted and promised to set a time to go out for drinks after work when I finished my case.

As I got out of her cruiser at my station, my smile left, and I focused on the case in front of me. Justin Cartwright may have been a US marshal, but he was a suspect in my murder case. I needed to find out what I could about him, so I went to my desk and started a background check.

As expected of a US marshal, he had never been arrested for any major crime, and he had a minimal social media presence. His credit report showed that he had almost nine thousand dollars in consumer debt, a nineteen-thousand-dollar loan for a car, and a two-hundred-thousand-dollar mortgage on a home in Affton, Missouri, a middle-class suburb in south St. Louis County.

I leaned back on my desk chair and stretched. Cartwright was in his early forties. If he had spent most of his career with the US Marshals Service, he would be making sixty or seventy thousand dollars a year. It was a decent salary, but he had a good bit of high-interest debt. I didn't know whether that changed my case, but I had to keep it in mind.

I called up the license bureau's database next to get his home address, and then I looked it up on Google Maps. He had a two-story brick house with a big garage and a covered front porch. It looked like a nice place, the kind a mother and her two boys would feel comfortable hiding in. I checked that my phone had a full charge and that I had a spare magazine for my pistol before signing out an unmarked SUV from our department's motor pool.

I hit rush hour on my drive north, which slowed me down. By the time I reached Cartwright's neighborhood, the sun was going down. It looked like a new development with brick and siding-clad homes on undersized lots. Many of the front yards held wagons and trucks, while a well-landscaped, communal green space in the center of the subdivision held a playground and mulched play area as big as those at a public park.

Cartwright's house wasn't hard to find. The lot to the west was empty, but it had a For Sale sign in front. The house to the east looked identical to Cartwright's save for its bright pink door. If I had to guess, the builder only provided three or four standardized designs for residents to choose from. The practice kept costs low and allowed people to own houses larger than they could otherwise afford. I liked old houses, but I could see the appeal of a new home, especially for those who had kids.

I parked in front of Cartwright's house and got out of my car. A toddler cried in protest from the sidewalk as his mother carried him home from the playground across the street. Cartwright's home was quiet, but a light shone from the transom window above the front door. I took the concrete walkway to the front porch and knocked on the door. No one answered, so I waited two or three minutes and rang the doorbell. Then I waited for another couple of minutes before I heard the deadbolt unlock.

The door cracked open to reveal a petite woman in her midthirties. The sunlight reflected off her olive-colored skin, making her pink lipstick all the brighter. She blinked big green eyes and cleared her throat when she saw me. She looked nervous, so I pushed my jacket back to show her my badge.

"Hi, miss, I'm Detective Mary Joe Court with the St. Augustine County Sheriff's Department," I said, smiling. "I may be at the wrong house, but I'm looking for Deputy US Marshal Justin Cartwright. Is he in?"

She cocked her head to the side.

"What's this about?"

Her voice was soft, and it had a slight warble. Even though she had seen my badge, her posture never relaxed.

Plenty of people became nervous when a stranger knocked on the doors, but that nervousness usually dissipated once they learned I was a cop. She kept one foot behind the door, and the other near the doorframe. If she sensed a threat, she could slam that door in my face and lock it well before I could stop her.

"I've just got questions for him. Do you know Marshal Cartwright well?"

She hesitated. Then her eyes flicked to my left and behind me. My breath caught in my throat. My hand shot down to my firearm, but before I could draw it from my holster, I felt the barrel of a weapon pressed to the back of my head.

"Tracy, get the kids and go. Detective, put your hands in the air. If you make any sudden moves, I'll shoot you in the head."

I swore under my breath. It took the average person about half a second to recognize and respond to a physical threat. Cartwright had training at least as good as mine, and I had to assume his reflexes were sharp. If I tried to duck or spin around, he'd pull the trigger and blow a hole in the back of my skull and paint his house with my brain matter.

"I'm just here to talk," I said, raising my hands like he'd asked.

"We're way past the point of talking," he said, pushing me forward with the barrel of his gun. "Step forward and put your hands flat against the wall."

The garage opened to my left. I heard the squeal, but

I couldn't see it. Once his wife and kids left, I knew Cartwright would shoot me. I had to get out of there.

"This is a bad idea," I said. "People know where I am."

"Shut up and shuffle to the door," he said. "We're going inside, and then we'll talk so I can figure out what to do with you."

Going from a public position on the front porch to a private place without witnesses seemed like a bad idea considering he had a gun to my head. I tried turning my head to look at him, but he pressed the gun against my skull harder and then began patting my sides, feeling for my weapon. Once he found it, he pulled it from the holster with his right hand. He probably pocketed it after that.

"Go inside," he said. "Then walk down the main hall to the kitchen. There we'll take the stairs down to the basement, where we can talk."

I shot my eyes around the porch, hoping to spot a rock or decoration I could use as a weapon. The porch was clean, though. Cartwright had a wooden swing on a chain that dangled from the ceiling, a low coffee table, and a wicker sofa with red cushions. None of it would have enough weight to be an effective weapon, and none of it was substantial enough to provide cover if he started shooting at me. This was bad.

"Open the front door and go inside," said Cartwright. His voice had a hard edge to it now. My heart pounded, and my lungs felt tight. Muscles all over my body itched. It was the adrenaline. "We can talk in the basement where there are fewer distractions."

I shuffled over to the door and opened it, exposing a two-story entryway. A staircase led to the second floor, while a hallway led to a living room and kitchen in the back of the house. There was a dining room to my left and a hall table along the wall beside the staircase to my right. Fake roses covered in a thin layer of dust rested in a glass vase on the table. There were glass marbles in the bottom to give it heft and the illusion of water.

I could use that.

"What do you plan to do?" I asked, stepping forward. The vase was about ten feet from the front door. Cartwright had taken my firearm, but he hadn't taken my car keys or cell phone. If I could hit him with the vase, it should disorient him enough to give me time to escape and get to my car. "I just came to talk to you. I need to hear your side of the story."

As I took two steps forward, he shut the door.

"My side of what story?" he asked.

"Joel Robinson," I said, stutter-stepping forward and to the side so I could reach the vase. As long as I kept talking, he'd focus on my words instead of my hands. "Krystal Alvarez is your little piece on the side, and you're close to her kids. So, what happened? Did you find out Joel was visiting Logan and decide to scare him off? If so, I get it. Things happen. You were just trying to protect Logan. You didn't mean to kill Joel. We can work with that. Put your gun down and come with me. Your life isn't over."

He sighed as I continued walking.

"Stop talking and walk," he said.

My arms and legs tingled, and an empty, hard pit had grown in the bottom of my gut. If I didn't do something, I would die. I looked over my shoulder and licked my lips.

"Please don't do this," I said, forcing a quiver into my voice. "Please."

"Just walk," he said, shoving me.

That was it, the moment I needed.

I dropped to a knee as if I had fallen. Then I vaulted up and grabbed the vase with my right hand while spinning around. The vase weighed eight or nine pounds —heavier than I'd expected. I swung it as hard as I could, hoping to catch Cartwright off guard. Before I could hit him, he brought up a forearm.

Time seemed to slow. The side of his arm deflected my blow, but the vase was heavy enough and my swing was hard enough that momentum kept me going. The glass hit him in the temple and shattered. Blue beads fell to the ground, and blood trickled down the side of Cartwright's head. He staggered back, disoriented. I swatted his weapon away and stepped forward.

I didn't lift weights, but I was a runner. My legs were strong. I brought my hands to my face for balance and kicked him as hard as I could in the belly. He sucked in a deep breath and doubled over, bringing his face down to waist level. Without thinking, I brought my knee up to meet him. His nose crunched as my kneecap connected.

Cartwright's hands whipped from his thighs to his nose as he dropped to a knee.

I shoved him to the side and ran toward the front door. My right foot came down on a clump of glass marbles and lost all traction. It was like trying to run on ice. I fell to my side. Pain ripped through my rib cage as dozens of glass shards and marbles crunched beneath me. I gritted my teeth and pushed up in time to hear the marshal roar and see him charge at me.

I dropped to the ground and rolled, avoiding a collision with the enraged federal officer. Then pain burned through me as he kicked me in the ribs. Blood trickled down his face from the cut on his temple and from his nose. His eyes were as black and pitiless as midnight, and rage had contorted his face into an animalistic visage.

"You moron!" he screamed, rearing back to kick me again. His foot hit my ribs with a dull thud that knocked my breath out. He spit blood on the ground and sneered at me before pulling his leg back once more. "I tried to give you a chance."

He kicked me again, this time in my upper ribs near my shoulder. Pain like I had never felt ripped through me. If I didn't move, I'd die. I knew that. Before he could pull his leg back again, I wrapped my arm around it and drew my legs up and to my chest. I kicked his balls as hard as I could. He gasped and doubled over. I rolled to my belly and shot my eyes around the room.

He had dropped his pistol near the kitchen, so I dove

toward it. The marshal grabbed my ankle, so I kicked him in the face again and lunged forward with every bit of muscle I had. As my fingers wrapped around the stock of his pistol, I heard the sirens outside.

I whipped the gun around and pointed the barrel at Cartwright's chest. He drew himself to his feet. Blood covered his shirt and the floor, and he sucked down deep breaths. My entire body ached, and I could feel the cuts on my hands and forearms from the glass on the floor, but I ignored it all as I stood. I felt dizzy, but I forced that feeling down.

"Put your hands on top of your head," I said, fighting to keep the tremble out of my voice. "You're under arrest, motherfucker."

22

Someone must have heard our fight or seen us outside because there were three police cars in front of the house as I opened the front door. The uniformed officers outside ducked behind their cars when they saw my firearm. Two of them carried tactical rifles, while the third had a pistol. My heart had just stopped pounding from the fight with Cartwright, and now it began thudding against my chest once more.

I held my badge up in one hand and lowered to a knee to put Cartwright's pistol on the ground.

"I'm on the job!" I shouted. "I'm Detective Joe Court with the St. Augustine County Sheriff's Department, and Mr. Cartwright is a suspect in a homicide. He attacked me, and I defended myself."

"I'm a US marshal!" shouted Cartwright. "I have a badge in my back pocket. This lady came to my house and threatened me and my family. She attacked me and stole my firearm."

The uniformed officers looked at one another. One of the officers, a guy in his early fifties, stood straighter, but he didn't lower his rifle. He had sergeant stripes on his shoulder. More sirens blared in the distance.

"Both of you, place your hands behind your heads and step forward and onto the grass."

"I'm on the job!" I shouted again, doing as he said. Cartwright did the same beside me.

"Get on your knees."

I knelt down. The grass was cold. I looked to Cartwright.

"You're not talking your way out of this," I said. "You killed a man."

"Mouths shut!" shouted the sergeant. "Keep your hands behind your heads and lower your faces to the ground. If you listen, no one will get hurt, and we'll sort this thing out."

There was nothing to sort out. I came to Affton to question a suspect in a homicide. Cartwright snuck up on me and drew a weapon, so I defended myself. That was it.

And it was stupid.

He had already been a suspect in a murder investigation, but now I'd have him for assault in the first degree. Considering I was a police officer, that meant he was facing ten to thirty years in prison. I would have preferred if he talked to me peacefully, but ten to thirty years gave me an awful lot of leverage over him.

I lowered myself down. Within moments, a fourth police cruiser arrived, and a uniformed officer patted me down for weapons before handcuffing my wrists behind my back. It wasn't comfortable, but the officer was a professional. Once they had both me and Cartwright secured in the rear seats of two different squad cars, the officers conferred with one another a few feet away.

About twenty minutes later, a uniformed lieutenant from the St. Louis County Police Department walked up to the squad car in which I sat. He was fifty or fifty-five, and he looked familiar. He blinked at me and then opened my door.

"Can you tell me your mom's name?"

It would have been an odd question except that my mother had retired less than a year ago as a captain in this guy's department. I gave him a tight smile.

"Julia Green," I said. "And I'm Detective Joe Court with the St. Augustine County Sheriff's Department. My supervisor is Sheriff George Delgado. You can call him to verify my identity."

He nodded and held the door open for me.

"I thought you looked familiar," he said. "Stand up and turn around so I can get these cuffs off you."

I did as he asked and thanked him as he unhooked me. I rubbed my wrists as I looked toward the house and the vehicle in which Cartwright sat. He still had his arms behind his back, but a uniformed officer with blue nitrile gloves was cleaning the blood from his temple.

"You've got some blood on your hands and forearms," said the lieutenant. "Once Blake's done with Marshal Cartwright, he'll clean you up and make sure you don't have any glass in those cuts."

I looked down at my hands. Blood had soaked into my shirt and sweater, but the cuts weren't too deep. It looked much worse than it felt.

"I'd appreciate that," I said. "Did you find my pistol? Cartwright took it. I'm not sure what he did with it."

"We've got it and will get it back to you once we sort things out," he said. Then he sighed. "This is a mess."

"I'll make it simple," I said. "Arrest Cartwright for assault, and then I'll take his weapon back to my crime lab to see whether it fired the rounds that killed a man in St. Augustine. If it all goes right, I'll close my case, you'll close your case, and we'll put a violent murderer behind bars for the rest of his life. Sound good to you?"

The lieutenant smiled.

"Let's hope it goes like that. Sit tight. I've got some work to do before I arrest anybody. Sheriff Delgado isn't answering his phone, so is there anybody else you'd like me to call?"

I almost asked him to call Mathias, but that would have just worried him. I shook my head.

"I'm fine, but thank you."

He nodded and wished me luck before walking to the other cruiser with Cartwright. I sat down and closed my eyes for a little while, enjoying the break. Then I heard footsteps outside.

"Up and at 'em, Sleeping Beauty."

It was a woman's raspy voice, but I didn't recognize it. The instant my eyes opened, she grabbed my arm near the shoulder and pulled hard enough to drag me from the car. Instinctively, I shot my hand to my holster, but the county police still had my weapon. Once my feet were on stable ground, I shrugged her hand off and motioned toward the nearest uniformed officer. He hesitated before walking toward me.

"Thank you for coming, Officer. I need you to stay with me while I talk to this woman," I said before looking at the lady who had grabbed me. She was forty-five or fifty and had thin shoulders and an angular face. Her eyes were like little black beads. A tie held her long black hair from her face. "Who are you, and why are you touching me?"

She stepped closer to me, invading my space as if she were trying to intimidate me. It'd take a lot more than that to cow me into submission. My back straightened, and my jaw tightened. I dropped my right leg back but kept my hips squared to her.

"I don't know what you're doing, but I'd suggest you give me some breathing room," I said, balling my hands into fists.

The officer I had called over put up his hands and spoke in a calm, reassuring voice.

"Let's de-escalate this. You're both professionals, and you're both here to do a job. Both of you step back."

I glanced at him and sucked in a deep breath before forcing my shoulders to relax. I stepped back. She didn't. Instead, she crossed her arms and glared at me.

"I'm Chief Deputy Marshal Kelly Babcock," she said. "You're lucky to be alive after showing up at the home of a US marshal unannounced."

"And Cartwright will be lucky if he doesn't get life in

prison," I said. "He and his girlfriend are the prime suspects in my homicide investigation."

The muscles of her jaw clenched, and I counted to ten before she spoke again.

"Stop talking, Detective."

"I don't think so," I said, shaking my head. "My victim was Joel Robinson. He's the father of Logan and Evan Alvarez. Logan witnessed his father's murder, but when I went to interview him, your officer intervened and prevented me. Furthermore, he tried to prevent me from speaking to Logan's mother, with whom he has a very familiar relationship. He wouldn't have done that without very good reason. If I had to guess, he was covering his ass.

"When I tried to interview Logan at school the next day, I learned that Krystal Alvarez, Logan's mother, had called him in sick. When my boss and I went to the Alvarez house to speak to Logan or Krystal, we found the house emptied. Because Justin Cartwright, your employee, has a close relationship to both Krystal and Logan, I drove here in the off chance the Alvarez family had joined Cartwright at home.

"When I knocked on the door, he snuck up behind me and pulled a gun on me. Fearing for my life, I defended myself and disarmed him. I don't know whether Mr. Cartwright murdered Joel Robinson, but I know he assaulted a police officer. If you want to help him, call an attorney and get out of my way."

Her eyes narrowed, and she ran her tongue around

the inside of her cheeks as she considered me. Then she stepped back and reached to her belt for a pair of handcuffs.

"Detective Mary Joe Court, you're under arrest for assaulting a federal officer intending to commit murder. You have the right to remain silent, but if you speak to me, we can use anything you say against you in a court of law. You have the right to an attorney. If you can't afford one, the court system will provide one for you free of charge. Do you understand your rights?"

I scoffed and shook my head.

"This is unbelievable."

She didn't blink. She just stared at me with those cold, beady eyes of hers.

"Do you understand your rights?"

"Fuck you," I said.

She looked to the uniformed patrolman.

"Officer, please take Detective Court into custody and put her in the back of my vehicle."

He held up his hands and took a step back.

"I'm not comfortable with this," he said. "I need to call my supervisor."

She rolled her eyes and looked at me.

"Detective Court, turn around and place your hands on top of the vehicle. I'm going to put you in handcuffs, and then I will drive you downtown to the federal courthouse. If anyone obstructs me, they can join you in a federal holding cell."

I looked to the uniformed officer and shook my

head. He backed up even further. We'd have to let the court system figure this one out. The marshals wanted to flex their muscles, and that was fine. They'd tire themselves out, and then I'd get back to work. I just hoped nobody got hurt until then.

I turned and allowed the marshal to cuff me.

"Let's just get this over with so I can get back to my job."

The marshal leaned forward.

"You just took a hard left turn in the right-hand lane, honey," she said, her voice barely a whisper. "You're not going back to work anytime soon. I'll make sure of that."

23

It had been a longer walk than Logan had expected, so both he and his brother felt exhausted. Houston had decent public transportation, but things had become a lot harder when they left the city limits. Their bus had dropped them off at a giant park-and-ride in Westfield. They could have taken a cab or a private charter bus from there, but they didn't have the money.

Instead, they had walked twelve miles north alongside an access road that ran parallel to the interstate. It wasn't fun, but it could have been worse. There were plenty of gas stations and stores along the way, so they stopped and used some of Evan's money to buy bottles of water and use the bathroom. When they asked for directions in a gas station, the clerk even showed them Google Maps on his phone so they had a better idea of where to go.

When they reached the outskirts of The Woodlands, they followed Sawdust Road past gas stations and banks and grocery stores until it narrowed and became Grogans Mill Road. Gradually, they ran across fewer and fewer strip malls and parking lots and walked alongside a busy road through the woods. Houses lay tucked behind and amongst the trees. It was a pretty area. Logan could see why their dad and Daisy had moved there.

Then they hung a right onto Crystal Lake Lane and walked deeper into a neighborhood for the next fifteen minutes. With every step, Logan relaxed more and more. They had made it. It wasn't home, but it would have been one day. Logan's dad had shown him dozens of pictures of their backyard and the house and his bedroom. He would have had a bedroom with blue walls. Evan would have been down the hall.

As soon as he turned eighteen, he would have left his mom and the stupid Witness Protection Program and moved in with his dad and Daisy. It would have been great.

As he walked, his feet seemed to become heavier as his exhaustion caught up with him. Logan hadn't stopped moving since Diego murdered his father. Soon, he would. For days, everything that happened to him had felt surreal, like he was re-enacting the events of a movie instead of experiencing his life. Finally, his adrenaline was waning, and the profound nature of his loss was setting in.

His eye felt glassy and wet. His dad had saved him in the park. He hadn't seen that before, but now he couldn't stop seeing it. After a few more feet, a weight began pressing down on him, crushing him, threatening to break him. For a few steps, he pretended like nothing was wrong, but then the weight grew heavier and heavier until it was all he could feel. His vision began swimming and growing more and more narrow until all he could see was a tiny corridor in front of him. He willed his feet to keep going, but then he couldn't do it anymore.

He sat on the ground on a bed of pine needles and put his head between his knees.

"We're almost there. What are you doing, Logan?"

Logan ignored him at first, but then Evan repeated the question.

"I just needed a break, okay?" he said, his voice trembling. "I just need to breathe."

Evan sat down beside him in a similar posture. A big car slowed as it passed, but it didn't stop. That was good. Logan didn't want to talk to anybody. As he closed his eyes and breathed in the pine-scented air, he found his eyes growing more and more watery. The sob welled up in his gut before he could stop himself. His shoulders and back shook.

"Don't cry," said Evan, his voice small. "I don't want you to cry."

"Shut up," said Logan, rubbing the backs of his hands across his eyes. "I'm not crying. I'm fine."

Evan said nothing. Logan kept taking deep breaths until his shoulders stopped trembling and the tears left his eyes. He didn't feel better, but at least he had control of himself again. He focused on the pine needles on the ground so he wouldn't have to look at his brother.

"Before we get to Daisy's house, you need to know something," he said, after swallowing hard. "I killed Dad."

"No, you didn't," said Evan.

"Yeah, I did," said Logan. "I didn't shoot him, but he

wouldn't have been there if I hadn't bought that stupid phone from Eric Murphy. He didn't even know where we lived until I told him. He didn't want to visit, either. I had to beg him."

"Shut up," said Evan.

"No," said Logan. "I killed him. It was my fault. When he saw Diego coming toward us, Dad told me to run. He was protecting me, but he shouldn't have even been there."

"Dude, shut up," said Evan.

"Make me," said Logan. He smacked his brother on the face. It wasn't hard, and he didn't even know why he did it, but he felt compelled anyway. Evan's mouth popped open.

"Why'd you do that?"

"Because I could," said Logan, smacking his brother again, this time harder. "You want to make me stop?"

"I don't like this," said Evan, starting to push off the ground. "I'm going to Daisy's house."

"You're not going anywhere," said Logan, ramming his brother with his shoulder. At first, Evan didn't even try to push him away. That made Logan even madder. He put his hands on his brother's chest, shoved his back to the ground, and then swung his leg over his abdomen to sit on his stomach and prevent him from moving. "Fight me."

"I don't want to," said Evan, shaking his head.

"Fight me," said Logan, fresh tears coming to his eyes. He slapped him in the face. "Hit me, asshole."

Evan, instead of fighting back, brought his arms over his face to protect himself. Logan sucked in two deep breaths and then punched the soft, sandy ground beside his brother's head. The pine needles cushioned the blow and prevented him from breaking his knuckle, but the force of the strike traveled up his arm and into his elbow and shoulder, anyway. It hurt, and he deserved it. He shook his hand out, swung his leg off his brother, and lay beside him.

Neither said anything for a few minutes, but they both breathed easier.

"Sorry," said Logan. "I don't know what happened."

"It's okay," said Evan. "You didn't mean it."

Logan shook his head and blinked again as more tears came to his eyes.

"You're too nice, man," he said. "That'll get you hurt."

"Being kind to other people isn't a weakness," he said. "It's a strength."

Logan scoffed and rolled his eyes.

"They tell you that in preschool?"

"I'm not in preschool, butthead. I'm in sixth grade."

"Same difference," said Logan. He paused and softened his voice. "I'm sorry I hit you."

"You already said that," said Evan.

"Yeah, well, I am sorry," said Logan. He shook his head and picked up a handful of pine needles and tossed them in the air. Evan sputtered and spit and brushed them off his chest and face.

"Cut it out."

Logan didn't apologize this time, but he lowered his hands to his sides.

"Do you like Mom?"

A minivan passed on the road but didn't slow. Its driver probably didn't even see them in the pine trees' shadow. Logan looked to his brother and repeated the question.

"She's our mom," said Evan, furrowing his brow. "We have to like her."

"No, we don't," said Logan, shaking his head. "All of this is her fault. I hate her. I wish Diego had killed her instead of Dad. At least then we'd still have a home."

Neither said anything for a moment.

"Daisy will give us a home," said Evan. His voice was so soft Logan barely heard it. He was almost pleading. Logan wanted to tell him he was right, and that they'd live with Daisy, and that she'd raise them as if they were hers. And if they didn't live with Daisy, they'd live with their grandmother. And if their grandmother didn't want them, they'd go live with their uncle Travis. He wanted to tell him the same comforting, soft lies he had told himself over the past few days, but after running, after having a knife pressed to his throat, after having his cell phone and wallet stolen in a shelter for homeless kids, after everything that had happened to him, he couldn't. His life no longer had room for soft, comforting, childish lies. It only had room for hard truths.

"We don't know Daisy," said Logan. "She's not our

mom. She was Dad's wife. Dad would have given us a home, but Daisy's a stranger. We'll stay here for a night, but then we'll move on and find our real family. I'll take care of you until then."

Evan blinked a few times. Logan thought he'd argue with him, but he just seemed to think. Then he nodded.

"Okay."

The weight Logan had felt earlier began pressing on him again. He'd get used to it, though. He stood and reached down to help his brother to his feet.

"You ready?"

"Yeah," said Evan. "Let's find Daisy."

They walked for another five minutes before coming to a two-story brick home with a two-car garage and bright yellow flowers in pots beside the front door. Logan had seen this house in pictures, but to stand in front of it and see it in person and know he'd never call it home made his throat and chest grow tight enough that it was almost hard to breathe.

He forced himself to cough, clearing his throat, before walking down the concrete walkway to the front door. A pair of big pecan trees on either side of the curving walkway cast shade over most of the lawn. Logan picked up a pecan from the ground but couldn't crack the brown shell. He handed it to his brother, anyway.

"Do you remember these?" he asked. "We used to have pecan trees at our old house in Katy."

Evan nodded.

"I used to like running over them on my bike to hear

their shells crack."

Logan shook his head and drew in a deep breath.

"You always were weird."

"And you were stupid," said Evan.

Logan wanted to tell him he was a butt, but they needed to make a decent impression on Daisy. Fighting on her doorstep wouldn't have done that.

"You've got pine needles on your pants," said Logan.

"You've still got a butt face."

"I'm serious," said Logan. "Brush your pants off. We don't want to bring a bunch of crap into the house."

"Oh," he said, looking down and brushing off his pants. He looked a little better, so they resumed their walk up the walkway. When they reached the door, they stopped, and Logan rang the bell. Within moments, the door opened, and they caught sight of a familiar face. Evan grabbed his brother's forearm and squeezed tight. Logan tried to push his brother behind him, but the kid wouldn't move.

"Hey, guys. Funny seeing you here, isn't it?"

The voice belonged to Gloria, the woman who had tormented them on the train. Logan swallowed, but he couldn't force his legs to move. She stepped forward.

"Don't be afraid," said Gloria. "All that shit you guys did is in the past now. I forgive you."

The pine needles behind them crunched. Logan looked over his shoulder to see Diego walking from the side of the house to stand behind them. Logan started shifting to his right, but Diego matched him footstep for footstep. Even if he and Evan ran in opposite directions, Diego would follow one and Gloria would follow the other. Logan could feel his brother tremble behind him.

"What'd you do with Daisy?" he asked, trying to force strength into his voice. Diego chuckled.

"She's fine, kid," he said. "Her husband just died. Neighbor says she went to her mom's house."

Logan stepped closer to his brother.

"We've got to run," he whispered.

"I'm tired of chasing you. If you guys run, I'm just going to Tase one of you, and Diego will shoot the other. We only need one of you alive," said Gloria, reaching behind her for a bright yellow Taser. "Learn to whisper a little quieter."

Logan looked at her in the eyes. They were black and hateful, but they held something else, too. She wanted him to run. She wanted the excuse to shoot him. It was over. All of it. Everything that had happened to them had been for nothing. Logan blinked glassy, wet eyes.

"If I give up, will you let my brother go?" asked Logan. "He'll disappear."

"Logan, don't," said Evan, gripping his arm even tighter. Diego chuckled. Gloria tilted her head to the side and smiled.

"That's so sweet, guys," she said, shaking her head. "But no. You're a package deal. You'll be easier to control that way. Now get inside the house."

Logan stayed still until he felt a heavy hand on his back.

"Go inside, or we'll kill your little brother in front of you," said Diego. "Move."

"I'm sorry," whispered Evan.

"Don't be," said Logan. "We have to go inside. If we listen to them and do what they want, they won't kill us. Right?"

"Sure," said Gloria.

Logan knew it was a lie, but he nodded and started walking, anyway. He would finally get to see the inside of his dad's house. He just wished he could have seen it while standing beside him.

24

The Marshals Service contracted with St. Louis County for detention space, so Babcock drove me to the St. Louis County jail in Clayton. I knew a lot of police officers in Clayton, but I didn't know many people in the jail, so nobody recognized me right away. That was fine. I was pissed, and I wouldn't have been a great conversationalist given the circumstances.

Babcock dropped me off, and a uniformed female officer with the St. Louis County Department of Justice Services brought me inside for processing. First, a nurse technician checked my vitals, drew my blood to test for drugs and other substances, and asked whether I had or suspected I had any serious illnesses or ongoing health concerns. She also asked whether I was pregnant or could be pregnant. I told her no.

Then a uniformed officer led me to a windowless hallway, where she had me place my hands on big yellow handprints painted on the wall while she frisked me for weapons. The county police had confiscated my firearm and badge at Cartwright's house, so I was unarmed. Then the same officer who frisked me tried to lead me to a temporary holding cell with four women already inside, but I shook my head.

"Not going to happen," I said. "Get me a private cell."

The officer sighed and appraised me. Then she raised an eyebrow.

"I'm having a lousy day, honey," she said. "I don't want to sit here and argue with you. Give me one reason I shouldn't hit the alarm and have a dozen of my colleagues carry you in there kicking and screaming."

I narrowed my eyes at her and cocked my head to the side.

"I'll give you two reasons: First, this isn't an emergency, so hitting the alarm so your colleagues would rough me up would be unprofessional and an abuse of your position. Second, I'm a detective with the St. Augustine County Sheriff's Department. You can't guarantee my safety inside a general-population jail environment. If those ladies find out who I am, they could attack me."

The officer looked me up and down again before taking the walkie-talkie from her belt.

"Sergeant Taylor, I'm outside the ladies' temporary holding cell, and I've got a situation I need your help with."

A voice squawked an acknowledgement. About three minutes later, a heavyset man in a navy uniform stepped into the hallway. He looked at me but focused on his officer.

"Is she causing a problem?"

"She says she's a detective from St. Augustine County," said the officer.

The sergeant looked at me but then narrowed his eyes and looked to his officer.

"What's her paperwork say?"

Had I not understood what was going on better, it would have annoyed me that they were speaking about me as if I weren't there, but given the situation, they couldn't believe a word that passed out of my lips. For all they knew, I was a schizophrenic woman who stopped taking her meds or a professional con artist who hoped to talk her way out of a night in jail. Still, I crossed my arms and sighed as the uniformed officer looked at a document on her clipboard and then shook her head.

"She was picked up for assault with a deadly weapon enhancement. She's a federal prisoner," said the officer, peering at me. "Who'd you hit?"

I closed my eyes and sighed.

"A US marshal attacked me. I defended myself, but his boss got to the crime scene before mine did. That's why I'm here now."

They both exchanged glances before looking at me.

"If you're a detective in St. Augustine County, who's your supervisor?" asked the sergeant.

"Sheriff George Delgado," I said. "He's preoccupied tonight. If you want to confirm my identity, call Detective Mathias Blatch. He works out of the South County Precinct Station on Sappington Barracks Road."

"I've seen Blatch's name on arrest reports," said the

uniformed officer. The sergeant nodded and looked to me.

"You sure Detective Blatch will vouch for you?"

"Yeah," I said. "He'll also probably come down here looking for me. He's my boyfriend."

The sergeant blinked but otherwise didn't respond.

"Good for you," he said, his voice flat as he looked to his subordinate. "Put her in a private room and make her comfortable. I'll sort this out."

The officer nodded.

"Will do," she said, gesturing. "This way, ma'am."

I followed the officer down the hall to a small, windowless room with a metal table and four metal stools, all of which someone had bolted to the floor. On a normal day, the jail likely used these rooms for prisoners who needed to see their attorneys. Today, it'd serve double duty as a temporary holding cell.

I sat at the table and thanked the officer for her courtesy, but I couldn't even force myself to smile.

"Can I get you anything?" she asked. "Water, soda, sandwich?"

"I'm fine, but thank you," I said.

"Sit tight," she said. "We'll work as quickly as we can. If you need me, knock on the door. We don't have cameras or recording devices in here, but I'll be in the hallway."

I sat at the table. She shut the door, but I didn't bother checking to see whether she had locked it. I wasn't going anywhere. At first, I sat at the table with my arms crossed, but after a few minutes, I put my head down and closed my eyes.

I drifted in and out of a light sleep for a while, but eventually the same uniformed officer I had spoken to earlier opened the door and popped her head inside.

"You still doing okay, Detective?"

I lifted my head and nodded.

"Yeah. You're calling me Detective now. Did you confirm my identity?"

She nodded and then sighed.

"Yep, and I can't recall the last time we had so many phone calls about one prisoner," she said. "So far, my boss has spoken to the county prosecutor, your mom, your boyfriend, two US attorneys, the sheriff at your station, the chief deputy of the US Marshals Service, and even an FBI agent. You're popular."

I exhaled a long breath through my nose.

"Popularity alone doesn't get you out of jail."

She shook her head.

"Sure doesn't. That takes a court order, and we haven't received one of those."

"Can I make a phone call?" I asked. "I need to ask somebody to feed my dog."

She hesitated but then blinked a few times.

"I'll see if I can arrange that."

I thanked her, and she stepped out. Once she left, I stood and stretched my arms over my head. It felt good to move, but every time I thought about why I was in that cell, fresh waves of heat passed over me. I ground my teeth. Cartwright might not have killed Joel Robinson, but he knew far more than he let on. I tracked him down and went to his house because that was my job. I didn't deserve this shit.

About ten minutes after I asked the officer for a phone call, she came back and led me to a bank of pay phones. I called the landline at my mom's house collect, figuring that'd be my best chance for getting in touch with somebody who could help. My dad answered the phone on the third ring and accepted the charges.

"Joe, hey, you okay?" asked Dad. "Detective Blatch called a little while ago. Your mom's downtown right now trying to talk to somebody in the prosecutor's office and find out what's going on."

"I'm fine," I said. "This is all a misunderstanding. It'll work out, but I need somebody to feed Roy. He's home alone."

"Okay," said Dad. Already, I could hear the floor creak as he walked. "I'll head down and pick him up."

"Don't worry about it. I don't think I'll be in here that long," I said, shaking my head. "Call my station instead. Jason Zuckerburg will be working the desk, and he knows everybody. Ask him to call Preston Cain. Preston lives in St. Augustine, and he and his fiancée have taken care of Roy when I'm not home."

Dad paused, probably to write the name down.

"I can do that," he said. "Do you need a lawyer?"

I sighed and nodded. "Probably. When you call my station, ask Zuckerburg to call the union. I was arrested for doing my job. They'll send a lawyer out."

Dad paused again and then sighed.

"I'll make that call," he said. "Are you doing okay, hon? Is there anything I can do?"

"No, but thanks. I'm sure Mom and Mathias are raising enough hell."

"I imagine. That Mathias guy seemed steamed to know someone had arrested you. Is there something going on there?"

I closed my eyes, but I couldn't help but smile just a little.

"Dad, I'm in jail," I said. "I don't think now's the time to talk about my love life."

"Sure," he said. "Everything will be okay. We'll figure this out."

There wasn't a lot Dad could do, but his support still meant a lot to me. I grew up in and out of the foster care system and didn't meet my real family until I was in high school. When Doug and Julia took me in, I was angry, depressed, and jaded. My previous foster father had drugged and then raped me on the couch in his sun room. He went to prison, but that didn't change what had happened. Neither Julia nor Doug could change that, either. With their patience and support, though, I became more than the broken young victim who first came to their home. I became a survivor, and I learned to love myself—and them. They were my family, and I'd do anything for them.

"We will," I said. "I'll see you soon, okay, Dad?"

"I love you, sweetheart."

A lump began to grow in my throat, so I swallowed it down.

"I love you, too."

I hung up a second later. After that comforting conversation, the jail's bright white walls and steel bars seemed even more foreboding. A uniformed officer led me back to my private room. Now, though, the door was propped open. As I walked in, I found the uniformed sergeant I had spoken to earlier inside. He smiled at me and then handed me a transparent plastic tote that held my purse and other personal items.

"Okay, Detective," he said. "You're getting out of here. The US attorney has dropped all charges against you, and there's a guy outside waiting to pick you up."

I bet it was Mathias. My shoulders relaxed, and I breathed a little easier.

"Great," I said, reaching for my purse and checking to make sure everything was inside. Then I glanced up at both the uniformed officer and the sergeant. "Thank you both for your professionalism."

"And thank you for not swearing at us," said the sergeant.

I couldn't smile at him, but I raised my eyebrows and nodded.

"You guys were just doing your job," I said. "Now lead me out of here. I want to see my boyfriend."

The sergeant handed me a piece of paper, which I signed to show I had received my personal possessions. Then his officer gave me a tight smile and led me through the building. As I left, she wished me good luck, and I told her I hoped I didn't run into her in a professional capacity again. She agreed.

Outside, night had fallen hard. I walked toward a black SUV, the kind St. Louis County provided its plainclothes detectives. Despite the situation, I smiled at the thought of seeing Mathias. Then the window rolled down, and I found Special Agent Bryan Costa staring back at me. Apparently, the FBI leased the same kind of vehicle as the local police.

"Hey, Joe," he said. "I know that smile's not for me, but how about you climb in anyway?"

My smile slipped, and my shoulders relaxed just a little. I probably shouldn't have felt disappointed to see a colleague, but I was anyway. I also wondered where my boyfriend was.

"So you're the one who got the charges dropped," I said, opening the passenger side door. Costa nodded.

"The situation's complex," he said. "We're going for a drive. I've got a few things to tell you about Ms. Alvarez and her kids."

25

I had expected us to drive to the FBI's field office on Market Street in western St. Louis, but we drove east in silence for about ten minutes instead until we hit Forest Park, a massive public park that held St. Louis's art museum, history museum, zoo, and dozens of other attractions. If the city had a soul, we had just driven to it.

Costa turned onto Lagoon Drive and then drove until we hit Fine Arts Drive. A moment later, we parked in the art museum's lot. Before us, Art Hill sloped downward to the Grand Basin and upward to the massive, neoclassical museum. Surrounding us was a formal garden complete with fountains and a massive bronze statue of Louis IX, the namesake of St. Louis.

"The museum and park are closed," I said, glancing at Agent Costa as he opened his door. He nodded.

"They are, but I wanted to take a walk, anyway. Come on."

I got out of the car. Outside, the air was crisp and clean, and the streetlights cast everything into a deep orange incandescence. My breath was frosty, and I pulled my jacket tight around my chest. Had I known we'd be going for a walk outside this late at night, I would have brought a scarf. Agent Costa grabbed a briefcase from his backseat before walking toward the statue of Louis IX and the limestone viewing platform that overlooked the Grand Basin.

It was a clear night. Spotlights lit the statue but left shadows elsewhere. We were alone. The FBI agent leaned against the limestone wall that separated the platform from Art Hill and looked down at the grass and fountains below.

"This is my favorite view in town," he said. "My wife proposed to me by the statue. She said she got tired of waiting for me to ask her."

I nodded and leaned against the limestone beside him.

"You told her yes, obviously?"

"Yeah," he said, chuckling. "We went ring shopping the next day."

I said nothing for about a minute. Then I crossed my arms.

"I don't suppose we came here to talk about your marriage."

"Nope," he said, shaking his head, and opening his briefcase. "We came to talk about your investigation and arrest. After you were taken into custody, the US attorney called my office to ask about you. I thought it was a joke."

"It's bullshit, but it wasn't a joke," I said.

"I got a one-sided story from the US attorney. He said you were out of control and had threatened and then assaulted a federal officer at home. That didn't seem like you, so I called your station and talked to a guy named Dave Skelton. He told me you were working a homicide involving Joel Robinson. After that, I called your boss. He filled in a few more details for me."

"And you got me out," I said, nodding. "Thank you."

He nodded and considered me.

"Based on the facts of your case, Justin Cartwright's behavior made little sense. Neither did his boss's."

I shrugged.

"Cartwright's a murderer, and his boss is a witch. He was trying to protect himself, and she was protecting her officer."

"It was more than that," said Costa, reaching into his briefcase and pulling out a manila file folder. "On a hunch, I looked up your victim in our database. Joel was mentioned a few times, but Krystal has an extensive file."

He held the folder out for me, so I used the limestone wall as a table and browsed. The file was thick, but the vast majority of it had thick black lines over the text. A stamp on each page suggested readers contact an agent in DC if they needed more information. I could see a few things, though.

"Your file needs an update. This says her name is Krystal Robinson. I know her as Alvarez."

Costa shook his head.

"Robinson was her last name before she went into witness protection. Joel was her husband, but she didn't change her name after they divorced."

I straightened and gave myself a minute or two to process that. Then I sighed as my case came into clearer view. When Justin Cartwright refused to let me speak to Logan, I had thought he was trying to protect himself. Instead, he was trying to protect the kid from an unidentified woman who showed up on the family's porch after they learned Krystal's ex-husband had died.

Then, when I showed up at Cartwright's house unannounced, he had assumed I was a threat and reacted. It would have been easier if he had just talked to me, but he didn't know me. For all he knew, I worked for whomever Krystal had testified against. Even if he believed I was an honest local cop, he couldn't have talked to me without compromising the family's security.

"Fuck," I said, covering my mouth with my hand. "I'm the asshole."

"I wouldn't go that far," said Costa. "You were in a difficult situation. So was the US Marshals Service."

I gave myself a moment to think.

"Did the marshals know Joel Robinson was in town?"

Costa hesitated before answering.

"I doubt it," he said. "Witness protection has strict procedures and rules concerning contact with those outside the program. Logan and Evan would have been able to talk to their father, but it would have been monitored, and it would have taken place under strict conditions to ensure they didn't accidentally reveal things they shouldn't."

"Would they have allowed Logan to own a cell

phone?"

Costa blinked and then shrugged.

"If he did, it would have had a lot of restrictions. He could have used it to call his mom and maybe the marshal in charge of his security, but he wouldn't have been able to call his friends or father."

And he wouldn't have been able to use social media on it, either. The kid must have purchased a burner.

"Here's what I know," I said. "Logan contacted his father via Facebook. He used a fake name to avoid scrutiny. He and his father spoke on the phone and via text message. They also met in person for regular outings. Logan was there in the park when Joel was murdered. A witness says he took off running. I've been trying to track Logan down ever since then, but Cartwright's prevented that every time. Now I know why. He thought the kid and his family were in danger. Joel's current wife, Daisy Robinson, claimed he came here to go fishing, but he came to see his kid.

"My theory was that Cartwright and Krystal were dating and that Cartwright killed Joel either out of jealousy or in some misguided bid to protect Logan from his father. Cartwright had nothing to do with Joel's death, though."

Agent Costa nodded.

"Doubtful."

I let the focus leave my eyes as I stared out over Art Hill. This changed my entire case. Local cops typically investigated murders, but if Joel's family was in witness protection, and he was killed to get to them, we'd have a different case altogether. I didn't even know whether I had jurisdiction over it anymore. I swore under my breath and looked to Costa.

"What can you tell me about Krystal Robinson?"

"Before I say anything, you know the drill. The information I have to share with you is confidential, and it's important it stays that way. I shouldn't be sharing it with you, but you deserve some answers after what you've been through. Plus, you're already consulting with the FBI on a separate matter, so we know we can trust you."

"Thank you, and I understand," I said. "I won't compromise an investigation or her safety."

"Good," said Costa. "She married Joel Robinson in 1994. They had their first child, Logan, ten years later in 2004. She was an attorney for a major oil and gas exploration company in Houston and specialized in international freight logistics."

I nodded and crossed my arms.

"And what does that mean?"

"It means she helped her company move machinery across international lines with minimal fuss."

I brought a hand to my face.

"Considering the government put her in witness protection, I'm guessing she did more than that."

"Yeah," said Costa. "Around the time her son was born, Ms. Robinson began using her expertise and her position at her company to smuggle cocaine from Colombia to the United States. Shipments she arranged arrived weighing two to three hundred kilograms more than when they departed from Colombia. Considering she was shipping drilling equipment that might have weighed fifty or more tons, the difference was considered negligible."

I narrowed my eyes.

"That's a lot of drugs."

Costa nodded.

"Over a seven-year period, we believe she and her network smuggled somewhere around fourteen metric tons of cocaine to the United States."

I didn't know the exact number, but that would have been worth a few billion dollars at least. I whistled.

"That's a lot of blow. How'd you catch her?"

"Stupidity and greed," said Costa. "It took a lot of people to move the quantity of drugs Krystal did. She had employees at the Port of Houston, at the port in Cartagena, Colombia, at the US Customs Service, and at shipping companies worldwide. A dockworker in Houston on her payroll got fed up with his job, so he quit and bought a quarter-million-dollar Ferrari with cash. The dealership sold him the car and filed a form with the IRS to report a large cash payment.

"Since the dockworker only made about sixty grand a year, the IRS investigated. They thought they were looking at a money-laundering case, but as they dug, they figured out it was bigger than that. Once they found the drug angle, the IRS investigators brought in the FBI and DEA. We worked the case together and arrested almost a hundred people and confiscated four hundred million dollars in assets in the United States and abroad. It was a big bust."

I stood straighter and put my hands flat on the wall.

"Jeez," I said. "And she was the ringleader, huh?"

"One of them," said Costa. "We had her dead to rights on several hundred felonies. We could have put her away for the rest of her life, but she cooperated and testified against her superiors for a suspended sentence. Because of her, we disrupted a major drug pipeline into the United States and dismantled a major drug cartel's money-laundering operation."

I raised my eyebrows and shook my head as I let out a long breath.

"I can see why her former partners want her dead," I said. He nodded but said nothing as I started pacing along the low wall. A new theory began coalescing in my mind. "So, Krystal's former employers wanted her dead. When they couldn't find her, they started watching her ex-husband and noticed that he had made several inexplicable trips to a small town in Missouri. They followed him and found him talking to Logan in Sycamore Park.

"When the bad guys approached, Logan recognized that something was wrong. He ran, and Joel fought with an attacker to slow him down. The attacker killed Joel, but not before Joel saved his son's life. The man died a hero, but nobody can know because of his ex-wife. That sucks."

"It will suck even worse if you can't find his

murderer," said Costa.

I glanced at him and chuckled but then shook my head.

"Thanks, Bryan. I needed that."

26

Agent Costa and I spent another fifteen minutes at the park, but I didn't learn much new. Krystal Alvarez or Robinson or whatever she called herself had pissed off some very dangerous people, and her ex-husband had died for it. My newfound knowledge changed my perception of the case, but it didn't change my job. Logan had seen everything. I may not have known a lot about the Witness Protection Program, but the best way to protect him was to put the guy who killed his father in prison. I hoped the Marshals Service understood that.

Once I ran out of questions, Agent Costa and I climbed into his SUV, and he drove me to a tow lot in Valley Park, Missouri, where the St. Louis County police had sent my department's SUV. The lot was dirty, and the attendant was creepy, but I found my vehicle and paid a hundred and ten bucks for the privilege of having it stored during my detainment in the county jail.

As I searched to make sure no one had taken the tools and other equipment in back, Costa waited beside the hood. Thankfully, no one had taken anything, so I nodded to the FBI agent.

"Thanks for sticking around and for driving me here," I said. "We still going to Terre Haute tomorrow to work the Brunelle case?"

"Yeah. I'm driving back tonight," he said, nodding. "So far, we've arrested nine guards and three independent contractors who work with the Department of Corrections. We think they've been smuggling drugs and contraband into the prison for years, so there's no telling how long or how many times they've smuggled people in to see Brunelle."

I crossed my arms and nodded. Bright lights, the kind I would expect to find on high school football and baseball stadiums across the country, lit the tow lot in an uneven yellow incandescence and cast long shadows on the ground. Some small animal scurried nearby, but no human being approached us.

"This is a mess," I said. "Has Brunelle said anything?"

A tight smile sprang to the FBI agent's lips as he shook his head.

"Just that he's in love with you and continues to refuse to speak to anyone without you present in the room."

I tilted my head to the side.

"Hard to believe he loves me when he's having trysts with another woman in the prison laundry room."

Costa shrugged.

"Mr. Brunelle is a man with a lot to give. He can't allow a single person to tie him down."

"Right," I said, chuckling and shaking my head. I drew in a deep breath and looked around the lot before focusing on the FBI agent again. "All right. Looks like I'm going home for the night. Drive safely to Terre Haute."

"You, too," he said.

I thanked him, and we both got in our separate cars and left the parking lot. I followed him for a little while, but then I merged onto I-270 South to head home. My drive was boring and dark but uneventful. Once I reached my station, I returned my department's SUV and drove to my property on the edge of town, where I slept fitfully and alone in the guest bedroom of my friend Susanne's home.

It was cold the next morning, but I changed into a pair of yoga pants, a thermal top, and a sweatshirt anyway and went for a quick run. It felt good to get my body moving. Afterwards, I showered, packed a bag, and drove by Preston Cain's house to drop off some dog food and to check on Roy. The dog seemed happy, and Preston assured me he was glad to keep him for a while. I thanked him and promised to bring him a souvenir from the prison.

After that, I drove northeast for three and a half hours until I reached Terre Haute. On previous visits, I had met Agents Costa and Cornwell in a Denny's on the strip, but today, I drove straight to the prison. Once I signed in, a guard at the front gate directed me to a warehouse facility off of West Bureau Drive.

There, half a dozen semitrucks had parked in the

expansive lot out front, while two black SUVs had parked nearer the red brick building. None of the three loading-dock doors were open, but a gray metal folding chair held open a door for pedestrians, allowing me to see the dimly lit interior.

I parked beside the SUVs and entered the building. Rows of plastic-wrapped pallets lined the walls. A pair of white tarps covered the ground in the center of the room, but on the tarps lay the contents of Peter Brunelle's cell. Agents Costa and Cornwell stood near the pallets. Each had a cup of coffee. Costa nodded to me, but Cornwell pretended not to have noticed I had arrived.

I looked at the tarp as I passed. Someone had stacked Brunelle's books, papers, blankets, mattress, and other delicate items on one tarp while the second held the disassembled pieces of his steel toilet and sink. At a glance, the sink and toilet assembly had half a dozen or more spots where he could have hidden something if he had access to the interior, but it didn't appear that he had.

"There's an office, break room, and restrooms on the other side of the building," said Costa once I joined the two FBI agents near the pallets. "Coffee's not bad."

"I'm not thirsty, but thank you," I said, looking out at the tarp. "What do we have?"

"Not much," said Cornwell, putting her coffee on top of a pallet of macaroni and cheese before picking up a thick manila folder and walking toward the pile of stuff. "His cell had two dozen books, a couple hundred letters from fans, and a few magazines, but nothing that mentions any of his victims or future murders. Most of the people who write him seem to think he was innocent and that the criminal justice system railroaded him."

"He walked into a police station wheeling a cooler containing the heads of three women," I said, shaking my head and narrowing my gaze. "He confessed to their murders. How could anyone think he was innocent?"

Cornwell shrugged and then tilted her head to the side.

"They either don't believe the official account, or they're crazy," she said, opening her folder. "Either way, they're not our concern. We need to focus on Brunelle, and I've got a list of questions for you to ask him. I also have my original list of questions you refused to ask him the first time you met him a few weeks ago."

I lowered my chin and glanced at her.

"You mean the detailed questionnaire about his sexual history, his relationship with his mother and grandmother, and the questions about his masturbatory habits."

Cornwell raised her eyebrows.

"Among other questions, yes," she said. "Since we've only recovered the heads of his victims, we can't discount the possibility that Brunelle's murders have a psycho-sexual component. Because of that, we have to ask questions concerning his psycho-sexual history and mindset."

"And you think asking him what he thinks about as he jerks off will help us find a murderer?"

Cornwell closed her eyes and sighed. When she looked at me again, she spoke the way she might have spoken to a child.

"Detective Court," she said, a tight smile on her lips. "I need you to respect my expertise and understand that a dozen or more very skilled, very well-educated law enforcement officials have vetted every single question in that questionnaire. My colleagues have PhDs in psychology, sociology, and criminology, and we are experts in this field. That you don't understand their questions doesn't reflect ill on them. It shows that you lack the education and experience to appreciate what we do."

"I see," I said, nodding and crossing my arms. "Let me ask you: As a federal officer, do you feel that talking down to your co-workers and treating us like idiots is an effective management strategy? Or do you think it's possible that you're alienating the people whose cooperation you most need to do your job?"

She pressed her lips into a thin line but said nothing. I looked to Agent Costa and then to Cornwell.

"I understand what you're doing," I said, raising my eyebrows. "You are part of an ambitious research project that hopes to catalog the proclivities and histories of serial murders from the United States and surrounding countries to create a behavioral database that will allow you to find patterns and commonalities amongst various types of murderers. The project's goal, as I understand it, is to create a decision procedure that would allow you to intervene in the lives of at-risk individuals before they snap and kill innocent people. It's a great project, but it's not my top priority.

"I'm a small-town cop. More than that, I'm a woman who had three heads buried in her backyard. I'm here to see whether I can find the person who did that before he or she hurts anyone else. When I speak to Brunelle, I plan to ask questions that will help me find a murderer. That's my job, and I'm good at it. Our projects aren't at odds, but we don't share the same goals. Please don't make assumptions about me or my abilities simply because I focus on a different problem than you do."

Cornwell looked away and sighed as she crossed her arms.

"You're here because a serial murderer has a crush on you," she said. "He gets off on seeing you work this case. I hope you understand that."

"I do," I said, nodding. "But it changes nothing. Brunelle's partner is killing people. I'm here to find and stop him. If I can help your project along the way, I will. If I can't, that's too bad."

Cornwell shook her head but said nothing. I looked to Agent Costa.

"Unless there's something I need to see here," I said, "I say we pay Brunelle a visit."

"Sure," he said, reaching into his pocket for his cell phone. "I'll call the warden and have Brunelle brought into a room."

"I'll be staying here," said Cornwell. "I'd hate to

interfere with Detective Court's project."

I nodded to her.

"Good. Brunelle thinks you're a bitch."

She rolled her eyes but said nothing to me. If she wanted to act like a sullen teenager, that was fine with me. About ten minutes after I arrived at the warehouse, Agent Costa and I left. Agent Cornwell could analyze the shit out of a suspect, but she was a liability in an interrogation room. With a manipulative, intelligent, and downright evil man sitting across the table from me, her presence was the last thing I needed. We were better off without her.

As Costa and I climbed into his SUV, I steeled myself for the job ahead. It was time to talk to a murderer and shut him up for good.

27

Brunelle was already in the interrogation room when we arrived. He was pudgy and had dark hair buzzed close to his scalp. Like every inmate in the building, he wore a bright orange prison jumpsuit that would make him easy to spot on the lawn if he somehow escaped the prison's walls. Thick gray shackles on his wrists and ankles and a matching gray chain connected his upper body to his lower body, forcing him to shuffle whenever he moved and preventing him from being able to swing his arms and grab anyone else. A metal ring welded to the steel table in the center of the room kept him stationary.

"Afternoon, Mr. Brunelle," I said, sitting across from him at the table. Agent Costa sat beside me. I put my notepad down and crossed my arms. "I've got some ground rules. Special Agent Costa and I are here to talk, but the moment you ask me to remove any of my clothing or send you nude pictures, he and I will walk out and never come back. If you ask me theological questions, Agent Costa and I will leave. If you reference any part of my anatomy or the anatomy of any other woman, I will leave. If you lie to me, I will leave. In fact, if you annoy me, I will leave, and you will never see me again. Clear?"

Brunelle tilted his head to the side as he appraised me. Then he closed his eyes and screwed up his mouth.

"Do you think you're in any position to dictate terms to me?"

I picked up my notepad and stood. Costa stood beside me.

"Goodbye, Mr. Brunelle."

I started toward the door, but before I could reach it, Brunelle sighed.

"Fine. I agree. Since it bothers you so much, I won't flirt with you. You should consider why a little attention riles you up so much, though. Sounds like a bit of a personal problem."

I flipped pages on my notepad but didn't look up.

"You're a douche, and your constant attempts at witty banter get on my nerves," I said. I found a clear page, so I wrote down the date and details of the interview before glancing up. "Okay. I'm here to talk about your recent visitors."

He leaned back and narrowed his eyes at me.

"You called me a douche," he said. "I don't appreciate that."

"I don't care," I said. "Who's the girl with the black hair?"

He blinked and then smiled as he looked around.

"We're in prison," he said. "You may not have noticed, but the male-to-female ratio in this place is high. There's a lot of sausage but not much bun, if you get what I'm saying."

"An idiot would get what you're saying. You're not subtle," I said, pretending to jot something down on my notepad. Agent Costa gave me a sidelong glance, but Brunelle leaned forward.

"Are you trying to piss me off?" he asked. "Because it's working if you are. This isn't fun."

"I don't care whether it's fun. I'm here because your girlfriend buried a bunch of heads in my backyard. Does she know you like me?"

"So you get to make jokes, and I don't," he said, raising his eyebrows.

I kept my lips straight and my eyes on his as I shook my head.

"That wasn't a joke," I said. "It was a question. Does your girlfriend with the black hair know you hit on me when you see me?"

He frowned and then squinted at me.

"What are you talking about?"

I looked to Agent Costa. He put a manila folder on the table and opened it to show Brunelle a picture of the dark-haired woman in the laundry room. Brunelle had been in the shot, but they cropped him out.

"Who is she?" I asked. "You met her and had sex with her in the laundry room. I hope you enjoyed it, by the way, because it's not going to happen again."

He considered me before leaning back.

"If you've seen the video, you'd know we both had a good time. You can't fake the smile I gave her."

"It's cute you think that," I said, smiling at him before

drawing in a breath and looking at my notepad again. I allowed my smile to disappear before looking at him again. "Who is she?"

"What do I get for telling you?"

I shrugged.

"What do you want?" I asked. "We can bring in some food from the outside, we can bring you cigarettes, we can get you more yard time. What do you want?"

He considered before answering.

"You take away one piece of ass, it seems like the polite thing to do would be to replace it with someone else."

I nodded and closed my notepad before standing.

"Congratulations, Mr. Brunelle," I said. "You broke my rules. We're done here."

He scowled.

"I didn't break your rules," he said, holding up a hand and counting off on his fingers as he spoke. "I didn't talk about your tits, I didn't ask to fuck you, I didn't talk about anybody else's tits, and I didn't talk about God. Tell me the rule I broke."

"You've annoyed me," I said. "I came here as a favor to you and your girlfriend. If you give us her name, we'll contact her and allow her to turn herself in. If you make us find her on our own, we'll kick down her door with guns drawn. I can't guarantee she'll survive that. If you care about her, you'll do the right thing and tell me who she is."

He thought for a good thirty seconds. I folded my

hands in front of me and leaned forward but said nothing, giving him time to think. Then he snorted and shook his head.

"Sasha Ingram," he said. "I think you'll like her. When we're feeling frisky, we like to role-play. Sometimes she even pretends to be a cop. She says she works for the St. Louis County crime lab. It's hot to be picked up by a cop."

At first, I didn't register the name. Then a feeling like frost spread from my fingertips to my wrists and then my forearms. Goosebumps rose on my skin. My fingers began trembling.

"Say her name again, Brunelle," I said, hoping to keep my voice strong and confident. It sounded shaky, though. Costa looked at me and frowned before standing.

"We'll end the interview here," said the FBI agent. Brunelle grinned. Heat began to replace the cold shock.

"What's the girl's name?" I asked. "Say it again."

Brunelle said nothing. His grin grew even broader. I reached across the table and yanked as hard as I could on his restraints. He grabbed my forearm and squeezed.

"Sasha."

"That's it," said Agent Costa, pulling me out of his grasp. I stood and crossed the room. "This interview's over. Nobody say another word."

"Fuck you," I said, ignoring my partner. I crossed to the door and slapped the metal with my palm. The guard outside opened it. Agent Costa and I stepped out. "We're done with Brunelle for the day, so you can take him back to his cell."

The guard leaned his head toward the microphone on his shoulder and whispered. Then he listened and nodded before looking at us.

"A colleague will be by to escort you out."

"No need," I said. "We already know the way."

The guard seemed a little perplexed, but he nodded anyway and stepped into the room with Brunelle. I started walking toward the first security gate, and Agent Costa hurried to walk beside me.

"What the hell was that about?"

"I can't talk just yet," I said. "I need to call somebody first."

Costa considered me as we waited outside the security checkpoint. Then he blinked.

"Okay. Fine. Make your call. Then we'll talk."

Even though Agent Costa and I were law enforcement officials and the prison staff did everything they could to accommodate us, it takes time to leave a maximum-security facility. By the time we reached the lobby and the locker in which I had stowed my firearm and purse, skin all over my body felt hot. I pulled out my cell phone and dialed my brother Dylan's number. His phone rang almost five times before he answered. I sighed with relief when I heard his voice.

"Dylan, it's Joe," I said. "Can you talk for a minute?"

He paused before responding.

"I'm in school, but we've got to talk," he whispered. "That woman you hooked me up with, Sasha…she was fucking insane."

"You have no idea," I said, thinking back to the surveillance pictures I had seen of her. "Just so we're on the same page, she had jet black hair and a tattoo on her rear right deltoid?"

"Her shoulder," said Dylan. "It was a rose."

It was her, then. Brunelle had sent his girlfriend after my little brother. I blinked and nodded.

"Okay. I'm on my way to your area, but I'll call Mom and have her pick you up from school."

"I can't talk, Joe. The teacher saw me on the phone."

He hung up before I could say anything else. Agent Costa looked around the lobby and smiled to a corrections officer before focusing on me again.

"Give me another minute," I said, already hitting the button to call my mom. She answered before Agent Costa could respond.

"Mom, it's Joe. I need you to do something for me, and it won't make sense, but you need to do it anyway. I'll explain everything when I get to town."

"Okay," she said. "What do you need me to do?"

"Get a pistol and pick up Dylan from school. If he protests, call the school resource officer and have him taken into custody. If you feel as if someone's following you, particularly a woman in her early to mid-twenties with black hair, call the police. She's dangerous."

Mom paused, but then I heard the floor creak as she ran.

"I'm getting my gun now," she said. "Are you safe?"

"Yeah," I said. "I'm in a prison."

Mom didn't even hesitate before asking her next question.

"How about Audrey and Ian?"

Audrey was my adoptive sister, and Ian was my half-brother. I winced and swore under my breath as I closed my eyes. I hadn't thought about them.

"Call Audrey and have her go to the campus police station for now. She's probably fine, but better safe than sorry. I'll talk to her as soon as I can. I'll also call Ian's parents. I'm sorry this is happening."

"Don't be sorry," said Mom. "Stay safe. I love you, and I'll talk to you soon. I'm on my way."

Before I could even thank her, she hung up. Agent Costa crossed his arms as I thumbed through my phone's directory to find Ian's mom's number.

"What's going on, Joe?" he asked. "I don't think I've ever seen you this worked up.

"One of my brothers hooked up with Brunelle's girlfriend," I said, putting my phone to my ear. "I'm having my family put in protective custody before that crazy bitch hurts somebody."

28

As I walked out of the prison, I called Miriam Staley, Ian's adoptive mother. We didn't talk long, but she heard what I had to say about Brunelle and Sasha Ingram and promised to take care of Ian. I suggested she, Ian, and her husband head out of town for a few days, but she told me she'd handle things on her own and didn't need my help or suggestions. I hoped she was right.

Costa and I took his SUV to the warehouse that held everything the corrections officers had taken from Brunelle's cell. Agent Cornwell was inside, cataloging Brunelle's books.

"You find anything, Philippa?" asked Agent Costa once we stepped into the room.

"Nothing interesting," she said, glancing up and then focusing on me. "You looked perturbed, Detective. Meeting go poorly?"

I ignored her and focused on Agent Costa.

"You want to come to St. Louis or stay here?"

He looked to Cornwell.

"I'll stay here and see what we can find in his letters and notes," he said. "We've still got days of surveillance footage to view, too. Drive safely. If you need me, I'll have my cell phone on me at all times. You have a little sister in Chicago, right? If so, I'll have somebody from the field office in Chicago and talk to her and make sure she's okay."

"Yeah," I said, nodding. "Audrey's in Chicago. I'll get you her address."

"Why would Detective Court's sister not be okay?" asked Cornwell, narrowing her eyes.

"Because Brunelle's coming after my family," I said. "Does the database you're developing have anything about imprisoned serial murderers who use partners on the outside to harass and threaten people they'd otherwise never have the chance to interact with?"

She considered me and blinked as she thought through what I'd just asked.

"I've never seen that precise scenario, but twenty percent of serial murderers work with a partner," she said. "Typically, one partner is dominant and provides direction for his or her followers. The subordinates provide adulation and validation to their superior. It's a symbiotic relationship."

"Talk to Agent Costa about Brunelle and Sasha Ingram," I said. "Maybe you'll have some insight we don't. I've got to go."

I gave Costa Audrey's address and phone number and then hurried toward my Volvo. The nearly two-hundred-mile drive from Terre Haute to my parents' house in Kirkwood, Missouri, usually took a hair under three hours.

I pushed my Volvo hard, though, and made it in just a little over two. The sun was still up as I parked in front of my mom and dad's house, but already the shadows from nearby trees were growing long.

The front door was locked, so I knocked and waited for my dad to answer. He pulled the door open.

"Hey, Joe," he said. "Are you alone?"

"Yeah," I said. "Agent Costa and Cornwell are still in Terre Haute. Are Mom and Dylan here?"

Dad nodded and led me to the kitchen, where Mom stood at their granite island, chopping an onion.

"Hey," I said. Mom looked at me and sighed.

"Hey, Joe," she said. "You want to tell me why I pulled my son out of school early?"

I filled her in on my meeting with Brunelle and the little we knew about his accomplice. Mom closed her eyes and swore under her breath. Then she looked to the basement door.

"Dylan, get up here," she called. "Your sister needs to talk to you."

"In a minute," said Dylan. "I'm playing *Madden*."

"Turn off your damn video game and get up here," said Mom, her voice sharp.

Dylan grumbled, but he climbed the stairs a moment later and looked at me. He wore jeans and a navy T-shirt. He had abrasions on both of his wrists. Mom looked to me.

"Joe, tell your brother who he hooked up with."

I nodded and flipped through the images on my cell

phone until I found a photograph of Sasha Ingram. It wasn't a great picture because it had come from a surveillance camera, but it showed her form and hair well. Dylan covered his mouth but said nothing.

"Is that her?" I asked.

Dylan looked to our mom. She rolled her eyes.

"Just answer the question," she said. "You're eighteen, so you're an adult. As long as you take precautions and you're with another adult who consents to whatever you do, I don't care about your sex life."

Dylan looked at me then and nodded.

"That's her," he said. "And please don't set me up with anybody again. She was a psycho."

"What happened?"

Again, he looked to our mom before answering.

"Can I have some privacy?"

"I'm your mother," said Julia. "And I'm a retired police officer who specialized in sex crimes. So, no, you cannot have privacy."

"Okay," he said, drawing the word out before looking at me. "So, I met her at work. She sat at the bar and flirted with me. We decided to get some drinks once I got off."

"Okay," I said, nodding. "Where'd you go?"

"Blueberry Hill," he said, glancing at our mom. "I've got a fake ID."

"And I'll be confiscating that," said Mom. "What happened at the bar?"

"We had drinks and started having some fun. She was grinding on me and stuff. Then, things started getting serious, and we left. When we got to her car, I put on the blindfold and—"

"Hold up," said Mom, shaking her head and holding up a finger. "You got into a car with a stranger and blindfolded yourself?"

Dylan paused and drew in a breath as his face grew red.

"She was touching me," he said. "I didn't want her to stop."

Mom closed her eyes and shook her head as she stood straighter.

"I was wrong. I don't want to hear this anymore. Talk to Detective Court."

"Joe's my sister," said Dylan, lowering his chin and glancing at me. "Isn't she? I don't have to call her Detective, do I?"

"She is your sister," said Mom, "but for the moment, she's Detective Court, and she's here to do a job. And learn to think with your head instead of your dick. Life will go a lot smoother."

Dylan nodded, and Mom left the room. I crossed my arms.

"What happened after you blindfolded yourself?"

"She drove me to some kind of house. It wasn't far. She led me inside, and we had sex."

"Where was this?"

"I don't know. I wore the blindfold until we got inside. Then she took it off and tied me to the wall. Then we had sex again, and she left the room. When she came back, she had a belt and started hitting me with it."

I lowered my chin.

"She tied you up and hit you?"

"Yeah," he said, lifting his T-shirt to expose welts all over his back, belly, and ribs. "Like I said, she was a psycho."

"Mom's right. You need to think with your head. You could have died there. Do you understand that?"

"Yeah," he said. "I get that."

I shook my head, crossed my arms, and leaned against a bank of cabinets beside the sink.

"How'd she tie you up? Did she use a chain, ropes, ribbons, scarves, what?"

"Rope," he said. "There were rings screwed into the wall."

That explained the abrasions on his wrists, at least.

"You get the impression she had done this before?"

"Oh, yeah," he said. "She was fast."

I added that to everything else I knew about her—which was very little.

"Aside from hitting you with a belt, did she hurt you in any other way?"

"That's bad enough, isn't it?" he asked. "There wasn't even anybody around. She tied me to the wall and hit me. Afterwards, she kissed me on the forehead and told me to tell you hello for her. Then she walked out. I only got out because I ripped the ring out of the wall and found my clothes."

If she had left him to die, she wouldn't have given

him a message for me, and he wouldn't be talking to me today. I said nothing as I let my mind process the information.

"Who is she?" he asked. "And don't lie to me. You wouldn't have driven here if she was just some nobody."

"She's not some nobody," I said, blinking. "If we went for a drive, could you find the house she took you to?"

"Yeah," said Dylan, nodding. "Who is she?"

I tilted my head to the side and considered whether he could handle the truth. The longer I stayed quieter, though, the redder his face became.

"Just tell me, Joe."

I sighed and closed my eyes.

"She may be a serial killer. If she's not one, she's working with one."

"That's not funny," he said, shaking his head.

"I'm not trying to be funny," I said. "The picture I showed you earlier came from a surveillance camera at the United States Penitentiary in Terre Haute, Indiana. She snuck inside in some laundry to visit a serial murderer named Peter Brunelle. It's likely that she buried the three human heads Roy found in the woods behind my house."

He ran his hands through his hair and turned around.

"This is so fucked up," he said.

"I'm sorry," I said. "We didn't know this woman existed until recently, and we never expected her to come after you."

"This is way beyond sorry," he said. "A serial killer

tied me up and left me to die in an abandoned house to get to you."

"If I knew it would endanger you, I never would have agreed to work with the FBI to interview Brunelle."

He shook his head and walked to the basement stairs. I started to follow, but my mom walked in from the living room to stop me. She must have been listening in.

"Let him go, Joe," she said. "I'll deal with him. You go home. It's getting late."

I nodded and looked to the stairs.

"You'll make sure he understands I didn't mean for this to happen?"

She hesitated and then looked down.

"I know you didn't mean for this to happen, but it did," she said. "We can't change that."

I blinked a few times.

"Are you okay, Mom?"

She crossed her arms but didn't look at me. Neither of us spoke.

"I love you, and that will never change," she finally said. "If that woman had killed my son, though, I don't think I could have ever forgiven you."

"I didn't mean for this to happen," I said. "You understand that, right?"

She looked at me. Her normally jovial eyes were dark and angry.

"My son could have died," she said. "You may not have intended that, but you're partially to blame. I need some time. Okay?"

"Okay," I said, my voice soft. "I'm sorry."

"I know," she said. "I'll see you later."

I swallowed a lump in my throat.

"Yeah," I said. "I'll see you later."

I left the house and drove home on a dark highway. I couldn't remember feeling quite that alone in a very long time.

29

I didn't want to spend the night alone, so I called Preston on my drive to St. Augustine and asked whether he'd mind if I stopped by to pick up Roy. He said that'd be just fine, so I stopped by his house before going home. I hadn't planned to stay long, but Shelby asked me to come in, and it was a nice evening. She and I sat on rockers on the back porch while Preston tinkered in the garage with an old tractor he had purchased.

"He thinks he can take it apart and rebuild that old tractor so it's as good as new," she said, sipping on a glass of sweet white wine. "Preston's good with his hands, and he builds great cabinets and furniture, but I don't have the heart to tell him he has less mechanical ability than your dog."

I smiled and sipped my glass of white wine.

"If you did tell him, I'd like to be there to watch," I said.

She snorted. Roy snored near my feet, and we sat and rocked for another few moments.

"You doing okay, Joe?" asked Shelby, a few minutes later.

"Yeah," I said, forcing myself to smile. "Why? Do I not seem okay?"

"You seem tired," she said. "That's all."

"I've had a long day," I said. "I was in Terre Haute this morning, but then I had to come home." I sipped my wine and considered what else to say. Then my lips started moving before I gave them permission. "I've been interviewing a serial murderer, but we found out the guards at his prison have been allowing a girl to come in and see him. We think she's killing for him. Long story short, she picked my little brother up at work and seduced him. My mom's mad because she thinks my work almost got my brother killed. So, you know, long day."

She reached for the wine bottle to pour me another drink. I thanked her and rocked for another few minutes.

"Is your brother okay?"

"Shaken up," I said, nodding. "She tied him up and whipped him with a belt."

Shelby tilted her head to the side.

"I don't mean to make light of it, but some people pay good money for that kind of thing."

I smiled and tucked a stray lock of hair behind my ear as I nodded.

"Yeah. I guess some people do."

We rocked for another few minutes.

"Preston misses the job, but after hearing about your day, I'm glad he's out of it."

"He was a good cop," I said. "He would have gotten through it."

"You will, too," she said.

Even though Shelby and I had only met a handful of times, I appreciated hearing that.

Preston came out of the garage a few minutes later. Thick, black grease covered his hands, but he looked happy even if he had gotten little done on his tractor. Police work gave my life meaning. I didn't know what I'd do if I lost it like Preston had, but I was glad he had found something—and someone—to fill the void in his life. The three of us chatted for another few minutes, but it was getting late, and I needed to get to bed.

Roy and I left at nine. I hadn't played with him much lately, so I threw him a ball in the yard before heading inside. I ate a sandwich in the kitchen before going to bed. Roy slept at my feet. He was a good dog, and he seemed content. I was glad to give him a home.

The next morning, he woke me up at about six by yawning, standing, and rocking the bed as he stretched. Then he licked my face until I opened my eyes.

"I love you, but sometimes you're a butt," I said, gently pushing him away. He jumped off the bed and landed on the hardwood with a thud and a surprised yelp. Where my old dog Roger had been graceful even in old age, Roy was more of an awkward but lovable brute.

I stood, sighed, and grabbed a bathrobe before letting the dog out and making coffee. Roy came back in a few minutes later and sat beside his breakfast bowl as he looked at me and then the bowl and back. He was subtle like that.

We had a nice morning together. Since it was still

early, we did some obedience training. Roy had been in training to become a cadaver dog before he moved in with me, so he knew a lot of commands. Unfortunately, he was both stubborn and lazy. Still, he came when I called and sat and waited for me when I needed him to. He would have been a terrible cadaver dog, but he was a good friend.

At a quarter to eight, I walked Roy from Susanne's house to my house and let him into the dog run. There, he had a doghouse, a bed, and room to stretch. He'd have a nice day.

I drove to my station. The construction crews on the first floor and basement had started working on the electrical and plumbing systems, so the lights on the second floor flickered, and only one bathroom in the building had running water. At least our computer systems and dispatcher's station had a generator and uninterruptible power supply.

Sheriff Delgado led the morning briefing, but I let my mind wander. I had a lot of paperwork to catch up on, so that'd occupy most of my morning. We were also hiring two new uniformed officers and a new detective, so we had a couple dozen applications for each position to look through. Delgado would decide whom to hire, but he had asked for my opinion on the men and women applying for the detective's position. I didn't want to spend my day reading resumes, but it was important that we hired the right person. Everyone in my station had seen what happened when the wrong person was given a badge.

After the roll call meeting, I stretched and walked toward the coffee maker. Delgado was already there pouring himself a drink. He held out the carafe.

"You got a mug?"

I grabbed a paper cup from the table, and he poured me a drink.

"Thanks," I said, nodding and sipping. "Coffee's good today."

"Trisha made it before roll call," he said, nodding and sipping from his own mug. "Glad to see you back. How's life outside the St. Louis County jail treating you?"

"Has its ups and down," I said. "Unfortunately, my investigation into Joel Robinson's murder is shot to hell. I haven't decided yet how to proceed on that one."

Delgado nodded and put his coffee down on the table beside him. I did likewise.

"I've talked to the US attorney in St. Louis. I don't know what happened at that marshal's house, and I don't want to know, either. If the federal government wants to keep secrets, that's their business. And that's something you've got to understand. You can't drive to a US marshal's house and harass him because he refuses to aid your investigation. You just can't do it, Joe."

My skin felt hot, but I forced myself to smile anyway.

"Got it, boss. Thanks for the advice."

He narrowed his eyes and straightened his back.

"And what's that mean?"

"It means whatever you want it to mean," I said. "I did my job. I followed the evidence and tried to talk to a potential witness. Shit went sideways after that, but that happens sometimes. By your own admission, you don't understand the situation. The US attorney dropped every charge against me, which should tell you everything you need to know. I did nothing wrong, and I don't need a lecture."

He drew in a slow breath through his nose before raising his eyes.

"You are on very thin ice, young lady."

I narrowed my eyes at him.

"Please don't call me young lady," I said. "It's patronizing. Okay?"

"I have tried to be patient with you," he said, shaking his head. "If I had another detective on staff, I'd fire you right now."

"And if you did that, my union would sue. I did my job. If you penalize me for doing my job, then you don't deserve to be in yours," I said, picking up my coffee. "Unless you've got something else to tell me, I'll be going to my office to fill out some paperwork."

He glowered but said nothing. I walked to my office while clenching my jaw. Delgado had solved a lot of cases when he wore a detective's badge, but he had never been a leader. The sheriff's job just wasn't in his skill set. Some days, I felt sorry for him, but most days, I just wished he'd retire early and allow someone better suited for the position to take over.

Once I reached my office, I spent the next few hours transcribing my interview notes, filling out after-action reports, and catching up on my email and voicemails. If Delgado or the Marshals Service came after me, I'd have a record of everything I had done, why I had done it, and what had resulted from my actions. Sheriff Delgado may not have agreed with my decisions, but I could justify everything I had done. Maybe I could have brought backup with me to Cartwright's house in Affton, but I didn't see the immediate danger. He was a suspect in a homicide, but he was also a federal officer. I couldn't have predicted what had happened at his house.

After two hours, my desk phone rang. I picked it up without looking at the caller ID.

"Yeah. It's Joe Court."

"Detective Court," said a woman's voice. "You got a minute to talk?"

I blinked a few times as my mind placed the familiar voice with a name. Then things clicked, and I felt an angry pit grow in my belly. It was Kelly Babcock, Justin Cartwright's superior officer.

"That depends," I said. "Are you going to have me arrested again, Ms. Babcock?"

"No. We're past that," she said. "This morning, I received a phone call from a deputy director at the FBI. I didn't realize you consulted with them."

"I do," I said. "Now what can I do for you?"

"Director Alexis Koch told me that one of her agents briefed you on Krystal Alvarez."

"That agent called her Krystal Robinson, but yeah," I said. "I know who she is, and I know why your officer acted the way he did when I asked to talk to her. I'm not holding any grudges, and I hope Cartwright doesn't, either. He and I were both doing our jobs. Unfortunately, those jobs came into conflict."

"I'm glad you see it that way," she said. She paused. "Are you still working Joel Robinson's murder?"

I leaned back in my chair and nodded.

"I am."

"If you'd like to talk to Krystal Robinson, Justin Cartwright's in your parking lot right now in a white SUV. Leave your weapon, cell phone, and handcuffs at your desk. He'll drive you to see her. She will answer any question you ask of her, but her answers are for your ears only. You may take notes, but you may not record the conversation. In your notes, call her Jane Doe. Clear?"

I didn't like the stipulations, but it'd be my only opportunity to talk to an important person of interest in my homicide.

"Can I talk to Logan?"

Babcock paused and exhaled.

"Talk to Krystal about that."

I nodded and blinked a few times.

"Is she sober?"

Babcock snorted.

"By the grace of God, yes," she said. "She's not happy about it, either."

"All right," I said, nodding. "Tell Cartwright I'll be right out."

Babcock agreed before hanging up. I locked my pistol

and cell phone in the center drawer of my desk and then hurried to the dispatcher's conference room. Trisha sat behind the desk, sipping on a cup of coffee. She smiled when she saw me.

"Hey, Joe," she said. "I was just about to call in my relief. Want to go out to lunch?"

"I would, but I've got something to do. Can you call up the video feed from the parking lot?"

She furrowed her brow but then nodded and set her coffee down before clicking her mouse. Then she looked at me.

"Is there a white SUV out there?" I asked.

She looked to her screen and then nodded.

"Yep. It's there."

"Print a picture of it and try to get its license plate. If you haven't heard from me in three hours, send your picture of that car to every officer in the state and tell them they've abducted me."

She furrowed her brow.

"I don't know what you're up to, but I've got a feeling the sheriff wouldn't like it."

"That's how I know it's the right thing to do," I said, forcing myself to smile. "See you later. I need to talk to some US marshals."

30

Justin Cartwright stepped out of his SUV as I reached the parking lot. The sun beat down on the asphalt, warming it on a cool day. A heavy flatbed truck laden with stacks of sheets of drywall idled beside the exit, leaving the air heavy with diesel exhaust. Cartwright saw me and nodded.

"Morning, Detective," he said. "We're talking because an FBI agent told my boss I can trust you. Just to be clear, I don't. In my business, you have to earn trust, and you haven't earned shit."

"Thanks for sharing," I said, nodding toward the car. "Is Jane Doe in the front or the back?"

"She's not here," said Cartwright. "I'll pat you down and make sure you left your firearm and cell phone in your office like my boss asked, and then I'll drive around for a while until you're disoriented enough that you don't know where we are. Then, and only then, will you be able to interview Jane."

"I know this part of the state pretty well," I said. "You'll have to drive around for a long time before we run into roads I don't recognize."

He crossed his arms.

"We figured that," said Cartwright, nodding. "That's why we plan to blindfold you."

I laughed and shook my head.

"Not going to happen. I'm not into that kind of kink."

He shrugged.

"No blindfold, no interview."

I smiled.

"No interview, I arrest you," I said. "After the shit you've done, I'm taking a big step by leaving my weapon and cell phone in my station. If you think I'll put on a blindfold and get into a car with you, you're an idiot. By refusing to allow me to talk to a person of interest in my investigation, you're hindering the prosecution of a murderer. That's a felony. So what do you want to do? I'll meet your reasonable conditions for the safety of Jane Doe, but blindfolding me and driving me around for an untold amount of time isn't reasonable."

"After the way you showed up at my house with a gun, I should arrest you."

I tilted my head to the side.

"You already tried that," I said. "And you're just mad because I kicked your ass and disarmed you. I'm working a case, and you're hiding a material witness. That's it. End of story. You don't let me talk to your Jane Doe, we're all going to have bad days."

He blinked and considered me for about thirty seconds. Then he sighed.

"Let me make a call. You stay out here."

"Sure. Make your call," I said.

He climbed back into the driver's seat of his SUV and spoke to somebody—probably Kelly Babcock—on his cell phone. I waited outside and enjoyed the sunshine and exhaust fumes. About two or three minutes later, he rolled his window down.

"We're moving Jane Doe to a temporary location. I will drive you to her, and you will have fifteen minutes to interview her. Because we can't secure our temporary location, we have to limit the time we spend there. If you wear a blindfold, though, I'll drive you to the safe house, and you can spend all day with her. What do you want to do, Detective?"

"Fifteen minutes is plenty," I said, walking around the front of his car and climbing into the passenger seat. "Let's drive."

Cartwright put the heavy SUV in gear the moment I sat down and put my seat belt on. He didn't tell me where we were going. He just drove to the edge of town and then kept going. I hadn't been bluffing when I said I knew the area well, so I recognized that we were driving in a circle on back country roads. He may have been trying to confuse me, but then again, he may have been giving Krystal time to get to our rendezvous location. It didn't matter to me either way.

After about an hour, he turned on his blinker and hung a right across a cattle guard and into a grassy field. Barbed wire ringed the exterior, and even from my seat in the car, I could see piles of cow manure on the ground outside. We drove for an additional few minutes on rough terrain before coming to a four-door black sedan with dark-tinted windows beneath a sassafras tree. Cartwright parked beside the other car and looked at me.

"Krystal's in the back. You've got fifteen minutes."

I opened my door and stepped out. The ground was spongy and damp. A woman in a white button-down shirt and gray slacks stepped out of the driver's seat of the sedan and nodded to me before climbing into Cartwright's SUV. The marshals may not have trusted me, but it looked as if they planned to give me some privacy, anyway. They had probably bugged the car, but I appreciated the pretense all the same.

I sat in the front passenger seat and looked behind me toward Krystal. Her hair was unkempt, and she had big bags beneath her unfocused, tired eyes. She wore no makeup. When she saw me, she crossed her arms and swallowed hard.

"Justin said I have to answer your questions."

"You don't have to, but it'd help me a lot if you did," I said. "I'm investigating the death of Joel Robinson. I understand he's your ex-husband."

She nodded but said nothing. I pulled a notepad from my purse.

"As you know, someone murdered him in St. Augustine," I said. "Can you tell me anything about it?"

She shook her head but said nothing.

"Joel came to St. Augustine to visit Logan. Did you know your son had a cell phone?"

She shook her head again. This time she blinked.

"If I had known, I would have told Justin," she said. "I want to give my kids freedom, but we're not like most families. They know that. They're good boys."

"I'm sure they are," I said, nodding. "Have you seen any sign that your son was in contact with Joel, or have you seen Joel around?"

"No," she said. "If I had seen him, I would have told Justin. Joel shouldn't have known where we lived. The kids visited him once a year, so it wasn't as if they never got to see him. We called it Christmas. He should have just waited. He understands the procedures, and he violated them. We're divorced, but I've never wished ill on him. He brought this on himself, though."

I wanted to roll my eyes and remind her it was her criminal activity that led to Joel's separation from his children, but I looked down to my notepad, pretending to read something.

"Have you or the kids seen anyone suspicious around your house?"

"No, ma'am," she said. "If I had, I would—"

"You would have called Justin," I said, interrupting her. "I get it."

"I know you don't like me, Detective, but I don't care," she said. "My debt to society is paid."

I didn't bother glancing up.

"You smuggled several billion dollars' worth of cocaine into the United States and avoided spending a single night in prison," I said. "You haven't paid for a thing. That's not why I'm here, though. I'm trying to solve your ex-husband's murder, and you have been singularly unhelpful. Where's Logan? He witnessed everything."

She said nothing, so I glanced up from my notepad at her. She was looking out the window. Her jaw was clenched, so she took quick, shallow breaths through her nose. As I watched, her throat bobbed as she swallowed.

"Mrs. Robinson?" I asked. "Where's your son?"

When she looked at me, her eyes were glassy, and her bottom lip quivered.

"I don't know," she said, sitting straight and rigid. "Logan and Evan disappeared the same day their father died."

I lowered my chin and furrowed my brow.

"Excuse me?" I asked.

"You heard me," she said. "They're missing. I don't know where they are. I don't even know whether my babies are alive."

She couldn't hold them in anymore, and tears began falling down her cheeks. That explained why the kid wasn't at school. I swore under my breath.

"Have there been any ransom demands?"

She shook her head before reaching into the purse beside her for a pack of cigarettes. She lit up and blew a long stream of smoke to her right.

"This is my ex-husband's fault," she said. "I wasn't keeping him from his kids. All he had to do was wait for Christmas, and he would have seen 'em. He brought this on himself."

"Did he work for the same drug cartel you did?" I

asked.

She furrowed her brow at me.

"Excuse me?"

"Did he smuggle drugs for a cartel, too?" I asked. "Because I've been working this case for several days, and everything I've seen says Joel was a stand-up guy. You were the criminal, and yet, because of a quirk in the judicial system, you got sole custody of your kids and disappeared."

"He agreed to the custody arrangement," she said, opening her eyes wide and pointing at me with her cigarette.

"If he hadn't, a drug cartel would have murdered his children to get to you," I said. "How is that a choice?"

"You don't know what the hell you're talking about," she said, after taking a long drag on her cigarette. "I'm a good mom."

"No, you're a drunk," I said. "Your husband was a good man and a loving father, and the government ripped his kids away from him because of what you did. If he wanted to see Logan and Evan, he should have gone through the right channels. I agree with you there, but I can't blame him for wanting to see his kids. He made a mistake, but you forced his hand. I am sorry that your children are missing, and I will do everything I can to find them, but don't blame your husband for this. If you want to find out whose fault this mess is, look in the goddamn mirror."

Her face seemed to crumble inward, and sobs

wracked her shoulders.

"I'm sorry," she said. "I'm so sorry."

"Me, too," I said. "Now if you'll excuse me, I have to see what I can do about finding your kids."

I got out of the sedan, slammed the door shut, and knocked on the passenger side window of Cartwright's SUV. The female marshal opened her door.

"You get what you need, Detective?"

"No," I said, "but thank you all the same. Ms. Doe is pretty upset. Sorry about that."

The marshal sighed and looked to Cartwright.

"You stock up the liquor cabinet?"

He closed his eyes and nodded.

"If I hadn't, she'd sneak out to a bar."

The female marshal rolled her eyes and shook her head but said nothing. I looked to Cartwright.

"You mind driving me back now?" I asked.

Cartwright nodded, and the female marshal slid out of the SUV.

"Good luck, Beth," said Cartwright. She nodded but didn't seem bolstered by the comment. As I climbed into the SUV, she got into the driver's side of the sedan. Once I shut my door, Cartwright looked at me. "Want me to drop you off at your station?"

I nodded.

"Yeah. I'm done here, and I've got work at the office. And no need to go through that hour-long drive to get back. Just hang a right out of here and then the first left. It'll look like a little farm road. Follow that for ten minutes, and we'll run into a McDonald's. From there, you'll recognize where we are."

He smiled just a little.

"You knew where we were the whole time?"

"Yeah. Like I said, I know this part of the state pretty well. Now let's go. We've both got work to do."

31

Sasha had last stepped foot in a high school seven years ago. For some people, high school was the highlight of their lives. Men sat around in bars and restaurants, reliving their exploits on the football field and their adventures beneath the bleachers with young women too naïve and stupid to say no to their advances. Adolescence was magical for many. For the first time in a young person's life, she was given the freedom to make important choices for herself.

By the time Sasha entered high school, though, she had already experienced more tragedy and pain in her short life than most people ever would in eighty or a hundred years. She had been glad to leave school and her childhood behind.

Today, she wore dark jeans, a purple hooded sweatshirt, a gray T-shirt, and a gray pair of canvas shoes, and she carried a green canvas backpack. Her simple clothes felt comfortable against her. They made her look younger than she was and should allow her to fit in very well. More than that, her sweatshirt allowed her to conceal a pistol in a holster on her hip, and her backpack allowed her to carry half a dozen magazines, each of which held seventeen nine-millimeter rounds.

Ian Staley and his family lived in St. Charles, Missouri, a suburb northwest of St. Louis. Sasha had little reason to visit, but it seemed like a pleasant enough town—especially for couples with children. Joe Court and Ian were half siblings. Unlike Joe's other siblings, Ian kept his private life off the internet. A search of the local newspaper told her Ian had won a spelling bee at his elementary school in sixth grade and that he was involved in an engineering club at his high school that had built a solar-powered go-kart. Beyond those brief mentions, she had found nothing.

That was enough, though.

Sasha parked on the street near the cafeteria. The kitchen's exhaust fans thrummed, and the air smelled of grease and French fries. She waited on the sidewalk and glanced at her watch. It was almost time. The school's red-brick and stacked stone foundation had a timeless look, while its athletic fields and track were modern and more than functional. The expansive lawn out front held big trees and healthy grass.

Sasha followed the sidewalk toward the vocational arts building. The architecture matched the rest of the school, but it lay across the street, disconnected from the main campus. That kept the noise of its table saws and other machinery from disturbing students in math and English classes, but it forced the school to open its doors for several minutes each hour. That was the entrance she needed.

Sasha waited near the side of the building. Right on time, the school's bell rang, and dozens of students—boys mostly—emerged from the workshop and classrooms. She clutched her backpack and kept her head down as she followed them. Though she was in her twenties, Sasha looked young enough that she could pass for a high school senior at a glance. She only needed a few minutes.

Once she reached the school's interior, she walked to the first girls' restroom she found and locked herself into a stall. Once the bell rang, she found herself alone in the bathroom with another girl in the stall beside her. She waited another few moments, expecting the other girl to hurry to class, but then she heard the familiar bubbly, crackling sound of an e-cigarette. Sasha sighed.

"When I was in high school, we just smoked in here," she said. "That vaping shit will kill you."

"Who the fuck are you?"

"A substitute teacher on her break," said Sasha. "Go to class. If I take you to the office, I've got to fill out paperwork."

"Shit," said the girl. She fled the stall, leaving Sasha alone. She opened her backpack and withdrew two magazines, both of which she slipped into the front pocket of her sweatshirt. Before leaving the bathroom, she chambered a round on her pistol and slipped it into its holster on her side.

Outside, lockers lined the empty hallways. A few classrooms had their doors open, but most were closed. It was quiet. The carpet muffled her footsteps. Sasha had complete control of the situation, so she wasn't nervous. Her muscles felt tight, though, and her heart thumped in her chest. Her body anticipated the violence to come. Every student, teacher, and staff member in that building would remember today for the rest of their lives. They thought they knew what it felt like to be afraid, but they didn't. Some of them had survived tornadoes and floods and car accidents, but few of them had faced death firsthand.

They would today.

If Sasha ran into Ian in the hallway, she'd kill him and whoever he was with, but she didn't count on getting that lucky. For almost fifteen minutes, she wandered the hallways but saw no adults. Then, a fit man in khaki pants and a white button-down shirt came toward her. He was bald, and he had the chiseled features of a man who exercised regularly. His eyes locked on her as he walked.

"Shouldn't you be in class?"

Sasha said nothing, and his footsteps slowed as he drew near. He stopped about ten feet from her and put his hand over the walkie-talkie on his belt.

"You're not one of my students. Who are you?"

Sasha looked down at his left hand. He wore a simple gold band on his ring finger.

"You're married," she said, smiling. "I bet your wife calls you Mr. Clean."

He pulled the walkie-talkie from his belt.

"Ms. Gonzalez, please call the police and let them

know we've got an intruder in the building."

Sasha brought her hand to the pistol at her hip.

"Why'd you do that?" asked Sasha, sighing.

"Get out of my school," he said.

"Do you know Ian Staley?" she asked.

He brought the walkie-talkie to his mouth again.

"Lockdown," he said. "Lockdown."

"That should have been your first move," said Sasha, pulling her weapon from her holster. Mr. Clean lunged toward her, but she brought her hip back and raised her weapon before he could cross the distance between them. He gasped almost the instant she pulled the trigger. The sound echoed up and down the hallway as Mr. Clean fell. She had shot him in the gut. At one time, it would have been a mortal injury, but with modern antibiotics and surgery, he'd survive.

"Please tell Ian Staley I said hello," she said, holstering her weapon and hurrying to the nearest fire alarm. Just as someone came over the PA system to tell the school to lock down, the fire alarm blared. The classrooms nearest her stayed closed, probably because they had heard the gunshots, but on the floor above her, she could hear movement. Sasha looked to the principal. "Ian Staley. Remember that. I came here for him."

The principal groaned and spoke into his walkie-talkie.

"Lockdown," he said again. "I've been shot and need help. We have an armed intruder. She pulled the fire alarm. Lockdown."

As the first lines of students began coming down the stairs, Sasha sprinted toward the exit nearest her car. In the distance, she could hear the first sirens, but they didn't bother her. She reached her car within three minutes of shooting Mr. Clean and was on Missouri 370, the nearest highway, within five minutes of that.

If she had wanted, she could have killed dozens of young people. This was a targeted raid, though. If Mr. Clean did his job, the police would know that. So would Joe Court. The detective's world would soon become much smaller. Sasha couldn't wait to tell Peter the next time she saw him.

32

Neither Cartwright nor I said anything for a few minutes. Then I glanced at him and cleared my throat.

"Thank you for setting this up," I said. "I know it took some work."

He nodded and glanced at me before focusing on the road again.

"My boss made me," he said. "Sorry I punched you the other day."

"Forget about it," I said. "You couldn't tell me who Krystal and her family were. I get why now. Sorry I disarmed you and beat you up in your own home in front of your wife and children."

He snorted and shook his head, and I couldn't help but smile a little. We settled into another silent minute before I glanced at him once more.

"Tell me about Logan and Evan."

He hesitated before answering.

"They're good boys, and they stay out of trouble. They had a good dad. I wish they had a better mother."

I nodded.

"Were they abducted, or did they run?"

"We're working with the FBI to figure that out," he said. "Because of their mom's enemies, though, we've got to keep things a little quiet. If they have just run, we don't want to tip off the cartel's men to look for them. And if someone took them, their kidnappers are doing a very good job of keeping them hidden."

I crossed my arms.

"That's rough," I said. "Logan's got a Facebook page under the name Oliver Klothesoff. Have you seen it?"

"Oliver Klothesoff," said Cartwright, snorting. "That sounds like Logan. I'll look into it. How do you know about it?"

"A kid at his school showed me his page," I said. "By the time I saw it, Logan hadn't posted for several days. If you're lucky, he'll have logged in and checked his messages or something."

He grunted.

"I rarely get that lucky, but it's a help. Thank you."

"And I'm sure you've checked out his cell phone, too."

He nodded.

"We monitored it."

"How about the burner phone he used to contact his father?"

He cocked his head to the side at me.

"We didn't know he had one," he said.

"I've got the number."

He thanked me, and we drove the rest of the way to my station in silence. Once there, I flipped through my notepad until I found Logan's number and read it off so he could jot it down.

I got out of the car feeling like someone had scraped out my insides with a melon baller. My investigation was over. If a cartel hit man had killed Joel, the shooter was long gone. I couldn't close every case I worked, so that didn't bother me too much. Missing kids did, though. Wherever they were, I hoped Logan and his brother were okay.

Once I reached my desk, I settled into my chair and unlocked the center drawer for my phone and pistol. My trip to interview Krystal had taken a little over an hour and a half, so I figured I'd have an email or two to answer. I didn't expect two dozen text messages, almost all of which had come from my family.

Mom had texted and asked about Ian. Then she texted me to ask me to call her. Dad, Audrey, and Dylan had left me similar messages. Special Agent Costa had sent a message, too, telling me to call him but warning me he was already on his way to St. Charles and that he didn't have any news yet. That made my heart beat a little faster. Finally, I found a message from Ian.

I'm okay. Call me later.

I furrowed my brow and dialed my little brother's cell number. It rang six times and then went to voicemail, so I called him again. Once more, it went to voicemail, so I left him a message.

"Hey, Ian, it's Joe. I got the message that you're okay, but what's going on? Call me."

I hung up and started pacing my office, hoping he'd call me back. He didn't, so I called Agent Costa. He picked up before it finished ringing once.

"Bryan, it's Joe," I said. "I've been out, so I just got back to my office. My cell phone's been blowing up. What the hell's going on in St. Charles?"

Agent Costa drew in a deep breath. When he spoke, his voice sounded calm and measured.

"Are you somewhere we can talk?"

"Yeah," I said. "What the hell's going on? Talk to me."

"Are you sitting down?"

"I'm in my office," I said, my voice sharp. My heart pounded, and skin all over my body tingled. "I'm fine. Just talk to me."

"There's been a shooting at Ian's high school. We don't have a lot of details yet, but the vice principal confronted an armed intruder inside the building. He called for the staff to lock the school down. Then he was shot. He's still in surgery, so we haven't been able to talk to him."

I swallowed hard and nodded. That was why everyone had asked me about Ian and why he had texted me to say he was okay. It didn't explain why Agent Costa was driving in from Terre Haute, though. School shootings were, depressingly, common enough that they shouldn't have drawn an FBI agent from a priority assignment two hundred miles away.

Then, a cold feeling began seeping into my chest and

then into my arms and legs. I fell into my chair.

"Who was the shooter?" I asked.

"We don't have a positive ID yet."

"Cut the shit," I said, shaking my head. "You wouldn't be driving from Terre Haute without a damn good reason. Sasha Ingram already came after Dylan. Did she come after Ian, too?"

He hesitated and then sighed.

"Yeah. She shot the principal in the gut and told him to tell the police that she came to the school looking for Ian Staley."

At once, my office felt small and hot. My head swam, and I almost fell off my chair. I took half a dozen breaths, hoping that would help things. My fingers trembled.

"You still there, Joe?" asked Costa.

"Yeah, but not for long," I said. "I'm going to St. Charles. I'll talk to you later."

I hung up and then stood as I dialed Ian's number once more. As before, it went to voicemail.

"Ian, it's Joe. I heard what happened, and I'm on my way."

I left my office at a run and signed out a marked cruiser from our motor pool before driving north to the city. St. Charles was just about seventy-five miles away, and I made it to the high school in a little under an hour. The police had closed the roads for two blocks around the school to keep the press away, but that didn't stop the helicopters from hovering over the building. I parked near the corner of Vine Street and Park Avenue, just outside the police barricade. It was a residential street. Since I didn't know anybody with the St. Charles Police Department, I'd have to use my charm.

Before getting out of my car, I hung my badge around my neck on a lanyard and called Agent Costa to let him know I had arrived at the school. He was on I-70 near Normandy, Missouri, which meant he was about twenty minutes out. I didn't want to wait for him, so I asked him to call the senior-most FBI agent at the school and let him or her know I was on my way in. He agreed, so I hung up, got out of my car, and walked toward the barricade.

The street on which I had parked was quiet and residential and lacked a clear view of the high school, limiting its appeal to the news media. A single uniformed officer stood at the barricade. He nodded as I walked toward him.

"Area's closed, and even if you have questions, I don't have answers," he said. "For your own safety, you need to return to your vehicle and go home."

I reached to my badge. He saw it and nodded.

"You think the shooter's still in the area?" I asked.

He hesitated before answering.

"We don't know," he said. "I appreciate that you're law enforcement, but we don't have room for tourists or looky-loos."

"I'm expected," I said. "Call your CO. Let her know Detective Joe Court is here."

He leaned his head toward the radio on his shoulder and whispered. After a few moments of back-and-forth conversation, the uniformed officer straightened and nodded toward me and then pointed down the road.

"Make sure your badge is visible at all times. Our command post is on Bennett Avenue. You can't miss it. Agent Stallweather is expecting you."

I nodded and thanked him before stepping past the blue and white police sawhorses the officer had erected. There should have been kids laughing and walking home from school, but the area was quiet and empty. With the shooter still at large, the local police would have evacuated every house for several blocks, but it felt like people were watching me anyway. A helicopter hovered somewhere overhead, but I couldn't see it from my present location.

The houses on Ferguson Street were mostly single-story and had well-kept yards. There were no sidewalks, so I walked along the edge of the road. Without streetlights, it would have been dark at night, but in the late afternoon, it was pleasant enough.

As I approached the end of the street, a uniformed officer in a puffy navy coat saw me and nodded.

"Detective Court?" he asked. I nodded. "Right this way."

I followed him to the left down Bennett Avenue. A few cars had parked alongside the road, but police barricades prevented anyone from leaving. Their command center comprised a blue party tent and a six-wheeled armored vehicle that would have looked more at home traveling the deserts of Afghanistan or Iraq than it did on a suburban street.

Beneath the tent, half a dozen uniformed officers and three plainclothes officers stood around a pair of folding tables, talking and staring at a map. As my escort and I walked toward them, a woman a few years older than me left the group and nodded a greeting to me.

"Detective Court?" she asked. I nodded, and we shook hands. "Gina Stallweather. Bryan Costa says nice things about you."

"Bryan's a good cop. I like working with him."

She nodded and looked toward the high school before focusing on me.

"I know little about what you're working on, but he told me to give you the same access to the scene and our information that he'd have. We don't do that for local cops often. So who are you, and what are you and Bryan working on that would compel you to drop everything you were doing and drive to St. Charles to work a school shooting?"

She smiled, but her voice had an edge to it. She didn't enjoy being in the dark about key aspects of her case. I knew what that felt like.

"It's complicated. This school have any surveillance cameras?" I asked.

She considered me and then crossed her arms before nodding.

"A few in the main hallway. You want to see the shooter?"

I nodded, so she and I walked to a laptop on the folding tables. The crowd around us quieted, probably wondering who the hell I was and why I was there. Stallweather clicked a few times and then opened an image file. The picture was grainy, but I recognized Sasha Ingram. I couldn't see her firearm, but she had a bulge on her hip where she would have carried a holster.

"Where is she now?" I asked.

Stallweather shook her head.

"No clue. She had this planned pretty well. She was long gone by the time our first responders arrived. Who is she?"

Cops surrounded me, but I didn't know them. Most of them were probably trustworthy and honest, but if I told them the truth, someone would tell his or her spouse, and that spouse would tell a friend or two. The information would spread like a virus. We'd have parents across the state terrified that a serial murderer was targeting their kids.

"She's dangerous," I said. "She's also the subject of an active homicide investigation in St. Augustine."

Agent Stallweather crossed her arms and frowned.

"Anything else you can tell me, or are you here to waste my time?"

"She's not killing at random, and I doubt she'll go after another school."

Stallweather cocked her head to the side and raised her eyebrows.

"And you know that how?"

"Because she came here to kill Ian Staley. He's my half-brother," I said. "She went after my other brother a few days ago. She's sending me a message."

Stallweather blinked a few times. Her mouth opened, and she raised her eyebrows.

"I don't know whether to believe you or call the paramedics to give you a psych eval."

"I'm glad you're not in charge, then," I said. "Bryan Costa will be here soon. If you've got questions, ask him. I'm going to my little brother's house to make sure he's okay."

33

Ian and his family lived in a yellow American Foursquare in a quaint neighborhood on the north side of town. The houses were all built within the past decade, but they had historic designs and features to mimic neighborhoods from long ago. Trees lined the road, but none looked older than the surrounding homes. It made me wonder whether the area had been a farmer's field in the not-too-distant past.

I parked in front of the house and stepped onto the covered front porch. A rocker swayed in the slight breeze. Wood smoke wafted from a neighbor's chimney. Ian's mom, Miriam, opened the door when I knocked. She was in her mid-seventies and had short, fashionable white hair. Though she was on the older side to have a fifteen-year-old adoptive son, she and her husband were both healthy. The way Ian described her, Miriam would outlive us both.

I smiled hello to her. If he had even half a chance, my little brother could change the world. He could become a world-class mathematician or physicist or something else entirely different but still amazing. Miriam wanted her son to flourish and use all of his considerable talents. In her mind, though, I was still an open question. She had dreams for her son, and she didn't know where I fit in those dreams yet. I just wanted my brother happy. Everything else was window dressing.

"Is Ian home?" I asked. "I tried calling him."

"He gave his phone to the police in case that woman called," she said. "He was in class at SLU when Mr. Korfist was shot."

"Good," I said. "I'm glad he was okay."

She closed her eyes and shook her head.

"He's not okay, Joe," she said. "A serial murderer came to his school and shot his vice principal while looking for him. How can you ever expect him to be okay?"

I stepped back.

"You're right," I said. "I spoke poorly. I'm glad he's physically unharmed. Can I talk to him, please?"

She considered me and then sighed before shaking her head.

"No. I'm afraid not," she said. "My son is in danger because of you. If he had been at school, he'd be dead now."

I wanted to argue with her, but I couldn't, so I just nodded.

"That's possible," I said.

She sighed again and looked down.

"Please leave before I call the police. My son is your brother, but he's a minor under my care, and you endanger him and everyone around you. My husband is at the St.

Charles County Courthouse filing a petition for an order of protection against you. If you visit this home again or try to contact Ian, I will call the police, and they will arrest you."

My throat tightened. It felt like a slap, and it was all the worse because I deserved it. I nodded and stepped back, blinking rapidly. Ian and I hadn't known each other long, but he mattered to me. He was my brother. Your family was supposed to be permanent, an anchor or safe harbor. Ian and I weren't there just yet, but one day, I had hoped, we would be. I had thought we were on our way.

Then again, I'd also thought Julia Green and I were family, too, and she had sent me away. I couldn't blame her, either. I had endangered Dylan, her actual kid. As much as I had wanted to believe that I was as much a part of her family as her biological children, I wasn't. If anything, I was more like their ward. They had watched over me, and they had cared about me, but I wasn't family. I shouldn't have let myself think otherwise.

My only real family was my mother, a drug-addicted prostitute who had lost me to the foster care system before I had even started kindergarten. Everything else was a lie, and I had been naïve and stupid to believe it.

My throat tightened, so I coughed to open it up.

"I'm sorry."

"Sorry doesn't keep my son safe," she said. "Please leave."

I swallowed hard and nodded and tried to tell her that I was sorry again, but my throat had tightened once more.

I couldn't speak, so I turned and walked back to my car. It felt as if someone had clamped my gut into a vise. Every part of my body felt heavy. My arms felt shaky. I didn't want to cry, but I couldn't stop myself, and I knew I wouldn't be able to drive safely once tears started coming. I drove to a park along the edge of the Missouri River and followed a trail in the woods until I was sure I was alone.

Then, as I walked, I let go of everything and cried until I couldn't even see the trail in front of me through my tears. When I couldn't walk anymore, I put my back against a tree and slid down until my butt hit the cold, damp earth. I put my head between my knees. Dylan and Ian were alive because they got lucky. Sasha Ingram never should have even known their names. Now, they'd never forget hers.

From the moment I had met both of them, I promised myself that I'd be a good big sister. I'd take care of them when they needed me, and I'd support them and be in their corners for whatever they needed. I had thought that was the right thing, but now I knew better.

My entire family, everyone I loved in the world, would have been better off if they had never met me. That sounded like an overreaction, but it wasn't. I chose to work with the FBI on Peter Brunelle's case, I knew he was working with someone on the outside, and I chose to antagonize him into action. Because of me and my choices, my little brothers could have died. Because of my choice, the vice principal at Ian's school had been shot. Because of me, Dylan had been tied up and beaten.

Because of my choices, I was alone now, and worse, I deserved it. That tore me up.

I stayed in that park long enough that I ran out of tears. Eventually, my breath came easier, and I heard things I hadn't heard before, including the roar of a street nearby, and a beep coming from my cell phone. Someone must have called. I wiped my eyes and looked at the screen before dialing Agent Costa's number.

"Hey, Bryan," I said. "It's Joe Court."

He hesitated, so I cleared my throat, hoping he didn't notice the catch in my voice.

"You all right?"

"I'm fine," I said. "What do you need?"

"I'm in St. Charles, and I just talked to Agent Stallweather. Are you still in town? I'd like to talk to you about our next steps."

"Sure," I said, nodding. "I'm at a park overlooking the Missouri River. It's by 370. I'll meet you by the playground. It's by the corner of North Main and Tecumseh Streets."

Costa, once more, hesitated.

"I can find that," he said. He paused. "Are you sure you're okay? I can call somebody for you if you want. I think I've got your mom's phone number."

The lump in my throat grew tighter. I swallowed it down.

"No. Don't call Julia. She has a lot going on. I'm fine," I said. "Thank you. I'll see you when you get here. I'm on a trail, so if I'm not at the playground when you arrive, I'll be walking toward it."

"See you in a few."

"Yeah," I said. "See you soon."

I hung up and slipped the phone back into my purse before looking at the river again. It was peaceful in that park, but I couldn't stay. Life didn't stop moving because I needed a break. More than that, Sasha Ingram wouldn't stop until we made her. I needed to focus on her. Maybe she was content with just scaring my brothers, but I doubted it. If we didn't catch her, she'd go after my dad or my sister or my mom. Nobody in my family was safe until I solved the problem I had created.

I swallowed hard, stood, and brushed dirt and leaves off my legs and jacket before heading down the trail toward the playground and asphalt lot in which I had parked. The walk took about ten minutes. It didn't make me feel better, but it hardened my resolve and gave me a moment to compose myself. I was a cop. This was my job. I'd find this bitch, and I'd put her in prison for murder. And if I couldn't do that, I'd put her in the ground.

Agent Costa arrived about five minutes after I reached my cruiser and sat down. He parked his big SUV beside mine but stayed in his car, giving me a moment more to compose myself. I took a deep breath and forced a smile to my face.

"You're fine, Joe," I said. "Everything will work out."

I sucked in another breath before opening the door. Agent Costa rolled down his window.

"Why don't you have a seat inside? It's cold out

there."

I nodded and walked to the passenger side of his SUV. For a few moments, neither of us spoke. Then Costa cleared his throat.

"Did you talk to Ian and his family?"

"Briefly," I said, nodding. "He takes some math classes at St. Louis University, and he wasn't at the high school when Sasha shot Mr. Korfist."

"I'm glad," said Costa. "We need to shut Sasha down before she kills again."

I nodded and crossed my arms.

"What do we know about her?"

"The name is a fake," he said. "We don't know who she really is, but we know she's not Sasha Ingram. We've also run her face through every facial-recognition database we've got, but we haven't found a match yet."

"You have access to pictures from the Department of Revenue's license database?"

He blew out a breath and then sighed.

"Not officially," he said. "If she were a terrorist, we could get access, but it's a legal gray area."

I nodded. Some tension left my shoulders. Being a cop wasn't always easy, but when I assumed that role, at least I knew who I was and what I was supposed to do.

"If we can't ID her from her picture, let's think about her victims. At this point, it's fair to assume she buried the heads on my property on Brunelle's orders."

"That's our working assumption," said Costa. "We've tried to ID them, but we've had little luck there without the rest of their bodies. They're all Caucasian males, and our coroner estimates them each to be between twenty and forty. None of them have had major dental work, although one of them had two missing teeth. Two had broken their noses, and one had a deviated septum. It would have caused problems breathing through the nose, but he never had it fixed."

I reached into my purse and pulled out a notepad to jot down some notes. Then I thought.

"Did you check missing-persons reports?" I asked.

"Yeah," he said, nodding. "We went back two years, but no one reported our victims missing anywhere in the country."

"That's telling," I said, nodding and raising my eyebrows. "It's a pattern. She's hunting outcasts. Her victims have no family and friends, or they live in communities that don't trust the government."

Costa considered and nodded.

"Okay," he said. "What else?"

"To meet these people, she has to fit into their communities. She knows who they are and how they think," I said. "We don't know Sasha's name, but she's pretty, she's white, and she's got a few tattoos. She looks like she could be in a biker gang."

"Or the Aryan Brotherhood or many other separatist organizations," said Costa. "It's a good thought, but we need more."

"We do know more," I said, nodding. "She's confident, she's smart, and she knows the St. Louis area. I think she's local, which means her victims might be local, too."

Costa considered before nodding.

"It's worth looking into," he said, blinking. He paused. "I'll contact the Bureau's Gang Intelligence Center and see what we've got on biker gangs and white supremacist organizations in Missouri. Maybe we'll get lucky and find a directory that has pictures."

"You do that," I said. "I'll call my brother and see whether he can remember anything else about her."

He wished me luck, which I appreciated. I walked to my cruiser, sat in the front seat, and drew in a slow breath before calling Julia Green's number. She answered on the third.

"Hey, Joe," she said, her voice subdued.

"Julia, hey," I said. "I'm with Special Agent Bryan Costa from the FBI, and I need to talk to Dylan."

She paused. I waited for about thirty seconds before I blinked.

"I know you're not interested in talking, but I'm working a case," I said. "Dylan might know something."

"I understand," she said. She paused again, but this time it was shorter. "You called me Julia instead of Mom. It threw me."

"It seemed appropriate," I said. She started to say something, but it would have hurt to hear her agree with me, so I spoke over her. "If Dylan's not available, I can call later."

"He's here," said Julia. "Give me a minute. He's in the

basement."

"Thanks," I said. As I waited, I felt a heaviness settle into my chest. I didn't allow myself to dwell on that, though. I had shit to do. Dylan told me hello a moment later.

"Dylan, hey," I said. "Sorry to bother you, but I've got some questions about Sasha Ingram."

"How's Ian?"

"He's fine. Thank you," I said. "When we last spoke, you mentioned that Sasha had a tattoo on her shoulder. Did you remember her other tattoos?"

He paused.

"I don't know," he said. "She had barbed wire on her bicep, I think."

"That's helpful," I said, nodding. "Anything else?"

"A bunch of triangles on her left shoulder. She had a rose on her right shoulder, but the triangles and barbed wire were on her left side."

If we made an arrest, those tattoos could help confirm that she was the woman who seduced and then abandoned Dylan, but they were too nondescript and common to ID her. I blinked a few times, considering what to tell him.

"The FBI and I are pursuing a theory that Ms. Ingram might be a member of a fringe group or community. Did she have any tattoos or other body marks that seemed unusual to you?"

He paused.

"I don't know what you mean."

"Did she have a swastika tattoo?" I asked.

"Whoa, whoa, whoa, hold on," he said. "I wouldn't hook up with a Nazi no matter how hot she was."

"I know," I said. "I just have to be sure. Okay? Sometimes gang or prison tattoos are subtle. Unless you know what you're looking for, they'd look like normal tattoos. Anything you can tell me helps."

He hesitated.

"She had some numbers on her side," he said, his voice low. He paused again. "I didn't see them until she took off her dress."

I raised my eyebrows.

"What numbers were they?"

"1488. She said it was about an explorer who sailed around Africa."

I closed my eyes and swore under my breath.

"It wasn't about an explorer, was it?" he asked.

"No," I said, closing my eyes and swearing again. "Fourteen refers to the fourteen words: 'We must secure the existence of our people and a future for white children.' It's a guiding principle of the Aryan Nation. Eight refers to the eighth letter of the alphabet, *H*. When you put eight and eight together, it means *Heil Hitler*."

Dylan paused.

"Fuck," he said, his voice low. "She was a Nazi."

"Or she's pretending to be one," I said. "Thanks. This will help us find her."

Dylan swore again. A couple of days ago, I might have told him it wasn't his fault or that he had done nothing wrong. He didn't need to hear that from me, though, and it wasn't my place to say it, anyway.

"If you or your mom have questions, you've got my number," I said. "Good luck."

I hung up before he could respond. For some reason, that short conversation had left me feeling far more drained than it should have. When he was a kid and I had lived with the Greens, Dylan and I had talked dozens of times a day. It had been easy then. Dylan had some quirks, but he was resourceful and charismatic. Audrey, his sister, was kind and patient. They had bright futures and would do just fine. They didn't need me.

I left my cruiser and walked to Agent Costa's SUV. He was on the phone with somebody, but he put his hand over the microphone and raised his eyebrows at me as I opened the passenger side door.

"Got anything?"

"She's a white supremacist," I said. "Her victims probably were, too. That's why no one reported them missing. Their friends don't trust the government."

Costa nodded, removed his hand from the phone, and focused on his call.

"Tyrone, let me call you back," he said, glancing at me. "Detective Court just gave us a lead."

34

Agent Costa shifted and slipped his phone into his pocket before looking at me.

"Okay. Tell me what you've got."

I filled him in on my conversation with Dylan. Afterwards, Costa nodded and crossed his arms.

"The white supremacy angle is too bad," he said. "We've got better intelligence on biker gangs than we do hate groups."

"What intelligence do you have?"

He raised his eyebrows and sighed.

"Not a lot," he said. "We have files on individual white supremacists who've committed crimes, but it's not illegal to be a racist or to associate with a racist organization. Until people commit crimes, we don't watch them too closely. What does your station have?"

"I'm the only detective in a small department in a rural county in Missouri," I said. "We're lucky to have gas in our cruisers. We don't have an intelligence unit."

He nodded and sighed.

"Looks like we've got our work cut out for us, then," he said. "It'll be easiest to start online with racist

Facebook groups and go from there. Maybe somebody will recognize her and turn her in, especially if we let them know she's killing men in their communities."

I nodded and considered.

"That's a good idea," I said. "There's a church in St. Augustine County that might help us, too."

He furrowed his brow.

"Why would a church help?"

I tilted my head to the side and drew in a breath.

"They're not a real church," I said. "They call themselves a church to avoid paying taxes. Their minister is a former Klansman. He ran for Congress about twenty years ago on a pro-segregation platform and won way more votes than he should have. If Sasha is hunting anywhere near St. Augustine, he might know her."

Costa nodded.

"Sounds like a plan," he said. "I'll go back to my office and put a team together for this. You go visit your racist minister."

"Will do," I said, already opening my door. "Good luck."

"You, too," he said.

I didn't know whether we'd accomplish anything, but it felt good to move and focus on the case. The drive to St. Augustine was easy, although the sun had begun to set by the time I arrived. I called my station to let my boss know I was in the area and that I planned to visit the county's chief racist, Richard Clarke. He wished me luck.

The Church of the White Steeple sat on what should

have been a pretty piece of farmland. Unfortunately, Richard Clarke and his crew had driven metal rods into the ground and strewn corrugated steel barriers and rusted barbed wire around their property as a fence. A metal gate, similar to the ones found on a cattle farm, closed the driveway from the road. Behind the cattle gate were solid, wheeled gates they could roll into place if they needed privacy.

If our department ever had to come to that farm in force, we'd run into problems, but the Church hadn't given us a reason so far. Their white supremacist ideology was repugnant, but they weren't violent, and they didn't advocate violence. Mostly, they just carried protest signs at rallies and special events in town.

I pulled to a stop outside the main gate and honked my horn, just as the spray-painted sign beside the gate suggested. Within a few minutes, a kid on a four-wheeler made his way down the driveway. He was fourteen or fifteen, and he had curly brown hair. He wore a navy jacket and jeans, and he carried a hunting rifle slung across his back. I stepped out of my car, and his eyes traveled up and down me.

"You a cop?" he asked.

I still had my badge on a lanyard around my neck, so I pulled it over my jacket and nodded.

"Yeah. I'd like to talk to Richard Clarke if he's available."

He considered me again.

"You know the bishop?"

A lot of secretive organizations had signs and countersigns used to identify members. He may have just been asking whether I knew Clarke, but he also may have been testing me. It didn't matter to me, either way. I didn't pretend to be something I wasn't.

"If the bishop is Richard Clarke, I've met him twice," I said. "He said I'd make beautiful Aryan babies, so I think he likes me. He around? I need to talk to him. Tell him Detective Joe Court is here to do him a favor."

The kid nodded and revved his four-wheeler's engine before turning around and driving back the way he came. I leaned against the hood of my cruiser to wait, but it got cold, and Clarke was taking his time. I sat down and used my vehicle's laptop and 4G data connection to look up additional white supremacist organizations in this part of Missouri. They weren't hard to find.

About ten minutes after the kid left, a white minivan drove toward the gate. The driver was somewhere between forty and fifty, and he wore jeans and a yellow vest over a plaid button-down shirt. I didn't know him, but he opened the gate and smiled at me.

"Evening, Detective," he said. "My dad's in back. He'd like to talk to you."

I shook my head.

"As much as I'd like to talk to your father, I won't get in the back of a stranger's minivan."

As I spoke, the rear door slid open. A thin man in a gray suit stepped out. His thick, steel gray hair looked almost like plastic, and his leathery, jaundiced skin stretched taut over his cheekbones. His cool, cornflower blue eyes took me in at a glance, and a smile split his lips.

"Detective Court," he said, holding out his hand. "It's nice to see you again, and on my property, no less. Are you here for the Teaching While White seminar?"

"No," I said, reaching into my purse for my phone. I flipped through pictures until I found one of Sasha. "I'm here to talk to you. I'm hunting a murderer, and I wondered whether you've ever seen her."

I walked toward him and showed him my phone. He furrowed his brow and looked at the screen before stepping closer to me. His cologne smelled like cedar and musk. It wasn't bad, but now I'd forever associate that smell with a racist old man. It kind of ruined it for me.

"Never seen her," he said. "Should I have?"

"She had 1488 tattooed on her side. You know what that means."

"Allow me to stop you there," he said, smiling. "Neither I nor my people are Nazi sympathizers. True, we're interested in securing the future for our white children, but we don't believe that future has to come at the expense of lesser races. We don't advocate violence, merely segregation."

"Good for you," I said, trying not to allow my revulsion into my voice as I thumbed through additional pictures on my phone. "Maybe you'll recognize these men. Considering my murderer's background, I'm guessing they're members of communities like your own. She's hunting people with sympathies similar to your own and dumping their bodies nearby."

I flipped through my pictures and showed him individual pictures of each of the heads Sasha had buried in my yard. The old man shook his head.

"I don't know those men, but it's a horrible thing that's happened to them," he said. "If you send those pictures to my son, he and I will ensure that the men and women in our community understand the potential danger they're in."

I glanced at the guy in the plaid shirt. He gave me his phone number, so I texted him the pictures of Sasha and her three victims. A moment later, he confirmed that he had received them.

"If you see that woman, please call the police."

Clarke drew in a breath through clenched teeth.

"We'll call the police, but if she's a threat to our people, I can't guarantee her safety."

I forced myself to smile.

"You have every right to protect yourself and your loved ones, but murder is murder. If you shoot her while protecting yourself, you might be okay. If you kill her in her sleep, though, I'll arrest you and everyone involved in her death. Clear?"

"Clear as crystal," he said, grinning at me and exposing uneven white teeth. He could have used braces, but he must have brushed his teeth reasonably often. At least he had that going for him. Then his grin left, and he considered me. "You would make beautiful white babies. You should put your womb to better use."

"Thanks for the tip," I said, turning to go back to my cruiser. Clarke might have known something, but I couldn't help but feel that I had just wasted my time. As I drove back to my station, I called Agent Costa to let him know that Clarke had denied recognizing Sasha Ingram or her victims. Costa, unfortunately, wasn't faring much better.

On any other day, I would have worked through the night. After everything that had happened with Ian and Julia and Dylan, I needed a break. I dropped my cruiser off at work and drove home. As soon as he saw me, Roy barked and bowed from inside the dog run. Then he jumped and put his front paws on top of the fence as his tail wagged. I petted his cheek.

"Hey, sweetheart," I whispered. "How are you?"

He barked and seemed to grin.

"I'm glad to see you, too," I said, opening the gate. He jumped down from the fence and hurried out. "You want to play with the ball?"

He bowed, which was his way of saying yes. Since it was getting late, we didn't play long, but I tossed him a tennis ball for a few minutes. He retrieved it four times before lying down on the porch beside me with his head between his paws. That was good for him. When he first moved in with me, he wouldn't even run after the ball once. Slowly, though, he was learning to tolerate exercise.

As we walked into my house, my loneliness hit me again. I checked my messages on my phone, but nobody had contacted me. My stomach rumbled, but I didn't give it food. Instead, I got some ice from the freezer and poured myself a glass of vodka. Roy sat at my feet in the living room while I watched the ice crack and melt.

I liked alcohol and the way it made me feel, but it couldn't give me what I needed at that moment. My throat felt tight, and I looked to the dog. As much as I loved my dog, he couldn't give me what I needed, either. I cleared my throat, and he cocked his head at me.

"You want to go out tonight?"

He jumped to his feet and panted.

"Come on," I said, standing and walking to my bedroom. There I packed an overnight bag before leading Roy to my Volvo. He sat in the backseat, and I got in the front. Detective Mathias Blatch lived in a two-bedroom condo in Mehlville, a suburb in south St. Louis County. It wasn't a long drive, but I drove fast anyway. I was lucky I didn't get a ticket. I needed a hug, though, and Mathias was the only person I knew who'd give me one.

I parked in the visitor spot of his building, grabbed my bag, and put a leash on Roy. Then we walked to his door and knocked. A big smile split Mathias's face when he saw me. I couldn't help but return it. I reached out and touched his hands with trembling fingers. His fingers intertwined with mine.

"Hey," he said, looking to the dog. "I finally get to meet Roy, huh?"

I nodded and stepped into him and put my arms around him. He hugged me tightly, and for the first time that day, I felt some of the weight leave my shoulders. I breathed just a little easier. I stayed there for a few moments, and then I lifted my head and kissed him delicately and lightly, and then harder. Before anything could happen, Roy whined, and Mathias pulled away.

"Wow," he said, breathing deeply.

"I had a bad day," I said. "I needed a friend."

He slid his arms to my waist and pulled me closer. I put my head on his chest. He squeezed gently before stepping back.

"I don't have any food for the dog, but are you hungry?"

"I've got stuff for Roy, and yes," I said, taking his hand, "I am hungry. We'll order pizza in a little while."

Roy followed us as I led Mathias into the condo. I hadn't been there before, but it wasn't a big place. I dropped my bag beside Roy and wrapped my arms around Mathias's shoulders to kiss him again. Eventually, I took my lips from his and stood on my toes to whisper in his ear.

"Take me to your room, please."

He pulled his head away but kept his arms around me.

"Are you sure?"

I kissed him again and then nodded.

"Yeah. I'm tired of being alone."

He nodded and slipped his hand to mine. I kissed him again, and then we walked to his room.

35

Sasha didn't care for the white supremacists or their ideology, but they were useful in so many ways. Peter had suggested using them as a hunting ground, a purpose for which they were well suited. Because of their beliefs, they often lived apart from the rest of polite society. They distrusted outsiders, but with an appropriate introduction, she was in for life. They even provided references when she moved to different communities.

Most of the racists saw only what they wanted to see, and in her, they found someone capable of parroting their ideology and beliefs. That she was young and attractive made her even more enticing—especially to the young men of the community. She promised them babies and a future of romantic, subservient bliss, but she gave them death.

Sasha had murdered six neo-Nazis in four different states since joining their movement, and only one had ever even been reported missing to the police. The neo-Nazi community was so transient, no one probably even missed the other five. They likely assumed those men had gone home—or maybe back to prison. Murdering them had been easy. She wished Peter had discovered them before going to prison. He could have killed hundreds and never been caught.

Tonight, she was staying in the spare bedroom of a decrepit trailer overlooking the Meramec River. She had an apartment of her own in St. Louis, but she didn't dare return to that. When Peter asked her to destroy Detective Court, she had known it would be a one-way trip. A life well lived was one spent in preparation for death. Had she not met Peter when she had, she would have ended it sooner. He had given her hope for a time, but then he had given her something even more precious than hope: he had given her a purpose and a reason to die.

The woods around the trailer were deep and thick, and to reach the compound, her host had driven her across streams, gravel roads, and fields. Since the river was so prone to spilling over its banks, the land was worthless to farmers and developers alike. The couple she was staying with were likely squatting on it. Sasha planned to kill them both before she left, but for now, they were asleep in the room beside hers.

She yawned and settled into the pillow. Tomorrow, she'd drive to Kirkwood, Missouri. She hadn't decided how she'd murder Detective Court's adoptive parents, but she was leaning toward burning them alive in their home. Joe's father had been a fireman before retiring, so that seemed fitting.

Her mind drifted as she closed her eyes. Then, someone pounded on the trailer's door, and she shot to her feet. She slipped out of bed. Her room's only window was too narrow to wriggle through. Worse, nothing in the room would stop a round if someone shot at her.

She knelt on the far side of the bed. If this was the end, Peter would be so disappointed. She should have killed Joe right away. Her heart pounded, and her breath caught in her throat as Chloe and Josh answered the door. They spoke to somebody outside, and then Chloe knocked on her door.

"Hey, Sasha, Bishop Clarke is here to talk to you. It's about somebody named Joe."

Since she got there, Chloe and Josh had gone on and on about Bishop Clarke. They said he ran a church for people like them, but it sounded more like a cult. He charged gullible racists hundreds of dollars to hear his theories of education and his sermons on the supposed Biblical origins of the supremacy of the white race. He even had a couple dozen people living with him in a compound in St. Augustine County. Sasha had planned to hunt amongst his congregation, but it didn't look like she'd get that chance now.

"I'll be there in just a minute," she said, pulling a bra out of her bag. She put it on and adjusted her T-shirt before grabbing a knife from her bag and stepping out of the bedroom. The bishop was an older man with dull white teeth and wiry gray hair. He was ugly, and she hated the way his eyes traveled down her T-shirt and shorts. Normally, men like him paid to visit women like her. Sasha didn't like this newfound power dynamic.

"Sasha Ingram?" he asked. It wasn't her real name, but everyone called her it now. "Let's talk outside."

She nodded and looked to her hosts before slipping her knife into the waistband of her shorts. They barely took their adoring eyes from Clarke, their guru and teacher. How anyone could look at a disgusting piece of shit with such love, she never understood. She was lucky to have Peter in her life. She didn't need diversions like this supposed man of faith.

Outside, the moon was bright and cheery. The Meramec River lapped against the shore not a hundred feet away. Leaves crunched under Clarke's feet as he shifted his weight from one foot to the other. He appraised her and then looked to the trailer.

"Shut the door," he said. "This is for your ears only."

She should have brought a pistol. She could kill the old man with her knife easily enough, but she'd get blood all over her.

"All right," she said, shutting the door. There were two bricks on the ground. Josh had wedged them on either side of his trailer's rear tire to act as an emergency brake. Her knife had a razor-sharp two-inch blade, but the brick gave her a better chance. After bashing in his skull with the brick, she'd go inside to kill Chloe and Josh, and then she'd steal the bishop's minivan to leave. It'd take ten minutes at most, but it'd open her to risks she'd rather not take. Still, she preferred having a plan should the worst come to pass.

"What can I do for you, Mr. Clarke?"

He considered her before crossing his arms.

"You're a pretty little thing, aren't you?" he asked.

She gave him her best coquettish smile and pretended to dig the tip of her shoe in the mud. In actuality, she was sliding the brick toward her. Clarke didn't seem to notice.

"It's true," she said, her voice soft and almost girlish. "I am dangerous. I'm a wild horse that no one has ever broken."

"You just need a real man," said the bishop. "Someone strong, someone who can bend you over his knee when needed."

"Ain't no strong men left, I'm afraid," she said. "Take Josh, for instance. He's a good man, but he's already got Chloe. I'm just a girl who's alone in all the world. Some days, I don't think I'll ever find anybody."

The bishop said nothing. When she looked up, she found him standing over her. Her lips were thin and straight, and his eyes were angry.

"Does that bullshit work on other people?" he asked. "I know who you are. I've seen pictures of what you've done. When I heard two of my parishioners took you in, I had to come out here and see it for myself before you killed them."

"I've never killed—"

His hand was on her throat in an instant. She grabbed his wrist with her right hand and whipped her knife toward his throat with her left. The blade glinted in the moonlight and drew a bead of red blood with its tip.

"Let go of my throat or I will open yours up," she

whispered. "And then I'll kill Chloe and Josh and everyone at that stupid compound of yours. Do not test me, old man. You won't live to regret it."

He relaxed his fingers. She kept the knife at his throat.

"You have a gun on you?" she asked.

"Holster behind my back."

She kept her left hand with the knife near his throat and reached around his waist with the right. His pistol was larger than those she usually held, but she could still fire it. She pulled it from the holster and stepped back.

"So, what do you want?" she asked.

"Believe it or not, I'm here to offer you a truce," he said. "You've killed three soldiers in the good fight. That's a stain on your soul you'll never escape, but with suitable recompense, you can avoid earthly punishment for now."

She shrugged and raised the pistol.

"I could just kill you now and pick off your followers one by one," she said. "Then I wouldn't have to worry about punishment today or tomorrow."

"You'd never escape God's wrath, though," he said. "Plus, my son will share your photograph with men and women across this great nation of ours. You'll lose your safe harbor."

She blinked.

"I could live with that," she said. "But what's your counter?"

"Work with me, and I'll assist you in whatever way I can in your work," he said. "Every organization like mine has chaff to be culled from the wheat. Since you seem to enjoy murdering men of a certain persuasion, I'll give you access to the wayward of my flock."

"I'm not interested in your flock," she said. "I'm going to kill a detective in St. Augustine. Once I've done that, you'll never see me again."

He considered and then tilted his head to the side.

"If that's your goal, I'll help you, but you've got to do a favor for me," he said. "One cop for another. There's an officer in St. Augustine County I'm tired of seeing in uniform. Marcus Washington. I want him dead. If you can help me make that happen, I'll help you with your other problem."

She already had a plan for Detective Court, but she could modify it to take out a second officer, too.

"How big is the St. Augustine County Sheriff's Department?" she asked.

"Forty or fifty officers," said Clarke. "Not very big."

He was right; it wasn't very big. If she played this right, she could take the entire department out in one swoop. She looked at Clarke.

"All right," she said. "I've got an idea to kill all our birds with one very big stone. Let's kill them all."3

36

Mathias and I took Roy for a walk at seven the next morning. Normally, my morning walks with the dog were quiet times for self-reflection, but I started to think I'd grow to enjoy sharing them with him now and then. Unfortunately, we both had jobs to do, so we couldn't goof off together in his condo all morning. At a little before eight, I kissed him goodbye, put Roy in the car, and headed out.

I hit some rush-hour traffic, but most people were driving to the St. Louis metro area instead of out of it, so I didn't slow down too much. I reached my house at nine, changed, put Roy in the dog run, and went into work.

I had two big cases, both of which were on hold pending new developments. Sasha Ingram was the FBI's responsibility, while the US Marshals Service was busy looking for Logan and Evan. Joel Robinson's murder was still my case, but I doubted I'd ever solve it. The cartel shooter who killed him was probably out of the country by now.

I was passing the dispatcher's conference room on my way to the storage room that had become my office when Trisha called out. I stuck my head in her room and smiled.

"You missed the morning briefing," she said.

"I wouldn't say I missed it."

Trisha narrowed her eyes.

"You made a joke," she said. I nodded.

"It happens sometimes."

"No, it doesn't," she said, shaking her head. "You're smiling, and you're happy. Tell me you didn't shoot George Delgado in the parking lot."

I shook my head.

"I didn't shoot the boss. I had a crappy day yesterday, but I had a nice night. That's it."

Trisha tilted her head to the side, and her own smile grew.

"I hope you have more nice nights," she said. "It's good to see you happy, Joe."

I smiled and thanked her before walking to the communal coffeepot and pouring myself a cup. Then I returned to my office, where I settled in and started writing and editing after-action reports, reading through witness statements, and ensuring that my interview notes were understandable.

The criminal justice system fed on paperwork. Ten years from now, a detective I had never met could read through my paperwork and understand everything I had done on a case, and if I did my job right, he or she could pick up that case where I left off without missing a beat. More importantly, paperwork forced us to follow the rules. That mattered to me. We didn't beat confessions out of suspects, we didn't harass witnesses until they told us what we wanted to hear, and we did our best to arrest the right people. Good paperwork showed the world that we were the good guys, and as much as I hated filling it out, it was an important part of the job.

For half an hour, I sat down and typed and read through reports. Then my cell rang. I didn't recognize the number, but I gave out a lot of business cards and received a lot of calls from strangers. I answered after two rings.

"This is Detective Joe Court. What can I do for you?"

"Morning, Detective," came a scratchy voice. "This is Bishop Clarke at the Church of the White Steeple."

I forced a smile to my lips and hoped it came through my voice.

"Good morning," I said. "What can I do for you?"

"You asked me to call you if I heard anything about that young woman, Ms. Ingram," he said. "I have it on very good authority that she's in the county right now."

I leaned back.

"Oh, yeah?" I said. "What's she doing?"

"Getting ready to kill a bunch of Mexicans at church," he said. "Darryl, a young man in my congregation, ran into her at a meeting. They hit it off as young people do, and she asked whether he'd like to become involved in her project. He told my son, and my son told me."

"What can you tell me about this plan of hers?"

"I didn't know the details, but she asked Darryl whether he had any firearms and how much ammunition he had for those firearms. She had her own guns, but she wanted to make sure he could come armed."

I nodded and felt a growing unease build inside me.

"So she planned to shoot up a church?"

"That was Darryl's impression," said Clarke. "St. David's at Nuevo Pueblo."

Nuevo Pueblo was a small town built by Ross Kelly Farms to house its immigrant workforce. The town had a company store, at least two churches, a post office, three bars, and a laundromat. The area was pretty, but the chicken-processing plant next door stunk. I nodded.

"Okay," I said. "Thanks for calling. I'll check this out."

"You had better check it out soon, miss," he said. "As I understand it, the priest at St. David's holds a Mass every morning. You don't get over there soon, you might have fifty or sixty dead Mexicans to deal with."

I didn't trust Clarke, but I doubted he was stupid enough to lie to me. If he did, I'd never listen to him again. Still, muscles all over my body twitched, and my heart had already started beating faster. This didn't feel right. Sasha Ingram had at least one neo-Nazi tattoo, but, as best I could tell, she only hunted white men. I could see a neo-Nazi shooting up a Hispanic Catholic church, but Sasha wasn't a neo-Nazi. She just played one to get close to her future victims.

"Thank you for your call, Mr. Clarke," I said. "I'll check it out."

"You stay safe, Detective Court," he said.

I thanked him again and then hung up and walked to the dispatcher's station in the conference room down the hall. Trisha looked up at me and smiled.

"Hey," she said. "You're not smiling anymore."

"I just got a tip that a white supremacist plans to shoot up the Catholic church at Nuevo Pueblo during Mass this morning."

Trisha sat straighter and began typing at her computer.

"Okay," she said, nodding, her face and voice serious. "What time is the service?"

"Soon," I said. "I'm not sure. I don't trust my tipster, but we need to check it out, anyway. Send me six officers and let them know what's going on. Also tell them I've also got some misgivings about this. Something's not right here. Put paramedics on standby. And call the security office at Ross Kelly Farms. They'll have their own armed teams, and they'll know the local area better than we do. I think they've also got surveillance cameras around."

Trisha nodded as she typed.

"I'm on it, Joe," she said. "Take an SUV and get your vest. If necessary, your SUV can act as an emergency ambulance."

It was good advice, so I nodded and grabbed a set of keys for one of the station's two unmarked SUVs.

"Thanks, Trisha."

She picked up her phone and nodded to me before dialing. I left her office and hurried down to the locker room in the basement to grab my vest. Within five minutes of Clarke's call, I was driving to Nuevo Pueblo.

Ross Kelly Farms had built Nuevo Pueblo on a rolling hundred-acre piece of property near its chicken-processing plant. I didn't know how much property the company owned, but deep woods surrounded the town and ran all the way to the Mississippi River half a mile away. A rail line led to the plant, while a two-lane piece of blacktop cut through the trees and town and to the highway.

As I approached, I found flashing blue and red lights. One of our cruisers had parked on the only road into town. There was a black SUV in front of it. Lorenzo Molina, the head of security at Ross Kelly Farms, leaned against his car and smoked a cigarette. I parked behind the cruiser and stepped out. Molina nodded when he saw me.

"Morning, Detective," he said. "I hear you're the one who got my people all worked up."

Molina was a snake who abused his position to intimidate his migrant workforce, but as best we could tell, he stopped just short of breaking the law. If he stepped over the line, he was mine, but for now, we had nothing on him.

"We received a credible threat against the church," I said. "I know you monitor your employees pretty well. Have you seen anything that would give you concern?"

He lowered his chin and narrowed his eyes.

"What do you mean by monitor?"

I rolled my eyes and pointed toward a telephone pole holding a pair of surveillance cameras not ten feet away.

"You watch your people," I said. "It's not a crime, so I don't care that you do it. I'm here to prevent someone from shooting the people who live in this town. Have you noticed anyone unfamiliar walking around lately?"

He considered me before shaking his head.

"No more than usual, but a lot of people move through here. Hikers, employees, the family members of employees. We don't know everybody. The cameras are there in case we have a problem. They provide a record of events."

"Fine," I said. "My team and I will check out the church and surrounding area and talk to the residents to see whether they've seen anything. If we can't find anything, we'll leave. Sound good to you?"

"Sounds just fine. Before you go, though, let me give you something," he said, already walking to the rear of his SUV. He pulled open the door and took out a black walkie-talkie. "This will allow you to talk to me and my team. We'll be watching everything that goes on, so if we see a threat, we'll contact you via that radio."

"That's helpful. Thank you."

"No problem, Detective," he said. "Good luck out there."

I thanked him and secretly thought, not for the first time, that he was a schmuck before turning to Marcus Washington.

"Marcus, let's get everybody together and figure out how we want to search the town."

He nodded and then tilted his head to the side to speak into the radio on his shoulder. Even as our team assembled, I looked at the woods and then the town just beyond. There was only one road in. It was a good place for a last stand. Molina thought we were wasting our time—and maybe we were—but I couldn't help but feel we were walking into a trap.

37

My team met around the hood of my SUV. Trisha had called in six uniformed officers and warned each of them to wear a bulletproof vest. Three of my colleagues carried tactical rifles, while two others had shotguns. Only Officer Katie Martelle and I carried pistols alone. Unless Sasha had an entire squad of racists with her, we'd have her outgunned, at least.

"Anybody here spent significant amounts of time in Nuevo Pueblo?"

Nobody nodded or said yes, so I continued.

"Okay," I said, turning to a piece of clean white paper on my hood. "The town's built as a simple grid and has, maybe, a hundred homes, a grocery store, a couple of bars, at least two churches, and a laundromat. I rarely make it out here, so I'm probably missing something. We'll patrol in pairs, and everyone will stay in radio contact at all times.

"We've received a tip that a woman named Sasha Ingram plans to attack worshippers at the Catholic church during Mass. Trisha's already called ahead, and the priest has cancelled the service. Sasha is in her early to mid-twenties and has black hair, light-colored skin, and multiple tattoos on her shoulders, arms, and torso. I'm told she's attractive. We believe she's committed multiple homicides, although this is the first mass shooting we've heard of her being involved in."

I took a pen from my pocket and started drawing a crude map on the paper as I spoke.

"Bob and Shane, I want you patrolling Main Street. Take your car. Emily and Marcus, take a cruiser to the Catholic church and check that out. Dave and Katie, I want you patrolling Buenaventura and Los Feliz Streets. They're residential, and hopefully you won't run into too many problems. There's only one road in and out of town, and I'll cover it in case Sasha shows up and tries to make a run for it. I'll also be coordinating with the security staff at Ross Kelly Farms.

"With any luck, nothing will happen. If you see something suspicious, though, call it in. We'll figure it out from there. Unless you need to get out to talk to somebody, stay in your cars. They'll give you some cover in case something happens. Questions?"

Nobody asked me anything, so I wished them luck and then settled into the front seat of my SUV while they did their jobs. For half an hour, I hung out in my SUV, listened to my team on the radio, and communicated with the security staff at Ross Kelly Farms. It seemed like a sleepy morning. In the entire time I sat there, nobody drove into the town, and nobody left.

Eventually, I picked up my radio.

"Hey, guys, we'll hang out for another half hour, but this is looking like a prank. Keep your eyes open, but I think we may have gotten lucky."

All three teams checked in and told me they understood. I picked up my second radio and called the security team at Ross Kelly Farms, but they had spotted nothing out of the ordinary on their surveillance system, either. This was a waste of time.

About fifteen minutes later, though, my radio crackled to life.

"Hey, Joe, you know anything about a parade down Main Street?"

I sat straighter and cocked my head to the side as I picked up my radio. It was Sergeant Bob Reitz. He was a good cop, and he knew what he was doing.

"What do you mean about a parade?"

My radio crackled again.

"Some women just led a long line of kids out of a storefront. There are, I don't know…" Bob paused. "Fourteen little kids and four adults. The kids are holding a rope. How do you want to handle this?"

"Talk to them and find out what they're doing."

I paused and heard a door open and shut. Then I waited another thirty seconds.

"Shane's out there now," said Bob. "He's with one lady, and he's looking back at me with his hands in the air like he's confused." Bob paused and then sighed. "I bet they don't speak English, and neither of us speaks Spanish."

I swore under my breath.

"Okay, Bob. Just hold on a minute," I said. I put that radio down and picked up the walkie-talkie from Ross Kelly Farms. "Hey. You guys know anything about a parade of toddlers down Main Street?"

Someone in the security office grunted.

"That's the employee daycare," came a woman's voice. "Everything's okay. They go to the church twice a week. The priest blesses them and reads them a story. Then they play on the church's front lawn."

I opened my door and stepped out.

"That's a regular thing?"

"Twice a week," she said. "The kids do better with a schedule."

I gritted my teeth and sighed.

"Sure, yeah, schedules are good. Was it not cancelled?"

The woman paused.

"I guess not," she said. "Sorry."

I tossed the radio to my SUV's front seat and picked up my police radio.

"Bob, those kids go to the daycare, and they're on their way to the church. Anybody know how to say *go inside* in Spanish?"

I waited a moment before a soft voice spoke.

"*Vamos adentro*," said Katie Martelle. "It's been a long time since I took Spanish in high school, but they should understand that."

"Good," I said. "Got that, Bob?"

"Yep," he said. "We're on it, boss."

"Good," I said. "Marcus and Emily, are you guys still at the church?"

"Yeah," said Emily. "It's all quiet here. We think the priest is inside in his office."

"Stay there and stay vigilant."

"Understood," said Emily.

I covered my mouth with my hand and breathed while I looked around. Deep woods surrounded me, but most of the trees had lost their leaves for the season, creating a thick, brown layer on the ground. The sky was blue, and the air was crisp. It was quiet.

I waited a few moments and then squinted. Something buzzed overhead. The sound was barely audible, like a bumblebee buzzing past. It wasn't summer, though, and I hadn't seen a bee or wasp for at least a month. As my eyes scanned the skyline, I found a dark spot hovering over the town and swaying in the breeze.

I kept my eyes on it so I wouldn't lose it and picked up the radio Molina had given me.

"Hey, does your surveillance team have a drone up right now?"

"No," said the lady I had spoken to earlier. "We've got cameras everywhere. We don't need a drone. Why?"

"Because there's one in the sky," I said. "Hold on."

I grabbed my police radio. The short hairs on the back of my neck stood on end, and I felt hyperaware of my surroundings.

"Shane, you're the best shot we've got in the department. Tell me you've got a rifle."

"I've got an M4 carbine," he said. "What do you need?"

My legs felt restless. I couldn't stay still, so I started pacing alongside my car.

"There's a drone over the town. Somebody's watching us. Given the circumstances, I don't like that. Take it down. Bob, try to warn the kids in the daycare that there will be a loud noise. We don't need to scare them."

Both men told me they understood. I bit my lower lip and watched. Even though I knew what was coming, I almost jumped as Shane fired. The sound echoed in the woods around me, and the drone tumbled from the sky.

"It's down."

Almost the moment Shane finished speaking, something boomed nearby. It was loud but not deafening, like a firecracker shot at a distance. My fingers trembled, and my heart pounded in my chest. I ducked down and pressed my back against my vehicle as my radio crackled to life.

"What the hell was that?" asked Bob. I held my breath and waited a minute for anyone to respond.

"It came from inside the church," said Emily, her voice strident. "The blast broke most of the windows, and there's smoke billowing out. The priest is inside. I'm getting him. Marcus is covering me."

My heartbeat raced, and I stood straighter before keying the button on my radio to clear the line.

"Stay where you are," I said, struggling to keep my voice under control. I squeezed the radio tight to keep my hands from shaking as adrenaline flowed through me. "If you hear the priest call for you, get him. If you don't, assume he's dead and stay outside. We don't know whether the building's stable. Bob and Shane, you stay with the daycare kids wherever you are. Dave and Katie, I want you at the main entrance to the town where we met earlier. I'm going to the church to evaluate it. Everybody move."

I didn't wait for a response before climbing into my SUV. Almost the moment I put the heavy vehicle into gear, a second explosion roared. This one was loud enough that it hurt my ears. Muscles all over my body fired, and without thinking, I slammed on the brakes. My ears rang, and trees around swayed around me with the shockwave. Leaves fell to the ground, and a black cloud rose above the woods.

For a second, I stayed still as my body tried to process this assault on my senses. My skin felt clammy, and muscles all over my body tingled. Then my brain caught up with the world around me.

"Fuck."

I slammed my foot down against my SUV's accelerator. The hood lifted, and the tires chirped as I rocketed forward and grabbed my radio. Adrenaline coursed through me, banishing the sense of dread and anxiety I had felt earlier.

"Sound off!" I shouted. I waited just a second and felt my heart race.

"Shane and I are okay," said Bob.

"So are Dave and me," said Katie.

As I drove, the black cloud grew larger and larger. Unsurprisingly, it was over the church. I keyed my radio's microphone.

"Emily and Marcus, are you with us?"

Nobody responded. A tremble passed through my body, and I willed my car forward, knowing I had two colleagues who were likely hurt.

Nuevo Pueblo wasn't a large community, so it only took me a few moments to reach the spot where the church had once been. Now, shards of wood, glass, nails, and other bits of broken construction materials radiated out from a shallow crater in the ground. About fifty feet from where the church once stood, I found a marked police cruiser. Debris peppered one side. Glass lay all around it, every window having been broken by either the blast's shockwave or by shrapnel.

Marcus and Emily were outside. Marcus was moving well, but Emily was immobile. I slammed on my brakes. My tires screeched, and the SUV skidded across the pavement. The moment it stopped, I threw open my door and ran toward them. Neither Marcus nor Emily even registered I was there until I was on top of them. Then they looked at me. Their eyes were open, but they looked dazed.

Emily tried to sit up, but she fell backwards. Blood trickled out of her left ear. Marcus looked better, but he had a cut on his brow and a dazed expression on his face. Their cruiser had taken the brunt of the blast, but they were clearly hurt.

"Can you hear me?" I shouted.

Marcus nodded. Emily drew in a breath, shut her eyes, and nodded.

"You sound like you're under water," she said. I looked over her chest and side to make sure she wasn't bleeding anywhere else, but she looked okay. Marcus did, too.

"I'm getting help," I said, already running to my car for my radio. I keyed the microphone. "Marcus and Emily are hurt but alive. Bob, call for a pair of ambulances."

I tossed that radio down before Sergeant Reitz could respond. Then I grabbed the radio Molina had given me.

"What have you got?"

"An explosion," said the female security officer. "I've never seen anything like it."

"I realize there was an explosion," I said, not bothering to hide my annoyance. "Someone controlled that drone, and someone triggered that explosion. She's in town. Look for her."

"Oh, sure, give me a minute," she said. As she worked, she hummed. "There's a woman I don't recognize near the laundromat on Buenaventura Street. She's got black hair, and she's wearing bright red lipstick."

"Monitor her," I said, picking up my police radio. "Bob, where are my paramedics?"

"Fifteen minutes out," he said. "This is a remote area. The sheriff is on his way, and so are Scott Hall and Kevin Owens."

"Good. Our suspect is in the laundromat. Bob and Shane, stay with the kids. Protect them and keep them inside. Katie and Dave, you're with me. The laundromat's on Buenaventura Street. We're taking Sasha down before she hurts anybody else."

38

I had no idea where I was driving, so I turned onto Main Street, then took the first left onto a side street, passing two bars and the post office before reaching a stretch of residences. I turned around and went the other direction, crossing Main Street again. This time, I passed the House of Christ Pentecostal Church. I hadn't seen it before, so I knew I was on the wrong street.

I slowed and got on the radio to the security team at Ross Kelly Farms.

"Hey, it's Joe Court. I'm in a black SUV. Where's the laundromat?"

"Buenaventura Street," came the woman's voice. "You're on the wrong street."

I clenched my jaw and sucked in a breath through my nose.

"I get that," I said. "Where is it relative to me? North? South? Northeast?"

"It's right behind the post office. Just turn around, cross Main Street, and the post office will be right there. You can't park on the street, though."

I shook my head and pressed on the accelerator.

"Ticket me."

As I crossed Main Street, I picked up the police radio.

"Katie, Dave, put on your lights and siren. Let Sasha know you're there. I'm parked in front of the post office right behind the laundromat. I'm going in through the rear."

"Understood," said Dave Skelton. I stopped in front of the post office and jumped out of the car just as a police siren began blaring on the other street. The post office shared a wall with the bar next door on one side, but a strip of well-trod dirt separated it from the house on its other side.

I took out my pistol and crouched into a shooter's stance. Ross Kelly Farms had thrown the town together without a lot of mind to longevity. The buildings had vinyl siding and exposed pier-and-beam foundations, making them look similar to the homes I had seen on floodplains. The builder saved some money over pouring a full concrete foundation, but the homes and business he constructed would have been uncomfortable in the middle of winter or the height of summer. I doubted the shareholders at Ross Kelly Farms cared.

I crept between the two buildings. There was a small courtyard with a picnic table behind the laundromat. The staff probably had lunch out there on comfortable days. Today, it was empty. A set of wooden steps led to a rear door with a large glass panel. Unfortunately, a curtain prevented me from seeing into the building. Worse, the staff had locked the door, and my pick set was in my purse.

Hopefully Dave and Katie had Sasha occupied.

I elbowed the glass hard. The window broke and tinkled to the ground, but my jacket prevented any injuries. Every part of my body wanted to move and run. My fingers tingled, and sweat dripped down the small of my back despite the cold air. I held my breath and waited, holding my firearm in front of me.

Sasha didn't come, so I reached through the hole in the glass and unlocked the deadbolt. The door opened to a storage room with wire rack shelving. The almost overwhelming scent of detergent washed over me. My heart thudded against my chest as I inched forward, being careful to avoid the glass. A flat, white door with a brushed nickel knob led outside.

"Now or never, Joe," I whispered as I grasped the knob. I twisted the knob and stepped out with my firearm held in front of me. The front of the laundromat was a big room with dryers along the walls. In the center of the floor, there were washing machines like aisles in the grocery store. A woman with black hair, porcelain skin, and bright red lipstick huddled behind one of those washing machines. She held a pistol in her right hand. Our eyes met, and she tilted her head to the side.

"Fuck," she said, a scowl on her face. She sighed. "It's you. I guess this is it, then."

"Drop your weapon!" I shouted. She didn't move, but Dave and Katie must have heard me because they came through the front door. Dave had a rifle, while Katie had her pistol. They walked down the aisle, but I motioned them back. If Sasha started firing, I didn't want anyone in the crossfire.

"He loves me, you know," she said, shaking her head. "Peter."

"Good for you," I said, slipping my finger from the trigger guard to the trigger. "Drop your weapon. You make any sudden moves, I'll shoot you. Put your gun on the floor. Then kick it to me and lie face down on the tile."

She appraised me, blinking.

"I don't know what he sees in you, anyway," she said. "I'm prettier than you, and I bet I'm a lot better in bed. You can ask your brother about that."

I shifted my right shoulder back, minimizing my profile.

"I won't ask you again. Put your weapon on the ground."

She tilted her head to the side.

"Oh yeah?" she asked, almost smiling. "What are you going to do? Shoot me? My arms are at my sides, and my weapon isn't pointing at you. I'm not a threat."

"Drop your weapon!"

This time, it was Dave Skelton. Unfortunately, he wouldn't have a clear shot unless Sasha stood. This was between me and her.

"Put it down," I said. "It's over."

"I'm not a threat to you. If you shoot me, it's murder," she said. "Then you'll be just like me."

I clenched my jaw tight and adjusted the grip on my firearm. If Dave, Katie, or I rushed at her, Sasha would shoot us, but that didn't mean I could shoot her first. Even though she hadn't listened to our clear instructions, she wasn't jittery, and she didn't seem scared or nervous. She seemed confident and relaxed. Shooting her now in these circumstances would be murder, or at least something close to it.

"If I lower my weapon, will you drop yours?" I asked.

She considered me for a moment and then looked toward the front of the store.

"Tell your partners to leave," she said. She smiled and raised her eyebrows. "Then we'll talk girl to girl. I'll think about dropping my firearm then."

I looked at Katie and Dave. Both of them nodded and began backing out of the laundromat. Outside, there were at least three police vehicles, so our backup had arrived. I locked eyes with Katie.

"Make sure the paramedics made it to Marcus and Emily. Emily has a head injury. Marcus might, too."

Katie nodded. I watched as she backed through the door. Then I looked to Sasha. My heart was beating fast.

"Why'd you go after my brothers?"

She shrugged, sat down, and drew her knees to her chest but kept her pistol pointed at the floor the entire time.

"Peter wanted you dead, but I couldn't get to you. I figured that if I killed one of your brothers, I could kill you and the rest of your family at the funeral."

She smiled, probably thinking it made her look scary. In actuality, it just made her look unhinged and stupid.

"I'm glad they're still alive," I said. "You want to surrender and kick your gun toward me, or do you want to draw this out? Maybe we can get a negotiator."

"Oh," she said brightly. "A professional negotiator could be fun. Think I could talk my way out of prison?"

"No."

She blinked a few times, and the smile slipped from her face.

"You're so goddamn boring," she said, shaking her head.

"Sane people usually are."

She nodded, although it didn't seem that she had heard me.

"I guess I've only got one play left," she said. "I didn't want it to end like this."

"Slide your firearm toward me."

She considered me and then opened her eyes wide as she shook her head. The barrel of her firearm began tilting toward me.

"Don't," I said, glancing from her firearm to her face. "Don't you do that. Don't you—"

I squeezed the trigger the instant the muzzle of her firearm pointed at me. My pistol kicked. Ten feet away, Sasha's body jumped as the round tore into her chest. She fell to her side, her eyes still open. The round probably hit her heart, so she would have been dead before she even felt the shot. My shoulders slumped, and my chest felt heavy.

Half a dozen of my colleagues in tactical vests rushed into the room. I held up my hands.

"We're clear," I said. "Suspect's down."

Dave Skelton was in front. He lowered his rifle.

"You okay, Joe?"

I nodded.

"Yeah. This is over."

As my colleagues relaxed and lowered their weapons, Sheriff Delgado entered the laundromat and looked around before walking toward me. He knelt beside Sasha and checked her pulse, but she was dead. Then he stood and looked to me.

"Can I have your firearm, Detective?" he asked.

It was standard procedure in an officer-involved shooting, so I handed it over without complaint or hesitation. He cleared the chamber and removed the magazine. Detectives from the Missouri State Highway Patrol were probably already on their way. They'd look into the shooting and determine whether it was justified. They'd also send my weapon to the state crime lab, where technicians would run ballistics on it to make sure it was my round in Sasha Ingram's chest. I wasn't worried.

Delgado sighed.

"Officer Martelle said you had the situation under control and that it looked like the victim planned to surrender."

"She didn't give up," I said. "Once Katie and Dave

left, Ms. Ingram and I spoke. I had asked her several times to drop her weapon, but she refused every time. She said she didn't understand what Peter Brunelle found fascinating about me, and then she told me she was great in bed and that I should ask my brother about it. It was a weird conversation."

Delgado nodded and crossed his arms.

"And then, once the witnesses left, you shot her."

I smiled and enunciated each word so he wouldn't misunderstand anything I had to say.

"I shot her after she raised her weapon toward me. Once I determined she was an imminent threat to my safety, I shot her to eliminate that threat."

"I see," said Delgado, looking down to her body. Sasha had slumped to the side. The weapon was on the ground near her hips. "It's interesting. Most people, when they point a weapon at somebody, extend their arms from their bodies. How was she holding it?"

"Between her legs," I said. "She was sitting with her back to a washing machine. Her feet were flat on the ground in front of her, and her legs were bent at an approximately ninety-degree angle."

Delgado considered me for a moment and then sat on the ground about fifteen feet from the body. He put his back against a washing machine and his feet flat in front of him. Then he held my pistol between his knees with both hands.

"Is this how she was sitting?"

I crossed my arms and nodded.

"Yeah," I said.

He drew in a breath and then blew a raspberry.

"You ever see anybody fire a gun from this position?"

I shook my head.

"No."

"And yet your story is that she tried," he said, grunting before blowing another raspberry. "If I wanted to shoot someone from this position, I'd raise my arm so it was in line with my eyes, and I'd sight down the barrel of my weapon. If the victim had her gun between her knees, she could point it in your general direction, but she couldn't aim it. Are you sure that's the story you want to go with?"

A cold feeling began passing through my chest and extremities.

"I'm not feeding you a story. I'm telling you what happened."

"And I'm telling you that your account makes no sense. This woman supposedly murdered multiple people. She knows what she's doing. You're an experienced officer. You know when to pull the trigger. Here, you discharged your weapon after every witness left the room, and you killed a woman who had tried to hurt your family. Then you gave me a story that doesn't make any sense. The woman you shot wasn't trying to kill you. She was trying to surrender."

My gut tightened, and I shook my head almost instinctually. Delgado leaned forward and lowered his voice.

"I heard what you said before coming to the laundromat," he said. "You broadcast it on the radio. 'We're taking Sasha down.' Those are your words."

I closed my eyes and felt some of the strength leave me. Before Sasha pointed the barrel of her weapon at me, she told me she had one play left, but she hadn't given me time to consider what that meant. Delgado was right about her hand placement. She may have been able to fire, but she couldn't have hoped to hit me. She wouldn't have heard what I said over the radio, but, contrary to what my boss thought, though, she wasn't surrendering. She was committing suicide.

I closed my eyes.

"Fuck."

"Are you admitting something?" asked Delgado. He almost looked smug. I had never understood what Delgado had against me, but from the day I had become a detective, he had shown me disdain. I hadn't realized how deep that grudge ran until now. He thought I had murdered her. Or at least he thought he could spin the shooting as a murder.

I shook my head, almost dumbfounded.

"Next time we speak, I want a lawyer in the room."

"I would, too, if I were you," he said. "Now get out of my crime scene and go home. I'll send people out to interview you at home."

39

I drove back to my station and wrote a narrative describing everything that happened at Nuevo Pueblo and what led me to go out there. Even with that written document, the detectives assigned to investigate the shooting would question me, but I was in the right. If they were at all objective, they'd see that.

Once I had the document written, I forwarded a copy to Special Agent Bryan Costa before calling him. He answered quickly.

"Hey, Joe," he said. "I just got your email, but I haven't had the chance to read the report. What's going on?"

"Sasha Ingram's dead," I said. "We received a tip she planned to shoot up a service at a Hispanic church in St. Augustine County. When we got there, we searched the town. I found a drone flying overhead. We shot it down, and then the church exploded. Moments later, there was a much larger explosion that destroyed the structure and injured two of my officers. It likely killed the priest who was inside the church."

Costa grunted.

"The first explosion was supposed to draw you to the church, and the second was supposed to kill the first responders," he said. "I bet the drone had a camera on it."

"That's likely," I said. "The area she was in had a significant surveillance system in place, so we tracked her down and found her in a laundromat. I shot her."

"Your team okay?"

"Two were injured," I said. "We called in paramedics, but I didn't get to talk to them before my boss took over. My shooting will get some scrutiny. People will talk to you about me."

"I'll tell them the truth," he said. "You're a good cop."

I forced myself to smile, but I didn't feel like I had anything to smile about.

"Thanks," I said.

The line went silent for a moment. Then Costa cleared his throat.

"What should we do about Brunelle?"

"Bury him," I said. "Lock him in a cell; deny him visitation, phone, and library privileges; and let him die alone. I'm done with him. Even if he identified his victims, the price for that knowledge would be too high. Let the dead lie. If God exists, he knows who they are. He can comfort their families."

Costa sighed.

"That'll piss off Agent Cornwell, but if that's what you want to do, I support you," he said. "Call me if I can help with Ingram."

"I will," I said. "Thanks."

I hung up a moment later and then sent text messages to Julia Green and Miriam Staley to let them know Sasha was dead, and the threats to their sons had passed. Neither of them responded, which was for the best. After that, I called my union and told them I'd need a lawyer. They promised to make the arrangements.

About three hours after going to my station to write my after-action report, I drove home. More than anything, I wanted to pet my dog and get drunk and pretend nothing bad had happened to me that day. Instead, as I arrived at my house, I found a car in the driveway. Every part of my body felt heavy, and a weariness that went beyond exhaustion pervaded even my bones.

As I parked in the driveway, the car's door opened, and a middle-aged woman stepped out. It was Krystal Alvarez. I closed my eyes and leaned my head against the seat rest behind me.

"Shit."

She knocked on my window, and I swore again before opening my door.

"This is a bad time, Ms. Alvarez. Or Ms. Robinson, or whatever your real name is," I said, stepping out of my car. As my foot hit the ground, I paused and glanced at her. "Where's your handler?"

"Justin thinks I'm in a safe house in St. Louis," she said. "The car's a rental."

I shut my door, considering her. Tears had streaked her cheeks. The whites of her eyes were bloodshot. She was about four feet from me, but I couldn't smell booze even when the breeze blew from her.

"Are you sober?"

She nodded.

"Yeah."

"I should call the marshals and tell them you're here."

She shook her head and furrowed her brow. She looked as if she were near tears.

"Please don't," she said. "They have my kids."

"Who?"

She shook her head.

"I don't know their names. They called and left me a message."

I furrowed my brow and allowed my voice to soften.

"Play me the message."

She fumbled in her purse before pulling out a phone. I waited about thirty seconds before she held the phone to me.

"Ms. Robinson, we've got Logan and Evan." The voice belonged to a woman, but I didn't recognize her. "They have no value to us. You do. Meet us, and we'll talk about letting your kids go."

I started to tell her we didn't know whether they had the kids, but she shushed me. Then a boy spoke.

"Mom, it's Logan. They haven't hurt us. Evan's scared. They killed Dad. I don't know what to do."

I squeezed my jaw tight and sighed as the first woman came back on the phone.

"If you want them alive, call us. Only you can save

your kids. If you come to us, they'll walk away and live long, happy lives. If not, we will kill them both."

Then the line went dead. I crossed my arms and looked at Krystal.

"Did you call them back?"

She shook her head.

"Not yet. I thought you'd want to. I need your help, Detective. If I told Justin about this call, he'd only want to move me to Alaska or something. I need my kids back. If it means I have to do the exchange, I will. I just want my kids safe."

She was pleading again. I didn't like to hear anyone beg.

"We'll talk about this inside. I've got to feed my dog."

She nodded and followed me around to the back of my house, where Roy was waiting in the dog run. His tail wagged hard when he saw me. Despite everything that had happened that day, I smiled when I saw him. I opened the gate and knelt in front of him. He licked my face and hands.

"Hey, buddy," I whispered. "I missed you, too."

Normally, I would have thrown a ball to him or changed to go for a walk with him, but I had Krystal Robinson with me, which meant I had work to do. The three of us went inside. I changed the water in Roy's bowl and put on a pot of coffee before sitting at my kitchen table. Krystal sat across from me.

"Play me the message again."

She pulled out her purse and played it. This time, I

took notes. For the first couple of playthroughs, I focused on the voice. I didn't recognize the woman, but she sounded confident. Logan sounded scared, but he didn't share any details that would tell me where he was. He had to be close, though, to do an exchange.

After I got everything I could out of the voices, I started focusing on the ambient noise. There were bells in the background. It wasn't just random ringing, either. Someone was playing a song, but I couldn't make it out.

"Stay here," I told Krystal. "I'll be right back."

She nodded, so I went to my bedroom and searched for the earbuds that came with my iPod. Once I plugged those earbuds into the phone and put them into my ears, the rest of the world seemed to disappear. Krystal put her arms on the table and lay her head down. I ignored her and listened, focusing on the bells in the background. They were playing a song. I listened again and again. Then, things clicked, and I listened to it once more. This time, I hummed along.

Krystal looked up.

"Why are you humming the theme to *Game of Thrones*?"

"Because that's the song in the background," I said. "It's coming from an instrument called a carillon. They're rare and expensive, but we've got one in town in the old Methodist church. Music students from Waterford College held a concert on Halloween and played the theme to Harry Potter and a bunch of other movies."

She shrugged.

"So what?"

"It means there's a good chance your kids are in town," I said. "And if they're in town, there's a chance we can find them. Let's go to my station. We'll figure this out."

She blinked a few times and focused on me.

"Are you going to call Justin?"

I considered but shook my head.

"No, but I'll bring in the FBI, though. We could use their resources."

"Not the marshals," she said. "I want my kids back."

"That's everybody's goal. If you want to help, do what we say, and start praying."

40

Krystal and I drove to my station, and once I got her settled into my office, I got the wheels moving on getting her kids back. Trisha traced the phone number and confirmed that the call was placed in St. Augustine. Unfortunately, the phone used to place the call was so old it didn't have a GPS chip, which forced us to triangulate its location based on the cell towers it connected to. That gave us a general location, but we couldn't get any closer than that. The bad guys knew what they were doing.

Special Agent Costa was at Nuevo Pueblo, supervising an FBI forensics team, but once I called him and explained the situation in town, he agreed to come in and offer whatever help he could. Sheriff Delgado promised Krystal that our department would do everything in our power to help her out. With limited resources and time, I didn't know what that would amount to, but Krystal seemed to appreciate hearing it.

At a little after nine, Krystal called the kidnappers back while we sat around the small conference table in my boss's office. The phone rang twice before a woman answered.

"I didn't think you would call. It's good to hear from you, Krystal."

The kidnapper sounded calm and confident. That was good. If she thought she were in charge, she'd be less prone to making irrational moves.

"Hi," said Krystal, her voice wavering. We had given her a script, but we couldn't anticipate everything the kidnappers would ask her. Hopefully she'd be okay improvising a little. "Please let my kids go. They're good boys. They wouldn't hurt anybody."

"They do seem like good boys," she said. "They're resourceful, too. We caught them in Houston. They were trying to go home."

Both Agent Costa and Sheriff Delgado glanced at me. If true, that changed the case. By taking the kids across state lines, the kidnappers had committed a federal crime, which put this within the FBI's jurisdiction. Knowing my boss, he'd shut this down as soon as the phone call ended.

I smiled at Krystal as my stomach tightened into a knot. Even with an FBI presence in town for the bombing at Nuevo Pueblo, it'd take them several hours to get up to speed on the case. Logan and Evan didn't have that kind of time.

"Houston isn't their home," said Krystal, shaking her head. "We live in St. Augustine."

"I don't care," she said. "Your kids are a means to an end. You're the goal. We want you."

"Please just let my kids go."

"We will," said the woman. "As soon as you're in our custody, your kids will walk. You have my word."

Krystal looked to me and then Agent Costa. He nodded and pointed to a line on the script we had given her.

"Um," she began. "I'll turn myself in, but I need time. The marshals put me in a safe house. I don't know where I am. I don't even know if I'm still in Missouri. Give me twenty-four hours."

"You have until midnight. You got a pen?"

Krystal looked up. Costa nodded and handed her a pen and paper.

"Yeah," she said.

"Meet us at the following coordinates. Thirty-seven degrees, fifty-six minutes, thirty-four seconds north. Ninety degrees, zero minutes, fifty-one seconds west. Come alone, or we will kill you and everyone with you before slitting Logan's and Evan's throats."

She hung up before Krystal could respond. The room went quiet. Costa looked to Trisha.

"Work with the bad guy's phone carrier to triangulate the call," he said before looking to Sheriff Delgado. "Find out where those coordinates are."

Delgado held up his hands as if he were directing a bunch of kids to stop running in a crowded hallway.

"Let's just take it easy and talk this through first," he said, not taking his eyes from Costa's. "I don't mind helping the federal government, but we're all jumping into the pool before checking how deep the water is. It seems like my station's providing an awful lot of resources for a federal crime."

Agent Costa nodded.

"I didn't realize this was a federal crime," he said. "I'll call in a team from St. Louis, but it'll take time for them to get here. These kids will die unless we get them."

"But they said they'd let them go," said Krystal. "If I turn myself in, they'll let my boys go. Let's just do that. You don't need to fight. I'll just go with them. As long as my boys live, it doesn't what happens to me."

Costa looked at me with a pained expression on his face. I looked down to the floor and forced a tight smile to my lips before speaking.

"There won't be a handoff," I said. "Your boys are bait. Once you take that bait, your boys cease to have value."

She furrowed her brow.

"If they don't have value, why don't they just let them go? It's easy. Logan and Evan can walk away. They could even leave the boys somewhere and then come see me."

I shook my head.

"That won't happen," I said. "As soon as the bad guys see you, they'll kill your boys so they can't identify anyone. Then they'll take you hostage. If they don't kill you immediately, they'll take you somewhere, torture you for information, and then kill you."

"You don't know that," she said, shaking her head. "They said they wouldn't."

I glanced to the sheriff.

"Can you take her outside while I talk with Agent Costa?"

The sheriff hesitated but then put an arm on her shoulder.

"Ma'am, why don't you come with me?"

She didn't look as if she wanted to go, so he pulled upward until she stood. Then he escorted her out. Costa looked to me again.

"Let's get some maps, and we'll talk tactics. I've got to call a team."

I nodded my agreement, and he pulled out his phone to make some calls. My station had old highway maps and surveyor's maps, but they were all in storage in the basement. I didn't want to dig for an hour in a dark, dusty room just to find a forty-year-old map that would have been so outdated it was useless, so I went to my office, downloaded a detailed road map of the town, and then printed it on eight separate sheets of paper that I then taped together.

When I got back to the sheriff's office, Costa was still on the phone, but he hung up as I laid my cobbled-together map on the conference table.

"My assistant's putting together a tactical team for us. Tell me what we know about the bad guys."

"They're not stupid," I said. "They're armed, they're dangerous, and they're professional enough to use a cell phone so old we can't use GPS to track it down. We have to triangulate its position with the cell phone towers it's connected to."

"What'd we learn from their conversation with Krystal?"

"Not much," I said, shaking my head. "The call earlier had bells, though. I think they were from the Methodist church in St. Augustine."

"Show me where the church is."

I studied the map for a moment until I found it.

"It's here," I said, pointing to a spot in the southeast corner of town. "The Mississippi River is half a block east. There's a big hill to the south, a residential neighborhood to the north, and a grocery store and commercial area to the west."

"So they're not to the east of the church unless they're on a boat," said Costa. "The hill to the south would muffle the sound of bells in that directions, so they're not to the south, either. Our search area is pie-shaped, north to west. What's there?"

"Houses to the north and northwest," I said, looking at the map. "There are a lot of businesses with a lot of foot traffic to the west."

"Excellent," said Costa. "These bad guys have two boys. One's a freshman in high school. A kid that age can make a lot of noise, so they'll maintain a low profile. I'm betting they're in a house or abandoned building. You know a good realtor?"

"I know a mediocre one," I said.

"Call him and get a list of every home for sale in that area," said Costa. "We'll send officers out to check each one. If the kids are still alive, I bet they're there."

"That's assuming the bad guys haven't moved since they called Krystal this afternoon," I said. "If you had kidnapped two people and then tried to set up a swap for a third person, wouldn't you be moving so the police wouldn't catch up to you?"

"Not if I were in a safe spot," said Costa. "Moving two strong, healthy boys is risky. You screw up even a bit, one of those kids could bolt or scream, and then you'd have an entire police department on top of you."

It made sense, so I nodded and hurried to my office. Rather than call my old realtor and have him try to sell me a more expensive piece of property, I went to his website and searched for every house for sale in those areas. The town of St. Augustine had a hundred and forty-three homes for sale, forty-five of which were in our search area. I printed out a list and hurried back to the conference room. Costa stared at his phone.

"I looked up the coordinates," he said. "It's an open field. If we show up there in force, they'll see us a mile away."

"Our best bet is to find the kids now, then," I said, glancing at my watch. "It's ten thirty. Assuming the bad guys leave to go to the field at a quarter to midnight, we've got an hour and fifteen to check forty-five houses."

Costa nodded and started walking toward the door. "Then let's go. We don't have time to waste."

41

Despite his belief that this was a federal case now and should be worked by the federal government, Delgado assigned twelve officers to me. I split them into six teams and gave them each six to seven empty houses to search. If they found signs that there were people inside, they were to look in the windows, talk to the neighbors to see whether they had seen anyone coming and going, and then to call me.

Agent Costa and I had our own list of seven houses to check out, so we weren't sitting on the sidelines. The first three were empty and dark. The fourth house had a few lights on, so I looked in the windows while Agent Costa visited the neighbors. From the neighbor's description, it sounded like the lights were on a timer, and since I saw nothing when I peered through the windows, we moved on.

While we were driving to the fifth house on the list, Paul Tidwell, one of our uniformed officers, called to let us know he and Carrie Bowen had found a house we should check out. It had a light on when they arrived, but then the light turned off, so we knew the house had people inside.

Carrie talked to the neighbors, and one described seeing an unfamiliar couple and two younger people going into the home through the back door. She thought the home had sold, so she even baked cookies to welcome the new family to the neighborhood. When she knocked on the door, they didn't answer. The neighbor couldn't identify Logan and Evan from the picture on Carrie's phone, but her description was close. It was the best lead we had.

Agent Costa and I met six uniformed officers about a block from the house. Three of the uniformed officers carried tactical shotguns, but the other three had just their service pistols.

"Okay, you guys know the story," I said, leaning against Agent Costa's SUV. "We're looking for Logan and Evan Alvarez. They've been abducted by a still unknown number of armed assailants. We do not know the capabilities of these assailants, but we can assume they're dangerous and will not hesitate to shoot. Protect yourselves, protect your team, and protect the boys if you find them.

"Carrie and Paul, I want you in the backyard watching the exit. Everybody else, we're going through the front doors. Stay with your partner at all times and watch each other's backs. We'll search room by room. Check every corner and closet. Questions?"

Nobody had questions, so we settled into position. The house was a white Federalist with black shutters and elaborate dentil molding on the roofline. Each of the five windows facing the street had a big cornice, and the narrow front door was inset, creating an overhang that would keep the rain from the heads of people as they knocked.

This wasn't an expensive part of town, but the home was pretty and well kept. I didn't want to kick down a front door that had likely survived the Civil War, but we didn't have much of a choice. My team lined up outside. Scott Hall would go in first because as the largest member of our team, he'd have the least trouble kicking the door in. Shane Fox and the rest of our team would follow.

My muscles tingled. I could feel the weight of my bulletproof vest, the cold of the air on my skin, the textured grip of my pistol. The air smelled of damp. Somewhere up the road, a car drove past. Shane held up a hand with five fingers. Then he started counting down. I drew in breaths to calm my racing heart. When Shane got to zero, Scott reared back and kicked the door hard enough that the sound echoed around us.

"Police officers!"

Scott's baritone voice bellowed, and the team rushed inside like water down a drain. The instant each of us crossed the threshold, we announced ourselves as police officers so no one inside could mistake us for home invaders or something similar. A staircase in the entryway led to the second floor, while a hallway led straight ahead to a kitchen. There was a sitting room to our right. Scott Hall and Shane Fox hurried forward to secure the kitchen, while Agent Costa and I headed to the right to check out the sitting room. Katie Martelle and Bill Wharton took the stairs to the second floor.

"Clear!" shouted Shane from the kitchen. I drew in a sharp breath as Agent Costa and I entered the sitting room. A family of four huddled in the corner. A middle-aged man had his arm around everybody.

"Hands in the air!" I shouted. "Hands up! Now!"

They didn't move.

"*Manos arriba*!" said Agent Costa.

They turned and raised their hands. Scott and Shane came through the attached dining room with their weapons raised while Katie and Bill continued clearing the second floor. Scott flashed a light at our detainees. The man was thirty-five or forty. The woman was a little younger. The kids were young teenagers.

"*Nos rendimos*," said the man, his hands shaking. I looked to Costa. He lowered his pistol.

"They're surrendering," he said. "These aren't our suspects. They're squatters."

I lowered my weapon.

"Shit."

We took the family into custody and questioned them. The man was Angel Hernandez, and he and his family had moved into the house after he lost his job at Ross Kelly

Farms a week earlier. Since he no longer worked at the chicken-processing plant, he had lost access to his company-provided house in Nuevo Pueblo. They had only planned to stay at the house until they could rent an apartment in town.

My muscles felt weak as I leaned against Costa's SUV.

"What time is it?" I asked.

Costa looked to his watch.

"Twenty to midnight," he said. He sighed, took out his cell phone, and dialed a number before motioning me to stand beside him. Since he had the phone on speaker, I heard it ring twice before someone picked up. "Where are you?"

"We're at the coordinates, but we're not seeing movement."

Costa nodded and looked to me. Since we already had teams of uniformed officers knocking on doors in St. Augustine, Agent Costa's team from St. Louis had volunteered to secure the site where the bad guys wanted to make the exchange. They had brought forward-looking infrared field glasses, cameras, and six FBI agents with tactical experience. Assuming they were coming, the bad guys would be there in the next twenty minutes.

"Lie low and observe," he said. "We need an accurate assessment of what we're up against."

"Understood."

Costa wished his team luck before hanging up. As he put his phone in his pocket, he glanced at me.

"What do you want to do?"

I shrugged.

"Stay here and hope for the best," I said. "That's all we can do. They're twenty minutes away, so we wouldn't make it before the drop-off time."

Costa considered me and then nodded and leaned against his SUV.

"Lousy day all around," he said. "I'm glad you weren't hurt out at Nuevo Pueblo and that your officers survived."

"Would have preferred if Sasha lived, but I'm glad the threat's over," I said. "Brunelle's done. I don't want to talk about him anymore."

Costa nodded, and we settled into an easy silence for a few minutes. Then my phone rang. I answered without looking at the screen.

"Yeah?"

The voice that answered belonged to Sergeant Bob Reitz.

"Hey, Joe," he said. "We've searched every house on the list and have found no signs of habitation in any of them except the one we raided already. Are you sure they were here?"

I started to respond but stopped when I heard a rumble on his end that was loud enough it would have drowned out anything I had to say. I waited until it passed before speaking again.

"No. We weren't sure," I said. "It was an educated guess. What was that rumbling noise?"

"A semi. I'm out by The Village Pantry. They were unloading bread at the loading dock."

The Village Pantry was our local grocery store. It wasn't a big store, but it had a good deli and decent produce. My mind had scrambled far beyond the store, though. I furrowed my brow.

"I appreciate the work you put in, Bob," I said, "but I've got to go."

I hung up before Sergeant Reitz could say anything. Then I looked to Costa.

"Two days ago, I read Agent Cornwell's notes on Brunelle. He confessed to three murders and said he had killed all three of them in the back of his company truck. It was enclosed, private, and portable, and it never looked out of place when parked near a construction site."

Costa furrowed his brow and nodded, but then straightened as he realized what I was getting at.

"You think our bad guys might have been keeping Logan and Evan in the back of a truck."

"Or something similar," I said. "They could have gagged them, tied them up, and thrown them in back. No one would have noticed. And if they had parked near that grocery store or the hardware store, nobody would have thought anything of them. They'd look like delivery drivers."

Costa considered and then crossed his arms.

"Call your sergeant back and ask whether there are any other big trucks loitering around."

I nodded and did as he asked. Bob, unfortunately, told me no, so I thanked him and looked at the FBI agent.

"There aren't many places you could hide a semi or

panel van in town," I said. "The railroad company has a big yard, but it's out in the boonies, and I don't think you can get a steady cell signal there. There's a diesel mechanic who works in a shop out in Dyer, but I bet he'd notice if there were an unfamiliar truck in his yard all day. Then there's Vic Conroy's truck stop and his strip club. Their parking lots are right beside each other, and hundreds of trucks move through each of them a day. If I had a truck to hide, that's where I'd put it. Even if a truck stayed a week, you'd never notice."

Costa nodded.

"We don't have a lot of time," he said. "If we get over there now and block the exit, we might stop them from leaving."

"Then let's go," I said, already hurrying around the back of the big SUV to reach the passenger side. Costa climbed into the driver's seat and put the vehicle in gear as soon as I had my door shut. As we drove, I called my station.

"Hey, it's Joe. I'm with Special Agent Bryan Costa. I need uniformed officers in marked cruisers at Vic Conroy's truck stop. We need to stop every truck leaving and inspect their cargo. Logan and Evan could be there."

Jason Zuckerburg, our dispatcher, typed for a moment before grunting.

"We're spread a little thin already," he said. "I'm calling in some help, but it might take a while."

"We don't have time," I said. "Just get them there as quickly as possible."

"Will do," said Zuckerburg. "Before you go, though, we've got a problem here. Krystal disappeared."

I blinked and shook my head, hoping I had misheard him.

"What do you mean she disappeared?"

"She and I were in the conference room, and then she said she had to go to the bathroom," said Zuckerburg. "Ten minutes later, I went to check on her, but she was gone."

"Damn it," I said. "Tell me you've got her cell phone, at least."

"I don't."

I clenched my jaw tight before swearing again.

"She's going after her kids," I said. "She thinks if she turns herself in, her kids will walk free. Call Bob Reitz and have him search the neighborhood for her. She can't have gotten far."

"Will do."

"Good," I said. I hung up the phone and looked to Costa. "Krystal Robinson is on the run. We need to find her kids before the bad guys catch her and make them expendable."

Instead of answering, Costa flicked on his SUV's siren and lights and floored the accelerator. I hoped it'd be enough.

42

When Agent Costa and I arrived at the truck stop, a pair of cruisers from the Highway Patrol had parked at each of its two exits, and six semitrailer trucks had lined up to leave a gravel parking lot the size of three to four football fields. Sodium lamps on tall aluminum poles lit parts of the lot but left other parts in shadow. I estimated there were well over a hundred trucks parked, many of which still had their engines idling.

Costa and I parked on the side of the road. I popped out and jogged toward the two nearest cruisers. A uniformed sergeant with the Highway Patrol nodded to me.

"Evening. You local?" he asked.

I nodded.

"Detective Joe Court, St. Augustine County Sheriff's Department," I said. "You searched the trucks yet?"

"Two so far," he said, nodding. "We hear you've got some missing kids. Is that right?"

"Yeah," I said, looking toward the SUV to see where Agent Costa was. He was carrying a thick plastic case as he walked toward me. I focused on the sergeant again.

"Someone abducted two boys from St. Augustine, and it's possible they're all hiding in the back of a semi. If they're here, we need to find them."

The sergeant nodded and crossed his arms.

"What's the truck look like?"

I sighed and shook my head.

"We don't even know if they're in a truck. To be honest, we're grasping at straws and hoping to get lucky. We've got about twenty minutes to find these kids, and they may or may not be here. If we don't find them, they will die."

The sergeant drew in a breath and nodded.

"Understood," he said. "If my department can do anything else to help, let me know."

"You're doing everything we can ask for already," I said. "Stop and search every truck before it leaves. We don't care about contraband, so you don't have to be too thorough. We're looking for kids."

The sergeant nodded and wished me luck before turning to rejoin a colleague at the checkpoint. I looked to Agent Costa, and he held up his case.

"It's a forward-looking infrared camera," he said. "We use it for surveillance. It should help us out here."

I nodded, and he opened the case on the Highway Patrol officer's trunk. Inside, foam hugged a device that looked almost like a small, black telescope. Costa pulled it out, flicked a switch on the side, and held it to an eye before twisting a focusing knob near the lens. Then he handed it to me. I held it over my left eye and closed my right. The camera showed me a world of reds, oranges, blues, purples, and every color in between. Agent Costa appeared in an orange hue, while the Highway Patrol trooper in the back of a truck appeared red.

I handed the scope back to the special agent.

"Have you only got the one camera?" I asked. He tilted his head to the side and gave me a tight smile.

"They're about ten thousand dollars," he said. "Even the federal government's budget has limits."

I nodded and raised my eyebrows.

"Better not break it, then."

He grunted, and, for the next ten minutes, we walked up and down the aisles of trucks. Costa checked out the trailers, while I peered into the cabs. I saw a lot of sleeping truckers, but I didn't see Logan or Evan. Unfortunately, Agent Costa had no more luck than I did. After ten minutes and after scanning about forty trucks, we met near the back of a semi to regroup and rethink.

"Are we wasting our time here?" I asked.

Costa shrugged.

"I can't say," he said, pulling his phone from his pocket. He ran a finger across the screen and scrolled through his messages before glancing up at me. "No one has showed up at the coordinates they gave us. The bad guys are still out there."

I nodded and pulled out my phone to read my text messages.

"Some uniformed officers from my department found Krystal Robinson three blocks from our station.

She was trying to steal a car."

Costa sighed and looked down.

"She trying to make it to the drop-off point and get her kids?"

"That's what it looks like," I said. "Jason, my dispatcher, says Krystal is begging everyone to let her go. They had to put her in restraints so she wouldn't hurt herself."

Costa nodded but said nothing. I paused and blinked a few times.

"This won't work, will it?" I asked, looking around. Dozens of trucks had parked around us, and more entered and left the checkpoint every few minutes. "Logan and Evan's abductors could have called Krystal from St. Augustine but then parked in a rest stop fifty miles up the road. Or maybe they're in a house we missed. Maybe they're in a car." I paused. "Maybe the kids are already dead."

Costa considered me for a moment before nodding.

"That's all possible," he said. "It doesn't change our job, though. We're here, and we need to keep working."

"That's not the pep talk I was hoping for," I said.

"I don't make pep talks," he said. "We get one shot at this. If we do it right and the kids don't make it, we'll at least know we did our best. I can sleep with that on my conscience. If we quit now, we'll both regret it. I don't think I could live with that."

I sighed and nodded.

"Me, either. Let's keep going, then."

Costa put his phone in his pocket and lifted the

infrared scope to his eye again as we resumed our search. In the next five minutes, we scanned twenty-four additional trucks and found nothing. I kept expecting my phone to ring with news, but nobody contacted me. My mouth held a sour taste, and my heartbeat felt sluggish. Agent Costa glanced in my direction now and then, but I avoided making eye contact. With every moment and every truck we searched, my certainty rose. These kids were dead.

Then we approached a truck that looked like a big moving van. Someone had stenciled a giant black and white cow onto the side. The cab was empty, but when Agent Costa looked through his scope at the trailer, he straightened and looked at me.

"You see something?" I asked.

He shook his head.

"No. I can't see inside at all. It's insulated."

I looked closer and pointed toward the roofline.

"There's a refrigeration unit above the cab," I said. "It's not on, though."

Costa considered.

"If they're moving milk or cheese, they'd keep the refrigerator running at all times, even in this weather," he said. "You don't park a truck like this overnight, either. It's for local deliveries."

I licked my lips and nodded.

"Maybe the driver made his deliveries and parked here and went to the strip club."

"Maybe," said Costa. "But I doubt it. The strip club's

got plenty of room for trucks."

He was right. My stomach felt fluttery as I nodded and started circling to the rear of the truck. The vehicle's rolling rear door was down, but the driver hadn't locked it with a padlock. Based on what we had seen so far, that was unusual. My heart beat faster, and a tingle spread from my fingertips to my wrists.

I nodded toward the door handle.

"No lock," I said, my voice low. "You think it's empty?"

"Maybe," said Costa. "You see the driver?"

I shook my head.

"Nope."

Costa considered and then placed his very expensive scope on the rear bumper of a nearby trailer. Then he took his pistol from its holster and glanced at me. I pulled out my firearm and checked to see that I had a round in the chamber before reaching to the milk truck's rear door handle. Before doing anything, I glanced to Agent Costa. He shifted his weight and aimed at the rear door. Then he nodded that he was ready, and I pulled hard and flung the door up.

Every muscle in my body quivered. We found three people: two boys and a woman. Silver duct tape secured the boys' arms and legs like shackles. A strip of black tape covered their mouths. The woman shot to her feet. She was older than me but not by a lot. The kids squirmed, but I couldn't focus on them.

"Federal officer!" shouted Costa. "Hands up!"

The woman's eyes shot to me and then to Agent Costa. She had a weapon in a holster on her hip. I slipped my finger to the trigger.

"Don't do it!" I shouted. "Hands up!"

She considered and then raised her hands. My shoulders relaxed a little, but muscles all over my body quivered.

"Drop to your knees," I said. "Then bend at the waist and lie on the ground."

The boys squirmed even harder. It looked like one of them was trying to shout something, but the tape over his mouth prevented him from speaking. He grunted, though, and kept kicking his legs as if he were trying to get my attention as he wormed his way toward the tailgate. I furrowed my brow at first, but then followed his gaze over my shoulder.

Then I saw the woman's partner.

He was thirty-five or forty, and he had olive-colored skin and muscles that stretched his sweater tight across his frame. He had dropped his left foot back and turned so that his profile was to me. His black pistol was aimed right at us.

"Shit!"

I dropped to a knee and fired without aiming. The shot went wide, but it was enough to throw him off. He squeezed his trigger twice and then ran but not before Agent Costa dove to the ground beside me. Before I could turn, the woman in the truck sprinted forward. Her footsteps pounded against the ground, so I spun around and stood in time to see Logan stretch out on the ground to trip her.

Her feet hit the kid's thigh, and she fell straight forward with a hard thud. Agent Costa stood and pointed in the direction the man had run.

"Get him. I'll get her."

I nodded and ran as the FBI agent stood and pulled himself into the back of the truck using handles built into the trailer's frame. By then, several uniformed Highway Patrol officers were sprinting toward us from their checkpoints. I ignored them and focused on the shooter. He was already halfway across the parking lot and running toward the strip club next door.

"Stop!" I screamed. He didn't stop, though. Instead, he whipped his arm around and fired, forcing me to duck behind a semitrailer. Three people waiting in line to get into the club started running, and the Highway Patrol officers dove behind their vehicles. Then someone shouted. Two more shots rang out. I peered around the truck. The shooter had run, but the club's bouncer lay on the ground.

"He went inside!" I yelled toward the patrolman. They pushed themselves up and followed me as I ran to the strip club. Five or six people huddled behind cars in the club's parking lot, but otherwise nothing moved. The rhythmic thud of music with a heavy bass line wafted through the open door. I doubted the clubgoers had heard the gunfire.

I sprinted forward and slowed only when I reached

the front door. The bouncer had a gunshot wound to his chest. Blood had already begun pooling around him. The Highway Patrol officers slowed beside me.

"Call an ambulance," I said. "I'm going in."

I didn't wait for them to respond. Dancers, truckers, and even men in suits crowded the interior of the dark, smoky club. The music was so loud I could feel it thump into my chest. Two naked women writhed together on the stage, while a third swung from a pole. There were dozens of small, round cocktail tables strewn about the room and maybe sixty men and women inside. The shooter must have pushed his way through the crowd because there were several people—including two cocktail waitresses—on the floor.

My lungs felt tight. I peered around the room for the shooter, but I couldn't find him. The bartender whistled for my attention and pointed toward a dark back hallway. It led to the restrooms, kitchen, and manager's office. I nodded and pushed through the crowd. My feet crunched on broken glass and a cocktail waitress's tray. Thankfully, people were already helping each other up, not understanding that the man who knocked them down had already shot at multiple people outside.

Then, when I was about halfway across the main floor, a heavy boom reverberated through the club. I dropped to a crouch—as did most people around me. The music kept playing, but the dancers froze. Then they dove behind the curtain at the rear of the stage. The noise was a gunshot. For a second, nobody moved.

Then people jumped from their tables and chairs and started pushing toward the exits. I tried to fight them at first, but it felt as if I were swimming against the tide. They'd knock me down and trample me if I kept trying to move through them head-on, so I slipped to the side until I reached the bar. At least I could hold on and stand there.

I held my breath as the club emptied. The club's patrons had knocked over tables, chairs, and drinks in their haste to leave, but no one lay on the ground. A few stragglers near the private rooms in back remained, but even they were leaving. Near the back hall, I saw Vic Conroy, the club's owner and St. Augustine County's resident gangster, standing with a double-barreled shotgun against his shoulder. He motioned me over.

I jogged across the room and nodded.

"He come back here?"

Conroy nodded.

"Yep. How's Gary?"

"Is Gary the bouncer?" I asked, lowering my chin.

Conroy nodded.

"I saw the shooting on my security system. Is he alive?"

"He was, last I checked," I said. "Paramedics should be on their way."

Conroy looked over his shoulder and then back to me.

"A big guy came into my office with a gun. I shot him in the chest."

I looked past him to a body on the ground. It was the

guy I had chased, but now he had a hole in his chest the size of a softball where his heart should have been. I looked to Conroy.

"Have you seen him before?"

He shook his head.

"Nope."

"I need your firearm," I said, holding out my hand. He handed me the gun.

"Are you going to arrest me?"

"No," I said. Conroy considered and then nodded.

"Can you tell me who he was?"

"It doesn't matter now," I said, holstering my pistol. "He's dead."

43

Krystal Robinson, Sheriff Delgado, and about a dozen uniformed officers from my department descended on the truck stop's parking lot about ten minutes after the shooting. Shortly after that, Agent Costa's team of FBI agents arrived from their position out in the middle of nowhere. Krystal Robinson held her kids and cried and thanked everyone she saw. Logan and Evan seemed a little reluctant to hug her at first, but then they started crying, too, and clung to their mom's side.

I watched while Kevius Reed, Darlene McEvoy, and two FBI forensic technicians combed the truck stop's parking lot for evidence. Two additional FBI forensic technicians were at the strip club. It was a big crime scene, and Vic Conroy had already complained about the disruption to his businesses. Lucky for him, the underage prostitutes who worked the truck stop had run the moment the Highway Patrol had arrived, or he would have been in jail beside Gloria Sanchez, the female kidnapper. Gloria's husband, Diego, was in the back of a federal coroner's minivan.

After a team from the FBI's Office of Professional

Responsibility interviewed us, Agent Costa and I sat in the front seat of his SUV. I wanted to go home, but Sheriff Delgado had questions for us he thought deserved immediate answers. After everything that had happened, I felt too drained to fight him. Not only that, my mind wouldn't stop working.

"You cold?" asked Costa, glancing at me as I leaned forward. I shook my head but said nothing. "You've got your thinking face on."

My lips crept upward.

"I've got a thinking face?"

He nodded.

"Yep. And it's the one you had on a moment ago. We did well today. Logan and Evan are safe, Gloria Sanchez is in jail, and the Robinson family's back together."

I nodded and slipped my hands into my pockets and tried to force the frown from my face.

"I guess you're right," I said.

Costa crossed his arms.

"That's not your I-guess-you're-right face."

Briefly, my frown disappeared as I smiled.

"I have one of those, too?"

He nodded.

"Yep. What's on your mind?"

I considered him and then looked out over the parking lot.

"Dinner."

"You're hungry?" asked Costa, bemused.

"No," I said, shaking my head. "Diego Sanchez was.

Gloria stayed with the boys while Diego bought dinner at the diner inside the truck stop. When he saw us, he set three Styrofoam containers of fried chicken, mashed potatoes, and coleslaw on the ground and then pulled his firearm."

"Who told you about the food?"

"Darlene McEvoy," I said "She's in charge of my department's forensics lab. The Highway Patrol was interviewing you when she told me, so you didn't hear. They're trying to piece together everything that happened prior to the shooting."

"Okay," said Costa, drawing in a breath. "Why is the food important?"

"Because it tells us they didn't intend to go to the coordinates they sent us," I said. "They weren't trying to pick Krystal Robinson up. It looks like they were planning to hang out in a truck stop parking lot and eat fried chicken."

"We'll ask Gloria and Krystal," he said. "It's possible they made alternative arrangements when Krystal disappeared from your station."

"That is possible," I said, nodding and raising my eyebrows. "Why are Logan and Evan alive, though? The instant Krystal agreed to swap herself for them, Diego and Gloria should have killed them. When Krystal showed up to do the exchange, they could ambush her, dump the bodies, and move on with their lives. Keeping them alive exposed them to unnecessary risk. It was stupid."

Costa nodded.

"Maybe they didn't want to murder children."

I shook my head.

"Krystal testified against a drug cartel. They don't hire squeamish kidnappers. Diego and Gloria kept these boys alive for a reason. There's something else going on here."

Costa looked out over the parking lot but said nothing as he considered the scene. Then he nodded to me again.

"We'll interview Gloria and see what she has to say. We've got a lot of work still ahead of us to tie up the loose ends, but we'll get it done."

"You might have to do it without me," I said, glancing at my boss, who was standing on the periphery of the crime scene near a lieutenant from the Highway Patrol. "I think my boss plans to charge me with the murder of Sasha Ingram."

"Didn't she pull a gun on you?"

I nodded and looked down.

"I told her to surrender multiple times, but she refused. Then she tilted her gun at me, but her position on the floor was awkward. Sheriff Delgado thinks the evidence shows that she was trying to surrender and that I murdered her because she came after my brothers. Before going to the laundromat where she died, I said something on the radio about getting her."

Costa grimaced.

"What'd your colleagues say?"

I shook my head.

"I sent them away, so they didn't see anything. Sasha wanted to talk one on one. I thought that was my best chance to force her to surrender."

Costa drew in a breath through his nose but said nothing for at least a minute. Then he glanced at me.

"Your boss is a dick, but you need a lawyer."

"I've asked for one. But I didn't murder her."

Costa nodded but said nothing. He didn't need to say anything. It was ugly, and we both knew it. He and I stayed on the scene for another hour and answered questions from several investigators before the investigators let us leave. Afterwards, we went our separate ways and didn't mention Sasha Ingram again.

Over the next week, Agent Costa and his team worked the case and filled in a lot of details I didn't know. He interviewed Logan and Evan Robinson and heard a story about their cross-country escape attempt. Considering the circumstances, they did well and escaped with little physical harm. But despite their health, they had both lost something profound and important. They weren't children anymore. The US marshals moved them once more. I hoped, wherever they ended up, that they'd be okay.

Costa and I spoke a few times and coordinated our separate investigations. We exchanged notes and files. Gloria Sanchez refused to talk to our investigators. She and her deceased husband had very long criminal histories in both the United States and Mexico. They should have been in prison.

Besides talking to Agent Costa, I talked to a criminal

defense lawyer from St. Louis who specialized in representing police officers. To his thinking, no jury in the world would convict me for taking out a scumbag like Sasha Ingram, but even though my lawyer felt confident, I still walked out of every meeting I had with him feeling more than a little disquieted. At my lawyer's advice, I refused to speak with either Sheriff Delgado or detectives from the Highway Patrol again.

About a week after the shooting, Agent Costa showed up on my porch. Roy and I were at home. I was reading a book and wearing yoga pants and a sweatshirt Mathias had left in my room the day before. Roy was dozing at my feet.

"Hey," I said, furrowing my brow as I opened my door. "Did we have a meeting scheduled today?"

"No," said Costa, shaking his head and gesturing toward my house's interior. "May I come in?"

I stepped back and nodded, so he stepped inside. Roy sniffed him and then sat down beside me.

"You want a cup of coffee or a soda?" I asked, shutting the door.

"Thanks, but no. You need to get dressed," he said. "We have to visit Krystal Robinson."

I lowered my chin.

"Do I have to go?"

"You'll want to," said Costa. "Trust me. And bring your badge and a firearm."

So, I dressed in a pair of jeans, a button-down shirt, and a navy blazer. It was cold outside, so I left Roy in the house. The marshals had moved the Robinson family from St. Augustine to Sunset Hills, an upscale suburb southwest of St. Louis. As we climbed into Costa's SUV, he handed me a thick manila envelope.

"Read this," he said. "You were right at that truck stop. Diego and Gloria should have killed the boys."

The drive took about an hour, and along the way, I read Agent Costa's file and asked questions when I had them. He answered without hesitating. The Marshals Service had moved the Robinsons to a single-story brick home with big front windows. It was pretty. A Ford pickup and a Toyota Camry had parked out front. Costa parked in the driveway beside a four-door Honda sedan.

The FBI agent and I walked to the front door without saying a word to one another. Chief Deputy Marshal Kelly Babcock and Marshal Justin Cartwright met us on the front porch. Both nodded to me.

"Good to see you, Detective," said Babcock before looking to Agent Costa. "You ready to get this started, Agent Costa?"

Costa nodded.

"Yep."

Babcock nodded and opened the front door. The home's entryway had little room for a meeting, so we walked to the living room, which stretched the entire width of the house and had windows to both the front and back yards. The room was open to the dining room and kitchen. Hallways branched off to the bedrooms and bathrooms.

Logan, Evan, and Krystal sat near one another on an L-shaped sectional sofa. Logan and Evan were watching a game show on TV, while Krystal stared at us.

"Can you turn off the TV, Logan?" asked Cartwright. "We've got some stuff to talk about."

Logan sighed and reached for the remote.

"I'm tired of talking," he said. "Let's just get this over with."

Costa looked at me.

"You want the honors, Detective?"

I stepped forward and pushed back my blazer so they could see the badge on my hip.

"Sure," I said. "Justin Cartwright, you're under arrest for conspiracy to abduct Logan and Evan Robinson, the murder of Joel Robinson, and the attempted murder of a bunch of other people. The US attorney will read you the formal charges. Krystal Robinson, you're under arrest for the same shit. You're both terrible people, and I hope you die in prison. Thanks."

Cartwright and Krystal opened their mouths in stunned surprise. I stepped back, and Agent Costa glanced at me.

"Short, but simple," he said. I shrugged, having done what I came to do.

"What the fuck are you talking about, Detective?" asked Cartwright, stepping toward me. Agent Costa stepped forward.

"A drug cartel would have killed Logan and Evan. Diego and Gloria Sanchez didn't," he said. Cartwright didn't react, but Krystal shut her eyes and slumped back on the chair. "You hid your money well, but you're a very wealthy woman, Krystal. Is that why you wanted to leave witness protection? So you could spend the forty million dollars' worth of drug money you hid in the Caymans?"

The boys looked at their mom, but she didn't open her eyes. Costa looked around and nodded.

"The marshals gave you a nice place, but this isn't the lifestyle you wanted, is it?" asked the FBI agent. "You earned that money. You should be able to spend it, right?"

She swallowed.

"It was mine," she said, her voice rough.

"But you couldn't spend it as long as you were in witness protection. You could have left the program, but then you would have lost that cushy deal you made with the US Attorney's Office. You would have gone to prison."

"Fuck you," she said, opening her eyes. I snickered, so she glared at me.

"You and Marshal Cartwright concocted a plan to help you disappear for good," said Costa. "You'd fake a kidnapping and trade yourself for your children. Your boys would then go to live with your ex-husband, and you'd disappear to live the life you've always wanted. The government would think you were dead, and you'd be free to spend your money. Justin Cartwright, for his help, would receive two million dollars, a portion of which would go to Diego and Gloria Sanchez."

Krystal sighed but said nothing. Cartwright covered

his mouth with his hand before shaking his head.

"This is bullshit," he said. "I did nothing wrong."

"Justin, put your hands on top of your head," said Babcock. "I'll take your weapon."

He shook his head and complied with the order, probably because we had him outgunned three to one. Babcock disarmed him and then cleared the round from the chamber of his pistol. Costa looked to him.

"We have bank records and the cell phones of both Diego and Gloria Sanchez," said Costa. "We've already got a team searching your house for additional evidence right now. You should have told Joel about the plan. He would have gone along with it."

Cartwright said nothing.

"Joel died to protect his kids from you," I said, staring at Krystal. "You didn't deserve him or your boys. I'm glad that you'll spend the rest of your life alone in prison."

Her shoulders shook as she sobbed. Logan and Evan both stared at their mom for a moment. Then Logan stood and looked at Justin before shaking his head and walking down the hall toward the bedrooms. His brother followed.

"I'm sorry," said Krystal, sobbing. "Joel wasn't supposed to die."

"But he did," I said, glancing from her to Marshal Babcock. "What happens to the kids?"

"They'll live with their uncle Travis and his family at the US Army Garrison in Ansbach, Germany," said

Babcock. "With Krystal in prison, any threat the family faced should be over. We can't guarantee they'll have a perfect life, but they'll be with people who care about them. They'll have a chance."

While Babcock spoke, Agent Costa stepped outside. A moment later, four more FBI agents in suits entered. They led Cartwright and Krystal to SUVs outside. They'd plea out before going to trial, but based on what I had seen, they'd spend at least the next twenty or thirty years inside a federal prison. Babcock turned to me.

"I owe you an apology on behalf of the US Marshals Service," she said. "Justin is an embarrassment to the Service. I hope his actions don't color your impressions of my agency."

I shook my head.

"They don't," I said. She nodded and then walked to the hallway in which the boys had disappeared. I looked to Agent Costa. "Well, thanks for this. I can get a cab home."

Costa shook his head.

"No, I need to drive you back. We have more to talk about. It's important."

44

For the second time, Agent Costa drove me to Art Hill in St. Louis. A cold wind whipped across the Grand Basin and whistled as it blew past the statue of Louis IX. I pulled my jacket tight as we walked. The last time Agent Costa and I had stood in that spot, he had shared with me something extraordinary that he had learned while browsing the FBI's mainframe. This time he shared something personal.

We talked for quite a while, but he couldn't answer all of my questions. I knew someone who could, but first I had preparations. At three in the afternoon, Agent Costa drove me home. With the property Susanne left me when she died, I owned over a hundred rolling, beautiful acres of Missouri countryside. Roy and I walked that land until the sun went down.

Then, I went home and made preparations to leave it.

It took a lot of work and a lot of meetings over the better part of a week, but I got my affairs in order, and I packed up most of my clothes. The hardest part was sitting down and writing letters to my family. Julia had called me twice, but I hadn't been ready to talk to her. I loved her, and I loved Doug. I wrote each of them a letter telling them what they meant to me and how much I appreciated having them in my life. Then I wrote letters to Audrey, Dylan, and Ian apologizing for how things ended. One day, they'd understand why I couldn't tell them in person. It just hurt too much.

Five days after we arrested Krystal Robinson and Justin Cartwright, I packed up the car with my clothes, put Roy's harness on so I could secure him with a seat belt, and drove to my realtor's office, where I dropped off the keys to both of my houses. The realtor already had multiple showings lined up for Susanne's place. Apparently, a couple from St. Louis were ready to make an offer based on the pictures alone. It was a nice house on a beautiful piece of land, so I could believe that. My house would be harder to sell, but somebody handy would want it. Until then, I could afford to let it sit.

After that, I drove north for my final task. My chest felt fluttery, and my muscles felt tight, but I felt a deep sense of purpose, too. I knew what I was doing and why I was doing it. This was important to me. I had imagined this conversation and how it might go for days. Now I just had to do it.

I drove to Comet Coffee just south of Forest Park in St. Louis and parked behind the building. Since I had Roy with me, he and I walked to the front of the shop, where I tied his leash to a bench before going in. The shop held the wonderful aroma of freshly roasted coffee beans. I ordered a cup of Kenyan coffee roasted by a company in

Denver and took it outside to wait beside my dog.

Mathias arrived about five minutes later, right on time. A smile lit his face as he saw me. Then he petted Roy's cheek.

"Hey," he said, walking to me. He tried to kiss me, but I turned my head and hugged him instead. His smile faltered for a moment, but then I reached out and squeezed his arm. "Good to see you. I hadn't heard from you for a couple of days, so I was worried."

"I've been busy," I said. The fluttery feeling traveled down my chest and into my stomach, but I did my best to ignore it. "Get something to drink. I'd like to talk to you for a few minutes."

He nodded and went inside, so I sat and scanned the area to make sure we had some privacy. Then I reached into my purse for a file Agent Costa had given me. Mathias came back a few minutes later with a cup of coffee. He sat beside me on a bench overlooking the road.

"How have you been?" he asked. "Your mom told me you were involved in a shooting."

"You've been talking to Julia?" I asked, raising my eyebrows. He nodded.

"We've both been trying to get in touch with you, but you haven't returned our calls. We care about you."

I nodded and looked down at my cup.

"I should have called you both earlier," I said. "I'm sorry."

"It's okay," he said, looking down as I held the file toward him. "What's this?"

"Open it."

He smiled a little and then tilted his head to the side as he put the file on his lap and opened it. Then his smile disappeared.

"This is from the FBI," he said. "How'd you get this?"

"A friend," I said. "It's my mother's file. My biological mother. Erin Court. Have you seen this before?"

He flipped through the pages and then glanced up at me.

"Someone's blacked this out," he said. "They've even marked out her last name."

"Bryan Costa filled in the details for me," I said. "Erin was an FBI informant. No one had ever told me that. Bryan found her file while filling out paperwork for the cases he and I just worked together. He looked up my name on the database, and Erin's file came up. It listed me as her next-of-kin."

Mathias nodded but said nothing. I turned a few pages in the document.

"Erin was a prostitute. She was addicted to heroin for most of her adult life, but there were periodic moments when she cleaned herself up. During the moments in which she was clean, she had a lot of high-profile clients. That was when the FBI found her.

"They paid her two thousand dollars to put a listening device in the office of a man in Chicago they had under investigation. If she refused, they'd send her to prison for trafficking in heroin. They had a warrant, but they couldn't get in themselves. They used her, but they didn't tell her that her client was a gangster who operated several hundred gas stations in dozens of states, or that he used his gas stations to help almost two dozen very wealthy Russian and Chinese families launder money. Erin had no idea who she was pissing off. They told her he was an investment banker who stole from his clients."

Mathias nodded.

"That's awful," he said, his brow furrowed.

"It is," I said, nodding my agreement. "The Bureau made a big case against the gangster, and he sent goons out to kill her. She escaped the bad guys and went into hiding. Her lawyer sued the federal government, and they settled out of court for eight-hundred thousand dollars. They refused to offer her protection, though, because they claimed the gangster she put in prison had lost influence in his organization. They said she was out of danger."

Mathias nodded.

"They were wrong," I said, continuing. "They came after her again. This time, they succeeded. Erin died after being shot twice in the chest, twice in the abdomen, and once in the shoulder by a .45-caliber pistol. That's a big round. When I first heard it, I thought it was overkill. A mugger would have just shot her once before running. Five shots with a round that large is personal."

Again, Mathias nodded. I had hoped for more reaction. I forced myself to smile at him even as my anger built inside me.

"How much of this story did you know before I got

here?"

He said nothing.

"A little?" I asked, raising my eyebrows. "A lot? All of it?"

He kept his gaze on the cars.

"Detective Mary Petrosini spent a week investigating Erin's death," I said. "She busted her ass. I know she's seen this file because Agent Costa showed me the log of everyone who's looked at it since the file's creation. Years later, your department assigned you to review Erin's case. It was cold, and you were doing the department's due diligence. I know you talked to Detective Petrosini about it. What'd she tell you?"

Mathias hesitated before looking at me.

"You know what she told me," he said.

I leaned forward and looked into his eyes.

"I want you to look at me and say it."

He kept eye contact with me for a moment, but then he looked down.

"I've seen the file. Mary had a copy."

His voice was so soft that I almost couldn't hear him above the sound of traffic. I balled my hands into fists as a tremble passed through.

"You let me believe my mother was murdered in a drug deal gone wrong," I said. "She wasn't, though, and you knew it. She was murdered because she helped put a gangster in prison. Even if you couldn't solve the case, you knew why she died."

He looked at me but then closed his eyes and held up

his hands.

"I wanted to tell you, but I couldn't," he said. "Everybody involved in your mother's case signed a nondisclosure agreement. That includes me."

"You may have signed a non-disclosure agreement, but this wasn't your secret to keep."

He didn't respond. In the recent past, I had enjoyed silences with Mathias. This one felt awkward. Finally, he looked at me again.

"I'm sorry," he said. "I wish I could have handled it differently, but I didn't have a choice."

"Bullshit," I said. "You've always got a choice. You made the wrong one and hid something from me that you had no right to hide. Because of you, I believed the worst things imaginable about my mom. I told my little brother that his mother died because she was a drug-addicted prostitute. I broke a kid's heart because of you. He didn't deserve that."

Roy must have sensed the pain in my voice because he whined. I reached to him and petted his side, which quieted him.

"I'm sorry," said Mathias. "I don't know what else to say."

"Then don't say anything," I said. I sipped the dregs of my coffee and threw the cup away in a nearby trash can before going back to the bench for my dog and the file. I started to walk toward the parking lot, but then Mathias called out.

"I heard a rumor you turned in your badge. Is that

true?"

I turned and nodded.

"I resigned to avoid being fired. My boss thinks he can make a case that I murdered the woman who shot up my brother's high school. I didn't, but I'm tired of fighting him. It's not worth getting out of bed every morning and putting on a badge if I have to fight every hour of the day just to keep it."

Mathias looked down and leaned forward.

"I knew you'd run eventually, but I had hoped I'd give you a reason to stay a little longer than this."

I scoffed and closed my eyes.

"You think I'm running away?"

He looked up.

"I know you're running away. And I get it," he said, standing. "You lost your job, you feel betrayed by me, neither of your brothers will speak to you, and your mom said things to you she shouldn't have, things that she regrets, by the way. That's awful, but as your friend, I don't want you making a decision today that you'll regret tomorrow."

I shook my head.

"I'm not running away. I'm leaving. There's a difference. Sorry this couldn't end as you had hoped."

I turned to leave. Mathias cleared his throat.

"Your mom will ask me where you're going. What should I tell her?"

I stopped walking and looked over my shoulder but didn't turn.

"My mom's dead. Tell Julia I plan to drive until I find out who I am," I said. "Because I don't recognize myself when I look in the mirror anymore."

He may have said something else, but I wasn't paying attention. Roy and I walked to my car and climbed in. I had strewn a hammock on the backseat to keep him comfortable as I drove, and I had filled my gas tank before leaving St. Augustine. I didn't know where I was going, but I didn't care.

As I put my key in the ignition, I knew my conversation with Mathias had been honest, but I also knew it had been incomplete. I wasn't running away from my life. If anything, I was running toward it. Life in St. Augustine no longer made me happy. I loved Julia and Doug Green; I loved Audrey, Dylan, and Ian; I even loved being a cop. None of those things defined me, though.

I was Mary Joe Court. My mom—my real mom, not the woman who had adopted me—was a prostitute who died doing the right thing, even if she didn't realize it. My biological father was a stranger who paid my mother for sex. My best friend was a dog who refused to run alongside me unless I carried a piece of ham in my pocket to entice him. Beyond that, I was a mystery. I didn't know what I wanted out of life or who I wanted to be. One day, I'd find those things that made my world meaningful, and then I'd be home.

But until then, I had a world to explore and a dog to explore it with. I had what I needed. At the moment, I couldn't ask for more.

Did you like *THE MAN IN THE PARK*? Then you're going to love *THE GIRL WHO TOLD STORIES*!

Former detective Mary Joe Court returns in a gritty story of betrayal and murder in the seventh novel of *New York Times'* bestselling author Chris Culver's Joe Court series.

Joe Court has moved on with her life. With her faithful dog at her side, she's left St. Augustine county and hopes to start a new career in a new state.

Then a young woman at a local university disappears.

Joe's never met the victim, but she knows her all the same. The victim was a storyteller. She runs a very successful true crime podcast and has fans across the country. She also has enemies.

Joe gave up her badge when she left St. Augustine, but she didn't relinquish her skills or her sense of right and wrong. When the young woman's mother asks for help, Joe can't refuse. But with every secret she uncovers and every clue she finds, she draws closer to a dangerous foe—and now, she no longer has a station full of colleagues to watch her back.

Paperbacks will be available on March 18, 2020!

Enjoy this book? You can make a big difference in my career

Reviews are the lifeblood of an author's career. I'm not exaggerating when I say they're the single best way I can get attention for my books. I'm not famous, I don't have the money for extravagant advertising campaigns, and I no longer have a major publisher behind me.

I do have something major publishers don't have, something they would kill to get:

Committed, loyal readers.

With millions of books in the world, your honest reviews and recommendations help other readers find me.

If you enjoyed the book you just read, I would be extraordinarily grateful if you could spend five minutes to leave a review on Amazon, Barnes and Noble, Goodreads, or anywhere else you review books. A review can be as long or as short as you'd like it to be, so please don't feel that you have to write something long.

Thank you so much!

Stay in touch with Chris

As much as I enjoy writing, I like hearing from readers even more. If you want to keep up with my world, there are a couple of ways you can do that.

First and easiest, I've got a mailing list. If you join, you'll receive an email whenever I have a new novel out or when I run sales. You can join that by going to this address:

http://www.indiecrime.com/mailinglist.html

If my mailing list doesn't appeal to you, you can also connect with me on Facebook here:

http://www.facebook.com/ChrisCulverbooks

And you can always email me at chris@indiecrime.com. I love receiving email!

About the Author

Chris Culver is the *New York Times* bestselling author of the Ash Rashid series and other novels. After graduate school, Chris taught courses in ethics and comparative religion at a small liberal arts university in southern Arkansas. While there and when he really should have been grading exams, he wrote *The Abbey*, which spent sixteen weeks on the *New York Times* bestsellers list and introduced the world to Detective Ash Rashid.

Chris has been a storyteller since he was a kid, but he decided to write crime fiction after picking up a dog-eared, coffee-stained paperback copy of Mickey Spillane's *I, the Jury* in a library book sale. Many years later, his wife, despite considerable effort, still can't stop him from bringing more orphan books home. He lives with his family near St. Louis.